# No Ordinary Fire

# No Ordinary Fire

Kaitlin,

So good it meet you!

Erika Jantzen

ISBN-13: 9781519537812
ISBN-10: 1519537816
Library of Congress Control Number: 2015919854
CreateSpace Independent Publishing Platform
North Charleston, South Carolina

## Dedication

For Donnie, my husband and best friend
– *with love and thanks*

The wound is the place where the Light enters you.

Rumi

# CHAPTER 1

IT WAS 1996. Atlanta hosted the Summer Olympics, and my third marriage ground to a halt. All the journaling, deep breathing, and attempts to get in touch with my inner child disintegrated before me. My co-dependent meltdown began when I tried to save my husband, Tom, from his current need to self-destruct.

"No, darling, you're not a loser," I would begin my mantras to bolster his ego. "You're brilliant."

I believed Tom would quit drinking, and we'd have a perfect marriage. He'd come home one day and announce, "I've been so foolish. I love you, and I want us to work."

But it never happened.

Instead, I climbed aboard the manic scream machine, displaying sincerity and good humor one minute, then rage over a simple miscommunication the next. I was one angry 38-year-old woman, with little hope on the horizon.

Our last night together was still a horrifying memory of my need for life-threatening drama. We lived in a two-story condo in Norcross, Georgia, a suburb of Atlanta, and Tom was enrolled at a local university, finishing a degree in biology. His plan was to enter a Physician's Assistant program the following year. His grades were good, but the drinking had started to increase, and I continually caught him in lies. He would lie about the garbage, the telephone bills, and why his workout clothes weren't sweaty after hours at the gym. We played tit-for-tat over every thought we shared, stabbing at each other with sharp words of bitterness and resentment.

I moved into the spare bedroom and became addicted to sleep aids. My friends were concerned about the escalating verbal abuse, especially after I told them I had an old .357 in my night stand. Suspicion and hatred oozed out of our pores. We weren't walking on eggshells; we were stomping all over them.

That night, I arrived home around nine, completely drained after a grueling ten hours at work. A massage therapist at one of Atlanta's most prestigious resorts, I'd had a long day. The guests had all been demanding and shitty. As I drove into the parking lot of the condo, my heart sank. Tom was home. All I wanted to do was become invisible, crawl up the stairs, take a hot shower, and go to bed. Opening the car door, I sat and took a momentary respite, letting my tired body sink into the worn blue cloth of the car seat.

I forced myself out of the car and stood for a moment. The sky was filled with white, billowing storm clouds. Random raindrops landed on my face and eyelashes. Resolve washed through me; this madness had to end. I didn't care anymore about the embarrassment of telling people we were on the verge of splitting. How could it be worse? I'd go into the condo, make nice, and go to bed. In the morning I'd get the paper and find my own place. But as I walked down the sidewalk, a haunting fear filled me, and my steps faltered. It was the same trepidation I'd experienced as a child afraid to go home after school.

Tom had secured both locks on the door. It was dark and I struggled to find my keys. "What a prick," I mumbled. "He could've left the porch light on." I noticed the For Sale sign was gone from our Jeep Wrangler's windshield. A down payment borrowed from my cousin had made it possible for Tom to have his dream Jeep.

The loan, the condo lease, and all the credit cards were in my name. Lucky me. My need to keep him happy had kept me stuck in this vicious cycle.

The car payment was taking a toll on our income. I was the primary breadwinner, but Tom had a weekend gig at the Green Parrot Bar and Grill that brought in enough cash tips for him to get through the week and buy booze. It was painful for him to give up the Jeep, but he eventually conceded. The Jeep fit the image of part-time bartender, return-to-college-cool-dude. He was handsome at six feet, with broad shoulders and an ever-so-slight beer belly that created his teddy bear allure. Crystal blue eyes, a chiseled face, and an angelic expression all camouflaged a tormented soul.

After two attempts the door finally yielded, and I stepped in, not knowing where he was, how much he'd had to drink, or what kind of mood he was in.

It was Monday night and he was in front of the television with a pizza box on the floor and five crushed beer cans dripping on the coffee table. I stood for a moment without acknowledgement.

Slipping off my jacket, hanging it on the antique coat tree in the foyer, I spoke in a low monotone. "Hey, sell the Jeep today?"

"Eight thousand dollars," he said, not looking away from the television.

"Eight thousand?" I was incredulous. My tone was full of disappointment; anger started to kick in. "We need ninety-five hundred to break even," I said. "We owe Karen fifteen hundred. Did you remember that? Do you have fifteen hundred dollars? Where's the money going to come from?" I was hot, in total disbelief. I wanted to rip his head off.

"You told me to sell the Jeep. I sold the Jeep," he said arrogantly as he stuffed his mouth and continued to stare at the football game.

I moved between him and the television and went on the attack. "What's the deal, Tom? Why are you putting the screws to me? What the hell is going on? Because of what you've done, I can't pay Karen back. Are you listening to me?" My voice was shaking.

For a fleeting moment, I knew I could stop this now, just walk away, and discuss it in the morning. But it was too late. My ears started to ring. I lost my peripheral vision. My big mouth went into overdrive.

"She went into her savings, you stupid mother-fucker! So you could have your precious Jeep! How could you? Who did you sell it to?"

He jumped off the couch and threw the remote across the room.

I spotted a pint of whiskey behind the side table, and my adrenals pumped out of control.

"How long have you been drinking?" I screamed.

"None of your business!" he blasted back in a jet of alcoholic fumes.

"It's my business when you're drunk, and you're fucking with my money."

"Your money?" he snorted. Looming over me, he reached into his back pocket for his wallet and fished out a check. He held it in front of my face with one finger in the air like a dog trainer giving the command to sit.

"Here you are," he snorted. "It's a deposit for five hundred bucks. The guy's name and number are on the check. Give him a call and get your cousin's fifteen hundred dollars. You are one sorry cunt!"

Oh no, the C-word. Of all the words in the English language, it's the one women abhor, despise, loathe the most, and he knew it. The big button had been pushed. I shoved against his chest with both my hands, ready for a fight.

"Shut up! Just shut up!" I screamed at the top of my lungs. I pushed against him again with no result. "Since you don't have the balls to do a simple business deal, I'll do it myself." I snapped the check from his hand and turned on my heel.

He grabbed my arm with a death grip and spun me around. "Apologize!" he shouted.

"Let go of me, Tom." I tried to pull away again, but he held on more tightly. My skin felt like it would burst. Our eyes locked, and I didn't care if he hit me. In fact, I wanted a knock-down-drag-out so I could kick him in the balls so hard his eyes would pop out. The relationship was ending. Might as well be tonight, I thought.

"I said, let go of me, you prick!" My voice shook from anger as hot tears streamed down my face.

He let go of my arm but quickly pinned me against the wall with his left hand. Pain shot into my shoulder, and my head bounced violently off sheetrock and then forward from the sudden impact.

"I want you to leave me alone," he said. Blue eyes glowed red.

"Stop it, you're hurting me." My spit sprayed against his face.

He raised a fist, and for a split second I thought I was a goner. I closed my eyes and felt his hand nick my cheek as it crashed into drywall. Dust flew, and I used the opportunity to escape.

He chased me in a drunken limp as I ran up the stairs two steps at a time. I stopped halfway up the stairs and turned as he reached for my leg to pull me back. Another second and he would have had me.

"Listen to me, you son-of-a-bitch!" I was hysterical, crying and screaming at the same time. "If you come up these stairs, so help me God, I'll blow you away. My gun is loaded. I've had enough! Do you hear me?" My ravings were full of defiance and contempt.

He froze in place.

Then without any warning, my voice became a whisper panting for breath. "I swear to God... I will kill you... if you come into my room tonight. Touch me... and you die. Understand?"

Then something very strange happened. We stared at each other like strangers for what felt like an eternity, and he started to blubber like a baby, lips quivering and pouting.

"My hand," he whimpered, looking down. His knuckles dripped bright red blood onto the carpet.

"Please, Tom, please," I pleaded, just leave me alone. I can't do this anymore. I mean it; don't come into my room."

Finishing my climb up the stairs, I entered the spare bedroom and locked the door. I actually thought about loading the .357. "Don't," I told myself. He could have put his fist into my face instead of the wall. Why was he crying on the stairs? I wondered. I had to stay in my room no matter what.

My head pounded, and tears flooded my eyes as I undressed and started the shower. Every muscle in my body ached. My hands rested on the edge of the bathroom countertop and I leaned into the mirror, surveying the damage. My biceps sported light blue finger marks. I spoke to my pathetic reflection. "Why are you doing this?"

Stepping into the shower I felt the heat of the water on my skin and prayed to God for a peaceful night.

# CHAPTER 2

*BANG! BANG! BANG!*

The bathroom door roared, sounding like it was about to explode. An authoritative male voice boomed, "Marianne Campbell, this is the Gwinnett police. Unlock the door and come out with your hands up."

"Real funny. Leave me alone, Tom."

"Mrs. Campbell, this is Officer McMahon; this is not your husband. Be advised, we are armed. Open the door with your hands up."

Jesus, he called the cops? The whimpering bastard called the cops on me, I thought with disgust. I turned off the water and stayed dripping wet as I put on my robe.

"I'm unlocking the door," I said. "I don't have a gun. Don't shoot." I unlocked the door and opened it a bit peering through the crack. Officer McMahon stood in the hallway with both hands holding his weapon, arms extended. The barrel pointed halfway up the door frame. A 911 domestic call, every oofficer's worst nightmare, I thought. Tom must've convinced them that I'm a murderer.

McMahon and I made eye contact. I opened the door and held up my hands. My robe cracked open and McMahon looked down at the floor, embarrassed.

"Mrs. Campbell, uh, you can put your hands down. We're going downstairs, you first." As I made my way past him, he holstered his pistol.

He was a twenty-something hunk with a Marine buzz cut, big brown eyes, and a buff body. I wondered what he thought of me. Walking slowly down the stairs, I saw Tom's blood on the carpet. I reached up, touched my bruised arm, and felt the connection. I hurt you; you hurt me; I hurt you more. Maybe he won this round, but he was not going to win the war. I was battle-ready from this last year, trying to control everything that moved into our sphere, however hurtful and shallow, a willing participant in my own demise.

When we reached the bottom of the stairs, the condo's front door was wide open, and I could see two other officers talking to Tom. Simultaneously, they all turned to look at McMahon and me in the foyer.

"Have a seat in here." McMahon motioned to the couch. "We need to hear your side of the story, but first tell me where the gun is, Mrs. Campbell."

I wanted him to stop calling me Mrs. Campbell and stick pins in my eyes instead. Mrs. Damned One was more like it.

"It's... it's... " I couldn't connect my mouth to my thoughts. The words were stuck. Why is the football game on, I wondered, if I was trying to kill my husband?

"Could you turn the television off?" I asked.

"Good idea." McMahon started to look around for the remote.

"He threw it against the wall," I said, pointing.

McMahon walked over to the set, hit the power button, and brought an end to the images of players scrambling for the goal line. I saw the virtue of maintaining a calm exterior.

"Officer," I said in my best victim tone, "the gun is in my nightstand, box of bullets in the closet between the folds of a blue blanket on the top shelf. The gun's not loaded. Our fighting has gotten worse since a woman's been calling here harassing me. It's not been good here for a long time."

So what if I was lying about the phone calls. I was going for the sympathy vote.

"Tonight when I got home from work, we fought. He bruised my arm, put a hole in the wall and threatened to kill me. I didn't know what else to do. I'm afraid of him, and I've had plans to move out this week. I have no family in Georgia; I'm embarrassed to impose on my friends. I felt trapped and angry, and he hurt me." I showed him my arm.

"I'm going upstairs for the gun," he said. "Stay put."

He leaned outside the door and called for one of the other officers. Blue rotating lights shone intermittently through the sheers hanging in the living room. I heard the dispatcher's voice over the police radio echo through the parking lot. Quite a show for the neighbors, I thought. I wonder what we'll do for an encore.

Another gorgeous boy-cop appeared in the foyer.

"This is Officer McFarland. He'll stay with you and take your statement."

Great, I was being held captive by the Notre Dame starting line-up. McMahon spoke into the tiny radio on his lapel as he went up the stairs to fetch the infamous .357 and those murderous bullets hiding in the closet.

I repeated my story to McFarland as he wrote quickly on a small well-worn spiral pad. McMahon reappeared within a few minutes with the gun and box of bullets.

"I never thought I'd threaten anyone," I said looking at my bare feet.

They looked at each other uncomfortably. McMahon broke the silence.

"I'm confiscating the gun for twenty-four hours. You can come by tomorrow with your permit and pick it up at the downtown Norcross police station. You both need to cool down."

Permit? What permit? I just lost my handgun.

"Your husband's not pressing charges," McFarland said.

"Pressing charges?"

"He made the 911 call. Do you think it's normal to threaten to kill someone you're arguing with?"

Yes, I do. I had heard it all my life. Why did it seem so foreign to these men?

"No," I lied. "You're right. Can you stay here while I get dressed and grab some things, so I can leave for the night? I think I'd better get a hotel room or I'll be the one calling you next."

McMahon nodded and I shivered inside my wet robe. Passing by the door, I saw Tom standing outside with his arms crossed against his chest, head down, listening to a third policeman's lecture.

I entered the bedroom and changed into jeans and a sweatshirt. The shirt was a souvenir from our first trip to the beach. We were both on our best behavior that weekend, smiling, polite, thoughtful and over-accommodating. We stayed in a run-down hotel so we could afford a hundred-dollar seafood dinner complete with a bottle of char-donnay and chocolate mousse. During the day we fed seagulls, flew a kite, and collected shells. At night we made love by candlelight and then talked for hours before drifting off to sleep in each other's arms.

After we returned to Atlanta, the vacation was the center of our conversations, our touchstone. Now, three years later, the shells were stored in a cracked Mason jar gathering dust, and I was leaving our home under police escort.

I rushed through my desk drawers for car titles, back-up credit cards, and the check book. I grabbed a medium-sized suitcase from the back of the closet, combed through my hair as best I could and remembered my toiletries and toothbrush.

I chose some of my favorite clothes: dress jeans, a silk blouse, run-ning gear, T-shirts, pajamas, and a pair of worn cowboy boots in case I had to kick some ass.

A thick silence fell over the circle of Tom and the policemen when I joined them downstairs.

"Do you have anywhere to go?" my buddy McMahon asked in a low tone.

"Yes, I'll be fine."

"Check her bags." Tom's voice was gruff and full of disgust. "She's got all our valuables."

"Stop it, Tom, just stop it."

"Mr. Campbell, we've had enough tonight." McMahon had taken on the role of mediator. "You can get things cleared up tomorrow. You two, get some counseling. And Tom, lay off the booze until you get things figured out. Being drunk and calling the police won't fix things."

"But she threatened my life," Tom shot back; his body bowed up.

McMahon met the challenge by turning to face Tom squarely; he put one hand on his hip while the other one rested on the handle of his Glock. The testosterone was flying.

"Who put the hole in the wall?" McMahon asked impatiently. Tom backed down and his shoulders collapsed in surrender.

"Mrs. Campbell, are you ready to go?"

"Yes."

My heart was full of gratitude. I wanted to get into the patrol car and hang out with McMahon and the boys, give them all a massage, talk about life and find out how to live without teetering on the edge. For the first time in my life, I wanted the rage and uncertainty to end.

Without a word to Tom, I walked out the door, deputies taking up the rear. In the parking lot, blue uniforms scattered to separate patrol cars, McFarland being the first to zoom away, careful not to make eye contact with anyone.

Unlocking my sedan and leaning against the door post, I called out to McMahon. "Thank you, Officer."

He opened his car door, turned off the flashing lights and rested his arm on the roof. The rain had stopped; a cool breeze swept past us.

"Be careful, Mrs. Campbell. I hope you get things resolved."

"I will. Thanks again."

"I'm just doing my job. You may want to think about selling that gun."

"Good advice." I smiled. "Be seeing you."

We ducked into our cars, and I slid my key into the ignition. My arm throbbed. I looked up and saw Tom standing in the window, drapes pushed to one side. I put the Volvo in reverse, and from the safety of my car, I threw him the bird.

# CHAPTER 3

IN A STATE of bewilderment, I drove randomly through the streets of Norcross. What had just happened? I wondered. The streets were wet, and barely visible; vapor formed clouds around the streetlights. Spooky. The night had taken on a Dali-like quality; trees and buildings melted along the sidewalks as I navigated through empty neighborhoods. It seemed as if I was the only human alive.

I finally stopped for gasoline, a pack of cigarettes, and a liter bottle of water. I parked my car on the far side of the convenience store and nervously unwrapped the smokes. During high school my relay partner and I smoked Marlboros because we were invincible. Our team went to state finals twice in three years and bonds were strengthened by rituals like trading socks before a meet, sharing lipstick and boyfriends. Defiantly smoking in public gave us a sense of power. Maybe it'll work for me tonight, I thought.

After the fourth inhale, nausea overwhelmed me, and I threw open the car door in time to vomit a rush of clear and yellow liquids onto the asphalt. I hadn't eaten in over twelve hours. My aching stomach felt hollow. My throat was sore from all the screaming and now the vomiting. I had to settle in somewhere for the night. Too freaked out to sleep in my car, the thought of a cheap hotel did not appeal to me. I had tons of plastic. Why not The Summit? I thought. If this is truly the night my marriage from hell ends, why not celebrate?

I started the Volvo and made my way toward Interstate 85 and then south. I looked like a bum, but in Atlanta after midnight everyone looked the same: ball caps, sweatshirts and blue jeans.

As I pulled up to the hotel's porte-cochere, a light-skinned black man ran to my approaching car. He wore a uniform of spit-shined shoes, black pants, and matching jacket and cap.

My window was down when the car came to a full stop. He tipped his cap and said, "Good evening, Miss. Welcome to The Summit. You visiting the lounge or are you planning to spend some time with us?" He sounded Jamaican. The cadence of his speech had a kind of sing-song quality. His smile was full of mischief. I began to feel human.

"I believe I would like to spend the night," I said.

"We are here to serve your needs, one night or many nights." His words brought a smile to my face, like a healing salve to my soul. I was in love. He spotted my suitcase in the backseat.

"One bag?" he asked.

"Yes."

His light-heartedness was contagious. "One bag for one night," he said, "then I'll be taking you to the front desk."

He opened the door and held out his hand for me. I was lifted out, light as a feather, by his graciousness. He handled the bag from the backseat, shut both doors, and walked behind me through the revolving doors.

I caught a glimpse of him as we moved together separated by thick glass panels. Did I see a halo? When we arrived at the front desk, he placed the suitcase next to me on the floor.

"Here you are, Miss. My name is Daniel. If I can be of further service, don't hesitate to ask."

"Thank you, Daniel." Fine service and a willing demeanor; I was never leaving The Summit.

After haggling for a reduced rate, I asked for a room on the highest level available and was assigned room 4206 on the forty-second floor, one floor below the penthouse. I handed over my car keys for valet service, was told twenty-four-hour room service was available, and was guaranteed a spectacular view of downtown Atlanta. Daniel appeared, as if by magic, and picked up my suitcase again.

"Please allow me to show you the way, Miss." We walked together to the elevator and he pushed the button.

"You certainly love your job, don't you?"

"This is my night job. My wife and I expect our first baby. I want them to have everything they need. My father is very strict about such things. A man must take care of his family and you need money to do this."

I wanted to empty my wallet and give him all my cash. Here was a man working his ass off, in love with his wife and joyous about his coming baby. His eyes glowed with love and pride. Maybe not all men are bastards, I thought.

*Ding.*

The heavy, polished brass doors parted and Daniel motioned me to enter. We zoomed from the lowest level of the building to who-knows-what floor balanced in the air by cables, but suddenly we stood still, doors shut in place. My stomach fluttered. He pushed the button on the panel again, still no response. Ironically, I had fled violence and injury, but now I was suspended in limbo.

The seconds entombed seemed like hours. I thought of the First Canto of Dante's *Inferno,* and the words Dante spoke to Virgil: "I thee entreat, by the same God whom thou didst never know, so that I may escape this woe and worse . . ."

The elevator shook and we rapidly began our ascent as if sucked up into a vacuum. Within seconds the car braked to a stop, another *ding* sounded, and Daniel announced, "Forty-second floor."

The hallway was long and carpeted in plush pile, reminiscent of a thick Persian rug. The wallpaper displayed pink and red roses; side tables along the walls held vases of flowers. Real or silk? I wondered.

We found my room. He opened the door with a pass key, deposited my bag just inside the entrance, and turned on the light.

"Have a good night, Miss."

"Thank you, Daniel….Wait." Fishing out a twenty from my wallet, I handed it to him and wished it could have been a hundred.

Breathing a sigh of relief, I locked the door. The room was a gorgeous display of maroon and deep blue floral fabrics, dark furniture, and crystal lamps.

I stood for a moment enjoying the skyline, settled in at the desk, and made the telephone call to cancel the credit card Tom still had, hoping it wasn't too late. I shut off all the lights, undressed and finished off the last of my bottled water.

Finally… peace.

It was after 1:00 a.m. and I didn't have to work for the next three days. I'd sleep late, eat a big breakfast, and begin to plan my future. Couch-hopping with friends could be an option. The thought of spending another minute under the same roof as Tom made me shudder. Shaking off the fear of seeing him again, I got under the covers of my very cool, king-sized bed, built a fortress of pillows around me and lay still, not trusting the silence.

Slowly the anxiety began to creep in. Turning on my side and hugging one of the over-stuffed pillows, I had to figure out how to get to sleep without my pills. Here we go… the old-fashioned way.

I took a deep breath, expanding my diaphragm and counting to eight, then holding four counts and exhaling eight. It took all of my concentration to repeat this pattern of eight in, eight out. Large numbers appeared on a blank screen in my head. After I drifted off to sleep, dark images appeared.

*I crawled on my belly, sliding back and forth, arms extended. There were vines of some sort surrounding me, tunnel-like, weighing down on me, layers and layers of thick branches. The air was dense with smoke. I couldn't see. It filled my lungs, and I began to grasp for breath.*

*Terror-stricken, I crawled faster to get away, trying to escape. I made no progress. Instead my legs began to slide under the surface.*

*Then another sensation… one of the branches covered with thorns fell against my back. The stinging pricks opened my skin; I felt the sensation of blood oozing out of me.*

*Streams of it covered my body and flowed into the ground. Suddenly, another branch moved, lifting me upward with violence. My mouth opened. I tried to scream, but there was no sound.*

I awoke in a panic, jumped from the bed, and fled into the bathroom turning on every light within reach. My heart pounded as if it would fly out of my chest. I turned on both faucets full blast and splashed water on my face, trying to catch my breath between gulps of air and water.

Running my hands over my arms and turning to look at my backside in the mirror, I was convinced there would be evidence of gouged, bleeding skin, but there was nothing.

"A dream. It was only a dream," I told myself. I grabbed a bath towel and covered my face, collapsed to the floor, folded my body into a fetal position, and cried out in pitiful sobs, trying to exorcise demons — the smoke, the thorns, and the blood. Propping myself up on one arm finally the tears stopped.

Positioned with my head resting on crossed arms on the toilet seat, I tried to slow my terror and reason the nightmare away. Maybe the thorns represent the pain of my marriage, I thought, and the heavy branches our relationship's emotional angst. But these explanations felt superficial. I struggled to my feet, turned off the lights and unplugged the phone. No wake-up calls for this poor wench. Once more I found the comfort of an overstuffed pillow and hid my head under the blankets.

I prayed the *Our Father* out loud and dispatched all the evil spirits present in my room back to the pits of Hell. All I remembered before dropping off to sleep was Daniel's smile.

# CHAPTER 4

"HOUSEKEEPING...HOUSEKEEPING."

I heard my door swing open.

"Sorry to disturb y' all, but it's twelve-thirty. Your check-out was eleven on the dot."

Peeking out from my cavern of cotton linens, I attempted to focus on the body dressed in a black and white maid's uniform.

"Twelve-thirty?"

"That's what I said," the fuzzy body answered.

A pencil-thin girl in her early twenties with a ruddy complexion and a bleached-blonde ponytail stood at the doorway with her hands on her hips.

"You have to clear out A...S...A...P." Her tone was defiant, almost angry, and her accent was straight from the north Georgia mountains. "Please," I said, "I'm so sorry." I sat up in bed and tucked the covers around my chest. "Last night was not good at my house. I had to leave and the nightmares kept me awake until four. Could you give me twenty minutes?"

Her expression softened. Her hands moved from her hips to cross in front of her flat chest. She had the body of a 12-year-old but her eyes reflected years of hard living.

"Just get out as soon as you can muster the strength." She paused and cocked her head. "Family trouble?"

"Husband, soon to be ex; he forced me out. It wasn't pretty." "Did he hit you?"

"No... Close, though."

"Oh." She looked concerned and her tone softened. "Are you hungry?"

I didn't understand her question at first and didn't respond.

She tried again. "I mean, are you ready for some food or maybe hot coffee? My cousin's working the kitchen today and her boss is off. She's running things, if you know what I mean." She winked at me. "How 'bout room service?"

This perfect stranger, another woman who fully understood my plight, was coming to my rescue. We were captured by this moment of chance meeting. Her heart held complete empathy. How could I be so blessed?

"Hot food?" my voice sang.

"Yes, darlin', hot food," she said with a grin. She was initiating some mischief, free food from the kitchen. I'm sure she felt powerful as she took control of the situation, and I was grateful.

She moved to the telephone, and I cautiously leaned over for the bath towel on the floor, wrapped up in it, and headed for the bathroom. Her voice was audible as I put on the hotel's cushy white robe and ran a wide comb through my hair.

"Marlene? It's Vi. I'm in room 4206 with a lady here all alone. Yah yah… that's right. How 'bout Dallas bring up a nice tray. She's lookin' kind of puny. Send hot soup, a nice big sandwich and coffee. You still got that special chocolate cake? Send a piece of that, too. Thank you, baby girl. I owe you one."

I came out of the bathroom; we stood looking at each other.

"Vi, I'm Marianne." I stuck out my hand to her. I was invigorated by her rough and tumble show of affection. Our hands locked. I knew this woman, and she knew me. No need for details.

"You got a place to stay?" Vi asked.

"I'll know later today," I answered.

"I'm fixin' to go," she said. "Finish up two more rooms then head back here. Take your time now; don't fuss too much. Groceries oughta be here directly." She held her hand to her heart as she spoke. "I got a brand new man, no beatin', no cheatin' and no name-callin'. You might like that, too."

She searched my eyes. "Okay, Vi, I hear you."

"You got it, sister." When she opened the door her fingers mimicked a pistol and took an imaginary shot at me. "When your vittles get here you gonna flat fall out over that cake." She shut the door behind her.

Ten minutes later another knock produced Dallas with a cart draped in white linen carrying three covered dishes, a coffee pot, cream, sugar, a bud vase of fresh flowers, and beautiful silverware.

"Wow," I exclaimed as he entered my room. Dallas was Vi's twin with gold wire-rimmed glasses. He wore the same uniform as Daniel, but did not possess Daniel's charm. I handed him a five, and he was gone in a flash. I inhaled the sandwich and licked the soup bowl clean. Three bites of the chocolate torte sent me into insulin shock. The sugar buzz gave me the energy to shower and get ready to face the world again.

I left a twenty dollar bill on the desk for Vi and scribbled on the hotel notepad, "Thanks for your help." It was the last of my cash.

While I finished enjoying the coffee in front of my forty-second floor window, I watched cars work their way through the maze of concrete below. I counted seven colorful dots waiting to cross the street. More dots arrived at the intersection and waited together. The cars stopped. The traffic lights must have changed. All the dots moved in unison. I stood hundreds of feet above observing them move in an orderly, responsible fashion.

Responsible. The word rang true, like a bell tolling to mark the changing hour. Last night's dream had pushed me into an awareness I had never experienced before. The horror of the blood, my blood, was overwhelming. This glorious afternoon of freedom, sweetened by Vi's compassion and Marlene's chocolate torte, marked the beginning of my journey into wholeness. I was now willing to be responsible, to look at my motives and intentions, and face what it was in my life that had to change.

———ɯ———

When I entered Ray's office, his receptionist, surrounded by an antique tiger-oak desk, was talking on the phone and taking notes at the same time. In her early sixties, and after two facelifts, Helen perpetually smiled with surgical perfection. She glanced up and I answered her acknowledgement with a wave, and then sank into the middle of an over-stuffed leather sofa. I ran both hands over the surrounding cushions in wide circles; the sensation tickled the inside of my palms. Smelling rich leather, I laid my head back and relaxed. The brown-skinned cushions were well-worn and soft, much like my relationship with Ray.

Ray and I were lovers when I met Tom four years ago. Ray's calmness, which I had perceived as a weakness, had not excited me like Tom's turmoil. At that time, turmoil was what I craved. But what I craved now was Ray's peacefulness, however uneventful.

He had absolutely the sweetest temperament of any man I had ever known. Only a few times did he lose his happy disposition, and one of those times was when I told him Tom and I were engaged.

"Engaged?" he scoffed. "That man doesn't love you." His tone was resentful and challenging. "He's a narcissistic little boy trying to be a man. He wants you because you give him some class. Without you, he's white trash with a small ration of brains." His voice dropped an octave as he leaned in closer to me. "They're the ones who are dangerous... he will hurt you."

He straightened up and became indignant. "You don't love him. You were in my bed two weeks ago. Does he know about me? Marianne, this isn't fair."

I was shocked at his distress. I had no idea Ray cared so much about me. We had shared intense physical chemistry. I thought we were just bedroom buddies, and the truth be known, he was boring out of bed. Tom and I shared great conversations; we played chess and racquetball together. How dare Ray call him white trash.

"Hey," I said playfully. "Snap out of it. We made a secret pact, remember? Friends forever, semper fi?"

I held out my fist so we could bump knuckles and say "taters," but it was all for naught. Instead he grabbed me and squeezed the air out of my lungs. "If this doesn't work out, or if you need anything, call me. Okay?"

I rested my head against his shoulder and suddenly became misty. "Okay."

Thoughts returned to earth when Helen hung up the telephone and gave me her full attention. "Nice to see you, child," she cooed. "Too late for lunch, aren't we?"

Straightening up in my seat I said, "Maybe Ray could buy me dinner."

His outer office was a huge room covered in cheap paneling, filing cabinets, and cardboard boxes ready to be shipped. Stuffed animal heads lined the walls. Ray had started an electrical company fifteen years ago that served the growing southeast. He was prosperous, and he liked calling himself TK, short for "transformer king."

"When is he getting an interior designer?" I joked.

"Heavens." She picked up the phone and pushed the button to the loudspeaker system in the warehouse. "Ray, you have a visitor."

Two seconds later the door opened.

"Helen, I was just…" He turned to give me his best smile and spoke while wiping his hands clean with a blue terrycloth rag. "Hello, sweetness. It's been awhile. What brings you to my neck of the woods?"

"Just the thought of you, Ray."

"Sure is getting deep in here," Helen teased. "Would you like some tea, darlin'?"

"Yes, ma'am, please."

"It'll be just a second."

"Ray," I tried to keep my voice from cracking, "I need to talk. It may take a while. Do you have some time?"

"Let's scoot into my office. Good to see you."

"Feeling's mutual." It *was* good to see him. In fact, it was terrific.

Ray closed the door behind us. His private office was wall-to-wall bookcases filled with technical manuals, trophies, photographs of family and friends and a stuffed armadillo named Harriet.

I sat in a lotus position in a wing-backed chair in front of him.

Ray extracted a thin cigar from a wooden box sitting on a bookshelf and settled into his chair. He reclined to the point of near calamity and propped his boots up on his desk.

"I like this time of the day," he said. "And I love the smell of tobacco." There was a knock on the door.

"I make the best sweet tea this side of Atlanta," Helen said. She delivered two yellow plastic cups covered in the Georgia Tech logo.

"Helen, hold my calls," Ray said. "We need some privacy. Don't worry if we go past five. I'll see you in the morning."

"Alrighty, then."

Ray held his cigar like a cigarette, slid it under his nose for a whiff but never put fire to it. I took a sip of the strong sugary tea and set it on the edge of his desk. Pushing my body deeper into the chair, I clutched the wooden armrests. I was nervous about telling Ray what had happened. I was embarrassed but desperate for help.

"Relax, Marianne. It's only me." Ray gestured with fingers spread open and his hands flowing in a downward movement while he spoke. It was reminiscent of a conductor signaling the orchestra to a decrescendo.

"Oh, God, Ray... oh, Ray..." I started to cry, but he didn't move to comfort me. He remained stoic and it created the space I needed to spill my guts.

"It's good to cry," he said. "I learned that from my mother and sisters."

Through the tears I told him the story of my last twenty-four hours: the Jeep, the bruise, the cops and Vi's kindness. He sat motionless--except for handing me a box of tissues--and listened intently. At last I dried my tears and he was silent.

Looking out the window, I witnessed the sun beginning to move into the western sky. There was a row of maples planted along the side of the building. Their leaves moved back and forth in perfect unison with the wind.

The turning leaves reminded me of all of the coming holidays: Halloween, Thanksgiving, Christmas. Where will I be? I wondered. Who will I be sharing these memories with? My heart sank.

"How can I help?" he almost whispered.

There was a reverence about his offer to help me. Not wanting to blurt out my needs, I wanted to respect it and honor our friendship by answering his question with self-restraint and temperance.

"I need your help... to stay calm. It's time to learn to back off and let go."

He leaned forward and looked into my eyes.

"I care about you, Marianne. A lot of us do. None of us understood why you married Tom. Frankly, I'm glad you're here. It's too bad you went through so much shit last night. Deb's in California with her dad. He's terminal with bladder cancer. No one can predict how much time he has left. Even when he passes she'll stay on to settle the estate. She's an only child."

Ray stood up and reached to his side for the plethora of silver keys on his belt. He was an inch or two taller than me, but at this moment, he seemed seven feet. In his early fifties, he had buzz-cut salt-and-pepper hair and milky white skin. I remembered lying beside him comparing the softness of his skin to mine and feeling calmed by his placid, pale-blue eyes.

Ray was a true blend of masculine and feminine characteristics with no signs of insecurity or apprehension. He held out a key for me.

"Back door to my house. I've got some paperwork to finish. It'll probably be a few more hours. You know how I like my nose slap-up against the grindstone."

I unfolded my legs to stand and reached over the desk for the key. Our fingers touched, and familiar electricity passed between us. I did a quick self-correct.

"And when Debbie gets back," I asked, "do the two of you have plans for the future?" I was hungry to know.

He shrugged his shoulders and continued with total apathy in his voice. "She's in no hurry to come back to Georgia. Before she left, she gave me an ultimatum. I've no desire to get trapped into marriage. I suspect she'll be moving out soon. Santa's not bringing her an engagement ring."

"Do you think she'll hold out for Valentine's Day?"

I knew so many women who stayed in relationships, wanting to get married, waiting for the holidays to rotate through their lives, wishing for a diamond ring to appear.

"Nope, I won't be changing my mind."

"Cruel, cruel man," I snickered.

"Cruel to be kind. Didn't someone write a song about that?" He moved around the desk and stood in front of me.

"Well, then, my dear," he said with affection as he put his arms around me, "we'll have the house to ourselves. It'll be good to spend some time with you. You can have the spare bedroom." He laughed and held me tighter.

"Oh, yeah?"

"I'm not fooling around with a married woman. Maybe all of this is happening for a reason. You can stay with me as long as it takes for you to decide what to do next. Absolutely no rush."

He rubbed my shoulders in a comforting fashion.

I pulled away to look at him. "I can cook for us tonight," I said with a smile. He let go of me and we held hands as we walked toward the door.

"I haven't had a home-cooked meal in over a month," he said. "Check the freezer for catfish. Greens in the 'fridge. Hopefully they haven't turned to slime." He raised my hand to his lips and kissed my fingers. My knees turned to Jell-O.

We said our good-byes. My heart was ecstatic, pounding. I sprinted through the parking lot to my car. The spare bedroom, I thought. How lucky. I had been hoping to impose on Ray for a night or two, but the realization that I would be in a safe, warm, loving place felt like a drug. It entered my veins and pulsed through my body. I was back on the roller coaster. This time, though, it was going to the top, and I planned to enjoy the ride as long as it lasted.

# CHAPTER 5

RAY'S NEIGHBORHOOD WAS a testament to the late Sixties. Brick ranch-styled homes lined the streets, and colorful flower beds dotted the landscape. His house was built on top of a high slope. I parked on the street, grabbed my suitcase, and locked the car.

Walking up the paved driveway caused my calves to ache from the pull of the incline. The black asphalt reminded me of my elementary school playground. One missed step meant scraped knees and elbows.

Bright quartz rocks, some the size of small boulders, covered the hill, and perennials and ivy thrived in the landscape. The rocks had come from his uncle's farm in Banks County, about two hours north of the city. They were a brilliant mix of clear and rose quartz. Flakes of mica made them appear to be laced with silver.

Ray once told me, "This rock creates a fortress against the worries of the day."

When I made my way through the metal gate and closed the latch behind me, I experienced non-stop sensory overload. His yard was surrounded by an eight-foot wooden fence covered in morning glories. A stone path paved the way to the back door leading to the kitchen. Flower beds filled with petunias, zinnias, marigolds and geraniums lined the walk. Just beyond, another path led to a lush vegetable garden that would have been the envy of any gardener.

Four tomato cages, still producing fruit, were symmetrically placed in front of the garden wall. Pepper plants, thick and bushy, held dark green, shiny peppers. Gourds and pumpkins lined the ground.

I stood for a moment and prayed. "God, thank you. You're the best."

The scent of oregano filled the air. Herbs, planted in pots partially buried in river stone, were situated in a circle outside the kitchen door.

"Home, sweet home," I whispered, sliding the key into the lock. The door opened easily and the alarm system beeped. Ray forgot to mention the alarm, so I hoped the code was the same after all these years. Entering 6969# stopped the beeping.

Would Ray ever change? I certainly hoped not.

Tonight nothing else mattered except a home cooked meal. How Zen of me to be in this frame of mind, I thought. When meals are prepared with this kind of love and gratitude, the food always tastes better.

Cooking that kind of meal became my focus. A bottle of Chardonnay was in the 'fridge, catfish filets in the freezer, and fresh herbs waited to be harvested. I found the wine opener and poured myself a glass of chilled wine. Tonight's dinner would be a celebration.

It was fun and easy getting around the kitchen. Ray had heavy stainless steel cookware hanging from a rack above the island stove and granite countertops. The greens turned out to be spinach, and there was a box of instant cornmeal mix in the cupboard.

The fish fillets softened under hot water, and a deep plate served as the dish for a lemon juice marinade. I washed the spinach, readied a pot for blanching, and prepared the cornbread. After placing it in the oven, I refilled my glass, went outside to the gardens, sat on a cast iron chair just beyond the kitchen door, and enjoyed watching birds land on the feeders.

Thirty minutes later the timer went off. With supper ready to go, there was nothing else for me to do, so I decided to relax on the couch. It was six-thirty and Ray would be home soon.

—⁓—

"Marianne, sweetheart, wake up." Ray spoke softly as he gently rocked my shoulder back and forth. I awoke to the smells of sautéed butter and broiled fish.

"I slept while you cooked?" I asked. "I didn't hear a thing."

"I can be like an elf when need be." He was smiling and had a kitchen towel draped over his shoulder. "You looked so peaceful I didn't dare wake you. Come on, girl, let's have some dinner." His voice was tender, full of affection.

What a change to be in a house with a man who was sweet and safe. We sat at the kitchen island on wooden barstools. Ray had stopped for two more bottles of white on his way home from work.

"You can never have too much wine," he said.

"Or too much good food," I replied. "This fish is delicious."

"You did all the hard work getting this together. Where did this cornbread come from?" He looked puzzled.

"Now that's a silly question. Have you looked in your pantry lately?"

"You mean past the peanuts, potato chips, and opened boxes of stale crackers? Ah, no." He looked at me with a sheepish grin. "More wine?"

"Ah…yes."

The wine buzz had begun, and it felt good. There was no driving in my immediate future, I wasn't waiting for the other shoe to drop, and there was rocky road ice cream in the freezer. Be still my beating heart.

I cleared the dishes and loaded them into the dishwasher. Ray opened more wine and talked about his day at work.

"Want to play a game of Scrabble?" he asked.

"Yes!" I almost shouted. Scrabble with Ray was fun, especially under the influence of Chardonnay. He found the box, and we moved to the dining room table.

I fished out an A square, and his was an X.

"Me first. Look out, loser boy. The odds are already stacked against you."

"X is my favorite letter," he laughed. "You don't scare me. Besides, A's are common. There is only one X out of 100."

"I'm shaking in my little Scrabble booties," I said. "Get the dictionary. I may have to defend myself."

We played, laughed, and teased each other. I was having a blast. I had forgotten about Tom, work, Debbie, and the fact that my life would be in total disarray over the coming weeks.

While choosing our tiles from the grey plastic bag, Ray asked, "Will you leave Tom for good this time?"

His words kicked me in the gut.

"Ray... what are you doing? Why ask me that now?"

My heart began to sink. All the trauma of the last forty-eight hours rushed over me like a breaking dam. I stopped breathing, my heart thumped, my face flushed, and tears welled up in my eyes.

"Oh, Jesus. I can't believe... I... stupid me, of course, you're still raw from everything. It's just that you seemed so ..."

"So what?" I became furious. "Seemed so what, Ray? So together? Oh, it's Marianne, the old girlfriend, back in the flesh."

I raised my voice and fired out words like a machine gun, "What do you want me to say, yes, I'm leaving Tom? Hey, Ray, want to fuck? How about now on the dining room table? Want to pretend it's five years ago and we're lovers, and Debbie and Tom don't exist?" I buried my face in my hands and sobbed like a schoolgirl.

And for the second time today, he let me cry. It seemed like an eternity but I finally gave up the whining. Then in true manic fashion

I picked my head up, pressed my fingertips against my eyelids and started to laugh.

"Got any valium?" I asked.

"Actually, I do. Two pills left over from knee surgery, five milligrams each. Should help you sleep. There are great healing powers in a good night's rest. No more wine, no more questions, and a down comforter for your bed."

"Oh, Ray, please hug me, and tell me I'm not crazy. I'm so sorry for saying those things to you. I had no... right."

We stood up together, and I leaned into his shoulder. His fingertips rested along the nape of my neck. His touch was soft and secure.

"Sweetheart, please know I want to be here for you, nothing more. We're past all the crap of being lovers, ex-lovers, whatever." He cupped my face with his hands and kissed my cheek. "Tomorrow is our friend."

Ray left me, made his way to his bathroom, and returned with a paper cup filled with water and a Valium.

Such a lovely shade of blue, I thought.

He kissed my forehead, and started to lick it.

"Gross, stop it, you nutcase," I said, wiping off my forehead with the back of my hand.

He mimicked a Creole accent with long and sexy tones, "I just wanted to see if you still taste the same, baby girl." He laughed heartily as he walked down the hall to the master bedroom. I swallowed the pill and chased it down with water. Thank God for drugs!

The guest bedroom had become an overflow room for Debbie's things. She'd placed her artwork on the walls, and her clothes still hung in the closet. I shut the bedroom door and stripped off my clothes. It felt good to walk around the room naked, happy and smiling. Was it the Valium? I entertained the thought of seducing Ray.

No, I decided, don't ruin a good thing; respect the friendship and set some boundaries. Run a bath, enjoy it, and go to bed.

There was expensive aromatherapy oil and a loofah in a basket on top of the toilet. The oil was lavender; its fragrance filled the air as soon as it hit the bathwater. I tested the water's temperature and stepped in. The loofah absorbed the bathwater and swelled into an exfoliating sponge.

Starting with my arms, I sloughed off dead skin cells, then moved to the rest of my body. My skin turned pink. Sliding down into the water, I rested my head against the back of the tub and began to question my sanity. Need to see Robin, I thought, as soon as possible. She understands me. Our last couple of counseling sessions had been rough, but I needed her tough insight and guidance.

Turning on more hot water, I tried to remember the last time I was truly happy. Memories of Palm Beach flooded my mind. In 1988, I had managed a boutique day spa with ten loyal employees, state-of-the-art equipment, and a beautiful view of the ocean. We all liked and cared for each other. My primary focus in life was to make other people happy, a perfect job for my co-dependent personality, and I could schmooze with the best of them, a prerequisite to success among the elite. It was *carpe diem* all the way.

My days at the spa were mostly happy and satisfying. I dated a few men, went to luscious Palm Beach parties and even made it once to the local gossip rag, the Shiny Sheet, in my little black dress and pearls. I was respected, but held at arm's length because, after all, I would never be one of *them*.

Enter attorney Randy Woods, a brown-eyed, full-throttled, womanizer son-of-a-bitch who stole my heart. What was I to do? He swept me off my feet and we instantly became an item. There was an air of competition and one-upmanship that drove us to keep pushing the envelope.

One night at a blues club, after finding the lead guitar player, I asked if I could sing *Steamroller Blues* with them on the next set. "Oh, yah!" he said. "In the key of C, we'll get it on."

We sure did. The crowd loved us. After I got offstage Randy took me home and made love to me all night long. Between orgasms there were lines of coke, joints, and Tequila shooters. This was an officer of the law? Who cared? He was gorgeous, and he was mine.

I started to use coke on a daily basis. It kept me thin and thirsty for sex. Randy was like a drug, too. It was crazy that I didn't lose my job. I was late, distracted, and grouchy after being up all night.

My cousin, Karen, who lived in Atlanta, called one day and wanted to visit. Instead of being happy to see her, I began to worry about spending time away from Randy.

When she arrived and hugged me, she was shocked at my weight loss.

"What have you been doing, Marianne? Are you sick?"

I didn't realize how much I had changed. Karen was a high school counselor and started to put two and two together.

We met Randy for drinks one night, and she hated him by the end of the first martini.

"I don't like the way he talks to you and manhandles you in public," she said. "He's trouble." And, of course, she was right.

Two months later Randy dumped me for an eighteen-year-old blonde who worked retail in a swimsuit shop. I was shattered. The cocaine withdrawal was the worst nightmare of all. I drank gallons of orange juice. The therapists at the spa gave me herbal body wraps, massages and pep talks. I tried to meditate at the beach and give up cigarettes. Jesus, would it ever end?

Finally one Sunday evening, in desperation, I called Karen and spilled my guts. She lived in a beautiful home in Roswell just outside of Atlanta, no children, and her husband traveled.

"Move in with us," Karen offered. "You need to get out of Palm Beach. If you don't, you'll die."

The realization that I had no roots, no connections, and my death would be a brief flash of departure, nothing more, scared me shitless.

I started to make plans for my relocation, and within two months was drinking coffee on my cousin's back deck, checking through the Sunday paper's classifieds. I found a job as a massage therapist at a spa/resort and enjoyed getting healthy again. I spent Thanksgiving and Christmas with Karen and Spencer, and in January I found an apartment near their home. It was 1992.

Lost in my thoughts, I hadn't realized that the bathwater had cooled. Now I pulled the plug, dried off in an oversized bath towel, and looked in the mirror.

"Hey, you... how's it goin'?" I asked. The image of tired, dark eyes was answer enough. My life was a mess.

# CHAPTER 6

WHEN I AWOKE in the morning, mouth dry and lips parched, it took me a minute to focus and remember where I was. Ray's house, I thought, Wednesday, September twenty-second, safe and sound. Got it. It was ten in the morning. The house was quiet. I lay in bed, comfy in my cotton pajamas, and reflected on the evening prior: dinner, wine, Scrabble, crying, laughing, Valium and a hot bath.

I got up and headed to the kitchen for a glass of water. My head was still a little soupy and it took me a minute or two to get oriented. The cool water was a welcome sensation, rousing me to complete consciousness. There was a note on the island: *Hold on to your key. Come and go as you please. Hope to see you tonight.*

Eventually, I located my address book, found Robin's information, and punched in the numbers to her office. She had a cancellation that day at four-thirty.

"Would you like that appointment?" the receptionist asked. Would I like a million trillion dollars? I wanted to snap back.

"Yes, please." I should have asked for a two-hour session. Robin would not be surprised by my stories; there was so much I needed to share. Last month she had cautioned me of my dangerous need to stir things up, if Tom wasn't giving me a daily dose of drama. "Try to stay calm around him especially when he's drunk," she had warned. "Don't provoke him."

Nervous and uncomfortable while dressing, I never looked in the mirror. I donned my run-away-from-Tom uniform: hair in a ponytail, an old sweatshirt, jeans and sneakers.

When I arrived at Robin's office, the waiting room was full. I signed in and found a chair near the door. An easy escape path always made me feel safe. Besides I didn't want to sit near all those crazy people. It was only five minutes before the receptionist called me back.

I did the zombie shuffle down the hall, feeling shallow and super transparent, kind of like rice paper. Grasshopper, break the paper while you walk, and you will fail.

"She'll be right in," the receptionist assured me.

"Thanks." I settled down into the pillows of an oversized pastel couch. Stuffed animals lined the bookcases along with self-help bibles and photos of smiling children. One book was titled *It's Never Too Late to Have a Happy Childhood*. "Yes it is," I replied.

Two quick knocks and my savior entered the room.

"Hello, Marianne, how are you?" Her voice was full of concern.

"If I was any better I would just burst," I smirked.

She stopped and gave me an honest appraisal. "You look like crap."

"That's funny, I feel like it."

"Let's get started," she said. "I haven't seen you in a month. What's going on?" She grabbed a notepad and pen and sat across from me in a straight-backed chair.

Jesus, what isn't going on? I thought. I recounted the whole mess, including the heavy drinking and the Valium the night before. Without looking at me, she jotted down notes. When I finished we sat in silence. I thought about our last session; she had told me there was a possibility I controlled situations by playing the victim. Could she be right?

Finally Robin spoke. "I'd like for you to start thinking from your gut, your center. Get out of your head. You are not your emotions." She looked at me oddly and said, "Marianne, are you breathing?" The exhale was loud, almost funny.

She smiled and said softly, going through the motions, "Let's breathe together, four in...hold for four... four out, three times. Ready?"

I closed my eyes and followed her cues. A minute passed; calmness filled the room. The magic of deep breathing was mysterious, but quite effective, like a soothing tonic.

I opened my eyes and said, "I don't know who I am anymore." My tone was flat, lifeless.

"Could you be comfortable not knowing who you are?" she asked.

"I'm not sure what you mean."

She spoke deliberately. "What do you think I mean?"

Oh, no, she answered the question with a question, I thought. I hate that. Caution and fear swirled inside my head. My attitude became humorous and trite, ignoring the gravity of the situation.

"I am a massage therapist. I can run three miles in under twenty eight minutes and I practice yoga twice a week."

"You're defining yourself by what you do. What else?" That one was easy.

"I'm preparing to divorce my third alcoholic, shit-head of a husband."

"You're a massage therapist, a body worker, yet you've forgotten to access your intuitive self; the power that rests here... and here." Robin put her hand on her heart and moved it to her solar plexus. "It's time to learn to trust your instincts again."

I squeezed my eyes shut and the tear machine started. She handed me a box of tissues.

"Repetitive behavior, especially negative behavior, has its roots in some past pain. It has a life of its own. We've talked about this. You're feeding it now by pretending not to care. Think about your nightmare. It was frightening but, on the other hand, it can mark the beginning of something that can offer clarity. The experience was painful, but there's no more running from the pain; it's time to walk through it."

Through the nose blowing I glanced at the clock. We had five minutes left.

Robin continued, "I'm recommending you take some time alone before you make any major decisions about your life and where you are headed."

Time slowed to a crawl. I felt calm. It was weird not pretending everything was okay.

"It's important for you to examine your thoughts, your dreams and journal again. It may be wise for you to reduce any pressure from outside influences like Tom, Ray, the spa, friends. Is that possible?"

"Well," I said, "right now I'm camped out at Ray's. I'll try to come up with a plan."

We stood together, and I asked her for a hug.

"Absolutely," she said. "You can have a hug anytime."

As we embraced my tears miraculously stopped. Her touch was firm and healing. I melted into the sensation, smiling all the way down to my toes. I pulled away and made an appointment for September the twenty-eighth at two.

The drive back to Ray's was effortless. Every green light yielded, and I was ever so happy to see his Silverado in the driveway. Hopefully, we would have dinner together. I locked my car door and glanced up to see a full moon hanging there, just above the tree tops. *Una luna loca*, I thought. That could explain all the craziness.

Inside the gate, a blue cloud of cigar smoke drifted in the air. Ray reclined on a wrought iron chaise lounge fitted with green and white striped padding. The patio furniture faced east and the moon was visible through the pine trees. Another chaise waited for me, as did a pitcher of ice water, glasses, napkins and a fruit tray on the table separating the chairs.

"Wow, check this out," I said and leaned over to kiss his cheek. "Backyard entertaining, just like in the magazines." The kiss was more like smacking and licking, tickling his face. "That's for last night."

"Catch this side." Ray pointed to his left cheek.

"Nope, one's enough. Are you growing strawberries and grapes now? This is just too sweet." Sitting down across from him, I poured a glass of water and drank half of it in one gulp.

"A little thirsty?" he asked.

"What a day," I said. "I had a session with Robin, my counselor. Change is on the horizon."

"I bet," Ray said. "Do you want to talk?"

"I need to talk. I was hoping you could help me figure out what to do next."

"You know I'm excellent at strategic planning, especially for bright promising futures."

"I want to cut my hair," I said.

"Hold on, girl. Your long blonde hair is, well, long and blonde. And you have blue eyes. You should keep your long blonde hair, even though your butt is your best asset."

"My butt?"

"Yes, ma'am, your butt. Don't look surprised. You know how cute your butt is. Why do you want to cut your hair?"

"To make some kind of a statement, mark a new beginning. I left Tom and cut my hair."

"Oh, I get it," Ray said. "Why not just shave your head? That would make a statement."

"Too radical," I said. "Maybe just shoulder length, something."

"Fruit?" he offered, as though desperate to change the subject. "Tell me about Robin, or is that confidential?"

"No, sharing is good. The most interesting thing she said was that I am not my emotions. I need to get in touch with who I really am. Ethan, my guru yoga instructor, would begin our meditations with some piece of universal wisdom. Let me see if I can remember something that would be relevant today." After a few seconds I said, "You have to say yes to suffering before you can transcend it."

"Are you ready to say yes?" Ray asked.

I picked up a strawberry and contemplated its color and shape. Instead of answering I popped it in my mouth, closed my eyes and chewed slowly.

"Are you becoming one with the berry?" Ray asked.

"Yes," I said. "And yes to the root cause of my rage, my dream, choosing alcoholic husbands, all of it. And yes to the suffering before the transcendence."

"I need a martini," Ray laughed, getting up from his lounge chair, putting down his cigar.

"Bring out the pitcher and an extra glass for me."

"There are spiritual and physical aspects to your situation." He spoke more loudly, walking away. "Let's make a list of what we can do to get your physical affairs in order. Then you can transcend away."

"Grab a notepad," I called after him.

"I'm on it," he said. "Think in two-week increments; don't hit overwhelm."

Is Ray that smart? I wondered. Or is overwhelm written all over my face?

When he returned, he set down the glasses and handed me the pad and a pen.

"It's the twenty-second," he said while pouring. "You want to get out of the condo by the end of the month?"

I knew I could. I was a pro at packing my belongings, throwing them in the trunk of my car and running away. The only difference now was, I had so much stuff.

"I'll start tomorrow," I said. "I'll call my boss and ask for the weekend off. Better yet, I'll have the flu and get a doctor's excuse on Monday. That way she can't refuse, and I'll have the next eight days to get the job done."

A veteran of disappearing acts, I knew exactly what to do. "I'll talk to the landlord first, lose the deposit and pay whatever I have to."

Ray sipped his martini, then rested against the chair with his hands behind his head, staring up at the moon.

I made notes. I was on a roll.

"Maybe Danielle can help," I said. "I love banana boxes for packing and storing. I'll make the rounds at the grocery stores, too. Fifteen ought to do it. Tom's not getting my china or cookware. He can kiss my ass."

"That's my girl."

"The trick will be getting this done while he's at work. His shift starts at two Saturday afternoon. He'll be gone all night."

Ray turned his head to face me.

"I have to be in Chattanooga this weekend for a bid, but I'll arrange for two of my men to go with you, help pack and keep you safe. I've got a box van and an empty supply room at the shop. They'll get you squared away."

"That's in three days," I gasped.

"Are you scared?" he asked.

"No, I'm pissed off and determined."

"Determined is good, but don't let the anger control you."

"What a joke," I said, making a pathetic snort.

"Let it go; don't feed the beast."

I reached over for my glass, took a long drink, and felt the vodka burn the back of my throat. It tastes like medicine, I thought.

41

"There's a story about a tribe's elder giving his grandson advice," Ray said.

"It's always an old man and a boy; why not an old wise woman and her granddaughter, or two Apache sisters having a shared vision after eating Peyote buttons?"

"Let me see how much I remember. One evening an old Cherokee told his grandson about a battle that goes on inside people. The battle is between two wolves inside us all. One is evil. It is anger, envy, jealousy, regret, greed, and arrogance. The other is good. It is joy, peace, love, hope, truth, compassion, and faith. The grandson thought about it for a minute and then asked, 'Which wolf wins?' The old Cherokee replied, 'The one you feed.'"

We were silent as Ray refilled our glasses.

"Now I see what you meant... not staying angry."

"Well, at least you never threatened to kill *me* when we were together. You're high-strung but not mean."

"Was I ever too intense for you?"

"Once or twice at parties; I'd watch you work the room and flirt. I never knew if you'd be leaving with me or someone else."

Sipping slowly, I held onto the glass and rolled it between my fingertips.

"I did it because I was insecure. Getting a man's attention made me feel special. I was trying to become someone I wasn't."

"Thanks for your honesty."

"This flying by the seat of my pants shit is getting old. Here's a question: Why did it take me so long to realize Tom would be the death of me? Why did it take so much violence?"

"Because the pain is deep," he said.

He was right. Images of the dream immediately washed through me. I was on my belly. My chest hurt. I couldn't breathe. Suddenly I sucked in a breath and startled Ray.

"I think I'm going to cry," I said.

"You can beat this. Embrace the beast and breathe," he said.

"Alliterations are so catchy," I said sarcastically.

"Yes, they are."

I started to laugh, looked up at the moon and drank the last of my martini.

Ray looked at his watch. "Did you know it's ten after ten? Five a.m. comes pretty early in these parts. You gonna be okay?"

"Maybe; can we go inside and dance just one dance?" I surprised myself by asking him. "Remember when we used to do that?"

"Absolutely," he sounded amused by the invitation. "Remember, I'm a Southern gentleman and don't take kindly to women trying to lead."

We made it to the kitchen and Ray disappeared into the living room. *Lady in Red* started to play, and Ray came into the kitchen.

"Miss Sobieski?" He held out his hand.

Oh my God, we *were* going to dance. I joined my hand in his.

It was a beautiful, haunting melody in slow, four-four time about a man coming to a party and seeing a woman he knows. She is dressed in red, surrounded by admirers. She sees him, smiles, and moves to his side.

Ray pulled me close but not too close. We danced in the kitchen. My left hand rested lightly on his shoulder.

I felt his fingertips span my ribcage, our faces six inches apart, heads turned away from each other. Every other beat my waist would barely touch his belt buckle and I'd move back, not wanting to make full contact. It was like dancing with your cousin at a wedding reception.

*Never seen you looking as lovely as you did tonight,*
*I've never seen you shine so bright.*
*Never seen so many men ask you if you want to dance, looking for a*
*little romance, given half a chance...*

I tapped into his energy, stayed on my tiptoes and kept pace with his movements. The song ended and he left me to turn off the CD player.

He stuck his head around the kitchen doorframe.

"Good night, Marianne."

"When will I see you again, my charming prince?"

"Let's do delivery pizza tomorrow about six. I'll buy."

"Fabulous."

Ray disappeared and I began my search for the martini pitcher.

# CHAPTER 7

THE ALARM WENT off at eight-thirty. I stretched long and deep, feeling muscles inflamed and knotted from the last three days of stress. In the bathroom I stumbled over the pile of running gear I had left on the floor. I pulled my hair into a ponytail and turned to look at my butt. Maybe Prince Charming is right, I thought. My butt is my best asset. Donning sweats and shoes, I drank a glass of lemon water and was disappointed not to find a note from Ray.

It felt great to hit the road and stretch my muscles into a full jog, the wind caressing my face. While running, I practiced my "sick with the flu" speech for Judy, the spa director bitch-from-hell. It was a challenge working for a woman who loved making our lives miserable. I survived by portraying sweetness and humor to everyone at work, while devising ways to kill her: choking and drowning in the Vichy shower, poison herbs in a body wrap, hot stones much too hot -- Ahhh, the possibilities.

"Please forgive me, Judy, you know I never ask off. I started puking about three this morning. Been sick all day. I don't want to put you in a bind. Just take me off the schedule and I'll bring in a doctor's excuse next week. I'm really, really sick." That should do the trick.

After my run, I showered and put on my robe. I went to the kitchen island counter, called Mr. Perry's office, and got his secretary.

"Marilyn, this is Marianne Campbell. I've got kind of an emergency and need to see Mr. Perry -- today, if possible."

"He'll be back at four; can you make it?"

"Yes, I can. Thank you so very much. I'll see you then."

I jumped up and did the Snoopy victory dance. I made a cup of green tea and stirred in a heaping tablespoon of honey while I dialed the spa. I asked the receptionist for the director.

"This is Judy. How may I help you?"

I explained my flu situation, trying to sound weak, but not too weak. I promised a doctor's note.

"If you don't bring me a note there will be consequences," her imperial majesty decreed.

"Of course, I understand." I was humble, unchallenging. Kiss my ass, was what I really wanted to say. Oh, and by the way, fuck you!

In spite of Judy's pissy attitude, everything was falling into place. Doors were opening to getting my affairs in order.

My last call was to Piggly Wiggly's produce department. I expected the manager would have fifteen banana boxes after five p.m. and I was right. He sounded cute. Our conversation was playful.

"Moving?" he asked.

"Yes, I'm going to cram the last three years of my life into fifteen boxes."

I rummaged through the 'fridge and found the ingredients to make a toasted Swiss cheese sandwich on rye smeared with Dijon mustard. I picked spears out of a kosher dill pickle jar and was tempted to eat one of the garlic cloves swimming in the brine. It was one o'clock. My waitress friend, Danielle, would be getting off at two-thirty.

After cleaning the kitchen, I dressed in sexy underwear for good luck, a white silk V-neck, jeans, and a navy doubled-breasted linen jacket I found in Debbie's closet. Thank you very much. The jacket was a tad too large; this pleased me immensely.

Dannie and I met in a yoga class when I was between Ray and Tom. We liked each other immediately; she was the kind of friend who never judged and always wanted the best for you. She rented a basement apartment in a Colonial-style home built on the edge of the Chattahoochee River. Her landlord, a gay dermatologist, was never home because his lover worked as a nurse in Savannah.

French doors from the outside walkway opened into an expansive living room complete with a fireplace and stone hearth. Max, Dannie's eight-year-old chocolate Lab, was constantly wet and shook off specks of mud when he wiggled up to beg for a pet. The river bank's red clay gave his coat brilliant highlights. Many a bottle of wine had been shared on her patio, along with intimate conversations and laughter.

On Thursday nights--amateurs partied on Fridays and Saturdays--we'd meet for happy hour at Fitzgerald's, a bar on Peachtree Street in downtown Atlanta, to flirt with the attorneys. Fitzgerald's was built in the 1940s when the heartbeat of Atlanta was deep in the city.

The building was red brick, four large, square picture windows evenly spaced from the entrance, hardwood floors, a decorative tin ceiling and mirrors behind the bar. How could you tell the rich barristers from the poor? We devised a shoe-quality rating system that seemed to work. Shined, resoled Florsheims were keepers; these men knew quality and made an effort to add longevity to their investment. Wingtips, maybe. Work boots, forget it.

Dannie and I would take turns dropping our credit cards on the heart-of-pine floors, leaning off bar stools in precarious positions to get a closer look at the shoes. We attended the annual Atlanta attorneys' flag football game at Piedmont Park in the spring -- Jews versus Christians. The WASP prosecutors almost always won; it was a testimony to the advantage of having more brawn than brains.

Once a defense attorney gave me the best advice. "Don't break two laws at once," he said. "If you are drinking and driving, don't speed. Always make sure your tail lights are working before you drive and smoke pot." They were profound suggestions I would never forget.

It was worth taking MARTA back to my apartment after drinking at
Fitzgerald's.

—m—

Thursday's lunch crowd was thinning when I arrived at the Texas
Longhorn Steakhouse. This was my kind of place. Patrons threw peanut shells on the floor and animal heads covered the walls. Tips were
great and the atmosphere was fun and casual. Dannie liked everyone
she worked with, even the cooks who were notorious for being nasty
to female and gay staff.

I caught Dannie's eye and she came over to give me one of her
infamous bone-crushing hugs. She was five-foot-six, 180 pounds of
pure affection, straight, jet black hair braided past her shoulders.
Dark, black-brown eyes reflected her Cherokee heritage. When she
smiled her face shone like an angel, halo and all.

"Where are *you* going, all spiffed up?" Dannie asked.

"I'm off to see the Wizard."

"Can I come? I've finished my side work and need to get my tips at
the bar. Really, where are you headed?"

"We need to talk. So much has happened this week."

"Good or bad?" she asked with a worried look.

"I think you'll like my answer."

Dannie never liked Tom. She called him "creepy" in a psycho
kind of way. "His expressions never change. He's a sociopath," she
had warned.

Dannie and I sat at the bar.

"I need chocolate," I said. "This afternoon is going to be a bitch."

"Need me to tag along?"

I said nothing, not sure how to answer. I glanced over at Jessica,
the svelte body-builder bartender, working a couple of businessmen
at the other end of the bar. She strategically placed her coffee cup on

the cooler, bent over just enough to show her cleavage, and sipped slowly, seductively. Jessie wore her dark brunette hair in carefree curls that hung in long ringlets, shoulder-length. She had jade-green eyes and a butt you could set a plate on.

Finally, Jessie noticed us and hustled over.

"Why didn't you throw a bottle of ketchup at me?" she asked.

"And miss you mesmerizing those poor unsuspecting men?" We all turned to look, and Blondie raised his beer bottle in a pathetic toast.

"They're cute," Jessie said. "What can I get you ladies?"

"Bring me a warm brownie, please," I said, "with extra syrup and vanilla ice cream."

"New diet, huh?"

"Set me up with a sea breeze," Dannie said.

Jessica smiled; mischief was in the air.

"Not working tonight, Dannie?"

"I don't work again until Monday lunch, if you can you believe it. The time off will help recharge my *nice* batteries."

"I'm jealous," Jessie said as she scooped ice into a glass and over-poured Absolut for Dannie's drink. "Just a splash of cranberry, if I remember correctly."

"You're correct."

Dannie turned on her bar stool to face me and scanned me up and down.

"Let me see… where is that aura of yours?" She looked above my head, trying to observe my energy field. "I see… it's a mix of red and orange… a bit emotional today?"

The concern in her voice gave me the courage to begin the *Tom and Marianne* saga. I digressed often, but Dannie kept up with a few questions.

The brownie arrived and Jessie asked, "How about a shot of Baileys over it?"

I slid the bowl across the bar to her and said, "Pour."

Dannie sipped her drink and asked, "So where are you headed next?"

"First stop, Mr. Perry's office. I'm breaking the lease, no matter how much cash it takes. I'm not letting that bastard have a free place to stay. We'll both be out by the thirtieth. Watch me."

"I don't doubt you."

I took a spoonful of melting ice cream, brownie, and chocolate syrup all swimming in the sweet, creamy liqueur, real medicine for a troubled soul. My taste buds exploded. I chewed slowly, closed my eyes and savored every second.

Dannie stared at me and said, "Another death by chocolate."

"What a way to go," I mumbled.

"When will you actually pack boxes and move out?"

"Tom starts his shift at two on Saturday afternoon. Ray has an empty storage unit I can use, and he's allowing me to stay with him until I can decide what to do next."

We sat in silence. Our elbows randomly brushed against each other as she drank and I swam in my sensual dessert experience.

"I'm off all weekend," Dannie said. "I can help. I haven't had a chance to tell you, but I started seeing a guy named Steve. He's ex-military, very handy in conflict situations. He's intense, but so much fun. He's a big guy; I don't feel fat around him. He tells me my body is comfortable. How sweet is that? I know, you could give us a gift certificate for a massage... a house call for both of us. He'd be all over that."

"Oh my God, you're kidding!" I said. "Pinch me."

Dannie pulled an inch of skin from my arm and pinched aggressively as I recoiled from the pain.

"Ouch! You bruised me, you bitch."

"I'm not a bitch, I'm your best friend, remember? What time do you want us at the condo?"

"Two-thirty. It won't take long. Ray has a couple of guys who are going to help. I'll get newspapers, boxes and garbage bags for my clothes. I want to get in and out fast."

I pushed the bowl away with a few bites left.

"You're leaving that?" Dannie exclaimed.

"Have at it;" I said. "After all, we want you with a *comfortable* body."

"Shut up, smartass. Maybe just a taste."

I left a ten on the bar for Jessica. "Wish me luck," I said.

"Give me a hug." Dannie spread her arms.

We embraced. Her clothes held aromas of greasy French fries and burgers from the kitchen, cheap hairspray and patchouli. Steve is right, I thought, she is comfortable. Saturday would be a breeze with her at my side.

"Thank you, Danielle."

Breaking free from her, I made my way to the door. The heavy sugar-rush pulsed through my body like my old Palm Beach friend, cocaine. I was flying now, and invincible.

# CHAPTER 8

MR. PERRY'S OFFICE was in a one-story white brick building with rows of professional suites. Magenta cloth awnings, each a semicircle, hung over the doorways. Dark reflective glass set in varying rectangular shapes looked like a stack of dominos; hedges of dark green perfectly manicured shrubbery bordered the sidewalks.

Perry Insurance and Real Estate shimmered in gold lettering on Suite 340's aluminum framed door. I arrived ten minutes early. Turning off the car, I practiced Robin's breathing exercise: four deep breaths in, four deep breaths out. It took a few moments to compose myself. Mr. Perry was a shrewd businessman. Playing the part of a crazed, scornful wife simply would not do. The brownie buzz was wearing off, and I was ready to talk to the man and negotiate.

Marilyn smiled when I entered the office. We had a lot in common. Over the past year she and I worked out at the same fitness club and ran several 5k's together. In her mid-fifties with short cropped, salt and pepper hair, she had the body of a thirty-year-old. Everyone loved Marilyn, the way men loved Dagwood's Blondie.

"Marianne, it's great to see you. How are things?" Her tone was genuine, full of good intention.

"Not good. Tom and I are splitting up." She looked shocked.

"But I just saw you two at the mall holding hands."

"Trying extra hard to fix an impossible situation. It's been exhausting."

She moved from behind her gray metal desk.

"Can I give you a hug?"

We embraced. Two hugs from two wonderful women in less than an hour! I'd hit the jackpot.

"I'm so sorry," she said, patting my back with short repetitive beats as if she were burping a baby. It felt condescending; she didn't really know how to relate. She'd been married to the same man for thirty years. "You're tough; you'll make it."

Marilyn pulled back and held me at arms' length, looking into my eyes with a magnetic stare. I almost giggled.

"Men, unless they are my husband, are a nuisance. Most of them are full of crap."

We sat together in the waiting area. Finance and real estate magazines covered the glass coffee table. Healthy philodendrons and ferns flourished near the entrance.

"Is that why you're here?" she asked. "To terminate the lease?"

"It's time to make a clean break."

"Mr. Perry will be disappointed, but I'm sure you can work something out." She stood and said, "He should be back any minute. Can I get you an iced tea?"

"No. Thanks."

The ringing telephone sent Marilyn back to her desk. I picked up a real estate magazine and decided on a modest Peachtree Country Club Tudor-style home for 1.3 million dollars. A lot of vacuuming, I thought.

The steel backdoor slammed. Mr. Perry entered whistling softly. A few minutes passed, and Marilyn headed back to his office. Sounds of laughter soon followed. What's so funny? I thought. Steady girl, don't get pissed. They're not talking about you. They emerged from the hallway together. Marilyn winked at me and sat down at her desk.

"Hey there, Miss Marianne," he said.

Mr. Perry's chubby, pale face gained was framed by black-framed glasses. Thin strands of faded blonde hair were combed over his nearly bald head, his red striped tie was open at the neck, and the sleeves of his medium-starch white oxford shirt were rolled up to his elbows.

"Come on back."

I followed his short dense frame to his office. He pulled out one of the black leather wing chairs in front of his desk.

"Please, have a seat."

It was obvious Mr. Perry had graduated from the University of Alabama. The Crimson Tide had rolled in and washed his office walls in BAMA regalia. He was no exception to the pigskin rule -- southern men live and breathe SEC football.

"Marilyn tells me you're having some trouble."

So they *were* talking about me.

"Yes, sir."

After a short pause, "You want to tell me about it?"

"Well, Mr. Perry, it seems my husband has been living a dual life. He's been moody and drinking more and more. Someone has been calling the condo and hanging up when I answer. Frankly, sir, I'm concerned for my safety."

He sat quietly for an eternally long moment.

"Marianne, do you pray?"

"Why, yes, Mr. Perry, I do."

"There's a heap of power in prayer. In fact..." He began a long droning about his faith and the problems he had encountered in his life. I'm sure his intentions were good, but I stopped listening after the second example of the way he'd survived unthinkable circumstances through the power of prayer. But I dared not interrupt.

"And so you see, no obstacle is too large for our Lord."

"Thank you for the advice," I said cautiously, "and for sharing your stories with me. I can't fix Tom. He has to want to get help. Can you recommend a pastor?"

Playing to his self-righteousness seemed a good offensive move.

"Yes." He looked pleased. "My church has an outreach program for men struggling with addiction. Reverend Alexander is a recovering alcoholic. Tom would be welcomed with open arms. I know several men who have healed their lives and their marriages. All things are possible with our Lord Jesus Christ."

I almost answered with a quick *Amen, brother,* but refrained.

Perry reached into his back pocket for his wallet. It was flat from the weight of his large buttocks; miraculously he wiggled a business card out of one of its slots.

"Here you are, young lady." He handed me the card. "Give this to Tom. Tell him to call any time day or night."

"That is very kind, Mr. Perry."

"Now let's decide what's best for you."

He put his fingers together at the tips and flexed his joints in and out. His palms came together in a prayer pose, and his index fingers touched his lips, and then went back to flexing. Before he spoke, his skin changed from pale to blushing pink, and then to red.

Despite his Christian rhetoric, Marilyn speculated that his skin was victim to excessive gin consumption, and the broken blood vessels around his nose were due to his daily six o'clock cocktails.

"If you break the lease today you'll lose the deposit and pay October's rent. Also, the condo must be empty by September thirtieth and in good order. If we can find another renter by October thirty-first, you'll be released from the remaining penalty. The lease is in your name and you'll be held responsible. The renter's agreement states that you must pay three months to break the lease, but you have been a good renter and a friend to Marilyn. She and I are very sad to see you leave. We hope you and Tom will eventually work things out and not divorce."

So that's what Marilyn's wink was about; she had run interference for me. I forgave her for patting me like a baby. The gesture was motherly, not demeaning.

I reached into my purse for my checkbook. Eight-hundred-and-fifty dollars was a walk in the park, but the hole in the drywall was another matter entirely.

Seven days and counting.

—m—

The Piggly Wiggly grocery store was busy at five-fifteen on a Thursday night. Executive moms were buying rotisserie chickens, deli salads and ice cream; handsome men were selecting wines, and elderly women were squeezing tomatoes.

I made my way to the back of the produce department, where huge white swinging doors with clear Plexiglas windows led to the storage area. A tall, thin man wearing an apron and a white baseball cap embossed with the Wiggly Pig himself smiled at me. Big brown eyes, I thought, long lashes, and a heavenly smile. Is he the produce manager?

"Fifteen boxes?" he asked.

"Are you the psychic produce manager?"

"You have that 'my world is about to change and I'm moving' look about you."

"I hate being so obvious," I laughed.

"You're not. You don't have a shopping cart, and you've been scanning the back area. I know your type."

"Right you are. But how'd you know..."

"You called me, right?"

He looked like an old hippie, with his dark ponytail coming out the back of his ball cap. His grin reminded me of my college philosophy professor's smile; an inner confidence, special knowledge. Or was it *You're so beautiful, let's have sex?* Did he think I was attractive, or did he smile at everyone like that?

"Let's head back and get a handcart to load the boxes. I'll help you out with them."

"Wow, thanks."

The storage area was chilly. I was glad I had worn the linen jacket; otherwise he'd have witnessed hard nipples against my silk sweater.

"My name is Marianne." I held my hand out to him.

"Mark," he said, flashing the eternal beacon of enlightenment.

He must be a Buddhist, I thought. Only the Dalai Lama grins like that.

We opened boxes and tucked them inside each other for easy transport.

"What are you driving?"

"An old 240 Volvo; it's built like a tank. It should be easy to load all of these."

He stacked the cartons on the cart and followed me toward the front of the store. Several high schools girls working as check-out clerks waved at him and giggled. Ah, the guru of happiness and joy, I thought. I bet Mark gets laid a couple of times a week.

"Here we are," I said, opening the trunk of my Volvo.

"This is a classic," he said with enthusiasm, "straight from a 1980s European thriller."

We stood assessing each other.

He lifted two boxes and put them on the front seat. I reached down for two more and he stopped me.

"I've got this, no worries."

I stepped back and watched him work. He had a muscular body and a great ass. My nipples were getting even harder now, but not from the cold storage room. It had been so long since I had kissed a man I found attractive, and I wondered if he was a good kisser.

I leaned against the back fender, waiting for him to finish. He shut the back door and moved in front of me, very close in front of me. Very close.

"All done," he almost whispered and smiled another one of those "let's fuck" smiles.

I glanced around and wondered just how ballsy I could be with Mark in the parking lot. No one was in direct view.

"I'd like to show you my gratitude," I said.

I reached up, wrapped my hands around the top of his apron, and pulled him into me. He didn't resist. We kissed, our lips parted, and his tongue explored every inch of my mouth. He wasn't a good kisser; he was a great kisser!

I moaned softly.

He slid his hands under my sweater, unsnapped my bra, and gently massaged my rock-hard nipples. My silk panties were getting wet. I straddled his leg and rocked my pussy against his jeans.

"Come on, baby," he whispered, "come on. It's yours if you want it. Come on..."

He picked me up off his leg, held me with one arm, and unzipped my jeans. I was in a trance, and close to climaxing.

He zeroed in on my throbbing clit, and the fast vibration of his middle and index fingers forced me to grind against them in oblivion.

"Jesus, Mark, do it. Just do it."

My panting quickened and my whole body moved to the rhythm of his strokes. I moaned and burrowed my head into his chest.

"I'm coming! Oh God, I'm fucking coming!" I gasped.

Electricity coursed through every inch of my body. Mark steadied me as he slid his hand out of my jeans, and the waves of orgasm subsided.

Deftly he reached under my sweater and fastened my bra. My panties were soaked.

I started laughing so hard I snorted. "Oh, no, I'm snorting."

It was a wonder release. I zipped up my jeans and ran my fingers through his hair.

"You sure know your way around women's lingerie. Please don't say anything tacky like 'tons of experience,' although you probably do have tons. How often do you help women out to their cars?"

I looked down at his bulging dick and pressed the palm of my hand against it.

"Time to reciprocate?"

"This was fun, but I've got to get back inside or I'll get fired."

"Wow... okay." Little Miss Tough Chic was feeling abandoned.

He put his fingers in his mouth then touched my lips and said, "I've got this to remind me of you throughout the evening. You know where to find me."

"In the banana section?"

"Bananas or cucumbers," he said, trying to keep a straight face.

We both laughed and kissed briefly.

He made his way back to the store, pulling the cart behind him. I sat down in the driver's seat, started the car and put it in reverse. Looking out the back window to navigate the parking lot, I saw him waving goodbye and our eyes met.

I might need more boxes after all, I thought. The lingering sensation between my legs made me smile. God, I sighed, I needed that.

Ray's truck was in his driveway. The prospect of a pizza dinner was comforting. I hoped it was topped with pepperoni, sausage, ham, peppers, pineapple, extra cheese, extra sauce, extra everything. Red wine and a slice of pie would be heaven.

I exited the Volvo, took off the linen jacket and placed it over my arm. The tough-girl uniform had worked. Mr. Perry and Marilyn had supported my decision, and Ray would be pleased I had taken the first step. I was proud of my progress.

Ray was on the couch in his gray sweats and blue Georgia Tech T-shirt watching the six o'clock news when I entered through the back kitchen door.

"Ray-Ray, my friend R-A-Y," I called out to him in a high pitched, sing-song voice that sounded like a muumuu-clad senior citizen with curlers in her hair.

He muted the television.

"Please don't make me get up from the couch."

I waltzed into the living room continuing to sing.

"It's been a wonderful day, oh Ray."

"Are you going to have one of your 'I can't stop laughing' fits? Oh, geez."

My voice took on a more serious tone. "How do you fix a drywall hole the size of a fist, so it looks like nothing happened?" I draped the jacket over the back of a dining room chair.

"Tricky. You'll have to repair the hole with wire mesh and mud, sand it down and paint the entire wall to match the patch. What color is it?"

"The whole condo is renters' beige."

"How big is the wall?" he asked.

I had to think. Tom's Monday night punch was between the staircase and the kitchen.

"It's triangular shaped. Eight feet high, and it follows the staircase down to the woodwork. Nothing major."

I sat on the couch by his feet, picked up his right foot, and began a reflexology sequence.

"Ahhh. If you keep rubbing, I may just get it done for you."

"Oh, won-der-ful, Ray. You're the best." I wanted to kiss his toes.

"Please stop singing like a six-year-old."

Extra pressure on the ball of his foot produced a yelp of pain.

"Okay, Okay, your singing is not that bad."

"I'm singing because it feels good to be silly."

"How about some pizza?" he asked.

"Let me finish your feet."

"Good idea." He laid his head back and turned the sound back on. We watched the news together, commenting on arrest reports and the weather. The weekend forecast was partly cloudy with low humidity, temperatures in the mid-seventies.

Saturday will be perfect for the move, I mulled.

After the news, we sat together at the kitchen island, drank merlot, and shared the best pizza on the planet.

"Where did this pizza come from?" I asked.

"Little Italy. A family from New Jersey relocated to Norcross, and we're the happy recipients of a fully loaded, fourteen-inch Sicilian."

"It's sinful. Thank you."

"Prego."

We talked about our day. Ray was stressed out about his trip to Tennessee.

"So much depends on our personalities, the bid, and if I can let them win at golf."

"That's a problem?"

"For me it is. If they aren't worth their salt on the course, I'll have to start slicing the ball and missing putts. I hate that."

"Can't you schmooze them at the barbeque?"

"Probably, but it's always a challenge."

I told him about my experience with Mr. Perry.

"Marianne, how long have you lived in the South? If a man's office is a shrine to his university, Jesus is not far behind. Did you piss him off?"

Erika Jantzen

"No... thankfully." I explained the agreement. "Norcross condos are a hot item. It should rent in thirty days."

"Andy and Charlie will be with you on Saturday. Put Andy on the wall; Charlie is a workhorse. You should be able to go back on Sunday and paint."

"Back on Sunday? Are you crazy? Let's not forget about psycho Tom."

"Oh... right. Let's remain calm. You've a lot going for you right now. One day at a time. I'll give Andy instructions about the repair. He's a good kid. Don't worry, it will look like new."

"Have I told you in the last thirty minutes how grateful I am for your help?"

"No, but you can clean up the kitchen."

"With pleasure."

"I've got paperwork to do in my office before bed. You probably won't see me in the morning. I have a ten a.m. meeting with Mr. Archer and his staff. I'll be staying at the Smith House downtown, if you need me. The number will be on the 'fridge. Saturday's golf, then an evening BBQ at the Chattanooga Country Club. I'll be home Sunday evening before six. Go to the office tomorrow and have Helen introduce you to Andy and Charlie. The storage unit is in the back of the shop. It's climate-controlled."

"You've got it all covered."

"That's what I do for a living, supply people's needs."

His tone was flat. He wasn't here, but somewhere else. We hugged briefly. Was it Debbie's impending return, the trip to Chattanooga, or the gravity of my presence in his home that made him uneasy? After my chores I went to bed and tossed and turned all night. I was thankful for Ray's help, but understood that I didn't want to compromise him.

The next two days would be in my control. I had to be strong.

# CHAPTER 9

SOMETIME DURING THE night I found a spot in the mattress that suited my body and a light, cotton-weave blanket that gave me just enough warmth to lull me to sleep. The neighbor's barking dog awakened me, and the cacophony of early morning sounds began: a groaning A/C unit, diesel trucks rumbling down the street, more barking dogs, birds chirping, and finally, Ray's truck coming to life and departing. As the sounds of his truck faded, I felt so alone.

It had been an uneasy slumber. My body didn't move but the racing head-talk sprinted into "what-if" thinking. What if Tom refuses to move out, the doctor won't give me an excuse for work, I get fired, Ray hates me, I have nowhere to live, Dannie changes her mind and doesn't show. So many nightmare scenarios.

It was a bleak future, grim and scary. What the fuck? I thought. Where's my backbone, my internal strength? Will I always depend on the kindness and compassion of the people who love me? Will I ever move forward without some friggin' man lurking in the background to come to my rescue?

Forcing myself out of bed, I made it to the kitchen. No note from Ray, I thought. There were only phone numbers in Chattanooga on a paper held by an Atlanta Braves magnet on the 'fridge. Have I worn out my welcome?

Searching the kitchen cabinets for an espresso blend, I prepared to make a cup of my favorite get-your-head-out-of-your-ass coffee. While filling the coffeemaker with water and spooning finely ground black powder into the bleached paper filter, my thinking shifted into a more positive mode.

As long as I paid for a visit to the doctor I'd get an excuse; everyone knew this unwritten rule. Hey, even getting fired wouldn't be so bad, I thought. It would force me to find a new job, grow as a body worker, and develop my gift as a healer in new ways. Dannie would be there on Saturday; how could I doubt her allegiance?

I hit the button on the machine and waited for the sounds of the brewing rocket-fuel to begin. Ray doesn't hate me, I concluded. The guy worships me, poor bastard. Why else would he put up with this shit? I needed to relax, stop taking things so personally. Finding a mug from the cupboard and flavored cream from the 'fridge, I filled the cup only halfway, knowing that espresso required a heavy dose of cream to be palatable. That is, unless you are Cuban. French vanilla swirls brought the liquid from darkness to light and the perfect cup of coffee was born.

I sat at the kitchen island feeling the warmth of the mug in my hands. Through the slats of the wooden blinds, diffused first light created aurora-like streams and patterns on the refrigerator and walls. Birds gathered at the feeder and a frustrated squirrel kept watch for falling seeds. Several hours of alone time loomed before me. I was determined to make good use of it by staying calm and enjoying the moment.

I arrived at Ray's office just past one o'clock. Helen was her usual beauty-queen self, checking her lipstick with a compact mirror at her desk when I entered.

"Well, hello, Miss Marianne." Her tone was not the cheery one I was accustomed to, but instead reflected a hint of hostility. "The boys are looking forward to meeting you, but more importantly, they're looking forward to time-and-a-half pay on Saturday."

I flopped down on a chair facing her desk, propped the heel of my boot on the toe of the other, and moaned.

"Helen, I can't believe I'm moving again."

"Well," she said, "it's my understanding your *things* will be *here*, but where will *you* be?" Her inflections drove the tension in the air even higher and more hateful.

Geez, I thought, what side of the bed did she get up on?

She raised an eyebrow and snapped the compact shut with one hand. How much had Ray told her about my situation? She had always been kind to me before; this kind of reception was unexpected. Her words smacked up against my vulnerable frame of mind, and hurt.

Once more I faced a whole list of shitty possibilities: emptying my savings, daily chaos, losing everything including my sanity. A bleak future loomed, and once again I was depending on someone else to pull my ass out of the fire.

"I'm not sure what will happen next," I said sadly.

"Oh, my, isn't that sooo pitiful."

I wanted to slap her.

She pressed the button for the shop's loudspeaker. As she spoke, her Southernese hit a new high, with vowel sounds going on for syllables. "Andy and Charlie, Mr. Andy and Mr. Charlie, please come to the front office." She gave me a hateful side glance. "Your boys are on their way."

I had had enough of her disdain.

"Actually, Miss Helen, they're Ray's boys, aren't they?"

She dismissed me with a click of her tongue against the roof of her mouth as Andy and Charlie entered from the shop door. Andy, handsome with blonde hair and a closely trimmed red beard, wore a black merchant marine cap. His slender frame fit nicely into bib overalls, and a red handkerchief was stuffed into the back pocket. Charlie lumbered in after him, a big bear of a man, his body pushed against the buttons of his blue work shirt, belly fat hanging over the belt. A NASCAR hat covered his dark curly hair and he was in need of a shave.

Helen stood and crossed her arms under her breasts.

"Andy, Charlie, this is Marianne Sobieski. I'm sure Ray has filled you in on the details of what she needs." She reached down to her desk and handed Charlie two keys and a credit card. Her instructions were delivered with drill sergeant precision.

"Truck key and storage key," she said, "number sixteen. The credit card is for gas and any building supplies you need. Everybody pays for their own food. Clock in when you leave and clock out when the move is done. Any questions?" She shot me another look that dared me to challenge her authority.

The guys spoke in unison. "No, ma'am."

"That does it for me," she said. "Y'all scoot... I have *work* to do."

Charlie spoke without an accent. "Miss Sobieski, let's show you the storage unit."

"Thank you so much," I said.

Helen never looked up from her computer. The three of us made our way into the shop and I followed them to the storage area.

"You piss her off, Andy?" Charlie joked, poking him with an elbow.

"No, sir," Andy spoke with a soft melodic drawl. "She's fussin' at *you* on account of you not makin' her happy last night."

"No, gentlemen," I said, "she doesn't care much for me these days."

"Oh... that explains it," Charlie said. "She's like a mother hen over the boss."

Andy mocked Helen in a high falsetto, "That devil woman is comin' to steal my Ray. Just how many women does he need?"

"You know Mr. Ray long, Miss Sobieski?" Charlie asked.

"Please, call me Marianne. Come on, I'm only a few years older than you two. I've known Ray since Christmas 1991... before Debbie."

"That explains a lot," Charlie said.

It was obvious that Charlie was a fellow Yankee. Andy had a sexy Southern accent that could melt butter. We continued to unit sixteen in silence. When we arrived Charlie unlocked the door, switched on the light, and we all stepped in.

"Wow. So much room," I said, "and it's spotless."

"Sensitive electrical components are stored in here," Charlie said. "That's why it's so clean... climate-controlled."

Here, I thought, my clothes, books, linens, art and furniture will be stored in boxes and bags... until I can find another clean and climate-controlled area to inhabit.

I forced my voice to sound cheery and uplifting, but the fact was, these two strangers were going to move all of my personal possessions into a concrete cell guarded by light sensors and an alarm system.

"Tomorrow," I said, "I'll have everything we need to pack. Just show up at two and we'll get started. The weather's going to be nice."

"I moved from Louisiana once in the rain," Andy said. "Couch and bed soaked clean through. Finally flung the mattress to the dump, all moldy and smelly." He reached for his back. "I slept on the floor for a month."

"Do you want to exchange phone numbers?" I asked.

"No, we're good," Charlie said.

"If we don't show," Andy said, "Mr. Ray will have our hides."

"You know the way?"

"Yup," Charlie said.

"Then I'll see you tomorrow. Thank you both so much."

"No thanks needed. We're lookin' forward to the paycheck." Andy grinned.

"Both of us like overtime hours," Charlie added.

"Then tomorrow will be a productive day for all of us." I forced a smile as I made my way out of the unit, having taken my next step toward freedom.

———

I drove to the grocery store and purchased three boxes of heavy-duty garbage bags. My plan was to go to the condo and begin the process of organizing linens, blankets, and towels while Tom was at work. It would save time tomorrow during the move.

I parked the Volvo at the end of the condo's cul-de-sac. No sign of Tom's two-door beater; thankfully the Jeep sat untouched in its parking space, even after the drama of Monday night. I approached the entrance; the door was slightly ajar. My heart raced from the fear of another confrontation. It was time for him to be at work; why was the door unlocked?

I gently pushed the door open with the toe of my boot; there was only silence and the stench of an extinguished fire. I peeked in, opening the door slowly. I stood in shock. "Holy shit!" I whispered. All of the living room furniture was gone. My round, claw-foot kitchen table remained, as did the four matching chairs. Floral drapes still covered the windows and our artwork hung on the walls.

"Jesus," I said aloud, walking to the fireplace. Our wedding photos were ripped into shreds and lay half-burned in the fireplace. Sitting down on the hearth, I looked at the hole Tom had punched in the wall Monday night. He had taken a black Magic Marker and drawn squiggly lines around it, adding the word "CUNT."

Heat rose up my neck and into my scalp. I tore off my right boot and used the heel to bash in the wall. *Bang! Bang! Bang!* I couldn't hit it hard enough.

"Bastard, you bastard!" I screamed, Sheetrock flying. I covered my eyes and bawled, sliding down to the floor. There was an evil force around me and dark visions flashed in the cracks of my mind.

*The boot in my hand became a broom handle, and suddenly I looked at my father's belt as I smashed the broom straws against his back.*

*"Stop it, stop, you're hurting her!" I wailed, not recognizing my own voice. He finally let go of choking my mother and turned on me.*

*"Give it to me, you little bitch." His eyes were bloodshot. He breathed like a dragon as he tried to rip the broom from my grip. He flung me around.*

*"Let... it... go!" he hissed.*

*Mom threw her body against his, pushing him into the refrigerator. Blood ran down one side of her face.*

*"Run!" she screamed.*

*I ran halfway out of the kitchen but stopped suddenly, paralyzed by fear for my mother's life. She became a terrific force taking control of the broom handle and driving it into his stomach knocking the air out of his lungs. He lost his balance and fell to the floor. Mom grabbed her purse from the kitchen table and me by the hand. We flew out the back door and sprinted to her 1966 Rambler.*

*"He's coming!" I shouted.*

*She backed halfway down the block before putting it in first gear and almost hit him driving away.*

The boot leather flexed under my grip as all evidence of Tom's graffiti vanished into a gaping hole. I rested my head on folded arms and cried like it was the end of the world. The flashbacks of my parents fighting had overwhelmed me. It was crystal clear, every detail magnified by the pain. Still breathing heavily from the adrenal rush of smashing the wall, I gulped huge amounts of air between sobs.

A strong hiccup caught me off guard; another one was followed by a third. The crying stopped but the hiccups persisted, too many autonomic responses for my body to handle. I slid my boot on, went to the kitchen cabinet for a glass, and discovered that half of the dishes were missing.

Filling a glass with water, I drank the entire contents quickly, hoping to stop the hiccups. I held my breath but the hiccups persisted. I started to giggle. After another deep breath the giggling turned into full-blown laughter. The extreme emotional swing over a period of only ten short minutes sent me into a freefall of total abandon. Roaring, deep belly laughs transported me from the depths of misery to a place of surrender. Smashing in the wall was cathartic, cleansing, and an act of purification. Finally, the laughter subsided and my breathing slowed. My crazed state quietly calmed.

I dried the last of my tears with the back of my wrist and made my way up the stairs to the bedrooms to see what else had disappeared. I looked down and spotted the dried blood from Tom's hand on the stairwell carpet. Sitting down next to the stain, I placed my hand over it, felt the hardened fibers against my palm, and pressed lightly down, moving back and forth over the surface. The Summit dream entered my thoughts. Sensations of blood dripping down my back and this dried blood; I wondered, are they related? How? Somewhere in my subconscious the answer was buried, like a coffin waiting to be exhumed.

I rose and continued to the second floor. Tom had taken all the master bedroom furniture. My clothes were dumped in a pile in the middle of the floor. Okay, I thought, this is good. I felt self-assured, as if I'd made a great drive off the first tee: a little apprehensive but spunky. My clothes were in a pile on the floor? Stick them in a bag, Marianne. No heavy furniture... the move will go quickly.

I was beginning to see how positive all of this was. Tom had essentially cut my work in half. He probably thought he was putting the screws to me, but really this was the best-case scenario.

The other bedroom was untouched; even my books and desktop were unscathed. As I stood in my office I felt pressure on my left shoulder, almost like a hand caressing me.

I turned to see that the Australian crystal hanging in the window had created giant prisms of light interspersed on the wall. Red, orange, yellow, green, blue and violet; it was exquisite. A sense of peace enveloped me. Without warning, my body temperature rose and a tingling began at the base of my torso. I recognized the sensations as Kundalini -- the same experience I'd had in deep mediation with a guru in Atlanta. My left hand shook as I steadied myself on the arm of my office chair. I sat down and gave in to the experience.

The awakened energy moved slowly up my spine. Waves of electricity coursed through my body and into my extremities. The crown of my head felt hot. It was dream-like. My breathing deepened, and with my eyes closed I watched as the colors from the crystal's prism brought back the chakra clearing I had practiced weekly, before I had become so wrapped up in daily struggles with Tom. The breathing and the colors reminded me who I was, a child of light.

I felt the pressure on my shoulder again. The electricity calmed to a low buzz and settled into my heart. I opened my eyes to find that the bright afternoon sun had faded. The clock read 4:46 p.m. An hour had vanished, but there was still plenty of time for packing.

In the kitchen I hit the jackpot. The coffee pot remained and the refrigerator was full; even the freezer had veggie burgers and frozen peas. Setting up the coffee to brew, I looked at the new and improved hole in the wall and thought, *Jesus, Andy's gonna be busy with that.*

I wasn't rattled anymore; the calm I felt was profound.

Rummaging through my purse, I found the Jeep's key. I dreaded the phone call to Mr. Carson telling him I needed fifteen-hundred more dollars or no deal. The Jeep started right up and I drove it to the other side of the complex. It would be safe there. Dannie would help me move it to Ray's office tomorrow. Then I considered my own safety. Packing would take most of the night. I could sleep on the first floor next to the phone, but the locks would have to be changed. If I could get a locksmith here this evening, I would stay. Too bad the cops still have my .357, I thought. I'd sleep even better with it under my pillow.

I retrieved bags and boxes from the Volvo and placed them strategically throughout the condo to simplify the packing. After pouring a cup of coffee, I found the phonebook in its usual spot. Under "Locksmiths" was *The Southern Gentleman, Opening Doors Every Day.* Who could resist? Harvey Chandler answered on the third ring and said he could be at the condo within the hour. I liked him already.

Packing the master bedroom and bath was a snap. Clothes and linens slid easily into bags, and everything else fit into boxes.

As I started down the stairs for more coffee, the doorbell rang. I opened the door to find the most adorable older gentleman I'd ever seen. He had long gray wisps of hair combed over a shiny head, and his face was lit by an infectious grin and soft, kind eyes. Suspenders held up khaki pants over an expanded waistline. His white shirt was pressed, and a brown fishing vest completed his ensemble.

"Why hello there, Miss. I'm Harvey Chandler."

He had an air of distinction and nobility. Yes, he was indeed Harvey Chandler, the great and powerful locksmith who made the world a safer place.

"Mr. Chandler, thank you for coming so quickly."

"Well, if I'd known you were such a pretty little thing, I'd a got here sooner."

Was I blushing? I bet he talked to all the women this way. Some men just get it, I thought. Flattery will get you everywhere.

"Please come in. There's only one lock that needs to be changed: the front door."

Harvey entered and paused, turning the handle back and forth. "This won't take but a few minutes. Be back in a jiffy with my tools.

I have new locks in my van. Rest assured, one of 'em will do the job nicely." His voice had a singsong quality. Together with his melodious Southern accent, it was all comfort and ease. When he returned he knelt down to begin his task.

"Don't mean to be rude," he said, "but have you left a pot on the stove too long?"

Should I tell him the truth? I wondered. Chances are I'll never see this man again. Besides, he'd see the hole in the wall and ask more questions. Lying was fruitless.

"I'm going through a messy breakup with my husband. A few nights ago it got crazy here. He punched a hole in the wall and I left the condo with an overnight bag. When I got here today, I found photos of us burned in the fireplace. Smells bad, doesn't it? I called you to change the lock so I could stay here tonight."

"Good Lord have mercy! What a sorry no-count rascal. Where's the hole?"

I walked him into the kitchen.

"I am shocked beyond belief," Harvey said. "Land's sake, that hole is big enough for a bear to climb through. And you are just the prettiest, nicest young lady. How could he do such a thing?"

"I appreciate you saying that."

"Well, I pray the good Lord will protect you. I see you're packing everything up. Do you have help?"

"They'll be here tomorrow."

"Good. Let me finish my chore, and... may I ask you for a cup of that fine coffee I smell brewin'?"

I was a little taken aback. Why did Harvey want to have coffee with me? Surely there would be no motive other than the caffeine. Maybe he had another call to make and simply wanted a cup without the trouble of stopping at a convenience store or café.

"Yes, of course," I said. "I should've offered you a cup already. How do you take it?"

"Black with two teaspoons of sugar, if you have it," he said.

Thank God he didn't make some kind of sly remark. *I like my coffee like I like my women: hot, creamy and sweet.*

"Comin' right up."

"You can wait until I'm finished," he said. "I'll be changing out the deadbolt as well... is that right? My word, I've forgotten your first name. Just cannot believe where my mind is these days."

"Marianne, Marianne Sobieski." I liked the sound of it. *Marianne Sobieski.* At that moment I vowed never to take the last name of a man again.

I began wrapping glasses and plates in newspaper, and Mr. Chandler entered his own quiet world of screws, tumblers, and bolts. In the blink of an eye the job was complete. He took his tools to the van, returned, and sat down at the kitchen table. I poured his coffee over sugar, refilled mine, and sat down across from him.

"I'd like to share some thoughts with you," he said in a caring tone. "I hope you don't find this silly." He sounded like a preacher making an altar call.

I was intrigued.

"I'd be interested in anything you'd have to say, Mr. Chandler."

"Do you fish?"

I laughed out loud. "For compliments."

His question threw me back in time to the fifth grade, when my Aunt Mary and her friend, Alice, took me fishing. The three of us climbed into an aluminum, flat-bottomed boat with sandwiches, an ice cooler, and a large red thermos of tea. A small motor was fastened to the stern.

He looked like he was still looking for an answer.

"Only a few times... as a child," I said. "In fact, I actually like sticking worms on a hook."

"Oh, you were doin' lazy man's fishin'. Ever used a fly rod?"

"No, nothing that sophisticated."

"Well, my pretty girl, it's not hard. Once you get your rhythm, casting is easy. It's like poetry in motion."

"It is beautiful to watch," I said.

"Using flies is a far cry from baiting hooks, but any kind of fishing will calm your mind, feed your soul. You're moving the fish from its world of water through the air and into your hands. For a few brief moments you and the fish are fully engaged. Then you decide its fate... back into the river or onto your dinner plate, where the two of you become one again."

He laughed and our eyes met and held. His laughter was musical, a healing balm. I soaked it in.

"You ever been to the Tallulah Gorge, just north of here?"

"No."

"The Tallulah River feeds the gorge, and its waterfalls are magnificent. The water is clear and cold and the trout thrive."

"Sounds like heaven."

"Fishin' is the closest to heaven I ever been. I believe that's why Jesus was called a fisher of men. His glory called to others like my flies call to the fish." He laughed again. "Besides the water and the fish, the mountain air is purifying, strengthens the body and the spirit. You'll feel brand new."

He glanced at his wristwatch.

"Will you look at the time? I've one more stop to make and then my work will be done for today."

We stood together. I noticed he didn't drink any of his coffee. "What do I owe you?"

"Not a penny."

"Harvey, no, that's not fair... to you."

"All that's happened in this house... the pain and the hurt... you paid enough. You remind me of my youngest sister when she had to end her marriage. I remember all the suffering she endured. You're precious and so is she. This is a gift, not charity. Please don't rob me of the blessing I will receive by doing this for you."

"Well, since you put it that way... I accept."

"Good girl."

We walked to the door together, and once outside, he put his fingers under my chin.

"Look up and look forward. You'll be on top of this mountain you're climbin' soon enough. Your best days are comin'."

I felt tears in my eyes when I said, "I believe you, Harvey. Thank you."

He entered his van on his way to be an angel to another poor soul waiting to be rescued. Why is it men always want to rescue me? I wondered. Lucky to have a man like Harvey Chandler opening doors. I certainly was.

# CHAPTER 10

I SAT STRAIGHT up, not sure where I was. I looked at my watch: eight a.m. On a mattress on the floor in the condo, I had slept soundly throughout the night. It was a deep, tranquilizing hibernation, after weeks of unrest. I brewed a pot of Earl Grey tea, showered, and dressed in layers, knowing the move would produce periods of exertion and sitting, sweating and cooling off. I did my best to finish packing.

The doorbell rang at one-thirty and Dannie opened the door.

"Anybody home?"

I shouted at her from the upstairs hallway. "Girl, you are so early!"

"I know we're early, but there was no sign of dick-head, so we decided to test the waters."

"We?" I said. Then I saw a very large man walk in behind her. "Come in. Let's get this party started."

I made my way down the stairs to Dannie and, yes, that must've been Steve standing in the foyer. It was easy to see they were a good fit. He towered above us, broad-shouldered, with close-clipped, dark brown hair and a three-day beard that made him look dangerous.

Dannie and I hugged.

Steve extended his hand, which was more like a giant paw, then placed his other hand over mine.

"Steve Hood, at your service."

All I could squeak out was a quiet, "Thank you."

"Have you had lunch?" Dannie asked.

"No breakfast or lunch."

"Let's go get cheeseburgers and fries, honey. You know, carbo-load for the afternoon festivities." Because of her enthusiasm the day took on the prospects of hard work and fun.

"I'll buy," I said.

"I'll make the burger run," Steve offered.

I found my purse and handed Steve two twenty-dollar bills.

"Please," I said, "get whatever you want. I'll take two cheeseburgers and a monster Coke."

"Make that two of us," Dannie said, "but I want a large fries. What's a burger without a shit-load of fries? Lots of catsup, please."

She turned to me and said, "Thank God you're not a vegetarian. The thought of soy burgers at this stage of the game...Yuk!"

Steve took off and Dannie studied the Tom and Marianne demolition project.

"Good night, Marianne, this hole is huge!" she exclaimed.

I explained yesterday's events and she continued to stare at the wall while I spoke.

"You've experienced so much emotion in so little time," she said. "You must be exhausted."

"I feel... I feel rested, actually. The locksmith who came here last night, an older guy, he seemed to really care about me. He changed the locks for free and told me the worst was over."

"A prophet?"

"From an unexpected source," I said.

"Those are the best kind."

Dannie turned her attention to my bed-on-the-floor.

"Wrestling this mattress down the stairs must've been a challenge. How did you do it?"

"Sheer determination."

We propped it up against the bare wall and brought down most of the bags and boxes from upstairs. When Steve returned from Burger Barn with four bags of comfort food, we were glad to take a break. We sat at the kitchen table and I asked him about his time in the military. He was a Ranger and had been a part of *Operation Just Cause*, the invasion of Panama, in December of 1989. He was wounded in action. During the first part of his story it was difficult for him to look up.

"The intense fighting lasted four days," he said. "The PDF didn't have a chance. What kept me clear about why we were there was the human trafficking. My sister was sixteen at the time, and the thought of some young girl like her being sold into a sex market made me sick, and fighting mad."

I learned that he had parachuted into a drop zone outside of Panama City with the 508th Infantry. During day three of the mission, he was nicked by a bullet to his right thigh.

"I was lucky," he said and looked up at Dannie as she blushed with pride. "I'm working as a security guard now, but I'm thinking about the Atlanta police force. Currently my mission is to keep this perimeter secure and assist in the evacuation."

We heard a truck pull up to the front door.

"Steve, thank you for everything you've been through," I said, "and thank you for being here today."

"It's my understanding," he chuckled, "I have a massage coming in the future?" He put his arm around Dannie and pulled her to his chest.

"You do indeed," I said.

I opened the front door to Charlie and Andy, and greetings and introductions followed. While Steve and Charlie discussed the logistics of packing the truck, Andy and I assessed the damaged wall. He pushed his cap to the back of his head and rubbed his brow.

"Miss Marianne, I didn't know it was that... huge. That'll take a few days."

"A few days, really?"

"A hole this size... it's a process," Andy said. "I'll need to cut the drywall, cut a back plate larger than the opening, secure it with adhesive, screw it in place, use joint compound, patch it, more joint compound, let all that dry like a bone, sand it, and paint it."

"Shit," I whispered under my breath.

Dannie walked by us with a box.

"Tom's completely out, right?" she asked.

"Yes, definitely. He can't get in unless he breaks a window."

"Make a key for Andy," Dannie said, "and let him come and go."

"If 'n we can do that, it'll be dried and painted by Wednesday, good as new."

That'll work, I thought. I can get the condo keys back to the landlord by September thirtieth.

"Could you do that, Andy?" I asked.

"That'll be fine, just fine."

It was three o'clock and the five of us hustled, carrying out the last of my things. No one stopped, we were in sync, and the condo emptied smoothly by five. I had what I needed to take to Ray's in my car.

The boys went on to the storage unit, Steve followed in his pickup truck, Dannie with the Jeep, and I went to the hardware store to make a copy of the key. As I drove away, it hit me: this is all happening without a glitch. Do I deserve such good fortune?

When I arrived at Ray's shop I found the big white box-truck parked against the concrete wall of the loading dock at the rear of the building. The guys sat in a row, feet dangling off the wall. Steve was smoking a cigarette; Andy and Charlie drank from shiny red cola cans. Seeing them gave me a sense of camaraderie. They were my pals, my buds.

I got out of the car.

Steve stood and whistled a catcall. "Gentlemen, here comes a fine lookin', sweet talkin', single young thing. Let's give her a hand."

The gang gathered at the loading dock's ramp and applauded as I walked up to them. Of course, I cried... big juicy tears, big happy tears.

"I like this feeling," I said, wiping tears away on the sleeve of my sweatshirt. "I like feeling single."

I walked up to each of them and delivered a deep, heart-to-heart hug and a smooch on the cheek. Andy blushed. When I hugged Charlie his enormous belt buckle slipped down into the waistline of my jeans, and for a moment, we were stuck. Then I wiggled free.

"Hey now, man," Steve joked. "Do I have to come down there?"

"My... belt buckle..." Charlie stammered.

"Are you sure that's all it was?" Steve teased.

It was my turn to blush. Dannie and I hugged for a long time and Steve acted up again.

"Ahhhoooo, ladies, do you need company?"

"You are such a slut," I said.

"He's a slut, but a loveable slut." Dannie blew him a kiss.

I turned to Andy and everyone else went about their business.

"Please keep a record of your time." I handed him the key. "Is ten dollars an hour enough?" I asked.

"More than fine."

I could tell by his grin he was happy.

"Mr. Ray has an account at Rick's Hardware. You and he can settle up when the job's done. I'll be sure to sweep up any mess I make. Sandin's the worst."

"Thank you, Andy. Thank you so so very much," I said.

We locked up the storage area and said our goodbyes.

Steve hugged and kissed Dannie and said, "I've got a tough assignment tonight. I better get going."

I imagined a secret transport of some kind, or him acting as a bodyguard for an Atlanta celebrity.

"He moonlights as a bouncer on Saturday nights at the Platinum Room," Dannie said. She did her best pelvic grind with her hands above her head.

Everyone knew the Platinum was a premier, exclusive location. Some of the girls there had posed in Playboy.

"See you tomorrow, babe." He got in his truck, drove away, and did not look back.

"Dannie, I'm so impressed with him," I said. "How did you two meet?"

"At work. The minute I walked up to his table my knees went weak. I tried not to be too obvious, but I had this big, stupid grin, like the one I'm wearing now. He said he loved my dark hair and eyes. And I... well, I love everything about him."

"How sweet," I said.

Dannie reached into the pocket of her work shirt and pulled out a joint. "Want to celebrate?"

Marijuana... I hadn't smoked in months.

"Yes," I said with a smile. "But only if I can crash at your place. God knows I won't be able to drive after that fat doobie."

"Perfect. Let's go."

During the drive to Dannie's we talked about Steve again.

"Did he have post-traumatic stress?" I asked.

"Steve definitely has issues but I don't know if it's PTSD. I haven't known him that long. But like today, he shows up to do a job and he's *on,* as if he's wearing an invisible suit of armor that makes him invincible... larger than life. He'll always see himself as a warrior."

"My dad fought in World War II," I said. "Army Air Corps. He was a waist gunner on a B-24."

"Jesus," Dannie said, "I just watched a documentary last night about the fleet of B-24s in the war. Can you believe the karma? I'm getting God bumps."

I took over the conversation. "He flew all of his missions safely but came home a drunk. My childhood was so screwed-up because of his drinking. And he drank really bad booze, rot-gut shit, Echo Springs, cheap bourbon. He died at 56."

"You know," Dannie said, "we've never really talked about your growing up, only some things."

"I don't like to talk details," I muttered, " just broad strokes."

"We can talk tonight, if you want to."

"I'll know better after I smoke," I laughed. "Oh no, it's starting already... the giggles."

"You're laughing because you're nervous," Dannie said. "Relax. Just look at what you're feeling about your childhood and put a name on it. Whatever...anger, resentment, disappointment. We'll deal with it after wine and munchies."

I drove the Volvo down the pebble driveway that faced the Chattahoochee River, cut the engine, and said, "I love it here."

"You need to come more often."

Max, the super dog, came bounding up to Dannie's side of the car. As she got out he was already on his back, wiggling on the lawn, waiting for her approach.

"Maxie, my Maxie," she said as she rubbed his belly. "Such a good boy, you're such a good good boy. Come on, good boy."

He jumped up and followed us to the entrance. I scratched his ears while Dannie opened the door.

"Don't go back to the car. My guest bedroom has everything you need, even a new toothbrush. You can wear a pair of my pj's. I know you'll drown in them but ..."

"Are you saying I can't bring my baggage in here?" I asked.

"Exactly."

We promptly stripped off our clothes, showered, and donned our cotton pajamas. She gave me a pair covered in tiny white flowers. She was in cammo.

"Camouflage? Are you kidding?" I asked.

"You know me; I love all that macho shit. Who cares about tiny white flowers? Don't forget, I have a Native American heritage."

"Who gave you these?" I asked, stretching out my arms. They were covered in a mile of fabric.

"My Nana. Every Christmas produces more pajamas. I don't have the heart to tell her I don't wear them."

We went about the business of drinking wine and smoking pot. Glasses, wine opener, lighter, ash tray in hand, we headed to the living room and found places on the floor across from each other at the glass coffee table.

Dannie lit the joint, inhaled deeply, and held the smoke in her lungs.

It was my turn to take a hit. I rolled the joint between my index finger and thumb, with some familiarity, admiring Dannie's ability to roll the perfect cigarette.

"How'd you get it rolled so perfectly?"

"Years of practice. Shut up and smoke."

My first inhale produced a burning sensation in my lungs and a sputtering cough.

"Come on, Marianne, you're not a rookie. Don't hit it so hard if you're going to cough... nice and easy."

I took her advice and inhaled gently, more controlled. I didn't cough. It was a neat sensation.

"Want to go to the patio?" she asked. "It's warm enough."

We moved out to the patio and got comfortable on the cushioned chairs that faced the river. Max followed, gazed at the river and lay down at Dannie's feet.

We listened to the river flow over rocks and small boulders creating tiny waterfalls and shallow pools. The babbling sounds were soothing. We passed the joint back and forth two more times.

"I'm done," I said.

Dannie stubbed the joint out in the ashtray.

"Me too." She grinned while she spoke, "The Buddhists make so many references to water, river of life, go with the flow, let it wash over you, we are only waves in the ocean."

"That go with the flow thing... Bob Marley," I said. "You know, our bodies are over ninety-percent water."

"So," Dannie said, "we're biochemical bags of water attached to bones."

"We're bags of something," I said, "some more than others."

We laughed and made more stoned observations about the human body. Dannie leaned over and scratched the top of Max's head. He rolled over to lie on his side and let out a long doggie sigh of contentment.

"How unhappy were you, growing up?" Dannie asked.

"I can remember being happy at home with my mom before first grade. In the beginning it was all good. Then the heavy shit started. My dad turned into a raging fucking drunk. He beat my mother."

"I never knew," Dannie said.

"It's not something I like to share," I said, draining my wine glass. "Robin's helping me a lot." I stood. "More wine?"

"Just bring out the bottle," Dannie said.

I retrieved the second bottle from the kitchen and returned, filling both our glasses.

Dannie was the first to speak. "Alcoholic father... alcoholic husbands. Do I see a pattern here?"

"Something like that. Sometimes I just don't... don't know why I do what I do."

"Come on, Marianne, you've got to have some new insights from working with Robin. Any gut feelings or dreams?"

I felt a jolt and answered, "I did have a terrible, terrible dream."

"Can you share?"

I told her about my night at The Summit. Dannie, my faithful friend, listened intently about the smoke, and the fear, and the pressure of the branches producing blood.

"I need a cigarette," she said, wide-eyed. She went into the apartment, came back with a pack of cigarettes, sat down and lit one up. "Blood and thorns... were you being chased?"

"Yes."

The blue haze from Dannie's cigarette floated up into the damp atmosphere. We sat in silence. I didn't want to talk about the dream anymore.

"Dannie?" I said.

"Yes."

"I'm really loaded."

"Me too."

We looked at each other and burst into laughter. Max lifted his head, looked at us like we were crazy, and then put his head back down.

"He knows we're stoned," Dannie said.

More laughter. I tried to stand and promptly sat back down. "Oh no, this is not good."

"Wheelchair assistance?" she asked.

"Hey, just because I haven't smoked in a while doesn't make me a rookie. The wine has me partially paralyzed."

"Okay, blame it on the wine," Dannie said.

"It's bedtime for the Marianne girl."

"Let's get you up and tucked in." She stamped out her cigarette.

She helped me up and steadied my walking with one arm around my waist.

"Dannie, you are such a good friend, my best friend ever. Let's get married."

"I thought you were through with marriage."

"That's men. Okay then, let's just live together," I said in a wimpy little girl's voice.

We made it to the back bedroom. She propped me up against the dresser, pulled back the covers and sat me down on the bed.

"Dannie?"

"Yes, dear?"

"I love you," I said, getting comfortable under the covers.

"I love you too, you nut."

"Can I have a glass of water?"

"Yes, dear."

# CHAPTER 11

THE AROMAS OF coffee and bacon roused me from sleep. It was ten o'clock in the morning and I was hungry. I hadn't slept this late in months. Stretching under the comforter, I wiggled with contentment -- no more crap, no more buttons to push.

After good morning hugs from Dannie, we ate breakfast together and lingered over coffee.

I drove back toward Ray's and found an '80s music station on the radio playing the song *Whip It*. I blasted the speakers up to the max and sang at the top of my lungs, bobbing up and down to the rhythm. *"Move forward, move ahead, and you must whip it, whip it good..."* It was my freedom song. Yeah, whip it! The guy next to me at the red light looked at me like I had snakes in my hair.

"Whip it!" I screamed at him and snarled.

He took off like he had seen a ghost and peeled out.

During the rest of the day I unpacked my car and settled in at Ray's. It felt a bit scandalous, kinda sneaky, maybe a bit sinful. I was here and Debbie wasn't.

The phone rang and the answering machine kicked on.

"Marianne, if you're there, pick-up. Marianne... are you..."

I dove for the phone as if it would explode.

"Hey, Ray... hey, yeah, I'm here."

"Good, I'm about to leave Chattanooga. Be home around eight. How's everything?"

"I'll tell you when you get here. That way we'll have something to talk about."

"Cute."

"I took the liberty of snooping through your cupboards. There's spaghetti and sauce."

"Sounds like a plan. Let me get on the road."

"Please be careful."

"I always am."

After we hung up I found the notepad with my list of chores. I was always a nut about making lists. This one was the roadmap for moving me from point A to point B.

*Marianne's Move Out and Move Forward List*

1. Time off from spa
2. Talk to Dannie/ Meet landlord
3. Get boxes/garbage bags
4. Look at storage unit
5. Set time with Andy and Chuck
6. Move out 2 p.m. Saturday
7. Get doctor's excuse
8. See Robin
9. Thursday, back to work

*LIVE LIFE TWO WEEKS AT A TIME!!!!*

Miraculously, items one through six were complete. Hey this might be something, I thought. It'd make a great article for COSMO: *Ditch Your Hubby and Live Two Weeks at a Time.* Subtitle: *How to Create the Ultimate Orgasm – Alone!* The timeframe felt doable, not overwhelming.

I was at the stove stirring spaghetti sauce when Ray arrived. He looked tired but he was all smiles. He put down his bags and we hugged. He rubbed my back with a reassuring rhythm and gentle pressure. Mmmm, he felt good.

"I thought about you a lot on Saturday," he said as we pulled apart.

"Your spirit was certainly with us," I replied. "The whole move start to finish was a breeze. When you're ready, we'll eat."

After dinner we sat on the couch, propped our feet up on the coffee table, and balanced wine glasses on our bellies.

"If you can believe it, Ray, I only have three items left on my move forward list."

"Help me remember... the last three were..."

"They'll be completed this week: doctor's appointment for my work excuse, a session with Robin, and back to work on Thursday."

"Good. It'll probably take a few weeks to start to feel normal. Are you comfortable here?"

"God, yes. But I don't want to be here long. What if Debbie comes back?"

"I talked to her while I was in Chattanooga. At least a month, probably longer, before she can even think about coming home. I may fly out to see her next month."

"Lucky girl," I said.

"Yes, she is. Are you nervous about your next session with Robin?"

"Yes and no. I've done some journaling, not much. She told me to try and reduce any pressures, any stress in my life while I try to get to the bottom of all this crap."

"What pressures?"

"The spa, Tom, concerned friends giving advice I don't need, Tom, the spa... Tom."

"A retreat?" Ray asked.

"Maybe."

"There are the monks and their abbey in Conyers," he said, "or there's my cabin in North Carolina."

I sat up, almost spilling my wine. "What cabin?"

"Bought it last year. It's above Dillard, maybe twenty miles further north, just across the border. It sits right on Betty's Creek."

"Holy shit! You'd let me stay there?"

"If you're serious about taking Robin's advice, the cabin's yours. It's gorgeous up there this time of year. Can you afford the time off work, maybe a medical leave of absence?"

"I never thought of that."

"It's rustic, but it has indoor plumbing, a kitchen, a bathroom with a shower, and wall heaters. You'll be comfortable; there's a fire pit between the porch and the creek."

"Wow," I said, not believing my good fortune.

"When we get up there I'll take you to the most beautiful river, the Tallulah. It runs through the Tallulah Gorge. The state park has a series of bridges to hike over the waterfalls. Breathtaking views."

Oh my God! I thought. What the... Tallulah Gorge? The hair on the back of my neck went up and my heart started to pound.

"That's funny," I said calmly, though I wanted to scream. "I just had a conversation with a man about the Tallulah River. He changed the locks on my condo. Sweet, older man with startling blue eyes and a kind, gentle manner. Harvey Chandler, yep, that's his name."

"No, no, you mean Noah Chandler, Harvey's son."

"No, Harvey Chandler, I'm sure of it."

"Don't be silly, Marianne."

"I'm not being silly. The Southern Gentleman, opening doors every day." My voice shot up a decibel, "H-a-r-v-e-y C-h-a-n-d-l-e-r, dammit, I know who I met."

Ray put down his wine glass, stood, and began to pace back and forth in front of me. He gave me a worried look then started pacing again.

"I knew Harvey well."

"Knew?"

"He and I belonged to the same Masonic Lodge."

"So? Nice guy, isn't he?"

"Marianne... he died in a fishing accident on the Tallulah River. That was last spring."

I gasped aloud and said, "No, that couldn't be. I just talked to..."

"His son was around the bend and out of sight when Harvey slipped and fell. The water was fast, roaring. His son heard nothing. Harvey's skull was crushed against a boulder. Noah found him floating in a small whirlpool between the rocks."

My skin began to crawl. Suddenly cold, I pulled the quilt from the back of the couch and wrapped up in it.

"But I... I saw him..."

Ray stopped pacing, sat down and put a hand on my shoulder. "The only thing that makes it less painful is... he died instantly. He was here one minute, gone in an instant." Ray buried his face in his hands. He rubbed his face then smoothed back his hair with his palms.

"I... I'm not sure what to say," I began. My anger at Ray turned to sheer empathy. "I thought it was weird that he didn't drink his coffee. And he wouldn't take any money."

"Are you sure..."

"Ray, he made me feel stronger, he gave me hope. His eyes were so clear and bright, heavenly."

"Angelic?" Ray asked.

"He told me to go to the Tallulah... He told me to go fly-fish for trout."

Ray looked in my eyes and said, "Then I recommend you do."

"You're being smug."

"Marianne, there is a lot of shit we don't understand. We are so much more than this shell we walk around in on this planet. Harvey had the biggest heart of anyone I've ever known, a prince of a man. You need to talk to Noah. He took over the business. Call him. He may be able to offer some insight. I'd like to think... if what you're saying is true, maybe Harvey *is* an angel."

"Oh... it's true all right," I said with a shiver. "But I wonder... when I call, who will answer?"

# CHAPTER 12

AFTER MY MORNING run I called the doctor's office. I needed that note. "We can squeeze you in at four," the receptionist said.

"Great."

I had the rest of the morning and afternoon to do whatever I wanted. The respite from all the craziness was appreciated, and I liked being in Ray's house alone. It reminded me of the years I had lived with my Aunt Mary after my parents died. I was thirteen when a fatal crash took both their lives. Family and friends speculated that Dad was drunk and drove them off the road. Did my mother know he was drunk? Did she try to stop him?

Aunt Mary was cool. She smoked Pall Mall cigarettes and drank black coffee; the combination kept her pencil-thin. When I came to live with her she comforted me as best she could. I was lost and sullen for more than a year, barely speaking to anyone. A few times she took me to her priest, and the conversations helped pull me out of despair and depression. Every time she looked at me, it was as if she was assessing our shared life for the first time. What now? What next?

Aunt Mary worked as a purchasing agent at a steel processing plant in Warren, Ohio. She was one of the few women in the industry who held that position. She loved the authority and responsibility her job offered, and I loved it, too. I was proud to be a part of her life. I would take one of her silk or linen suits out of her closet when she wasn't home and try it on. Modeling it in front of the mirror, holding an unlit cigarette, I'd pretend I was Mary Dziejak at an important meeting. "Yes, Mr. Jones, I said ten thousand pounds of half-inch, rolled blue steel... *by tomorrow!*"

Her home had a split-level floor plan and I was given the bottom half all to myself. It was my domain: bedroom and bath, sitting area with a desk and love seat. It had the added luxury of a fourteen-inch, black-and-white television. Shell-shocked from the loss of my mother--I didn't give a shit about my father--all of this space was unsettling, and my time there was a bit lonely, because Aunt Mary worked long hours.

Memories faded as I sat in front of Ray's television, mindlessly watching the Weather Channel. My discovery that the locksmith had been a ghost was nerve-racking to say the least. It took me until one o'clock to gather up the nerve to call Noah Chandler. This was all too bizarre – too many coincidences. Ray and Harvey had been friends; I met Harvey well after his death. What would Noah Chandler think of my story? Did I dare tell the truth?

I turned off the TV, dug out the phonebook, found the listing, and punched in the numbers.

"Southern Gentleman Locksmiths, this is Noah."

"Hello." My mouth went dry and I coughed. "Is this Noah Chandler?"

"Yes, ma'am, can I help you?"

"Noah... I'm... I...Um..."

"Ma'am, are you alright?"

"Yeah, hey, my name is Marianne Sobieski. Ummm, I'm a friend of Ray Gibson. Do you know him?"

"Yes, yes I do," he answered. "He was a friend of my father's."

"Yes, your father, Harvey Chandler, right?"

"That's right."

"Noah, I know this is going to sound insane, but your father changed the locks at my condo."

"Oh, so you knew my dad?"

"Yes... no... I mean... he was at my condo just last Friday night."
Silence.

"Noah?"

"Miss So... sorry I can't pronounce your last name."

"Just call me Marianne."

"Marianne, you may not believe this but you're not the first to call about my dad. May I ask, were you in some kind of danger when you called our business?"

"Yes."

"Since my father's death... it seems he's been answering calls from women in trouble. I didn't believe it at first, but now I do. Two weeks ago he changed the locks for a single mom being harassed by her ex-husband. She called the business to tell me he forgot to give her a bill. I didn't want to alarm her, so I just told her he was happy to do it for free, not to worry."

I whispered. "He didn't charge me either."

"Did he talk you into making him a cup of coffee?"

The conversation was feeling more and more eerie. "Yes."

"Figures," Noah said. More silence.

"He was so kind," I said, "told me the worst was over."

"Then it probably is.  He was a remarkable man."

"Was?" I said. "*Is* may be more appropriate."

"Be careful who you tell this to," Noah said softly. "I don't want a bunch of crazies coming around here. And people will think you're nuts."

But I am nuts, I thought.

We talked a little more about his father, and Noah wished me well. After we ended the call, I looked up from the couch and saw my reflection in the black screen of the television. My image was dull, like an apparition. I knew that if I turned on the television, the images would be clear and crisp, just as Harvey had appeared to me.

What separates our worlds? I wondered. Where did Harvey go when he wasn't answering the phone for women in distress? Is he a spirit? An angel? The answer was apparent.

I sat in silence for over an hour, trying to make sense of the whole affair. Two worlds or many worlds could exist simultaneously in the universe. I had watched enough Star Trek to know that. If it was Harvey's spirit that wished to remain here helping women in need, women like his sister, why not? His spirit was like the electricity that turned on the television. You couldn't see it, but it was there, bringing images, words, and sounds to life.

Harvey Chandler had turned on his light and appeared... for me. I accepted the fact that I was blessed beyond belief. Yes, Harvey was my friend, perhaps watching my progress... or maybe he was already off helping someone else. So many in need.

—∭—

By five-fifteen I was walking out of the doctor's office with an excuse for work. The thought of returning to the resort made my stomach do flip-flops. There was an undercurrent of discontent that permeated the spa's atmosphere, and Judy was the main instigator. I would talk to Robin about a leave of absence. I encouraged people all the time to quit their jobs, if they were miserable. Makes perfect sense, I thought, to leave an environment that's unhealthy or disrespectful, as long as you can afford to. I was ready to move on but wasn't sure when or where.

At eight-thirty I was propped up in bed reading. It was one of those sexy novels, with a southern belle on the front cover, embraced by a muscular beau. Who writes this shit? I wondered. I heard the front door open and slam shut. I chose to stay put, warm and cozy under the covers. Footsteps approached my half-opened door and Ray appeared.

"You decent?"

"Hey, hey, door's open."

He pushed open the door and stood in the hallway dangling an open beer bottle by its neck.

"Hey, girl," he said leaning against the door frame. "How was your day?"

"Amazing. Want details?"

"Sure."

"Come on in... sit." I patted the side of the bed next to me.

Instead, he chose to sit at the bottom edge of the bed at a safe distance and sipped his beer while I conveyed the story of my phone call to Noah.

"This is exceedingly profound," he said. "I do believe in angels."

We shared stories about déjà vu, or feeling a presence when no one was there, but neither of us had ever seen a ghost before -- or an angel, for that matter.

"This shit is weird," I said. "You hear things but who would believe it? An angel?"

Ray took a long steady drink, emptying the bottle, and asked, "What's next?"

"I see Robin tomorrow."

"Good girl. You're making headway. Andy finished the drywall at your condo. Told me he vacuumed and it looks good as new."

"Terrific," I said. "I'll go by on Wednesday, check everything out, and drop the keys off to Mr. Perry."

He stood and made his way to the door. "I'm off to bed. Goodnight, darlin'."

"Night night, Ray."

I wanted to tackle him, but he shut the door.

I tried to read but couldn't focus. I slung the paperback across the bed, reached over for the light, and snapped it off. The drapes were open and a streetlight partially illuminated the room. Masturbating might be good, I thought, but I dismissed the idea immediately. I needed the real deal, hard dick, especially after Mark had teased me. I remembered the times when Ray had made love to me; they were always sweet and satisfying. Why not? I thought. Why not tonight?

I brushed my teeth, gargled with strong mint mouthwash for a solid minute, and decided to slip panties on underneath my silk nightshirt. It was difficult not to giggle as I tip-toed down the hallway to his room. His light was on; I knocked lightly.

"Ray?"

"Marianne, are you alright?"

"Can I come in?"

"Yes, darlin', come on."

He pushed his reading glasses to the top of his head and put his newspaper on the nightstand.

"Can't sleep?" he asked.

"No," I said meekly.

"Do you want to snuggle?" He smiled and lifted up the quilt.

"Only you would invite a woman into his bed to snuggle."

I walked slowly to the bed and crawled in. He enveloped me and created a cotton cocoon around my body.

Ray was bare-chested and wore flannel sleeping shorts. I slid down to his waist, hugged his torso, and laid my head in his lap, putting me within striking distance of my target.

He played with my hair and said, "Everything's going to be fine..."

"You feel *so good,*" I whispered.

I rubbed his belly with feather-light, slow strokes and worked my hand down to the elastic waistband of his shorts, lifting it slightly off his skin.

We touched and stroked each other tenderly, and reminisced about old times together.

"There was never a minute of disagreement when we were together," I said.

"You're easy to spend time with," Ray said, and started to knead my shoulders.

"You want a massage?"

Holy shit! I thought. Do I ever. He wants to give *me* a massage? This was too good to be true. I didn't know how to reply. I wouldn't get too aggressive; I waited for Ray to decide what would come next. And maybe with a little persuading…

"Are you kidding? I'd love a massage."

He adjusted the sheets and comforter.

"Slip off your shirt and lie face down."

I did what I was told and he set off for the bathroom.

I wondered why, maybe for some outrageous sex toy, or better yet, a tasty lubricant. He left the bathroom light on and partially cracked the door, giving the bedroom a warm glow. He sat on the edge of the bed and put his hand on my head.

"Because of my back issues…" he started and I began to laugh.

"Oh no… oh no… Ray…" I roared.

"You're making fun of me?"

He slapped my ass playfully. It stung and felt devilishly good.

"Okay, okay, time out," I said. I turned over and hid my nipples, just barely, under the sheet. "I'm the professional here. What kind of oil are you using?"

"Organic coconut."

"If your back is hurting, you can kneel next to me or just straddle my ass. It'll take the stress off your SI joint."

I turned over and he pulled the sheets down.

"Nice. Nice panties."

I exhaled as he moved his legs on either side of my hips. I heard the bottle snap open and Ray's hands rub together.

I felt him lean over as he placed the container on the bed. His warm palms and the deep pressure against my muscles were soothing. I moaned in appreciation and then his hands traveled to my lower back. He poured oil directly on my ass and it dripped down my crack. My torso dug into the mattress, in rhythm with his fingers, and

I could feel his hard dick against my anus. He parted my cheeks with one hand and ran fingers down to the most sensitive spot on my body.

I quickly wiggled away from him and he lost his balance.

"Ray, you didn't ask permission to play the back nine."

We both howled with laughter.

He pulled me to him. We kissed lying side-by-side. His hands ran up and down my willing torso, and with my help he slipped off the lotion-soaked panties. Then he massaged my breasts with fervor. He pinched my nipples hard, and the pain was spectacular.

I tugged at his shorts, ran my hand inside the waistband, got on my knees and pulled them off. His dick sprang to attention and I fell back to his side, facing him.

"Suck my nipples, baby. Please, suck me," I pleaded.

He squeezed my tits together and sucked one nipple, then the other; then began pulling at them with his teeth, turning them into hard pebbles of flesh. I was hot and wet.

As he licked and caressed me, I fondled his lovely dick and huge, loaded balls. How long has Debbie been gone? I wondered.

He pushed the top of my head and I knew what he wanted. I slid down to his cock and licked up and down the rigid shaft. With enough spit on his skin I opened my mouth and got his dick as far down my throat as I could manage. My tongue swirled around his penis.

Ray grabbed my hair and pulled me all the way into his crotch. Back and forth I fucked his hard cock with my throat. I ran both hands between his thighs, grabbed his ass and pulled him in even tighter. He moaned. I pulled away to catch my breath then went back in. He moaned louder.

"I can't do this... much longer!" he screamed. "Gonna come." I pulled away again.

"I need you to fuck me, Ray. I need it now."

I moved to straddle his cock. We were both wet, but I was dripping. I held the head of his dick and rubbed it against my clit and pussy lips. It felt incredible.

"Sweetheart," I panted, "I'm on birth control, but do you want to use a condom?"

I surprised myself by being so level headed in the midst of absolute chaos.

"Marianne," he rasped, "I need to be in you, now."

He plunged his hips upward and took my breath away. He held my waist with both hands and lifted me up and down on his dick, slow and steady. Then he moved to my torso, pulled me down and sucked my nipples while fucking me at the same time. I screamed and pushed harder. It didn't take long.

"I'm coming... Jesus... Ray... I'm..."

We rocked together and slammed into a wall of bliss.

"I'm coming... fuck me, fuck me harder!" I shouted.

He grunted aloud and cried out my name. I could feel his essence filling me, a spurting whirlpool of pleasure.

"Oh... oh God!"

I moved my arms to his side and kissed him deeply while his final thrusts became less violent and eventually stopped. After the ecstasy washed through me like a storm, our matched breathing calmed.

"Wow, I don't remember you being this good," I said, rubbing the soft nap of hair on his chest.

"I've always been this good. You just don't remember."

"Maybe you could help me remember, again," I said, kissing him. "And again... and maybe again?"

# CHAPTER 13

THE SUN GLINTED through the windows of Robin's office. I sat on the couch remembering what a basket case I was the last time. She would be proud of my progress, just like I was. The bright sun reflected my optimism.

The door opened and Robin smiled as she walked in.

"I see you're still in one piece. Excellent. Looking *much* better."

"I feel fabulous."

"Something extraordinary happen?"

"Well, ummm…"

"Let's talk," she said. "Tell me, what's *really* going on?"

I was afraid to tell her about my seeing a real live—actually dead—ghost. It would surely absorb my whole hour, and she would probably think me insane. I told her about going back to the condo, smashing the wall, and having a flashback of beating my father with a broom. She remained silent as she made notes.

It took a few minutes, but she final looked up.

"Do you realize how brave you were… a little girl trying to protect her mother?"

"All I knew was that if I didn't, she would die."

"How old were you?"

"Ten."

Neither of us spoke. She took more notes.

"Just think how strong you were in an impossible situation… a warrior-child, defending your mom. That kind of strength is in you, Marianne, I know it."

The gravity of her words had a profound effect on me. While my parents were alive, I loved my mother deeply. Even at a young age, I thought of us more as friends, or sisters. We had fun together. I still played back images of us planting flowerbeds, shopping at thrift stores, going for groceries, making pancakes on Saturday mornings.

"I loved her so much."

"I'm sure you did. I can hear it in your voice."

"Last session," I said, "you told me to reduce any stress as much as I could."

"I remember that. What do you have in mind?"

"As fate would have it, Ray has a cabin in North Carolina. He offered it to me, but only if I'm serious about working with you."

"Where in North Carolina?"

"Just over the Georgia border, north of Clayton. It sits on a creek and even has indoor plumbing. Everything I'd need to be comfortable. Completely isolated."

"Are you thinking about weekend trips?"

"Ray suggested I take a medical leave of absence from the spa and stay up there until I get my life sorted out, concentrate on getting my head screwed on straight. Another good thing is, the cabin is less than two hours away."

Neither of us spoke. Robin finally broke the silence.

"Ray's a good friend."

"The best. Can you recommend a timeframe? Two weeks, a month, two months? What do you think?"

"I know this sounds callous," she said, "but how much time can you afford to be out of work?"

Geez, she must really think I'm screwed up, I decided.

I quickly reviewed my finances. No rent, no credit card bills, four thousand dollars in a secret savings account. I could manage eight weeks. Two months in the mountains; it would be paradise. My life was a fucking mess. And every time I turned around there was some man trying to fix it. In the end, though, every man was only out to please himself. It seemed every guy I knew either wanted to be a savior or a shithead.

I need space, I thought, lots of it. I need to find out who I am, solve my own problems. I'm seeing ghosts, for Christ's sake!

"I think I could manage a couple of months off work without pay."

"Are you feeling any fear about being alone?"

I sat quietly for a few moments, checking my gut reaction. "Frankly, I love being alone. I don't think Ray would suggest my staying there if he didn't think it was safe."

"Good. Then we agree."

"Yeah, it sounds great."

"I'll only be a phone call away, if you want a session. You could drive back to the city if you need anything. How soon can you go?"

"I don't have a clue. The sooner the better, I guess."

"Let's look at the calendar." She got up, opened her appointment book and turned pages. "How about through November thirtieth? Does that sound too daunting?"

"It sounds like heaven. What do I do?"

"Do I have all of your contact information? I'll need your primary care physician's number… and your HR department at work."

"I'll check with your secretary," I said.

"Next Tuesday is October fifth. I'll start the paperwork tomorrow. My secretary will call you when everything is in order. Then you can have a sit-down with your boss. Don't worry, we're in this together. Same time next week?"

"Yes, absolutely."

—⁓⁓—

It was a pleasure to go into the empty condo and find everything fresh and clean. Andy had taken it upon himself to empty the fireplace and vacuum all the carpets, on both levels; even the outside patio had been swept. I wondered if he had gone the extra mile and cleaned the bathrooms. I was so anal about housework; they had probably been pristine when we packed up on Saturday. The new wall was flawless and the fresh paint masked any odors from the burnt photos.

I walked slowly through each room, touching walls and looking out of windows, reliving moments of my life here with Tom. It wasn't all bad, and I certainly had a hand in our demise. It was time for me to face my unhealthy need for bad boys and chaos. As I walked down the stairs, for some unknown reason, I was expecting the doorbell to ring. Instead I opened the door and felt a strong breeze blow past me and into the foyer.

"Hello, Harvey," I said, and smiled.

———

Mr. Perry was not in his office when I arrived.

"Well, Marianne," Marilyn said as she stood up from her desk and moved to give me a hug. "You look so much better than the last time I saw you."

"Thanks."

"You looked rested."

"I feel rested," I said and surrendered my key. "The condo is move-in ready. I had the locks changed, so you may need to make copies of this one."

"No problem. So you pulled it off?"

"With the help of many friends. I'll be giving free massages for a long time to lots of people."

"Aren't they lucky," she said. "I'm the lucky one."

# CHAPTER 14

WHEN I ARRIVED at work I saw Judy in the back hallway of the spa, chewing out one of the maids. She loved getting started early, making people feel miserable, and she was so good at it.

I clocked in, found the doctor's excuse in my knapsack, and purposely waited for her to finish ranting. On the other hand, I thought, maybe my presence would cut her bitch time in half and poor Isobel could escape.

"Judy," I interrupted.

"Nice of you to join us," she said with sarcasm.

"The pleasure's all mine," I said, sporting the biggest grin I could manage. "Here's the note from my doctor."

I handed her the paper and she did a close inspection of the writing and letterhead, holding it up to the light.

"Looks fine. Have a nice day." She turned abruptly and marched down the hall, heels clacking against the stone tiles.

"It sucks to be you," I said under my breath.

We were slow that day, so I could take my time with my guests. This was the part of the job I loved, bringing them tea, more towels, giving them a few extra minutes on the massage table. Generous tips reflected my willingness to go a little above and beyond. Being of service to others was a gift, a calling. This was when I was the happiest.

I didn't get home to Ray's until seven that night. I found him at the kitchen island eating Chinese takeout. It smelled delicious.

"Yum," I said. "Did you get me any eggs rolls?"

"Two, in fact, and an order of Buddha's vegetables."

"Double yum."

I waited for him to swallow his food and gave him a big juicy kiss.

"Great sex," I said, "and my favorite food; I could get used to this."

"Me too," he replied. "I saved a message for you. Seems the resort has received the faxes for your leave."

I hit the Playback button on the answering machine.

"Marianne, this is Misty from Robin's office. You should be hearing from your HR department tomorrow; they have received our paperwork. The first day of your leave is October fifth, and it will continue through November thirtieth. If you need anything, please don't hesitate to call."

"My God, this is really happening," I said.

"Are you ready to head up to the mountains and breathe in all that fresh air?" Ray asked. "You're gonna love it."

The rest of the conversation was an easy exchange about what clothes I should take, maybe a new pair of hiking boots, and the possibility of buying a fly rod in Clayton.

"We'll go to Franklins," Ray said. "It's right downtown. The store has everything from candles, outdoor clothing and candy to shotguns. You'll be amazed."

"Let's see what my fortune cookie says." I broke open my cookie and pulled out the tiny paper.

"A new relationship is about to blossom," I read aloud. "You will learn many new things."

"Sounds promising. You're on a roll; even random cookies are cooperating."

"Ray," my voice reflected growing uncertainty, "about last night..."

"Yes?" he said. He moved in front of me and surrounded me with his arms. "Do you want an encore performance?" He rubbed my scalp and murmured in my ear, "You smell so good."

I had needed him to fuck me last night, no doubt about it. But now I wasn't sure what I wanted. Jesus, I was so tired of all this merry-go-round shit in my head: yes, no, come here, leave, fuck me, now stay away. Am I hungry, or thirsty? Dazed or focused? I wanted to run out of this burning building and scream *Help!*

I leaned against his chest and cried.

"Don't cry, baby," he whispered. "You have two more nights here. You know how much I want you, but I won't force anything. We'll move at your pace… don't cry."

I crushed him with my embrace and said, "Could we sleep together tonight… just sleep?"

"Of course." He continued to run his fingers through my hair. My tears stopped.

"Ray… my Ray."

—⚬—

The next day at work I was called into Judy's office. She looked up at me with cat eyes and said, "HR wants to see you. What's this about?"

Was she actually squirming in her chair? I loved the idea of holding juicy information from her, actually causing her undue anxiety… what fun.

"Not sure. When I'm finished with HR I'll let you know."

Within an hour I had my leave of absence. There was a trail through the woods that led from the admin offices to the spa. I sat down on one of the benches and spent time deciding how I'd deal with Judy. She was so toxic. If she sensed I was nervous or fearful, it would be like blood-in-the-water to a shark. I'd give her as much information about my situation as I could without being specific, not let her get to me, and exit gracefully.

I arrived outside her office and knocked gently on the door.

"Judy, it's me, Marianne."

"Come." It was not an invitation but a command: come, sit, speak, roll over.

I decided on non-confrontational. Whatever motivated her to be so nasty must have been a burden. I wondered what demons tortured her.

"My doctors want me to take a leave of absence."

"Doctors?" She scanned me up and down. "A leave of… that's absurd."

"Why is it absurd? HR approved it."

Her facial expression contorted as if in disgust.

"Judy," I said quietly. "I need time off."

I started to feel some sympathy for her. She was so wrapped up in the day-to-day crap, she lost sight of why we were here and why she was managing a spa, a place people came to relax. What is her deal? I wondered. Why is she so angry all the time? Maybe I should give her Robin's number.

"Time off… for what?"

"All I know is… I'm within my legal rights. I'm going to take full advantage of this. I need this, Judy."

She adjusted herself in the chair, brushed bangs out of her eyes, and clasped her hands tightly, causing her knuckles to turn white.

"But why?" Her voice toned down a notch, almost human.

"Because I need to get myself together. I've had so much happen in the last week, you have no idea. If I don't get some time off I'll go bananas."

"But you seem so happy all the time."

"I'm good at being the clown, the jester. But inside… I'm dying."

We sat in silence; she looked away for a few moments, then turned her gaze back to me.

"I understand."

I was shocked at her response. Where did my mean-spirited bitch director go? Was she sincere, or was she just worried about legal shit.

Did it finally sink into her thick skull that she had no say in the matter? HR had approved my leave of absence. I was on my way to North Carolina.

"Thank you," I said, standing up. "Today is my last day. I'll return to work on November thirtieth, in time for the Christmas rush."

Instinctively I held out my hand to her. She looked surprised, then offered hers to me. It was like shaking a cold, dead, slimy fish.

# CHAPTER 15

IT WAS TUESDAY morning and I followed Ray to work so I could retrieve my clothes and books from storage to take to the cabin. I was especially keen to find the folder marked "Dream Interpretation" from my boxes. Earlier, while Ray and I were having coffee, I had asked him to let me in through the loading dock entrance.

"Why?" he asked.

"Family comes through the back door," I said. "Besides, I don't think Helen likes me too much these days."

"What makes you think that?" Ray sounded so innocent.

"Her tone, the way she looks at me, all pretty hostile."

"Are you being paranoid?"

"Maybe. Please, just let me in the back door. Then everyone will be happy."

"I can do that, no problem."

I was instantly relieved. Helen had my number; she was such a mother hen over Ray's life. I had had enough of her icy displeasure.

By ten I had rearranged boxes and had my pile ready to go. Andy walked by the door and stopped.

"Well, Miss Marianne."

"Andy, wow, good to see you. Do you have a minute?"

"Sure."

"All the extra effort you put in, vacuuming the entire condo, even sweeping the patio -- I appreciate all the wonderful work. The wall looks brand new."

"It felt good to clean up that mess. Your husband is a flat-out fool."

"I couldn't agree more, but I was foolish to stay so long."

"There's just no tellin' why people do crazy things to each other. But, for now, *you* doin' alright?"

"I am. But what do I owe you for your work?"

"Mr. Ray, he already paid me. You and I… fair and square."

It took a second to register. Ray had done it again, taken care of me when I didn't ask or expect him to help. I felt a lump forming in my throat and tears about to start. I wasn't touched by Ray's help; I was angry as hell. It made me feel inadequate, guilty, and pissed off. Somehow I was able to keep it together until I could escape Andy's presence.

"You and Ray," I said as he walked off, "have made my life bearable this last week. I'll always remember your kindness." But what I really wanted to do was scream and pull out my hair.

—⁓—

At one-forty-five I entered Robin's office carrying a vase of red carnations.

"How lovely," Misty said. "For me?"

"Geez, sorry. I should have brought you flowers too, for getting me out of jail. You're the best."

"It makes me happy when things work out. Robin should be ready for you in about ten minutes."

At exactly two, Robin appeared in the reception area.

"Hey you," she said, smiling. "Are those for me?"

"I picked them fresh this morning."

As we walked down the hallway to her office, she continued to smell the flowers.

"Roses are overrated. Carnations smell so rich and earthy. They're my favorite."

"I'm so glad you're pleased."

She set the vase on her desk, grabbed her notepad, and pulled her chair over to face the couch. I sat down on the middle cushion, thankful to have the tissue box in front of me on the coffee table. This time a large stuffed teddy bear was on the couch next to me. I immediately snatched him up and brought him to my chest, hugging him ferociously.

"I see you found a friend."

"It feels so good to hug him."

"Good, he's yours."

"Really?" My question sounded more like an exclamation of disbelief. I held him out at arm's length, inspected him more closely, and brought him back to me. "I love him. You sure I can have him?"

"I wouldn't have offered if I didn't mean it. I have a closet full of stuffed animals. It's a part of my practice, getting in touch with your inner child, feeling safe while holding something soft and warm against your body, even talking to the animal and telling him things no one else can hear. All good therapy."

"Robin, I'm going to cry."

"Hug your bear. Let him help you stay calm. Feel your emotions and try to name them."

My eyes watered but no tears fell. I spoke slowly, measuring every word.

"I'm so surprised." I buried my face into the soft fur, squeezed him as hard as I could, and took a long, deep breath. "Such a treasure. He'll bring me comfort, and yet... there's nothing I have to do but hold him."

"What do you mean, nothing you have to do?"

"In all my relationships I've had this need to try and figure out what I'm supposed to do, to give. In my marriages I couldn't stop talking, thinking, and worrying about my shortcomings, and what my husbands were doing. I obsessed."

"You obsessed because? Take your time."

I hid my face in the bear's body; my breathing went shallow and quickened. "I'm feeling nauseous."

"Marianne, look at me. Let go of the bear and sit back."

I did what I was told.

"Now come to the edge of the couch, put your head between your legs, and breathe."

My elbows rested on my knees and my head dropped down. After four deep in-and-out breaths, the wave of nausea passed. I sat back on the couch and crossed my legs under me. The room seemed brighter, my bear bigger, and the couch cushion felt like a huge pillow.

"Holy cow. What the hell is wrong..."

"You were having an anxiety attack. Do you want to stop the session?"

"No, no," I said rubbing the tops of my legs. "Something happened this morning and I need you to help me figure it out."

"Good."

"I was getting some of my stuff out of Ray's storage unit, and I found out he paid for all the repairs at the condo."

"Did he tell you?"

"No, it was Andy, the man who did the work."

"What happened when you found out?"

"I tried not to show my anger... got away from Andy as quickly as I could. But I wanted to scream."

"Did you?"

"Not really. I went into the unit, shut the door, and paced. I talked out loud... stuff like: Why would he do this? What is wrong with me? Why would he be so generous?"

"I like everything you've told me about Ray. He's given you a safe haven, and now a chance to have time alone in the mountains. Why *do* you think he's being so generous?"

"Why does every man..." I shut up as quickly as I started talking.

I reached over for Mr. Bear and held him against my solar plexus. I didn't want to tell her about the sex. It was only the one night and Ray and I had this kind of fuck-buddy relationship. The sex and his continual, unlimited generosity didn't equate.

"Why don't you try and find some peace about his kindness. Ask him yourself. You may be surprised to find he genuinely cares about you as a friend. If Dannie was so giving, would that upset you?"

"Good question... maybe not. But I'm a mess... damsel in distress. Ray is being chivalrous. Dannie's more like my sister. Yes, with Ray, it's different."

"The pacing and the talking in the storage unit -- you were angry?"

"Hell, yes, and confused, and feeling overwhelmingly inadequate. I obsessed about what he had done."

"Okay, I think you're ready for my 'why-you-obsess' speech. Worrying and obsessing keep you so entrenched in your own head you can't solve your own problems. When you become so attached to what Ray has done, you detach from yourself. You forfeit your power and your ability to think. You were out of control. The pacing is a sort of bursting energy, the energy that is obsession. Your nausea just now -- same thing."

She stopped talking and looked down at the floor. I looked down, too. Everything she said made sense. But now what? I stood up and walked over to the window. I was shaking and scared. I started to cry and covered my eyes with my hands. I teetered on a tiny slice of mountain top. It was impossible for me to be still. The way down was dark and bleak. If I fell, I would die.

"Robin, I'm so afraid." I turned and faced her.

"When you were growing up, Marianne, you learned specific behavior to cope with an alcoholic father and a mother who enabled him. There were unwritten, silent rules that prohibited you from expressing what you were feeling. There was no open, honest communication in your home. And now, as an adult, you lack the skills to engage in a healthy, intimate relationship. You're stuck in the old patterns you learned as a child."

"That's why I keep marrying alcoholics?"

"Yes, that's part of it. But there's so much more. You understood you were angry when you found out Ray paid Andy. You were able to recognize your feeling. You gave it a name: anger. Then you paced and obsessed."

"So, at that moment I had a handle on my emotion. But then I threw it to the wind?"

"You grew up in a home that forced you to worry about the next fight, the next beating. You were in a constant state of fight-or-flight, gut-twisting anxiety. It's the emotional state that worry and obsession feed on: fear at its worst. Fear and anxiety force you to try to control situations, control other people's behavior. You can think of nothing else but what you can give, or what you can do to fix it. What you are experiencing is actually post-traumatic-stress disorder."

"PTSD? But I'm not a…"

"Yes, it's similar to what war veterans experience. You're still being affected by your father's alcoholism and his violent abuse. Look at me. You can do this, kiddo. You can break free, just one step at a time. When you're ready, I have some homework for you."

I wiped my eyes dry and stood another moment. I crossed my arms and rubbed them briskly.

"Homework?" I sat back down.

"Let's talk about how to detach. Detachment is based on the idea that each person is responsible for himself or herself. We can't solve problems that aren't ours to solve, and worrying doesn't help. We give other people the freedom to be who they are, wherever they are in their own experience. Then we give ourselves the same courtesy. It also means living in the present moment, the here and now."

"Here, now?" I said.

"Exactly. You're in a situation. Don't fantasize about what you think is going on. Be brave and get the facts. Detaching doesn't mean you don't care. You can learn to love and care about someone without going crazy. You can love in ways that help others and don't hurt yourself. Start with Ray. You'll be with him during the next couple of days, right?"

"Yes," I said, "but it should be easier to just accept what he's done instead of investigating his motives."

"But will you let it eat at you? Will you continue to obsess?"

I laughed. "You know me, I'm obsessing about obsessing."

"Now you're getting it. You'll figure it out. Journaling will help. As you encounter people and situations in North Carolina, write it all down, what you are thinking and feeling, how you react. Soon you'll be the observer, not the obsessed."

"I like the way that sounds."

—⚊—

When I got back to the house I was encouraged enough to call Ray at work and invite him to dinner, my treat, a gesture to extend my thanks and talk about *why* he was being so helpful. I was nervous dialing the numbers. Steady, girl, I thought; this is a fact-finding mission, nothing more.

"Dinner?" he asked. "You're buying? I'd love to, but I was planning on working late so I can take tomorrow off. How about this? I want to introduce you to a friend of mine who owns the Mountain View Bar and Grill in Clayton. You can take us to lunch."

"Perfect," I said instinctively. "What time do you want to head out in the morning?"

"I'd like to sleep in; how about nine-thirty?"

"Nine-thirty it is."

"Tomorrow we head north," he said, "and you start a new chapter in your life. Excited?"

"Excited? Yes, and about thirty thousand other things."

—⚉—

My perfectly packed vehicle was ready to go. I placed my bear on the front seat next to me and patted him on the head. I decided to call him Sam. "Ready, Sam? Let's get off to a roaring good start."

Ray pulled out first and I followed him out of Atlanta on Interstate 85. We traveled north for almost two hours, then exited onto Georgia Route 441. The sun's rays heated the interior of my car until it felt like a traveling oasis. I still had coffee in my travel mug, and the sight of Ray's truck in front of me was comforting.

At the top of the next hill the mountains came into full view. Some of the trees were beginning to change color; they made a patchwork of brilliant reds, orange-reds, and champagne on the mountainside. A small billboard announced, "Tallulah Gorge, Deepest Canyon East of the Mississippi."

Ray's truck slowed and the right blinker signaled me to follow. We pulled into the parking lot for the Tallulah Point Overlook Area. Without speaking we walked together to the railing and I leaned against him. He put his arm around my shoulder.

"This is it," he said.

The view was spectacular. The river snaked around the gorge through sparkling pools and a series of cascading waterfalls.

"Wow," I whispered.

We stood looking over the cliff, watching two hawks sail on the thermals below. Huge areas of exposed rock formations, carved out by ancient glaciers, stuck out among the trees. I felt tiny and vulnerable.

"Where was it?" I asked. "Where did Harvey... die?"

"His son decided not to tell anyone."

I understood how Noah would want to keep that information private.

"How close are we to Clayton?" I asked. "I'm starving."

"Ten minutes. Let's go."

The Mountain View Bar and Grill lived up to its name. Perched on the side of a hill high above downtown Clayton, it boasted a stunning view of rolling peaks and valleys. Inside, the bar's décor was a continuous display of wildlife. A coyote met us at the entrance; deer heads in all shapes and sizes lined the walls. Mallards hung from the rafters, suspended in flight, and a massive pair of longhorns protruded from the wall above the bar.

Behind the bar a pretty, middle-aged blonde in tight jeans and a Mountain View t-shirt enthusiastically called out, "Hey, Ray!"

She ran over to him and they hugged. It was sweet to watch their exchange. They clearly liked each other. I was proud to be with him.

"Let me look at you, you handsome devil," she said. "Where've you been?"

"Back in the city, making the big bucks. I sure do miss being up here, though."

"We miss you!" Her voice was warm and naturally good-natured. I liked her immediately and tried to avoid my vision of her and Ray rolling around in the back room. "Now... who is your friend?"

"Beth, this is Marianne. She'll be staying at my cabin for a month or so."

She held out her hand to me. It was soft, but there was strength to her grip.

"Ah, the Gibson retreat? You're a lucky girl. Many a beer has been shared on that porch. And you're here at the most beautiful time of the year." Her hazel eyes shone from a deep place of joy. I coveted her exuberant energy, wanting to be more like her. Judging by her toned arms and lean body, I thought, she must be into some kind of athletic training. Or maybe it's from lifting beer boxes all day.

"Are you here for lunch?" she asked.

"Where else is there to eat in Clayton?" Ray said.

"I heard that. Have a seat at the bar and we'll catch up."

They chatted, we ordered, and at the end of our meal Ray asked Beth to keep an eye on me.

"Why, of course, darlin', anything you need, you just come on by."

What's this darlin' shit? I thought. Why does everyone keep calling me that? I wondered if Ray had gotten the term from her.

"This is *my* place, darlin'," she said it again, leaning into me, "so I'm here all the live long day. If I can't get 'er done, I'll know someone who can."

Beth left the bar area with our empty plates. It was finally my opportunity to talk to Ray about his generosity and my confusion.

"Ray," I started, jittery about what to say. "I found out from Andy that you paid him for his work at the condo."

"That's right," he said, sipping the last of his iced tea.

"When I found out, I got a little crazy, and Robin suggested I talk to you about it."

"Crazy, how?"

"I'm not sure. It's just… you're helping me so much. Why?"

"Why?" He looked a little hurt.

"Yes, why?" I could hardly say it. "What… what do you expect in return?"

"Women," he said. "I really don't understand why you girls don't get men. Men are so simple."

"Simple?"

"Yeah, men only want one thing."

"Sex, you mean."

"No, silly. Men just want to be somebody's hero."

"Not all men," I said. "Some men are just bastards."

"They're only bastards because they've never found someone who makes them feel like a hero."

"Really?" I said. "Can't be that simple."

"Well, it is. Men just wanna be somebody's Knight Templar."

"Okay, but I may not feel that I deserve your kindness. I feel I'm... I'm floundering, unable to keep my head above water. And I resent needing a man to rescue me."

"I don't see you as floundering. You're moving forward. Changes, big changes, take time. It's simple for me. It feels good to help you, no strings. I've been in tight spots before. I know how it feels – not good. I remember once I had no money for dog food. When I emptied the last of the bag into Chance's dish, I said, 'We're gonna have to split our next meal.'"

Ray without money? I thought. Difficult to imagine.

"I don't want to brag," he said, "but the money I paid Andy was pocket change. You have bigger things to worry about."

"But you... you didn't give me a chance to pay. You just took it upon yourself."

"Jesus, okay, I need the truth. Have you been upset the whole time I've been helping out?"

The truth... a daunting task for me.

"Gosh, I don't know what I'm feeling most of the time. I go from crazy to calm, and then from unrealistic to completely reliable. I had to get this out; I don't like feeling so dependent. Gee, you really just want to be my hero? You're so important to me. It's like you're the first person I can experiment with, being honest, talking openly. This is uncharted territory for me. You've been my safe harbor, and I love you for that." Uh oh, did I say love, the big L word? C'mon, Marianne, control your mouth. I pinched myself. "This quest for healing... well, I have you to thank. And Robin. And now you're giving me another gift – the gift of solitude."

"You just answered your own question. This gift, a soft place to land, this is all so easy for me. Mine to give."

He reached over and kissed my cheek.

My heart was full of gratitude, but I still felt indebted. "My hero," I laughed.

—ⱳ—

I followed Ray out of the parking lot. We headed north again on Highway 441 and the terrain changed dramatically. Lush valley fields flourished on both sides of the highway; the cultivated soil was black and loamy. A roadside produce market displayed huge bins of apples, pumpkins and cabbage heads. It was a North Georgia garden mecca. The fertile soil was perfect; no wonder the vegetables looked so appealing.

Eventually Ray turned left onto Betty's Creek Road, and the same kind of topography appeared. Fields of horses grazed on both sides of the road. A-frame houses and small log cabins dotted the hills. Then after another sharp turn, the fields narrowed and the majestic Blue Ridge Mountains presented themselves.

Ray's brake lights brightened and he signaled left. Nestled against the wall of the mountain, a stone drive led us upward. I could hear the creek. Between the trees and the dense thicket, I caught glimpses of moving water.

We pulled into a wide driveway. A wooden sign read, "You are at 2,100 feet. Breathe Deep." We opened our doors simultaneously. I got out quickly and stood, stunned by the beauty before me. The cottage's cedar shingles were painted forest green, the windows trimmed in bright white paint. The sound of the creek was mesmerizing. The cabin was surrounded by rhododendrons, some as high as fifteen feet, and it was situated only ten feet from the creek's edge.

Ray walked over and stood next to me.

"Must be magnificent here in the spring," I said. "I've never seen such giant laurels."

"Isn't this the most amazing sound?" he sighed. "I love it here."

Brilliant white rapids dissolved into deep pools. The steady flow of water rushed over the rocks, their surfaces shiny and smooth. A gray and black granite boulder the size of a Volkswagen bug divided the creek, creating tiny waterfalls on either side. Heavy green moss covered most of the smaller river boulders. A fire pit had been dug between the cabin and the creek, complete with a low wooden bench and a shovel.

"Let me show you where I store the firewood," Ray said. "It's so damp here; it's difficult to keep wood dry unless it's in the cabin or under cover."

He led me to the west side of the building, farthest from the creek, to a huge plastic container.

"This bin used to hold marine equipment." He opened the lid and sure enough the stacked logs were dry. "Here's a small hatchet for kindling. Just don't slice off a finger."

"Thanks for the warning."

We made our way to the porch and stood against the railing, watching the water rush before us. Two red wooden rocking chairs and a broom rested in the corner. He turned to face me and said, "Ready to go in?"

"Ready as I'll ever be."

He unlocked the French doors. "Ladies first."

"Thank you, sir."

I hadn't been sure what to expect, but I was pleasantly surprised. The front room consisted of a couch, two end tables holding lamps made from deer horns, and a coffee table stacked with National Geographic magazines. The kitchen was at the other end of the room. An old table and chairs sat in the middle of the kitchen area.

"Oh, my God," I said, "it's the same green swirly pattern my aunt had in our basement in Ohio. Even has the big silver upholstery tacks, more déjà vu."

"The seats are super comfortable," Ray said. "Shall we continue to the east wing?"

Around the corner a tiny bathroom held a small sink, shower stall, toilet, and hanging shelves on the wall.

"Running water," Ray laughed. "All the comforts. And the water gets hot fast. Be careful."

The bedroom was big enough to hold a queen-sized bed, a desk and two bookcases. A closet ran the length of the room. On the shelves in the closet were large plastic containers of linens, extra blankets, and towels.

"There's a Laundromat on Main Street, not too far from Beth's. Clayton will have everything you need: grocery store, restaurants, Franklins, even a quaint bookstore and coffee shop owned by a retired philosophy professor from New York, Dr. Minogue. He's a trip."

"I just noticed – no TV?"

"There *is* a phone," he said and started to chuckle. "No television reception up here. Besides, you're supposed to be concentrating on you, not the six o'clock news. There's a CD player and radio on the side table in the front room. You're not totally isolated."

Fear, real fear, gripped my heart, and my hands went clammy. I could hardly imagine living without a TV... and a computer.

"How far is the next cabin?" I asked. "How long would it take the police... what if..." The reality of my new situation was raining down. I felt the blood drain from my face.

"Easy, girl. Let's get you a glass of water. It's from a well across the lane. Best tasting water you'll ever drink," he said calmly. He sounded like a priest offering communion. *Take this cup and drink it.* I followed like a lamb. I made it to a kitchen chair and sat down. Remembering Robin's coaching, I put my head between my knees and took in long, slow breaths.

Ray put a glass of water on the table and sat down across from me. I sat up and drank it slowly. My fears quieted.

"You really want to do this?" His voice was full of concern.

"I... I do. I just didn't fully grasp what it would be like to actually be here in the mountains... alone. I wish I had my pistol."

"There's a twelve-gauge under the bed."

"A shotgun?" I was shocked.

"Yep, a real live one. But the only thing you'll need to worry about around here is the occasional raccoon or possum, maybe some field mice. I wouldn't let you stay here if I thought you'd be in danger. This is not *Deliverance*. The people in these mountains are gentle and kind. We can head back to Atlanta, if you're afraid to stay."

"Oh, no. I've come this far. And I'm going to have to face a lot more than raccoons in the coming weeks. Let's unpack my car."

—◠◠◠—

Ray left me three numbers: Beth at Mountain View, Doug, the handyman, and the Rabun County Sheriff's Department. We walked out to the porch and embraced.

His body was comforting and I drew strength from it. It stopped me from running to my car and driving away.

"You're a plucky chic."

"Plucky?" I asked. "What kinda shit is that?"

"It means courageous or gutsy," he said.

"Please," I said laughing. "Plucky, Ray, really?"

He turned me around and kissed me deeply. His tongue surged through my lips.

I wanted him in the worst way, but I knew it would kill the deal. I had to stand on my own two feet. I was the first to pull away, leaving him panting.

"Time for you to go off into the sunset, Cowboy, before I rip your clothes off. This plucky chic needs to get unpacked."

"All you have is time," he said. "What about..." his right hand angled downward. "Not even an hour for me?"

He held my face in his hands, kissed me again, moved his hands around my ass and pulled me into him. The kiss lingered and I could feel his dick coming alive. My clit throbbed.

"Ray, no…" I said, breaking away again. "I'm here now. This is new for me, and I don't want to fuck it up. If you stay, the lines of demarcation will blur. I want to start fresh, here in the mountains. Besides," I looked at the bulge in his pants, "you'll be with Debbie soon."

"I hate it when you're so sensible." He sighed and hugged me again.

As I watched the truck's tail lights fade from view, a veil of peace enveloped me. An owl hooted in the distance, and the creek's music played on. The cabin's inside lights illuminated the outside. Reflections of the river stone in the path gave the walkway a luminous glow, making it easy to find my way back to the porch.

Well, there's a new one, I thought. I actually walked away from hot, steamy sex. My clit throbbed again. I hope I don't regret it.

Once inside, the work began. I hung clothes from the plastic bags in the closet and found a spot for my socks and underwear in the chest-of-drawers. All of my books, files and writing papers filled the bookcase. A juice glass from the kitchen served as a pen and pencil holder, and I hung my Australian crystal from the kitchen window. I found the coffee filters, plates and silverware in the cabinets. I opened the plastic containers from the closet and retrieved towels and a bath mat for the shower. Slowly, the cabin became mine.

Sam waited on the couch, watching my progress. I took an extra quilt from the closet and wrapped him up in it.

"Here, my brave bear, make yourself comfortable."

I shed my clothes and took a shower. Ray was right, the water got hot fast. I forgot to put soap or shampoo in the shower, but the water pouring over me was cleansing and invigorating. Who needs soap? It was water from the mountains that flowed over my body, making me feel pristine. Lyrics from Madonna's song came into my head. *Like a Virgin.* I began to sing, *"I was beat, incomplete. I'd been had, I was sad. But you made me feel shiny and new. Like a virgin, touched for the very first time."*

I wasn't sure how long I was in the shower, but the water temperature began to fade. It didn't matter. It was only me and Sam now, and he didn't care how long I took, to get ready for bed. I didn't have to do or say or be *anything*.   I was truly *Free At Last*.

After the shower I put on my favorite pajamas. Sam and I had arrived at Nirvana. We were totally contained in Otto, North Carolina, a new life for both of us. I found a place on the couch, moved him to rest against my leg, covered us with the quilt, and stroked his head. "You're not just another guy... trying to help me along, are you?" I had to laugh.

I leaned my head back and closed my eyes. My mind rambled. *On Friday nights Aunt Mary and I snuggled in her bed and watched television. She stroked my hair as I rested against her shoulder. Who cared what program was playing? I loved feeling so close to her. Her touch helped me understand how powerful our hands are, and she was the driving force behind my decision to become a massage therapist.*

# CHAPTER 16

I AWOKE TO the sounds of birds chirping. Small birds, I guessed; their songs were high-pitched and repetitive. I surveyed my surroundings and realized, I was on the couch and the front door was wide open. What time was it? When had I fallen asleep? Had any raccoons invaded my space? I felt disoriented. I got up, made coffee, and drank it black with sugar, because I refused to use powdered creamer. Sam looked over at me and smiled. I moved him to the bed and straightened up the couch.

By nine I had my grocery list and was heading for Clayton, hoping to find Franklins first so I could take my time exploring the store. After the first traffic light on Main, Franklins loomed before me. It took up an entire city block. Ray hadn't exaggerated; it had every conceivable item one could ever need in the mountains. The fishing and hunting departments took up half the store. I stood in front of a wall lined with plastic worms, tiny silver-spoons with feathers, trout flies, and fishing line. What in the world is a tippet? I wondered.

A young man who looked about twelve years old approached me. What was this, I thought. Child labor? He was shorter than I and had a full head of black, curly hair stopping at his collar. His name tag read "Pete."

"Good morning, ma'am. Thinking about doing some fishing?"

"Maybe. I've only fished a few times, years ago. It was in a boat; we used live worms."

"You catch any?"

"Only one. I remember how exciting it was, pulling it into the boat. I was afraid to touch it, but somehow I liked sticking worms on the hook."

"What would you like to fish for now?"

"Trout," I announced confidently. "The Tallulah River?"

"Plenty of trout in there. You need gear?"

"Everything."

Pete and I spent the next two hours picking out what I needed to fly-fish; the process was intimidating.

"Don't worry about being new to this," he said. "It's actually an advantage. You don't have any bad habits to break. With no expectations, your patience level may work in your favor."

He recommended a fly rod with medium action. "These are best for beginners, very forgiving and easy to cast." As he continued my orientation Pete began to tease me. "I got two questions: Does size matter? And what kind of action do you like?" Suddenly he looked older.

"Well," I said, trying to keep up, "size always matters, but if the action is good... who cares?"

"Just so you know," he actually winked, "shorter rods are stiffer, faster action and good in tight spots."

"Tight spots?" This was getting out of hand.

"Some areas on the Tallulah are narrow, with brushy banks."

"So short and stiff is what I need?" I choked down the chuckle.

"Yes, ma'am, short and stiff." Pete grinned, clearly enjoying himself. But his help was heaven-sent and I was willing to play along.

"Alright then, Pete, show me one that's *short and stiff.*"

"Sorry, I'm not allowed."

We both started laughing, and I said, "I had no idea fly fishing would be this much fun."

"Just wait 'til you're on the river and bring in a big 'un."

But the real fun started when I chose a vest, hip waders, polarized sunglasses, and a hat. Trying on everything right there in the aisle, I looked like a cartoon character. Dang, I thought, this is putting a serious dent in my survival budget.

"I'm starting to feel like a pro," I snickered.

"You certainly look like one."

After securing my fishing license and trout stamp, Pete rang up my purchases, then helped me carry everything to my car.

"Do you have a guide?" he asked.

"A guide?" Thoughts ran through my head: guided meditation, *A Guide to North American Birds*, *The Hitch hiker's Guide to the Galaxy*.

"Yup, a guide," he repeated.

"No. I'm pretty much on my own for the next couple of months. But a guide makes sense."

"My Uncle Jet, he's a guide -- hunting and fishing."

"Jet, did you say? That's an interesting name."

"Well, his given name is John Edward Thomas. In high school he was super-fast on the football field, so the coach called him Jet. It stuck, and he's been Jet ever since."

Song lyrics started in my head again – this time from *West Side Story*. *When you're a jet, you're a jet all the way, from you're first cigarette to your last dying day.*

"Do you have his number?" I asked.

"Yup." Pete opened his wallet and handed me a business card.

"Wow, Pete, this is so cool. Will Jet guide me to the fish, or will he guide the fish to me?"

"A bit of both, I think. Good luck."

After Pete and I said our goodbyes I got into my car and studied Jet's business card. It was heavy card stock, white, with raised black lettering.

John Edward Thomas Mountain Guide
Hunting, Fishing, Hiking Services Available Year Round
Highlands, NC 828-658-8888

I let my index finger run over the print and closed my eyes. Each bump of ink translated his name to my skin.

"Jet," I said. "I hope we like each other. Will you teach me how to fish?"

—⟋⟋⟍—

Grocery shopping was fun. I loaded up on all the essentials plus three boxes of veggie-burgers, lettuce and tomatoes, and vanilla ice cream. On the way back to the cabin I decided to refer to my new accommodations as "home." For all intents and purposes it *was* home. Live in the now, Robin had told me. Everything that mattered to me was in that cabin, and for the next two months I was in self-explore mode. What better place to do it than... home?

I stopped at the farm stand and tried not to overindulge. All the fruits and vegetables looked so fresh and succulent. I settled on apples, onions, yams, a head of cabbage, and three pumpkins to decorate my porch.

By two o'clock I was making a veggie-burger and fresh coffee. I set the plate and mug on the kitchen table, then went to the bookcase to retrieve the folder on "Dream Work," along with a legal pad and pen. No time like the present, I thought. I'm ready to dissect The Summit nightmare.

In the folder were notes from John Bradshaw's book, *Healing the Shame That Binds You*, and his dream analysis worksheet. Each quote seemed deeply felt and poignant. *The Talmud says, "A dream is an unopened letter to yourself." Dream work is work. The great error is to think it can be done quickly. Dream work is a powerful tool. The dream images have associations. These associations are parts of ourselves. They need to be integrated and owned.*

Apprehensive about revisiting my nightmare, I fled to the porch and sat in one of the rockers, paralyzed. Slowly I rocked back and forth. I noticed a red maple leaf swirling in a pool of water just below the rocks, stuck in the current, unable to move downstream. Would I continue to be tossed about by my fear, like this leaf trapped in a whirlpool? I remembered my mother, and the way we were trapped in our house by my father's abuse.

The dread of investigating the dream came from the deep and haunting horror I'd felt that night at the hotel. My hands gripped the arms of the rocker, and I pushed myself up. Like a zombie I made it inside, went to gather up Sam, and hugged him long and hard. The sensation of his head against my cheek brought me back to life. I was safe with him; he would protect me.

My mother, my loving mother, was taken from me in a deadly car accident. I sobbed into Sam's body and wailed.

"Why? Oh, God, why? He took her... The bastard killed her!"

I rose on my knees and began to beat my fists into the pillows. "You bastard... You fucking bastard!" This went on for several minutes and then I collapsed on the bed, exhausted. "Mommy, please make the pain stop... please."

—m—

I jerked awake. Sam lay beside me, and the bedroom was filling with light. The cabin was cold. I got up, kicked on the propane wall heater, and dove back under the covers. So much pain had surfaced the day before. During my childhood my father's behavior was unpredictable. Sometimes he didn't drink for weeks. I blamed myself for his return to drinking after those sober periods, convinced that I had done something wrong and was being punished.

While under the covers, I tried to remember his redeeming qualities. When I was twelve he taught me how to shoot a gun and started taking me hunting with him for pheasant and grouse. Mom made us bologna sandwiches and Dad carried a thermos of hot tea.

The pheasant feathers were beautiful, and I used them to decorate my bedroom mirror. We never talked much. He never asked me about school, my Confirmation classes, or my friends. He rolled cigarettes from loose tobacco and Bugler papers, and spat stray tobacco onto the ground.

I got up from my cozy nest, started a pot of coffee, and put on jeans, a heavy sweatshirt, and my new hiking boots. While I was lacing up the boots, my anger returned. Dad didn't taught me anything about life; all he taught me was how to fire a gun. Surely fathers were supposed to teach their daughters more than that. The coffee was done. Instead of pouring a cup I turned off the machine. The thought ate at me. *The only fucking thing I learned from him was how to shoot a gun!*

I went into the bedroom and retrieved the shotgun and a box of shells from under the bed. The anger was building up; I was like a pressure cooker, ready to blow. I went into the closet, put on the fishing vest over my sweatshirt, and loaded up the pockets with shotgun shells.

"Okay, then, *Dad,* let's see if I remember how to fire a gun. Hopefully, I can find something in the forest to kill." I was talking to myself, but it felt good. "I need to blow the shit out of something. Too bad your sorry ass isn't here. I'd be happy to start with you."

My pulse quickened after I opened the breech and rested the gun against my shoulder, holding the barrel with one hand. I headed out to the woods. Maybe I could blow some unlucky squirrel out of a tree. With a 12-gauge, he wouldn't stand a chance.

There was a faint path heading west. I walked slowly over a slight grade and then the path leveled out. Just ahead of me, an ant hill appeared, about two feet high. It was teeming with red fire ants. I loaded both chambers of the gun and closed the breech. As I pointed the end of the barrel at the hill, my right index finger felt the forward trigger and squeezed. *BANG!* The gun hammered my shoulder and almost knocked me down. I pulled the butt of the gun in tighter to me and spread my legs to brace myself. I found the second trigger, and *BANG!* The hill exploded into fine, sand-like particles and the nasty bugs went flying. I strode past them in a state of wonder, watching them scurry in panic. It was very satisfying.

Opening the breech, I continued up the path with the gun resting in the crook of my left arm. Off to my left I spotted a large red feather on the ground and picked it up. The spine was thick and white with varying shades of red. Mesh material covered one of my vest pockets, and the feather easily slid into the openings and was held in place.

While standing, I reloaded the gun, and continued walking. I was itching to kill something. The memories of my father were like a poison under my skin. I wanted to put his face on something I could destroy. My chance presented itself a good way into the woods. A large dead oak lay in the middle of the path, just asking to be blasted. I was sure I could see my father's angry mug there.

"How dare you!" I shouted. I aimed and fired both rounds into the log at the same time. The gun knocked me on my ass, just as Dad had done, and that made me even madder. With lightning speed I got up, ejected the empty shells and reloaded. Bracing against the shotgun with all my strength, I fired again and again, walking slowly toward the dead tree. The smell of gun powder and moldy, splintering wood spurred me on.

"This is my path, goddammit!" Repeating the pattern of ejecting and reloading, I fired two more volleys.

"I hate you!" Two shells out, two more in; I had eight shells left. I reloaded and paced around the tree. Like a madwoman, I started taunting my father's ghost.

"What are you gonna do now, you bastard? Just try and hit me, you fucking prick. I'll blow your ass away." *Bang! Bang!* Within sixty seconds I emptied what I had left in my vest. My ears were ringing, my shoulder was beaten to a pulp, and my palms were wet against the gun's metal.

Finally, I threw the 12-gauge to the ground, fell on my knees, and cried out a primordial scream.

# CHAPTER 17

I GOT BACK to the cabin around twelve-thirty, threw the spent shell casings into the trash, kicked off my boots, and felt glorious: strong and powerful. It was a don't-fuck-with-me kind of feeling, one I had never felt before. Who can hurt me now? I thought. No one. The release of all that pent-up anger had been invigorating, and I was famished. I wanted meat, a nice, big, juicy burger with all the fixin's and lots of mayo. I smelled of gun powder and felt gritty... I didn't care. I finally understood why some men got off on hunting and fishing, the power over life and death, and the ability to survive.

The parking lot was empty at the Mountain Grill except for an old pick-up and a silver Toyota hatchback with a bumper sticker that read "My Other Car Is a Broom." When I entered, Beth and another woman sitting at the bar turned to see who was invading their territory.

"Well hello, Miss Marianne," Beth said. "How are you, darlin'? Please join us."

"I'd love to," I said. "I skipped breakfast and I'm starving."

"Good," Beth said. "What'll you have?"

"Do you have dark beer?" I asked.

"Is Guinness dark enough?" Beth asked.

"Oh, yeah," I said.

I approached the bar and the dark-haired woman held out her hand. "I'm Sarah," she said as we shook hands. "Come and sit."

Sarah was beautiful; her skin tone was a deep olive, her wide eyes a brilliant green. She could have been a spy for the CIA, an international beauty. Was she Middle Eastern, Italian, Greek, or Eastern European?

"Thank you," I said and sat next to her.

Beth put the Guinness bottle in front of me.

"Can I have a warm mug?"

"Ah... a purist," Beth said.

"I learned to drink Guinness warm," I said, "while reading James Joyce."

"Well, lah-dee-dah!" Beth said with jovial sarcasm. "You need a menu?"

"Nope. I want the thickest, yummiest burger you have, tomato, lettuce, mayo, and onion."

Beth returned with a mug and quickly poured the beer at an angle. Foam rose to the top. I put my head down to the rim of the glass and sucked it, making heavy slurping sounds.

Beth and Sarah howled.

"So lady-like," Beth said.

"Don't drown," Sarah added.

"Stop, please stop," I pleaded, choking with laughter. I used one hand to reach for a napkin.

"Certainly a momentous first meeting," Sarah said.

"I agree," I said and wiped my eyes with the napkin.

"All right, girl," Beth said, "I'll be fixin' a burger with everything. Want fries?"

"Sure, extra grease, vinegar, and catsup. Oh yeah, and plenty of salt."

"I can do that. Inside twenty minutes you'll be havin' the best burger in Georgia. Sarah, Marianne is staying 'round here for a few months, gettin' away from the city."

"Good for you. Where?"

"Ray Gibson's cabin."

"Oooo baby." Sarah licked her lips.

"No, no, he's not here. Loaned me his cabin."

"Oh, I see," Sarah said, rolling her eyes. "We all have a crush on Ray. Wonderful man."

"You have your cards with you, Sarah?" Beth asked. "This may be a good time to offer Marianne some guidance… maybe a pre-burger reading?"

"I always have my cards."

"What cards?" I asked. "A reading?"

"Tarot cards," Sarah replied. "You familiar with them?"

"I am. Well, not first hand, but I could use some fortune-telling. This is perfect timing."

"It always is. Let's sit at one of the back tables in case someone comes in." Sarah picked up her purse, which was more like a small duffel bag, and as we walked together to the back of the bar near the pool tables, she grabbed an ashtray.

The bright afternoon light shone through the windows, giving us plenty of illumination. We chose a booth, and Sarah reached into her purse and extracted a bundle; Tarot cards rested inside a color-ful scarf. She winked at me as she unwrapped them and began to shuffle. I sipped beer from my mug, wondering what kind of mystery was at hand. She put the cards on the table facing me.

"This deck was created by Pamela Smith in 1909," she said. "I love the images; it's my favorite interpretation. So… here we go. I'd like you to pick up the cards, shuffle them slowly, and think about a ques-tion you may have. Don't ask yes or no questions," she added, "but rather, If I do X… what will the outcome be?"

I picked up the cards; they were heavy and worn, easy to shuffle. Many hands have touched these cards and sought answers, I thought, and now I am the seeker. With reverence I shuffled and contemplated my question. *If I stay… if I stay in the mountains will the meaning of my dream come to me?* A card jumped out of the deck and onto the table.

"Stop!" Sarah cried, holding out her hand.

"Oops! What did I do?"

"When a card jumps out, it's significant. We need to look at it before you shuffle again." She picked it up. "It's the Knight of Wands. Great card; a knight is coming to your rescue? It signifies an escape from difficulty or changes in your life."

"I'm definitely going through some changes."

Sarah's tone was matter-of-fact. "Change is in the air. You're beginning a long journey, entering or leaving a significant situation. You may be changing jobs or residences. There is promise in your future; not bad for a first card."

Sure, I thought. What a bunch of... We sat in silence. She reached into her bag and pulled out a pack of cigarettes and a lighter. "You want one?"

"No, I'll just enjoy yours."

She lit the cigarette and said, "Pick up the cards and shuffle again, thinking about your situation, asking the same question."

After I felt like I had spent sufficient time touching the cards, I put them down on the table in front of her.

"We have about fifteen minutes -- time for a five-card spread. It's very reliable. Go ahead and split the deck into three piles, left to right."

I did what I was told.

She picked up the piles in reverse order and said, "If the card image faces you, then it is in a positive aspect; if it faces me, it's bad news." She made large circles in the air with her cigarette while she spoke. "Don't worry... lots of cards in their negative aspects can actually be helpful."

With the cigarette dangling from her lips, she slowly flipped five cards over, arranging them in a line between us.

"First of all, these are all Major Arcana cards." She took a long drag and tapped the ash into the ashtray. Again she made large circles in the air. Smoke formed a cloud between us, and I coughed.

"Sorry," she said, putting out the cigarette. "When I see cards like this line-up I tend to get excited; this is big mojo. Let's talk about the first one."

I stared at the weird card. It was the Devil card, an image of a man and woman chained together standing in front of the throne of a beast -- half-man, half-goat.

"This card represents your immediate past. You're in bondage to unhealthy emotions, guilt, fear, lust and hopelessness. This next card is the Hermit. How cool. Here you are chillin' in the mountains; this is certainly your present situation."

It all sounded a little too convenient, but I played along.

The card showed an image of an old man, a sage, looking down at the ground. He held a staff in one hand and a lantern in the other.

"This card represents an internal search," she continued. "It would be wise to meditate, become centered, connect to Source, and be patient with yourself."

I started to tear-up and said, "That's why I'm here."

"The third card is the Tower, a very powerful card. It's hit with lightning and is destroyed. It's a swift, dramatic change – like a sudden death."

What's positive about a sudden death? I wondered. I drained my mug and felt as if I was becoming overwhelmed, so I asked Sarah for a break. In the ladies' room I splashed water on my face and looked in the mirror. I didn't realize my face was still so dirty. I washed off a light layer of soot, rubbed it clean with paper towels, and adjusted my ponytail.

God, what must they think I've been doing?

When I came back to the booth Sarah looked up at me and asked, "You okay? Do you want to keep going?"

"Oh my goodness, yes. All of this is making so much sense it's scary." I sat down.

"Only two cards left," Sarah said. "The fourth card is your advice card; what will likely manifest in the near future. And yours is an especially good omen: the great earth-mother, the Empress. She heals, nourishes, and gives birth to the ability to give and receive love."

I became calm instantly. The card had an image of a beautiful woman in a colorful gown resting on a settee. There was water flowing near her, with trees in the backdrop, and she wore a crown of stars.

I looked down at the fifth card and noticed that Sarah had turned it around while I was in the bathroom, and faced it toward her. Why would she do that? Didn't she say before that if the card was facing her, it meant something bad? What the…

"The last card is the best card in the entire deck," Sarah said, sounding a bit rushed. "The World. It's the last card of the Major Arcana and it indicates fulfillment, a journey's end, ecstasy, reaching your goal. All is well and success is at hand."

And the opposite of success? I thought with an eerie feeling.

This card depicted a woman holding batons of light in both hands. She was draped in a blue sash. An eagle, a bull, a lion, and the head of a man each decorated a corner of the card. The woman's expression was peaceful, confident.

I sat back against the booth and let out a huge sigh. I wanted to believe it.

"All good," Sarah said. "You have some work ahead of you… but you'll be fine." She seemed a bit rushed to put the cards away.

I wondered why she had lied.

—⟳—

It was after six o'clock when I sat in the chair next to the telephone to call Jet. The phone was ivory, heavy and awkward, a throwback from the 80's. I balanced it on my lap while holding Jet's card and punched in the numbers. I wasn't sure what to expect – Jet or his answering machine.

"James Thomas," a gentle voice said.

"Is this Jet?"

"Uh… not too many people call me that. Who the hell is this?"

"I'm visiting from Atlanta and want to learn to fly-fish," I explained. "Your nephew, Pete, gave me your card."

He dropped his guard. "Okay, yeah… sorry. When people call for hiking or hunting trips they ask for James.  Sorry."

There; he said it again. I hated the word "sorry." I had started to use the phrase, "I apologize," years ago, because sorry had so many negative connotations: your sorry ass, that's a sorry excuse, sorry piece of shit, I know, you're sorry -- how's your family?

"Not a problem," I said.

"Neither is fly-fishing. Your first time, is it?"

"Yeah, I don't have a clue."

"You are going to love it. I get a lot of execs from Atlanta up here. They say it's the only way to truly escape work-related stress."

"I'm staying in a cabin near Clayton. You're in Highlands?"

"It's right up 441 north, forty minutes or so," he said. "But we could get started at Franklins at eight in the morning. I'll bring lunch and drinks and check out your form, I mean your gear, before we head out. Any preferences for lunch? Anything you don't like?"

"The only things I don't eat are tongue and tripe. Everything else is fair game. How long is the lesson and how much?"

"By four p.m. you'll have at least one trout, guaranteed. There are several lessons we need to get through. The cost is one-hundred-and-fifty dollars."

"Is that the going rate?" I swallowed hard. I hadn't expected to pay that much just to get started. One-hundred-and fifty dollars -- that was a commitment. But if I don't hire a professional I'll probably be wasting my time.

"It is. You might find a cheaper guide, but I'm the best. Hometown boy. Spent years fishing and hunting these mountains. I know where all the fish are."

"All the fish?" I laughed. "All the time?"

"All the time," he boasted. "How soon you want to get started?"

"I have no plans, except to read and relax for the next two months."

"What... you some kinda rich city girl? Who has that kinda time?"

"No I'm just..."

He cut me off. "Well, I'm busy with hikers until Monday morning. Tuesday work for you?"

"Yes. Yes, Tuesday. Will you take a check?"

"Long as I know where you live," he said. "Let's meet at eight... Franklin's parking lot. I drive an old red Jeep Cherokee. Easy to spot. You're gonna need waders. You got waders?"

"Yes, I do. I'm excited, Mr. Thomas," I said joyfully. "My next big adventure."

"Who are you, Pee Wee? *Pee Wee Herman's Big Adventure?*"

"You're a riot," I said.

"By the way, ummm, what did you say your name was?"

"I didn't say."

"Well, it might be helpful..."

"Marianne, just call me Marianne."

"Okay, Marianne, see ya Tuesday."

—⟋⟋⟋—

The next morning I went for a long run, showered, and got ready for the day. The weather was gorgeous. A rusty Coca Cola thermometer mounted on the porch registered seventy degrees. The sun's rays were warm, the air was slightly cool, and there wasn't a cloud in the sky.

I waited until noon to eat. After a microwaved mac and cheese dinner, I took my journal out to the porch and read my last entry.

Now I had new experiences to record, and I started with meeting Pete at Franklins. Then, with objective clarity, I wrote about my emotional rampage and how I'd felt while firing the 12-gauge. Detached, I thought. It was as if I was describing a scene from a movie.

I put the journal down and concentrated on the rumbling sound and perpetual flow of the creek. With no television or Internet, I felt a bit lost and realized I didn't have anything new to read. It was time to head into town and find Dr. Minogue's book store.

—◊—

A brass bell jingled and announced my arrival at the Books and Fresh Coffee shop in downtown Clayton. It was situated in a row of storefronts; the building marker read "1885." The interior was delightful: high tin ceilings, dark oak baseboards, wooden floors, and rows upon rows of books. People were browsing, and two black wrought-iron tables and chairs were placed in front of a small coffee bar equipped with a shiny brass Italian espresso machine. A pungent smell of strong coffee hung in the air.

A man, slightly overweight, with short, curly gray hair, approached me with an unlit pipe in his left hand.

"Good afternoon, Miss. I'm Dr. Minogue." We shook hands.

"This place is amazing," I said.

"Thank you. I don't believe I'll ever die, because I'm in heaven now." He was so charming.

"What an appealing thought," I said.

"I like to introduce myself to first-timers. Am I correct in assuming that this is your first visit?"

"You are," I answered.

He was dapper in his sweater vest, crisp white shirt and flowered tie, and his voice was calm and soothing.

"Are you looking for something in particular?"

"I'm spending some time in the mountains to relax and reflect. I don't think I'm a candidate for true crime."

"Ah… reflection; you need Rumi. And maybe a story about insight and personal growth. *The Way of the Peaceful Warrior* comes to mind. Let me take you over to Self-Help."

"Okay," I said, following him across the room.

"Take your time," he advised. "Look closely at the content before you make a decision. The right one will speak to you."

I thumbed through several books and that drove me to the coffee bar. With a steaming latte in hand, I returned to find a book of Rumi's work. Dr. Minogue was right; his words were captivating.

In the fiction section, I found a familiar title, *A River Runs Through It and Other Stories* by Norman Maclean. How fortuitous – à book about fly-fishing. I rounded out my selections with a stack of glossy magazines. Picking them up and turning the pages made me feel as if I was choosing friends to stay with me at the cabin.

I didn't see the good doctor anywhere, and while checking out I asked the clerk if Dr. Minogue had left for the day.

"He has," she said. "Can I help you with anything?"

"No. I just wanted to thank him for recommending Rumi."

"Oh, everyone gets the Rumi speech; he's on a mission. I'll tell him. He'll be thrilled."

—⟋⟋⟋—

I stopped at the local liquor store and bought four bottles of wine: two red, two white. I felt like a princess – lots to read, a full refrigerator, and plenty of wine. Upon returning I put everything away and opened the red wine first.

Build a fire, I thought. I took out all the advertising inserts in the magazines for kindling. Excited and joyous, I was going to have fun all by myself. I took the bottle of merlot and the paper to the fire pit.

With unexpected ease I chopped logs into smaller ones and stacked the wood near the pit. The paper and chips of wood served as a catalyst that would bring my fire to life. It was a glorious feeling to build a fire and watch it grow. What is it about fire? I wondered.

Within an hour I had a strong blaze going. I relaxed and enjoyed the flames. I thought of Jet and tried to put a face to match the sound of his voice. "Rich city girl," I chuckled. Was this really my life now? It all seemed like a dream. I took a swig from the bottle and felt the alcohol warm my throat.

"Yes," I said in a loud voice. I reached to the stars with the bottle in my right hand. "I am strong... I build fire!"

# CHAPTER 18

THE MORNING SKY was overcast, making the cabin's interior darker than usual, so it had been easy to sleep in, and I was hung-over. But after a hot shower and coffee I was almost human again and decided to walk the path I had found on Friday.

My steps were slow and measured. I passed by my murdered tree and marveled at its destruction. Gee, what maniac did that? The path went steeply upward. I continued on and began to sweat and feel a little nauseous.

The path leveled off and I stood for a moment with my hands on my hips, head down, and tried not to puke. Then, out of nowhere, a shiny, jet-black crow landed on the ground thirty feet in front of me. He squawked and turned to face me. He hopped about, coming slightly off the ground, then settled down. Looking at me intently, he moved his head from left to right.

"Caw... caw..." He flapped his wings and his chest expanded with each call. He was a beautiful, majestic bird; his wings held a hint of deep purple. I'd never seen a crow at such close range. Then, in an instant, he shook his body, spread his wings and flew into the sky as quickly as he had appeared. All that remained was one of his feathers.

"Caw... caw..." He soared above me and circled twice. His cawing sounds became "Bye-bye" in my mind. I waved farewell.

The feather he'd left was a twin to the hawk's feather I'd found on Friday: a thick spine like an arrow, a vane soft and beautiful. This gift had just arrived out of nowhere – from the crow's body to my fingers. What did it mean?

Two feathers in three days. I had found one and the other was delivered to me personally by Mr. Crow--or was it one of Poe's dreary ravens? It all felt very cosmic, as if it might be some kind of a message, like my reading with Sarah. These feathers would become my fetishes, objects holding magical powers, reminding me I had the power to take flight.

It rained all day. Because of heavy cloud cover, the temperature never went above sixty degrees. At ten in the morning I lit the propane heater and snuggled up with Sam on the couch, poring over my new book of Rumi translations. Rumi was born on the eastern edge of the Persian Empire, in what is now Afghanistan, in 1207. He was a great mystic, a Sufi poet, and devoted his life to divine illumination and the love of God. Many of his poems spoke to me. After reading *Climb to the Execution Place*, I put on rain gear and ventured out to the creek's cold water.

*Grief settles thick in the throat and lungs: thousands of sorrows being suffered, clouds of cruelty, all somehow from love.*
*Wail and be thirsty for your own blood.*
*Climb to the execution place. It is time.*
*The Nile flows red: The Nile flows pure.*
*Dry thorns and aloe wood are the same until fire touches.*
*A warrior and a mean coward stand here similar until arrows rain.*
*Warriors love battle. A subtle lion with strategy gets prey to run toward him, saying, Kill me again. Dead eyes look into living eyes.*
*Don't try to figure this out. Love's work looks absurd, but trying to find a meaning will hide it more.*
*Silence.*

I rolled my jeans up past my knees and walked into the creek. The water was icy. It numbed my skin immediately, but I pressed on to reach the huge boulder in the middle. I sat down and rubbed my legs back to life. Rumi's words described my relationship with Tom. This ancient scholar knew the pain of love and betrayal. The rain started to pour down with a roar, beating against my body. I took off my jacket and stood on the rock's edge, spreading out my arms, my face to the sky. I drank in the rain.

"Cleanse me!" I shouted. "It's time!"

I set the alarm clock for six but I was up at five-thirty, anticipating meeting Jet and having my first lesson. I decided on a big breakfast, because I didn't know what the activity level would be for the day and what time we'd break for lunch.

One of the smartest purchases I'd made at Franklins was a pair of canvas pants with lots of pockets, and zippers at the knees. As the temperature rose during the day, one could unzip the bottoms and they instantly became shorts. Ingenious! My fishing gear was still in the trunk of my car, so all I needed was my sunglasses, brimmed hat, and vest. I was out the door at six-fifty, hoping to get to the parking lot before Jet.

But it was all for naught. The red Cherokee was parked with its back gate down. There sat a man who looked somehow familiar. Had we met? Maybe he had been a client at the resort. Surely I wouldn't forget a man this striking. He had thick, curly black hair, a deep tan, and a manicured beard cut close to his face. His long legs were extended in front of him, crossed at the ankles, and he was drinking from a Styrofoam cup, looking relaxed and content.

He wore khaki pants and a long-sleeved cotton shirt, and his fishing hat rested on the gate next to him. His eyes were hidden by sunglasses.

As I pulled the Volvo next to his vehicle, he stood and watched me through the windshield. I waved; he smiled. His Jeep was equipped with huge knobby tires, and had an arrow for an antenna, a winch on the front bumper, spotlights mounted on the hood, several bumps and dings in the body, and scratched paint. I got out of my car; he slid his sunglasses up to rest on his forehead, exposing deep blue eyes and long lashes, much longer than mine.

I extended my hand. "Good morning, I'm Marianne Sobieski." His grip, I noted, was both soft and strong. "I love your nickname."

"Jet?" he responded. "It was a gift from my high school coach... Served me well over the years. Beautiful day; a good day to fish, but every day is a good day to fish. Do you have gear?"

"It's in my trunk."

"Let's take a look," he said.

I opened the trunk and he was pleased with my collection. "Pete did a good job. Let's move this to the Jeep and drive to our first location."

We worked together to move my gear, and I used the opportunity to get a closer look at him. Jet was tall, well over six-feet, and physically fit, clearly an athlete or at least a serious outdoorsman. We stood together and he shut the gate.

"Let's get started," he said, and we entered his truck.

"What now?" It was all I could think to say.

"It should only take you a few hours to get your basic casts down," he said, starting the Cherokee. "We need to take our time and practice before we hit the river. I don't want you developing any bad habits. You need to relax and think about what you're doing and have fun with it."

Sounds good, I thought.

He drove us to a golden meadow surrounding a wide pond. On the hill, tall grass waved in harmony with a light breeze. He stopped at the edge of the pond, shut off the engine, and turned to face me.

"Most fly rods break from a car door or trunk, not a fight with a big fish. Always be careful with your rod around an automobile."

We got out and moved to the back of the Jeep. After opening up the gate, Jet said, "There are three reasons to cast: to place the fly without spooking the fish, by presenting it as naturally as possible; to keep the fly dry; and... casting is fun!" He was animated and eager to teach. I wondered how many times he had given this speech.

He picked up the grip of the rod and demonstrated how to hold it. "It's almost like shaking hands with someone," he said and handed the grip to me.

When he saw me struggling with the placement of my fingers, he moved in behind me and placed his hand over mine. If I had leaned back I could easily have rested my head against his chest. His calloused palm sent warm sensations through me. I stepped away quickly and blushed.

"That's okay," I said. "I think I've got it."

Jet picked up the remaining two pieces of the rod, twisted them together, and lined up the guides.

"Let's step out in the open and I'll show you your basic cast."

We walked into a portion of the meadow that was covered in short grass.

"Remember a few things," he said as he demonstrated. "Try not to use your wrist; let your forearm do the work. The tip of the rod should follow a straight line through the air, not an arc, during the entire casting stroke. Point the rod out in front and bring it up quickly to the twelve o'clock position. Wait for the line to travel all the way back, just a couple of seconds, then snap the rod forward again. If you can keep it going, back and forth, that's called a 'false cast.' Then you can let the fly land where you want it."

On the first try the fly connected with the back of my hat and the line fell all around me in a tangled mess.

"Oops."

"Try to visualize the line unwinding behind you and snap it forward when it's straight."

I tried again and did better. It was hard to wait the exact amount of time before snapping it forward, but I finally started to catch on. I practiced for about ten minutes, "false casting" over my head, and beginning to get the hang of it.

"It's getting warm," I said. "I'd like to unzip the legs from these pants."

"Okay," he said. "We'll go back to the Jeep, you can unzip your pants and we'll put on our waders. I know the water's chilly. The next step is to learn how to strip out line. Then we'll head over to the pond."

At the Jeep I took care of the pants. Jet let me thread the fishing line through the guides and showed me how to tie on a fly. Then we put on our waders. As I walked around with the rubber against my skin, the height of the waders felt like thigh-high leather boots.

"Oh… I'm feelin' sexy now," I said, grinning.

"Women in waders *are* sexy," Jet said. His smile and gentle expression put me at ease, and gave me a kind of quiet pleasure. "We won't use a streamer at first. I'd hate to see it stab you in the eye or the back. We'll stick with a tiny nymph."

"Ouch," I said. "A fly in the face? I'll be extra careful."

While standing in the shallows of the pond I learned about shooting and stripping line, the false cast, and how to cast to my target.

"You're a natural," Jet laughed.

"Sure," I replied. "I bet you say that to all the girls."

"Let's break for lunch," he said, "and then we'll head over to my favorite beginner's stream. You'll love it. It's one you can fish by yourself."

# CHAPTER 19

WE MADE IDLE conversation while eating our sandwiches, talking about where we grew up, our families and religions, our favorite music and best friends. I guessed Jet figured it was part of his job, idle conversation with strangers. He was good at it.

"Did you go to college?" I asked.

"I wanted to study engineering," he said, "but I was drafted in 1966. After two tours in Viet Nam I moved home to these mountains and never looked back."

Geez... Viet Nam, I thought. In 1966 I was eight years old and Jet was fighting in the jungles of Southeast Asia. The comparison was startling. He didn't seem like so many of the Viet Nam vets I knew. By all appearances he could have been a mild-mannered engineer.

"Why *two* tours?"

"I was an Army Ranger. We were called Lurps."

"Lurps?"

"Yeah, it's an acronym for long-range reconnaissance. Patrols were risky business, very risky; it became addictive."

"My father was in World War Two," I said. "He never talked about it... stayed drunk most of the time."

"Those vets had no place to take their pain," he said with compassion.

"How did you cope? You seem so calm – like Buddha."

"Help from friends and family, one friend in particular."

I kept quiet, and he didn't volunteer any more information. He drained his soda can, crushed it, and threw it into his cooler.

"Let's get you on the water."

We packed up, got into the Jeep, and buckled ourselves in. When we made it to the main road, he asked, "Want to listen to the radio?"

"Only if you do."

"You're gonna like this stream. There's a series of small to medium- height waterfalls. Lots of oxygen, so the trout thrive and some get pretty big."

The mountain road turned into hairpin curves with no guard-rails. I looked over the edge a thousand feet straight down and felt the first wave of nausea.

"Jet, I'm getting a little spooked over here."

"Carsick?"

"Just a little green."

"You're a flatlander. The winding roads take some getting used to. Keep your eyes focused on the road ahead, pick out a spot on the mountain until we pass it, then choose another focal point. I'll slow down a bit. Hang in, we're almost there."

Finally we turned down a gravel road on the left and began a steep descent with only a few dips and bends. At the bottom of the hill we turned onto a road, partially overgrown with weeds. I was thankful for the break and regained my equilibrium. Within a hundred yards an open space appeared, with a wide stream glistening in the sun.

Across the water, on the side of the mountain, tiered waterfalls fed the stream. The beauty was magical – something I'd never experienced before. As I stood taking in the scenery, Jet opened up the back of the Jeep and joined me.

"Every twist and turn was worth it," I said. "So beautiful."

"This time of year, after the weeds cover the road, people forget about this spot. I did promise you a trout by four."

"I can't wait!" I said.

Jet took a few minutes and explained how to "set" the hook. "There's a barb on the end of the hook. Unless the hook gets into the fish's mouth or jaw and sets itself, the fish will spit out the hook. When you first feel that fish take the fly, you gotta lift the rod quickly to set the hook. Maybe a little bit of a jerk. Don't be too timid."

I picked up the fly, studied its construction, and purposely stuck my thumb with it.

"Ouch! This will not be pleasant for the fish. It hurts."

"Of course it hurts." He shook his head and laughed. "Only a woman would try to be empathic about what a fish would experience. Let's get to it."

I navigated through the rocks, carefully made my way to the middle of the stream, and felt the water's pressure against the waders and my legs -- the deeper the water, the greater the pressure. The rocks were slick with moss.

"I think my waders are leaking," I called out.

Jet answered, "No, you're fine. The water's cold; what you're feeling is the change in temperature."

I started to cast, short ones at first, then out with a little more line. Five minutes later I felt a tug on the fly and jerked the line to set the hook. A colorful trout broke the surface, flung his back fin in the air, and splashed back into the stream. Holy cow, a real fish! I thought.

"Give him more line," Jet called out. "Let him run, then tire him out by reeling him in slow. You'll feel him lose power, and when he does, reel him in fast."

I did as instructed and was rewarded with a nine-inch Rainbow. It was a balancing act, holding my rod, reaching down into the water, grabbing his lip and lifting him up. The fish was a true rainbow of color. His body was speckled and had stripes of yellow, pink, and blue. I held him in the air triumphantly.

"I caught a fish! Jesus, I really caught one, Jet. He's beautiful."

"That's a keeper," Jet said. "He looks delicious."

"I don't know how to clean a fish," I said. "Should I let him go?"

"No. I'll teach you; it's not hard. Bring him over to me and I'll thread him on the stringer. Keep fishing. Try the rocks over there."

I caught two more trout, thrilled beyond belief. One of them was a Brook trout, even more colorful than the Rainbow. Red spots dotted his side, and yellow markings covered his body. It looked as if someone had taken a paint brush and randomly applied color.

"I feel strangely omnipotent," I said. "I'm bringing the fish out of their world and touching them. They... we together... are traveling between two worlds." What was it Harvey said? I tried to remember. "I and the fish are one?"

"Try casting with your eyes closed. By now you know the lay of the land. Trust your visual memory. You should be able to feel when the rod is in the twelve o'clock position and when it's time to make another forward cast. It'll do wonders for your timing."

"You're kidding. That sounds crazy."

"Do you trust me?"

"Yes," I said.

"Then trust what you've just learned," he said. "Close your eyes and trust yourself."

He was right. I kept my eyes closed and my physical sensations of the rod and placement of the line heightened. My forearm and cast were in perfect synchronicity. Not only that, but my sense of smell was enhanced; I took in the subtle perfume of the grasses and trees. I began to laugh joyously and opened my eyes.

"It works, Jet." I shouted, "It really works!"

I started to reel in the line and felt the muscles in my right arm and shoulder ache. "This is too much excitement for one day," I said. "I'm bushed."

"Come on in," Jet said. "See, you didn't get skunked. Let's call it a day."

Once on land, Jet and I headed over to the Jeep. I slipped off my waders and put on hiking boots. He had already positioned the fish and a large wooden cutting board on the tailgate.

Filleting a fish was tricky business using a very sharp knife. I watched Jet slit the belly and pull out the internal organs.

"We can throw these back into the stream to feed other critters."

He showed me how to hold the knife and angle the blade to remove the bones closest to the spine. He cut off the dorsal fin. "This is the fishiest part. You may learn to like it, but I don't."

"Aren't you going to scale it, skin it or something?"

"No, that would be bass. We don't remove the skin from trout filets. It's all good."

He held out his hand with two perfect filets and put them on ice in the cooler.

"Your turn," he said and handed me the knife. "Careful... sharp as a razor. Always keep the business end pointing away."

The blade of the knife was a little scary but the process reminded me of dissecting a frog in biology class. I persevered and managed to fillet both trout.

"Nice work," Jet said. "Time to head back. I'm confident you'll be able to carry on without me; you're a very fine fly-fishing lady. And only one lesson."

I felt proud, learning something new, something as exotic as fly-fishing. We traveled back to Franklins listening to a country music station and making more small talk. I found out he had two dogs, a pointer and a hound.

"The pointer's name is Luke, after my favorite apostle. The hound is a Walker, a pretty girl named Sue. They're both great hunters."

I started to plan how to say goodbye. Should I ask him to join me for dinner at the cabin? I pondered. I do have a bottle of white wine, perfect for trout. But he's killer handsome, he must have a wife or a girlfriend. He isn't wearing a ring, but then a lot of men don't. Could this fabulous guy be alone? Certainly not. I decided to keep my offer of dinner to myself. Maybe... just maybe, he'd make the first move.

We pulled into the parking lot and began the process of loading up the Volvo with my fishing gear and cooler of fish.

"This day has been so wonderful," I said. "A perfect day, full of surprises. I learned so much. Thank you."

"What made you decide to learn how to fly-fish?" he asked.

My God, I thought, what a loaded question. The roots of my decision, like the experiences in Norcross and Harvey telling me to fish, were too deeply buried. I didn't want to fess up to all the shit I'd been through. Perfect day, why ruin it?

"I don't know. It looks so much like poetry in motion. I knew I'd be around for a few months, so... why not?"

"Well, you'll be eating fresh fish while you're here, that's for sure. You're a feisty lady, Marianne. I had fun today."

"Me, too." I sensed he was cutting me off, so I made one more suggestion.

"I'll deliver your cooler to Pete."

"Oh, the cooler," he said. "Sure, yeah, that'll be perfect. Pete won't mind, and you can tell him about all the fish you caught."

———

I washed the trout filets, wrapped two in separate plastic bags, and stored them in the freezer. I steamed veggies and pan-fried the third in butter. Now I had three days of protein and, with the vegetables mixed in, I was right on track. My body was thinning. I liked the idea of trimming down. I was getting down to fighting weight, buff and ready to go.

After dinner I sat on the porch, enjoying the creek and a second glass of wine. I thought about my day with Jet. I wondered if he thought I was attractive. He was the perfect gentleman and teased me only a little, but never flirted, so it was hard to tell. I wondered, too, what it would be like to kiss him; even though the thought of kissing a man made me uneasy. Any involvement with a man would have been daunting, given my current emotional state.

I got up and began to pace back and forth slowly across the porch. I traced the railing's swirling wood grain pattern with my index finger. The sun set at seven and now twilight was becoming dusk. I was fixated on Jet; back and forth I paced, back and forth again. I went inside, poured a third glass of wine and found my journal and a pen.

I turned on the all the inside lights and sat down at the table. I found the entry after my last session with Robin, the one that dealt with the root cause of my obsessing.

*Don't fantasize. Detaching doesn't mean you don't care. While in North Carolina write down your feelings about people and situations you encounter.* I picked up a pen and began to write. *I know I look strong on the outside, but inside I still feel helpless. What's next? Rumi and more fishing? Maybe it's time to get an appointment with Robin – next week. I need to take care of my needs, no one else's. One day at a time, and if that doesn't work, one hour at a time.*

I turned off the lights except for the bedroom lamp. The forty-watt bulb gave me enough light to see and gave the cabin's interior a soft glow. I went back out to the porch, sat down on the floor, and moved into a lotus position.

I took in several deep breaths and spoke, "I am so happy and grateful for: Ray... Robin... Beth... Dr. Minogue... and Jet. I am grateful for the fish in my freezer; I am grateful for this beautiful creek and cabin and Sam."

I continued to be aware of my breath and spoke the Metta meditation prayer I had learned from my yoga instructor.

"May I be at peace. May my heart remain open.

May I be awakened to the light of my own true nature.

May I be healed. May I be a source of healing for others."

Then I recited some positive affirmations. "I am strong, physically and emotionally. I am happy and healthy." These words did not feel genuine, but I decided to "fake it 'til ya make it," as Robin had recommended.

I stretched my legs out in front of me and took in the night sounds and pure mountain air. I drew my knees to my chest and wrapped my arms around them.

Childhood memories of Aunt Mary swept into my thoughts once again. Whenever she was able to make my high school track meets, I could hear her cheers above everyone else's. When I was a sophomore, she presented me with an exquisite leather-bound copy of *The Complete Works of William Shakespeare*.

I stood, walked out to the lane, and scanned the heavens. Between the branches of the trees I saw clusters of twinkling stars and sent my voice into the sky.

"I love you, Aunt Mary. I love you!"

# CHAPTER 20

I LIKED TO eat lunch at Beth's after two p.m. The lunch crowd was usually gone and I would have the bar and Beth all to myself. I sat at the empty bar and called out, "Hey… Beth. I'm hungry!"

Beth emerged from the kitchen wiping her hands with a towel. "Oooh, mountain girl, I hear you been fishin' with *the man.*"

"What? Oh my God, how did you know?" I was incredulous.

"Please, girl," Beth said, "this is Rabun County. I know what time you went to bed last night."

It began to sink in. We're not in Atlanta anymore, Toto. I could feel my face get hot. I was blushing.

"Okay, now," Beth leaned in, "what all happened on this fishing trip?"

"I caught fish."

"Is that all you caught? Girl… you are blushing. You're giving yourself away. Don't worry; your secret's safe with me. Just a heads-up, you're in the mountains. Everybody knows everybody's business. It can be a good thing if you have mischievous teenagers in your house. They can't hide anything. Nobody uses their blinker around here, 'cause everyone knows which way they'll turn."

"Thanks, I got it. How about another one of your juicy burgers? I'm up for my weekly dose of red meat."

"Guinness?" she asked.

"No, sweet tea."

Two men came in and sat at the other end of the bar. Beth went about the business of cooking and serving. I reached over for a copy of the area newspaper that was waiting for the next person to read it.

It appeared we were all having burgers for lunch. Beth set plates in front of the men, then delivered mine.

"Here you are, little missy. What are you doing Friday night?"

"Friday night... hmm, let's see." I scratched my head. "Cocktails at five and then the limo will arrive at six-thirty so I can make it to the theatre by eight."

"Okay, smartass. There's a dance at the Clayton VFW this Friday. Want to go with me?"

"A dance?" I asked. "Like with live music?"

"Yes, that's why they call it a dance. There'll be music and people will dance. The band plays country rock and some old stuff from the 70's."

"Oh, so it'll be *Free Bird*," I said. "Lots of lighters in the air celebrating the Confederate spirit: the south will rise again? I think I'll pass." I cut my burger in half and was ready to take my first bite.

"My oh my, you are one uptight bitch," Beth said.

"Excuse me?" I said, putting my burger back on my plate. "I am not an uptight bitch... in fact, I'll have you know, I have smoked marijuana."

"So, if I score you a couple of joints, you'll go with me?" Beth asked.

"I don't take kindly to bribery, madam," I said. "But a couple of joints would sweeten the deal."

"Come on, Marianne, go with me," she said. "Don't make me beg."

"Begging is so unattractive," I said.

"I neeed a date," Beth begged. "It's the VFW; we'll have fun... please, come with me, pleeease."

"You know," I said, "I have the sweetest pair of Nocona boots. My favorite silk blouse and tight jeans, I'll be lookin' so fine."

"Sister," Beth said, "we are going to have a blast and break hearts. *Yeehaww!*" She gave me a big high-five.

—m—

Beth and I decided to meet before eight, so we could get a seat at the bar. There were advantages to this: easy access to the bartender and a better view of the stage. I chose not to carry a purse. Dannie taught me this, because purses are easy targets when you're on the dance floor. Instead I carried lipstick, tissues, and mints in my linen blazer and stuck three twenty-dollar bills in my jeans pocket.

I scanned the VFW's parking lot for Beth. Cars and pick-ups were filling up spaces – there was going to be a crowd. I spotted her sitting on a bench in front of the door. God knows how long she had been there.

"We have arrived at the perfect moment," Beth said.

"I'm buying the first round," I said.

"Well… lah-dee-dah!"

Beth was super-cute in a short denim skirt, light blue blouse, and boots.

"Looking for a cowboy?" I scanned her up and down.

"Any boy will do tonight," she whispered.

I lifted up my leg and showed off my boot. "Look, we're twins."

"You've got good taste," Beth said.

"Better taste in boots than men," I told her.

We entered the VFW and found the last two seats at the bar, but they weren't together. Beth took charge of the situation.

"Hey there, handsome, would you mind moving down a chair, so two of the best lookin' women in town can sit next to you?"

"I'd be a fool not to," he obliged. When he smiled, yellow teeth stood out in contrast with his shaggy red hair. I let Beth sit next to him. I was lucky enough to be on the other side of two older women who chose not to acknowledge me.

The bartender approached, a fifty-something gentleman, slightly overweight with obviously dyed black hair. He wiped the surface in front of us with a damp towel.

"Hello, ladies. What can I get for you?"

"Rum and coke for me," Beth said.

"Vodka on ice and a glass of ice water," I said.

Beth turned to face me and asked, "Vodka on ice? What's that all about?"

"What do you mean?" I asked.

"It's just... so serious," she said. "Like James Bond or something."

"Exactly," I said. "I've been drinking wine and beer all week. I want something... more serious. I'm a Sobieski; I'm getting in touch with my Polish roots."

The band climbed onstage and tuned up. The lead singer stood behind one of the microphones and shouted, "Hello Clayton, Georgia!" The crowd roared and whistled. Just as I had predicted their first song was a Lynyrd Skynyrd tune, *What's Your Name?* No one got up to dance, but people started to mingle. We turned our wooden stools around and watched the crowd. Beth clearly enjoyed being in this target-rich environment.

"So many cute guys, and so little time," she said. "I'm going out to prowl, but let's keep track of each other." She was gone in a flash.

"Beth!" I called after her, but she was already lost in the crowd in front of the stage.

I took off my jacket, hung it on the back of the stool, and sat with my arms crossed against my chest. After being alone in the mountains for ten days, I found that the crowd noise, loud music, and screaming laughter putting me into sensory overload. I ordered another drink.

"Want to start a tab?" the bartender asked.

"Good idea," I said. "Please put her rum and coke on it, too."

"Name's Dave," he said, and left to refill my glass. When he brought it back, the glass was filled to the brim. "Enjoy."

I took a sip and felt the burn. The band began to play a slow, sappy love song and a tall man sporting a long brown ponytail and a black leather vest came up to me.

"My name's Tom. Would you like to dance?"

Tom... Christ! I felt like someone had walked over my grave.

"Maybe in a little while; I'm still getting settled in. Mostly I like to watch other people dance."

"Come and find me when you're ready," he said. "Never seen you in here before."

"My name's Marianne." We shook hands and I noticed several thick scars on his thumb and the top of his right hand. He caught me staring.

"Motorcycle accident. You like to ride?"

"I do... with someone who doesn't have accidents."

He picked up a napkin and asked Dave for a pen. He scribbled his name and number on it. "This is in case we don't hook up for a dance and you'd like to go riding this weekend." He smiled at me confidently and strutted away.

He wasn't bad looking, but the thought of calling a man Tom... well, it was unsettling. Maybe I could call him Thomas or Tommy. Nah, too much trouble, too much crap associated with Tom. I needed to find a Bill or a Rick; those names I could live with.

Beth ran up to me and grabbed my hand, almost pulling me off the stool. "Come on," she said. "It's time to dance!"

We went to the middle of the crowded floor and danced like teenagers. We rocked out, moved seductively to the music, and bumped our hips against each other. At one point we joined our elbows and did a poor imitation of the Rockettes. When the song ended we hung onto each other, laughing. Arm in arm we made it back to our seats and two fresh drinks were waiting for us.

Dave came over. "Drinks are from the gentleman across the room, the one wearing the black cowboy hat."

"Brian!" Beth yelled out. "Get your butt over here, darlin'."

Beth leaned over to whisper, "He's an old boyfriend from last year. Not sure why we broke up."

She introduced us. Brian was short, maybe five-six, with a thin mustache. The top two buttons of his shirt were unbuttoned and light-brown curly hair protruded. I hated fuzzy men. Yuk.

"I missed you," Beth said with a slur. She pulled his face to her and kissed him passionately, and he responded.

It made me uneasy to watch them, so I left for the ladies room. When I got back, Brian's foot rested on the bottom rung of Beth's stool. Their heads were together, and they were deep in conversation, oblivious to their surroundings.

Beth looked up at me with drunken eyes. "Brian and I are leaving. Aren't we, darlin'?"

"Yes we are, baby girl," he slurred. "Let me bring my truck around. I'll be right back. Don't you move an inch." He kissed her lightly on the cheek and left.

"Beth, what are you doing?" I asked. "Is he okay to drive? If not, we can head out together right now. Brian can wait."

"Oh, no, sweetie, I *want* Brian to take me home. We've got a year of making up to do." She giggled and elbowed my arm. "Your presents are in your jacket pocket next to your keys."

"Presents?" I asked. "What presents?"

"You know the ones we talked about when I called you an uptight bitch. But now I see you are not an uptight bitch and a pretty good dancer, vodka girl." She hiccupped.

Brian appeared. I stood, and got right up in his face.

"If anything happens to her, you answer to me and the authorities."

He snickered. "Relax. Jesus Christ, I'm just takin' her home. Why don't you worry about the rest of *your* night?"

Beth slid off her stool and Brian took her arm to steady her.

"Fuck you, cowboy!" I shouted.

"Likewise," he answered.

Beth was not paying any attention to our words and waved good-bye as they walked to the door.

"What a dick," I said to myself and sat back down with an empty bar stool next to me.

The band was on break and I ordered yet another vodka. I was feeling the buzz big time, and liked it.

A man appeared out of the smoke and asked, "Is this seat taken?"

"It is now, if you'd like," I said abruptly.

"Thank you," he said and sat down. He ordered a beer. I didn't offer any conversation; I was still steamed up about Brian.

Finally he turned to me and asked, "Do you like the band?"

He looked Italian: dark brown eyes, black hair and a thick black moustache – the burly type.

"The music is fun. But I really like 80's."

"Eighties music is happy and playful," he said.

"I never thought of it that way, but you're right, it is."

I learned his name was Tony and he was a diesel mechanic. He lived alone in an apartment in downtown Clayton and he liked to fish.

"I just learned to fly-fish," I said.

"That's cool... a woman fly-fishing, very cool."

Maybe Tony was a good guy. "Do you smoke?" I asked.

"I gave up cigarettes years ago," he said.

"No, I mean do you... do you smoke pot?"

"Oh," he said and lit up like a Christmas tree. "I do!"

"My friend gave me a couple of joints."

"What should we do about it?" he asked, grinning ear-to-ear.

"I've got to go to the ladies room. Get some matches from Dave, and I'll meet you outside."

"You're not undercover, are you?"

"Do I look like I am?"

I gathered up my jacket, shot back the last of my drink, left forty dollars on the bar for Dave, and walked unsteadily to the bathroom. My lips were numb as I applied more lipstick. I felt smug. It seemed

167

every woman in the ladies room was overweight and had bad hair. Once outside, I found Tony leaning against the front entrance post, waiting for me.

"I didn't realize how beautiful you are," he said. "Now I see you in the light."

"Thank you, how sweet."

"I parked way in the back," Tony said. "We should be safe there. Too far to smell."

I started laughing. "You know, I'm a massage therapist and I smell people all the time."

"I'm sure it's better than smelling diesel fuel. But to me, diesel fuel smells like money."

We laughed together and I hung on to him as we made our way to his pick-up. He put down the gate, put his hands around my waist and hoisted me up.

"You are just the prettiest little thing. How much do you weigh?"

"How much do you weigh?" I asked while lighting up the joint.

"A lot," he said.

We passed the joint back and forth, not speaking. The feeling went right to my head. When it got close to the end I stamped it out and threw it to the ground.

"Beautiful night," I said, "so many stars." I leaned back expecting something to support me and fell into the bed of the truck. "Oh… oh. Wow, I think… I think I'm drunk."

"You are," Tony said. He rubbed my leg, then moved to lie next to me, lifted my head and placed his arm underneath it.

I had entered that weird place of semi-consciousness. I knew where I was, but I also knew there was nothing I could do about it. He started to kiss me. His mouth was wet and sloppy; spit entered my mouth and made me gag. I pushed against his chest.

"Hey, Tony, no. This is not good."

His voice became angry. "Hey, you're the one that wanted to get stoned. You wanted to be alone with me. I know you want it."

"Want what?" I sat straight up.

"You want me," he said and pushed me back down against the truck bed. He reached under my blouse, pushed my bra over my tits and started to suck my breast. It hurt. His heavy moustache was like sandpaper against my skin. "Don't fight it now, baby... you're mine now, just go with the flow."

I did fight. I took a swing at him and missed.

"Stop it, you fucking asshole, stop!"

Suddenly his body lifted off me. I tried to focus and pressed the back of my hand against my lips. I scooted out on the truck gate and saw Jet when I heard a loud *SMACK!*

Tony was on the ground.

"You are one sorry son-of-a-bitch... and a coward. You know she's drunk, and she told you to stop." Jet's voice was strong and commanding. "Now get outta here!" Tony jumped up and tried to throw a punch. Jet caught his arm in mid-air, twisted it, and popped him with a left hook, sending him several feet away from the truck.

Tony regained his footing and held his palm to his cheek. "Who the hell are you?"

"I'm her brother; and so help me God, if you don't get out of my sight you will curse the day you were born."

Jet feigned another punch and Tony ran towards the VFW building.

Then Jet turned his attention to me. "You alright?"

"I think so." I adjusted my bra and blouse, picked up my jacket and came off the truck gate. I took two steps forward, stumbled, and fell into his arms.

—⟋⟍⟋—

I woke up in the back seat of my Volvo, covered by my jacket. I sat up slowly, my head pounding; every muscle in my body ached. It was cold. Morning, already? Covering my face in my hands, I tried to remember last night's details. There was drinking, Beth and I danced, and I insulted her boyfriend. Then Tony and I smoked some pot... Tony... oh my God, what did I do? Jet showed up out of nowhere like some kind of magic. How did I get here? Was it Jet? It had to have been him. He was the last thing I remembered.

The car was locked, all four windows were cracked open, and I found my keys on the floor. I unlocked the door, crawled out like a hundred-year-old woman, and leaned on the side of the car, trying to get my bearings. It was still dark, but the floodlights of the VFW's parking lot illuminated the area.

Two other cars were in the lot, along with Beth's pick-up. Perhaps I wasn't the only one being naughty last night, I concluded. But it was more than being naughty; I had put myself, Jet and Tony in serious danger. My head ached. I was starving and thirsty. My mouth felt like it was full of cotton, more like tumbleweeds. I wrapped my arms around my torso and started to cry.

This is a new low, I thought, even for me.

When I got back to the cabin I drank a quart of water without stopping. I found the second joint in my jacket pocket and flushed it down the toilet. After taking off my clothes I considered burning them. Wearing them again would remind me of last night and what an idiot I had been. What a failure: a disappointment to Ray, my work with Robin, and myself. I should pack up and leave... but where? My head throbbed, and my mind went into a dark place.

*"Get out!" my father screamed at the top of his lungs. He threw me against the back door with a thud and grabbed me by my arms, shaking me. "I've had enough of you and your mother." He flung open the door and pushed me out onto the porch in the middle of a downpour. I heard the lock turn. Mom was with Aunt Mary and had left me home alone with Dad. I ran into the garage,*

*shaking and wet. I cowered in a corner behind an old tire, praying for him to stay in the house and for Mom to come home soon.*

The flashback made me realize that I had been running and hiding my whole life. I was in such a good place on Friday, and now this... self-sabotage, jumping back on the roller coaster, putting myself in a pile of shit.

After a hot shower, I put on some fresh pajamas and then moped around feeling sorry for myself. When I heard a truck pull up, I couldn't imagine who it might be. Ray? I slipped on a robe and went out to the porch. It was Beth.

"Hey there, lucky you," she said. "I wish I was still in my pj's. You feelin' as rough as I am? Girl, I am hung-over with a capital H."

"I'm staying in them all day."

"I have some interesting news for you, and a message that is for your ears only."

"Come in. Want some coffee?"

"I've already had enough to sink a ship," she said. "I love this view of the creek. Let's sit on the porch. Fresh air will do me some good."

We sat in rockers facing the creek and stared in silence.

Beth finally said, "Jet came by the grill this morning right at eleven asking about you."

"Jet? What did he say?"

"Only that he needed to share some things with you about last night. He looked serious. So I told him I'd deliver the message and you could decide what to do next. What happened last night?"

What took her so long? I thought.

"I acted like a drunken fool."

"Me, too. I woke up this morning and couldn't remember if Brian and I... well, you know. He drove me to my truck and it took me two hours to feel halfway normal. Saturdays are one of my busiest days. I'm screwed."

"Join the crowd," I said.

"No, no you're not. Jet's a good guy, one of the best. If he wants to talk to you, it's because he has something important to say. He doesn't make small talk."

"Maybe you're right."

"I'm always right," Beth said and stood. "I've got to get back before the late afternoon crowd starts piling in. If I see him tonight, what do you want me to tell him?"

"Tell him… I'll call him… Sunday, maybe Monday."

"Smart girl," Beth said. "Now give me a goodbye hug."

—⁂—

I finally went out for a run around five. I pushed myself and sweated heavily, detoxing. Walking up the lane back to the cabin, I felt so much better. The strong endorphin release was just what I needed.

I showered for the second time and redressed in my pajamas. I gathered up Sam, found Rumi, and the three of us settled in on the couch. After reading for an hour or so, I turned on lights, made myself some chicken noodle soup, and sat down at the kitchen table to eat it. I propped Rumi up against my journal and found *Four Interrupted Prayers*:

> *Four Indians enter a mosque and begin prostrations, deep, sincere praying.*
> *But a priest walks by, and one of the Indians, without thinking, says, "Oh, are you going to call to prayer now? Is it time?"*
> *The second Indian, under his breath, "You spoke. Now your prayers are invalid."*
> *The third, "Uncle, don't scold him! You did the same thing. Correct yourself."*
> *The fourth, "Praise to God, I have not made the mistake of these three."*

*So all four prayers are interrupted, with the three faultfinders being
more at fault than the original speaker.*
*Blessed is one who sees his weakness, and blessed is one who, when he
sees a flaw in someone else, takes responsibility for it.*
*Because, half of any person is wrong and weak and off the path.*
*Half! The other half is dancing and swimming and flying in the
invisible joy.*
*You have ten open sores on your head. Put what salve you have on
yourself. And point out to everyone the dis-ease you are.*
*That's part of getting well! When you lance yourself that way, you
become more merciful and wiser.*

I sat riveted to the chair and re-read the poem several times. I must
put salve on my head, tell everyone of my condition, and receive healing. Visualizing my other half dancing and swimming and flying in
the invisible joy gave me hope. And I was grateful, so grateful, that I
had tasted the sweetness of being warned.

# CHAPTER 21

I WAS IN the middle of a wonderful dream when the ringing telephone interrupted my sleep. I was a mermaid swimming among schools of colorful, graceful fish. The water was crystal clear and warm; I swam with the current and felt my hair flowing against my skin.

I got up quickly and stubbed my toe against the end table.

"Shit!" I screamed into the phone, hopping around on one foot.

"Hello?" My voice carried a hint of disbelief. Who could be calling so early?

"Good morning. You okay?"

"Yeah, just hit my toe." I still didn't recognize the voice. "Who..."

"Marianne, did I wake you?"

"Ray! It's so good to hear your voice." I sat down on the couch and rubbed my throbbing foot.

"How are you getting along?" he asked.

I talked non-stop for fifteen minutes. I gave him as many details as I could: my experience at the bookstore, learning to fly-fish, becoming friends with Beth and building a fire. I left out the VFW mess; no sense sharing my bad behavior. The lingering sense of wellbeing from my dream allowed me to skip that story without guilt.

"I'm planning a trip to California... to visit Debbie?"

"Oh, good for you," I lied.

"I called to make sure you had everything -- that you feel safe."

"I took your shotgun out for a test drive," I said. "Yes, I feel very safe."

"Good," he said. "You sound terrific. The mountains must agree with you."

"They do, Ray. You have no idea."

—m—

I was on the river by noon, walking along the bank, scanning the water through my Polaroid shades. I saw shadows of fish in a deep pool. After getting my fly-rod, I tried my luck -- and tried, and tried. Wrong fly? I wondered. I was so disappointed, I decided to stop torturing myself. I packed up and headed out to Books and Fresh Coffee for a cappuccino.

By four o'clock I was back at the cabin, thawing out a trout filet. If I couldn't catch one, at least I could eat one. They were delicious. Before I started to make dinner I called Jet. He answered on the second ring.

"James Thomas."

"Jet, ummm, it's Marianne."

There was a long pause, pregnant with possibilities. "How are you doing?" His voice was full of concern.

"Truthfully," I said, "I was a little depressed, but I'm much better today. I got out to the river earlier but didn't catch anything."

"I'd be depressed too if I didn't catch any fish."

I felt a smile coming on.

"I'd like to see you," he said. "You went through quite an episode Friday night."

"I did... I know; I feel so foolish. I will always be grateful to you; you may have saved my life." I was apprehensive about talking to him but I wanted to know how I ended up in the backseat of my car. What did he want to tell me?

"I wouldn't go that far," he said. "And don't feel foolish. I'm not judging you at all. When I got back from Nam I did a lot of stupid, crazy things."

I felt relieved. I knew I'd been drinking too much since I got to North Carolina, and smoking that joint on Friday had probably pushed me over the edge.

"How about coffee?" I asked. "Tomorrow morning?" The suspense was killing me.

"Can we go early? I'm meeting a group for lessons at ten."

"The bookstore in Clayton opens at eight; how about then?"

"Eight is good," he said. "And since you think I saved your life, you buy."

"Perfect," I said. "See you in the morning."

# CHAPTER 22

YET AGAIN JET was the first to arrive. He was sprawled out on a city bench, his face turned to the morning sun and his arms resting along the top of the seat.

"Hey," I called out. "Are you the homeless guy they warned me about?"

He quickly sat up and stood. "Who are 'they'? I've always wanted to know."

"The ladies' garden club, who else?" I laughed.

He held the door for me, and we went inside and ordered our coffee. I asked if we could go back outside.

"If we're going to discuss Friday night," I said, "I'll need lots of fresh air."

"*It's a beautiful morning.*" He sang off-key, but it was delightful. "*I think I'll go outside for a while... and just smile.*"

"Oh, the man saves lives *and* sings. Nice combination."

"You should hear my impression of Frank Sinatra," he said.

We found another bench in a landscaped area near the sidewalk. There was no one around.

"This is good," I said.

We sat and opened our coffees. Jet moved his coffee cup back and forth from one hand to the other. Was he nervous?

"During our first conversation," he said, "you told me you were here to rest and relax, and I was impressed. You're a gutsy lady to stay in the mountains alone. But then I wondered if you were here to

177

escape from something… or someone. When I got to the VFW Friday night, you and Beth were on the dance floor. Do you know how many guys were checkin' you two out?"

"No, but there were more men than women there anyway," I said defensively. "What's your point?"

"You were vulnerable, not all that aware of your surroundings. When I saw you stumble on your way to the ladies room, I decided to wait and see if you were going to try and drive home."

My voice softened. "Why didn't you just come over to the bar… before all that business with Tony started?"

"I was heading to the empty seat but he beat me to it. You didn't see me, but I was drinking a beer at the other end of the bar."

"I've got to know, Jet, did you get me to my car and lock me in?"

"Yes."

"Well, thanks, but that's a funny way to rescue someone. What if I choked in my own vomit? What about the cold?"

"I watched you for awhile, you were sound asleep."

"Watched me?"

I couldn't look at him; instead I stared at the cement walkway and counted the cracks between my feet and his: seven. I was bewildered and dismayed by my acting out. Jet was right; I had put myself in harm's way, drunk and oblivious to what I was doing.

"I left Atlanta for North Carolina to escape," I admitted. "You were right about that. Away from an abusive husband, a boss I hate, an empty condo, and all the pressures of a divorce that has to happen as soon as possible. My friend Ray is letting me stay in his cabin for a few months to get centered and plan my life forward."

"That's great," he said.

I looked up at him and smiled. "Yes. The cabin's free… no strings. That's why I can afford a one-hundred-and-fifty dollar fishing guide."

We both laughed; our eyes met. That feeling of knowing him reawakened and tugged at my heart.

"I need you to tell me," I said: "did you follow us to Tony's truck?"

"Yes," he replied. "I need to explain a few things. In Viet Nam my unit carried out secret missions across the border into northeast Laos. For weeks at a time, three of us would do recon in the mountains. What we did had a top secret security clearance – we weren't allowed to carry an ID, no dog tags, nothing. I learned to move about undetected. Because of my experiences in the war I developed a sixth sense. I can feel the kind of energy coming from someone, good or bad. I can tell if there's danger in a crowd, or if an animal is close by in the woods. That's why I'm a good hunter and guide."

"It's your training," I said. "You'll always be a Lurp."

"I knew you were in trouble by the way you hung onto that guy when you two left the bar. Then I smelled pot."

"Where were you?" I asked.

"Six cars over. I sat on the ground and leaned up against the bumper of an old Chevy and waited. When you cried out, I knew what had to be done."

I went back to counting the cracks in the cement. A full minute seemed to be a long time sitting next to someone without speaking. My eyes filled with tears.

"I'm so sorry…" Damn, damn, damn! I hate that word! But it's true.

"Hey, no, don't cry," Jet said. He moved next to me on the bench. "Marianne, you're okay, please..."

"It's just that… I'm so grateful… so lucky you were…" I struggled to get the words out. He put his arm around me; I leaned on his shoulder. We sat like that until I quit crying.

He slid back a little from me.

"There's more I need to tell you. Are you up for more Jet information?" He moved back a little more, creating a comfortable distance between us. "You want another coffee?"

"No, no thanks." I pressed my fingers into my eyelids, drying up the last of my tears.

"I'll be right back," he said.

He came back with a bottle of water, opened it and took a long drink. He screwed the cap back on, kicked back on the bench, and rested his hands with fingers interlaced on his stomach.

"When I got back from Nam I was a mess. I chased women, drank, took meds, and smoked a lot of marijuana. Everything was easy to get. Women got into bed with me because I was a vet. Doctors gave me any kind of drug I wanted. The whole country either hated us or pitied us. I used valium to get through the day and pain meds to sleep. I had nightmares and night sweats, jumped at any loud noise, lost my temper over any little thing, and picked fistfights with strangers."

He took another long drink from his water bottle.

"Am I upsetting you?"

"No... no," I said. "How did you get through it?"

"The friend I told you about, the special friend who helped me cope. Her Christian name is Lillian Wilson and her American Indian name is Laughing Deer. In 1970, the VA hospital in Asheville called me and asked if I'd be willing to try counseling. The doctors were concerned about my prescription drug use, and one physician smelled pot on my clothes during an exam. I jumped at the chance. Lillian worked at the VA hospital and on the weekends had a satellite office in Clayton. Now she has a retreat center next to her house, not far from here. I'm telling you all this because I'd like you to meet her."

"She sounds interesting," I said.

"She's a Native American healer, a shaman. She's also a clinical psychologist. Very smart lady... very wise."

"I like her already. I'd love to meet her."

"Good!" he said and jumped up, surprising me with a sudden burst of energy.

"I'll try to get in touch with her today. She's retired but still sees people at her place and holds weekend retreats and workshops. Call me tomorrow night after eight and I'll let you know what she said."

"Gee, thanks," I said. "I'll do it. I came here for answers, but I'm feeling so much right now -- anxious and tense. So much has happened in the last two weeks."

"Then you'll like this quote from John Wayne," he said. "Courage is being scared to death, but saddling up anyway."

"Yeah, that's a good one."

"I gotta go, but call me."

"I will."

---

The refrigerator was empty. It was time to hitch up the wagon and head into town for supplies. When I entered the grocery store I decided to be frugal. Beside the money issue, living alone taught me to be careful when cooking a meal; leftovers went sour quickly.

My last stop was the open-air farmers' market just outside of Clayton. I was inspecting potatoes when I heard motorcycles pull up. From the sound of the engines, I figured they had to be Harleys. I went to the end of the aisle, looked toward the parking lot and saw that one of the three bikers was Cowboy Tom.

"Oh, no," I whispered. "Small town. He's the last man I want to see." I was tempted to put my basket down and run for it. But Rumi's words echoed inside me. *Put what salve you have on yourself. And point out to everyone the dis-ease you are. That is part of getting well.*

I gathered my strength and continued to shop. Slowly the top of my head became warm, as if some hum of healing energy was producing a halo.

I was in the jams and jellies aisle when Tom came up to me and said, "Hey, good-looking, fancy meeting you here."

I gave him my best smile. "I love this place."

"The brothers and I stopped for apples. They're the best I ever tasted."

"I'll get some," I said. "I like yellow delicious."

"Quite a party Friday," Tom said. "I'm sorry we didn't dance. But you seemed preoccupied."

"I was, but for all the wrong reasons. I paid for it the next day."

"I been drunk plenty. Do you think you'd like to go for a ride? Did you even keep my number?"

"I've got it somewhere." I paused, took a deep breath, and tried that truth thing again. "Here's what's going on with me. I'm here for a few months to get my head screwed on straight. I'm filing for divorce, and I need time alone."

He was undeterred. "Keep my number, and if you have an epiphany while you're here, we'll go out and celebrate."

Had Tom the redneck biker just used "epiphany" in a sentence? I was almost speechless. "Wow, okay, cool. I may just call you."

"You *should* call me," he said. He reached out, touched my chin, and winked. "We'll have fun."

—ɯ—

I sat in the chair next to the telephone and stared at the clock. At eight-ten I dialed Jet's number and it went to his answering machine.

"Hello," the message began. "This is James Thomas, North Carolina fishing and hunting guide. Please leave me your name and number so I may return your call."

"Jet... it's Marianne. Just curious about Lillian... I..."

He picked up the phone and said, "Marianne. I was at the other end of the house. I'm glad you called."

"Me too."

"Lillian is free on Thursday and would love to meet you. She was intrigued when I told her about our fishing lesson. You free Thursday morning around ten?"

"Absolutely."

"If you're comfortable with me coming to your cabin, you can follow me to her place."

I gave him directions and he told me he would see me at nine.

"This is amazing," he said. "She's halfway between Highlands and Otto."

"Of course she is," I replied. "If I've learned anything recently, it's that there are no coincidences."

# CHAPTER 23

THE ALARM CLOCK went off and I hit the button to stop the annoying *beep... beep... beep.* Last night's sleep was deep and dreamless; maybe it was because of the chilly cabin and the mountain of blankets I was nestled under.

I crept out from under the covers, wrapped myself in a flannel robe, and turned up the propane heater. Then I pulled a kitchen chair over and warmed my hands. Jet will be here in two hours, I thought in a panic. I hadn't cleaned the cabin lately, and as soon as the place warmed, I got busy: scrubbed the bathroom, changed bed linens, and swept the floors with a broom. I didn't want him to see my usual mess.

While showering I wondered what Lillian would be like. Already in retirement -- she must be in her sixties. As a therapist I was acquainted with the concept of a shaman. Lillian was a Native American healer -- that meant big medicine. I turned off the water and heard raindrops ping against the tin roof. I assumed the day's temperature would stay on the cool side because of the rain, so I dressed in jeans, heavy cotton socks, a sweatshirt, and my hiking boots.

Suddenly, with no warning, fear raised its ugly head and glared at me. It was my father's voice. *"Who do think you are? No one gives a shit about you. You'll never amount to anything. You're a piece of shit. Get out of my sight." He picked me up by my shirt and tossed me across the room. I slid against the wall and scrambled out of the house. I ran to my secret place in the ditch, blackberry bushes scraping against my skin, and I fell against my tree, hot and sweaty from crying.*

Why can't I erase all those memories? Does Jet feel sorry for me? Is that why he wants to help? I went from excited about meeting Lillian to terrified -- another accelerated jump from emotion to emotion. I heard Jet's Jeep pull up to the cabin; it was too late to back out. From the window I saw him standing at the creek's bank, taking in the view, and I took the opportunity to get a glass of water.

There was a knock at the door. I put the glass down and steadied myself against the sink. After a deep breath, I opened the door and offered my best welcoming smile.

"Good morning," I said.

"It's a good morning if you like rain."

"I do." I was trying too hard to be cheery. "Come in. I'll give you the official tour."

"You've been crying?"

"No, no, I'm okay," I lied. "Got soap in my eyes in the shower."

"Great place."

"Yeah, I like it."

"Beth told me she's partied here."

"Yeah, she told me too."

"Amazing view from the porch... and a fire pit. All the comforts of home."

"Don't forget the indoor plumbing," I said.

"Oh, right," he said. "Running water does have its advantages. You'll need a jacket. It's gonna rain all day."

I went to the closet, found my slicker, grabbed my keys, and said, "We're off."

Putting on my jacket while we stood on the porch, I locked the door.

"I'm not sure why I do this," I said.

"Bears," Jet said.

"Bears? You're kidding, right?"

"Don't be naïve. There are bears all over these mountains. But if you lock your door," he laughed, "they can't turn the knob."

"Well then, that's why I lock it."

We walked off the porch and toward our vehicles.

"Bears," I said, poking him with my elbow. "Really, Jet... bears?"

He suppressed a smile, opened his door, and laughed. "Yes, bears."

I followed him on 441 south, then turned left onto Highway 246. We turned north on 106 and traveled to the Scaly Mountain community. The rain had stopped; I opened all the windows and turned the heater on low. It reminded me of driving around with friends in high school on wintry days. We'd blast the heater and open the windows, calling out to people on the sidewalks, "Check out our sled! Don't you wish you were with us?" We were such idiots.

We made a left turn onto a dirt road and began a steep ascent, with serious twists and turns. The road, a mirror image of the one I'd experienced with Jet during my fly-fishing lesson, challenged me to keep focused on the tail lights of his Jeep, not on the side of the mountain sheering downwards to my right. Several stretches of road consisted of only one lane.

I closed the front windows and began my pep talk, "You are fine, Marianne. We're almost there; keep looking forward. Volvos are the safest cars on the planet."

The road leveled out and I parked next to Jet on a graveled area large enough to accommodate ten cars. I closed all of the windows and got out. Jet joined me.

"Here we are," he said, stretching his arms out and breathing deeply, "at the top of the world."

"My my, it certainly feels like it."

We walked together around a large concrete-block garage and down a path made of flat fieldstone. The path was decorated with statuary on both sides representing various religions -- a Celtic cross, large Chinese lanterns, an Asian woman in ceremonial dress -- and with flower beds filled with brilliant chrysanthemums in red and orange.

We came upon a large wooden deck that faced the adjoining mountains to the north. Huge, translucent, billowing clouds, white and fluffy, surrounded the mountain.

"Is that fog?" I asked.

"No, clouds."

"Clouds? But..."

"We're at four thousand feet. We're actually standing on the clouds."

His words had a powerful impact on me. Jet had such a way of looking at nature.

"My God," I sighed, "I've never stood on clouds before."

The deck was another fascinating area. Four Adirondack chairs faced the mountain, a long wooden table surrounded by thirteen hand-crafted chairs sat in the middle of the deck, and an enormous amethyst geode, broken in half, rested in the corner near the entrance to the house. I went up to it for a closer inspection; it was tall enough to reach my waistline. The purple cavern was a magnificent display of many facets of crystals. Varying shades of color revealed themselves in the tiny mountains and valleys of the geode: violet, lavender-blue, plum, and lilac.

The first time I saw a geode, it was small and brown, with white quartz crystals inside. It confirmed to me an important message: outer appearances don't necessarily reflect the beauty within.

The door opened before we could knock.

"Jet!" a woman cried out enthusiastically. "I heard you pull up and saw you on the porch." They embraced; he lifted her up slightly off the deck. It was an all-out love-fest hug. "Too many moons since I've seen you," she said and pulled away from him. She tousled his hair. They held a gaze that was loving and pure.

"Lillian," Jet said as he turned, "let me introduce you to Marianne."

Lillian moved to stand in front of me and extended her hand. "Hello, my dear, so good to meet you."

Her touch was warm, soft, and comforting. She was an inch taller than me. A thick, shiny crown of black and grey curls flowed past her shoulders. She was statuesque and strikingly beautiful, with a long neck and strong chin. Her lips were full and her eyes deep pools of ebony. She wore a long red skirt that gathered around her feet, a simple white t-shirt, and a colorful shawl.

"Let's get in out of the weather," she said.

Jet held the door while Lillian and I entered. She was barefoot, so Jet and I took the hint and removed our boots. The entire left side of the front room was composed of six floor-to-ceiling windows that framed a view of the mountains. Along the windows, plants of varying kinds and sizes were placed on tables and bookcases of different heights. The bookcase shelves were filled with more geodes, rocks, and crystals. A huge oil painting of a galloping white Appaloosa, with black and brown spots on its rump, hung on the far wall. Just past the painting, French doors led into another room.

"Is it too soon for her to hear the gong?" Jet asked.

Gong? I thought. What is this?

"No, of course not," Lillian said with a straight face.

We followed her through the French doors into a room with an open-beamed ceiling, and I saw a huge gong about five feet in diameter hanging from one of the beams. It was red and gold and the striker sat on a table next to it. I stood still, uncertain what to do next.

"Marianne," Lillian said, "come and stand on the buffalo skin in front of the gong. It was a gift from my shaman in North Dakota."

With a great deal of trepidation, I moved to stand in front of it. My feet sank into the fur. It was so thick, parts of my socks were hidden from view. I looked at the gong and was intimated by its size. The only time I'd ever seen anything like it was in the movies. *King Kong* came to mind.

"Close your eyes," Lillian said, "and take a deep breath."

She struck the gong and immediately the vibration shook me – I could feel my bones, my heart, and the blood running through my veins.

As the reverberation settled, she said, "Once more," and struck the gong again.

With my eyes closed I saw myself riding a powerful Appaloosa alongside a buffalo. I reached out, touched the beast, and felt his mane in my hand. I wondered if I could kill it, or if it would kill me.

The three of us stood quietly until the gong fell silent.

"What did you see?" Lillian asked.

"A running buffalo," I answered.

"Good," she said. "It's time for tea."

We walked back into the main room. Along the back wall hung drums of varying sizes, bundles of sage, and several masks, one of which was decorated with sea shells and ribbons.

In the kitchen, an island with four chairs surrounding it stood in the middle of the room. A vase of fresh flowers was placed in the center. Jet and I sat watching her put the kettle to boil on the corner stove. Then she sat down across from me and looked directly into my eyes. I felt she could see all the way into my soul.

"Jet tells me you're here to get your mind clear and make some decisions about your life."

Jet looked at me sheepishly and said, "Hope you don't mind that I..."

"No, no, not at all," I replied. "I need direction. I have a counselor in Atlanta; that's part of the reason I'm here. She recommended I take some time off from the real world."

Jet stood and said, "I think I'll leave you two alone to drink your tea and share. Lillian, I'm fine with you telling her my story if you care to. If I can help in any way just let me know."

The kettle's whistle sounded and Lillian stood to give him another hug. "I'll call you," she said and kissed his cheek. She went to the stove and turned off the burner.

"See you soon, Marianne."

"Thanks, Jet," I said. "Thanks for everything."

He left us, and Lillian brought a tray with tea bags, honey, spoons, and two cups of hot water over to the island.

"What do you do in Atlanta?" she asked while making her tea.

"I'm a massage therapist."

"A healer," she said.

"I've never owned that aspect of myself. Right now it's a job. Work. I feel more in my own skin when I'm running or doing yoga."

"Why do you stay there, if you're unhappy?"

That was a loaded question. I dug deep into my being before I answered. "I've been stuck... for a long time." This was hard for me to admit. "It seems I'm afraid to move forward; I don't know where forward is."

We sipped our tea in silence. She gazed out the window, then asked, "What would it feel like if you weren't stuck, if you were strong and vital and in control of your life?"

My answer was immediate. "I would be ecstatic. I would eat cheeseburgers every day; I'd sing at the top of my lungs, and smile a lot."

She looked at me. "Cheeseburgers?"

Our laughter broke out simultaneously.

"You, my dear, are on your way to recovery," she said. "Laughter is a great gift. You've already started the journey in Atlanta, so tell me, why *are* you here?"

"How much time do you have? Do you really want all the details?"

"You decide. I have all day and, as they say, the devil is in the details."

I began my story with my crappy childhood and a short overview of my marriages to three alcoholic husbands. "My last husband put me over the edge. Our break-up was violent, the police were called, and I spent a night in a hotel room. That night I had a very disturbing dream. It's haunted my thoughts ever since."

"A dream?"

"More like a nightmare, all kinds of blood and stuff."

"Are you able to sleep?"

"I am. The other night I had a good dream. I was swimming in clear water and felt my hair flowing on my back. I felt free."

"Water often symbolizes our spiritual nature. If the water was clear; your spirit eyes were open."

I sipped my tea and looked up at the ceiling. Tiny glass birds, suspended from the rafters by fishing line, looked as if they were flying.

"Every corner of your home holds some kind of magic," I said. "I'm curious about the drums."

"You never drummed?"

"No."

She stood and motioned for me to follow. "Come."

We walked to the display of drums.

"Does one appeal to you?" she asked.

My eyes fell on the smallest one. It was light tan, about twenty inches wide. Lillian lifted it off its hook and handed it to me. She chose a much larger, darker drum and brought down a bundle of sage.

"Let's sit on the floor. This rug is very accommodating," she said. Before we sat she retrieved a box of wooden matches from the table and a shallow clay bowl. We sat facing each other.

"Before we begin to hear the voice of the drum, it is wise to clear the air." She lit a match and then lit the bundle of sage. As the smoke rose, she used her hand to guide it over her face and her heart and then she touched the floor. "Please do the same," she instructed.

I reached out for the sage. The bundle was feather-light and the smoke smelled sweet and earthy. I mimicked her gestures directing the smoke toward me, inhaling it, touching my heart-space, and then touching the floor, palm down. When I gave it back to her, she tapped the hot ashes off the end of the bundle into the bowl.

"If you do this alone, be mindful of the smoke alarms," she chuckled.

Next she handed me a drum beater. It was a stick with one end covered in padding and fabric. I lightly tapped the drum head.

"Drums have been with humankind since the beginning of recorded history," she said. "American Indians use them to have visions."

She began to drum. "Let your heart guide the rhythm; your hand will follow."

She rocked slightly back and forth; her drumming fluctuated -- loud to soft, slow to fast and back again. At one point it sounded like a heartbeat, then a steady tom, tom, tom, tom.

I joined her, closing my eyes, and my drumming hand took on a life of its own. The next minutes dissolved into beating sounds, splendid shared rhythms, fluid and blending. Lillian slowed, softened her beating and then stopped. With closed eyes I continued a minute longer, beating quickly and loudly before I realized I was the only one drumming. I stopped, a bit embarrassed.

"Coming out with a bang?" she asked.

"Wow. I like drumming... it's, I don't know, kind of bizarre."

"More can be learned through drumming," she said. "There is a drumming meditation that will help you find your power animal and spirit guide."

"Jet said you hold workshops?"

"I do, but none are scheduled until December."

She stood and held out her hand to help me off the floor.

"Would you work with me?" I asked. "Jet told me you saved his life."

"If you want to work with me, you need to talk to your counselor in Atlanta first."

"What do I say?" I asked.

"Tell her about me, give her my phone number, and we'll come up with a plan. In the meantime, have a cheeseburger or two, go running, enjoy your yoga, and meditate at least once a day. If you practice yoga I'm assuming you meditate. Correct?" She smiled and winked.

I nodded, filled with hope and anticipation.

"Lillian, this is all so cool." I had tears in my eyes. She came over to embrace me and gently stroked my hair. I don't know why, but I trusted her like no other.

"When it's time, you'll find your strength and your passions. I promise you this; as you begin this journey the Great Spirit will walk with you, give you the heart of a warrior princess, and show you the way... forward."

—m—

I cried most of the way back to the cabin. It was a release from the pressure of all the things I dreaded: the flashbacks, feeling sorry for myself, and the need to obsess. The tears were a valve that opened up and washed the anxiety away. When I finally stopped crying, I felt energized, almost electric.

As soon as I got into the cabin I found Robin's number and dialed her office.

"Good afternoon, Atlanta Mental Health Associates," Misty said.

"Misty, it's Marianne Sobieski."

"Well, hello, mountain girl," she said cheerfully. "Is it getting chilly up there?"

"The weather's been fabulous. Warm sunny days and chilly nights, the kind of weather that makes you feel happy to be alive."

"Nice," she said. "What can I do for you?"

"I need to talk to Robin. Before I left she said she'd be willing to do a session by phone?"

"I just saw her walk back to the break room. She has group work tonight at six. What's your number?"

I gave her the number and we said our goodbyes. The universe is kicking into high gear for my journey, I thought. What luck, Robin might be able to talk to me this very afternoon.

I moved to the porch and listened to the creek. Small animated birds chirped and played in the trees across the water; their sounds were perky and joyful.

The telephone rang and I jumped. I picked up on the second ring. "Hello."

"Marianne!"

"Robin!" I almost shouted.

"I was so happy to get your message. It's a perfect time. I have the next thirty minutes free."

"Robin, I met the most fascinating woman. She's a retired counselor and has a retreat lodge. She's also a Lakota shaman, and helps with post-traumatic-stress disorder."

"What's her name?" Robin asked.

"Lillian Wilson."

"I know her," Robin said.

"What?" I was incredulous. "How?"

"She's written landmark papers about sweat lodges and vision work for returning Viet Nam veterans. She held a workshop in Asheville in the early seventies. I'll never forget that weekend. She's still practicing?"

"She retired from the VA and has a center on her property, next to her house. Robin, you should see this place. It's on the top of a four-thousand-foot mountain and filled top to bottom with all sorts of shaman tools from all over the world. She showed me some drumming basics today. I just left her a few hours ago."

"How in the world did you meet her?"

"Long story. I'll give you the Reader's Digest version."

I told her about Jet and learning to fly-fish. I didn't spare any details about Beth and my night at the VFW dance. When I told her about Jet and I having coffee, she interrupted me.

"Marianne, I know you sound almost gleeful now, but you do understand… the risks you took?"

"I do, Robin. I think I'm still a little high from the drumming. Yeah, I screwed up, I know. I've been in self-destruct mode for years and I'm just now beginning to understand why."

"Anything else you want to tell me?"

"My flashbacks are getting worse."

"How are you coping?"

"Breathing… journaling."

"Good. Are you telling me you have a chance to work with Lillian?"

"She wanted me to call you, give you her number, so you two could decide if I'm a candidate for her healing work."

"I'd love to talk to her," Robin said. "You've certainly fallen into a pot of honey. Good God, I hardly believe it, Lillian Wilson."

# CHAPTER 24

I TOSSED AND turned all night long. I switched pillows, rearranged the blankets, and searched for the perfect spot in the mattress. Eventually, the clock read four-thirty. So I must have slept at least some of the night. Lying in bed, I stared at the ceiling and thought about yesterday. Robin was right; I had fallen into a pot of honey. It was time for tea and meditation, time to give thanks.

I got out of bed, stumbled to turn on the light, and found my way to the bathroom. There was a certain mysterious feeling in the air during these early morning hours. It was once explained to me that the planet powers itself down between the hours of three and five in the morning. The static energy of the human race subsides, and a higher consciousness travels to those who are awake and aware. I was certainly awake and my awareness was growing every day.

The nighttime temperature was mild, so the cabin was a pleasant sixty-eight degrees. After putting on a t-shirt and cotton pants, I rolled out my yoga mat and began a meditation. Deep breathing calmed my thoughts, and I visualized white light entering my crown chakra, traveling down my spine and back up through the remaining six chakras.

After two more rounds I felt quite relaxed.

"I am grateful for my journey. I am blessed, comforted by friends and wise counsel. I am grateful."

Twenty minutes later I started my yoga poses with ease and grace. So this is how the yogis feel, I thought, practicing yoga at five a.m.

Perhaps, while in the mountains, with enough self-discipline, I could get into a serious routine and embrace my inner yogi.

I brewed a pot of mate' tea, flavored it with honey and cream, sat on the porch, and watched the dawn light arrive through the trees. The creek's ever-present gushing and gurgling was hypnotic.

It was time to make a choice, a new direction. Chose a sane life free from abuse and anger, I thought; pray that Lillian will share her gifts of insight and experience. She knows the pain and power traumatic stress can have over someone's life; and now I am in her backyard. She gives me hope.

At seven-thirty I was on the main road, having a great run. I kicked it into high gear a few times and stopped to rest with my hands on my hips and my head bent over to my knees. A truck approached and stopped on the other side of the road. The driver was an overweight woman in her fifties wearing a flannel shirt. She had fried-blonde hair and smoked a cigarette.

"Are you sick, honey?"

"No, ma'am. I'm just out for some exercise." I stood up and shook out my arms and legs.

"Well, if you call that exercise, I just don't know. Looks like you're about to lose your breakfast."

"I appreciate you stopping to check on me."

"Land's sakes, I don't want nobody dyin' on my road. Can I give you a lift?"

"No, ma'am, really, I'm fine."

"Child, you crazy to be out here so early, by yourself. You could be et by a bear," she said and laughed. Her laugh was a high pitched hee-hee-hee. "You could probably outrun 'im, though."

"I'll certainly try."

"Alright, then," she said, putting her truck in gear. "You run back home now, and be safe." She spun off and waved through the window.

What a character, I thought. If this was Atlanta, some asshole with a truck that size might run me off the road. I liked the people of North Carolina more and more every day.

—⁊ɯ—

I sat on the front porch, reading Cosmo, discovering "new ways to please my man... in bed and out." How many ways are there? I wondered. A vehicle pulled into the drive, and I recognized the sound as Jet's Cherokee. I met him at the end of the porch.

"Oh," I said, "it's my best friend in the whole world."

"I'm glad you're home. I've got news."

We hugged briefly.

"Want something to drink?"

"Can't stay long. Got folks coming in from Raleigh at four. Busy weekend.

We sat in the rockers on the porch. Neither of us spoke for a few minutes, enjoying the creek's music and the sunshine.

"Lillian called me this morning," he said. "She didn't have your number. I wanted to make sure you were okay with me giving it to her."

"Of course. She's an awesome lady. She taught me a little bit about drumming yesterday."

"Wow," he said. "She's usually not that giving of her talents on an initial meeting. Must be because she saw your potential."

"Jet, I don't know if I'll ever be able to thank you enough in this lifetime for everything you've done for me."

"I'm just giving back to the circle of healing," he said. "You'll do the same for someone in your future. That's the way it works."

I rocked back and forth, staring at the creek.

"You're not going to believe this," I said, "but my counselor in Atlanta has been to one of Lillian's workshops."

"That's why Lillian called me. She's already got the go-ahead to start working with you. The two of them will exchange insurance information, if you like, so you don't have to worry about paying Lillian."

"My goodness, I hadn't even thought of that."

"Lillian's been doing this a while," he said. "She understands that her work is valuable, and that she should be compensated."

"Yes, of course, of course," I said excitedly. "What should I do now?"

"I've got her number; you can call her today." He handed me his business card with a phone number on the back. "Just leave a message if she doesn't answer. I've got to get going. The wildlife is calling me."

We stood and hugged again. I felt the side of my cheek against his chest and didn't want to let go. I squeezed him tighter.

"Lillian may want you sequestered during the beginning steps of your work. I stayed in a teepee on her property before she built the lodge."

I started to tear-up. He kissed the top of my head and rubbed my back with one strong hand; the other pulled the flat of my back into him. I felt a sudden surge of sexual energy. His flat belly felt good against mine, and my nipples hardened. Every inch of me wanted him, all of him.

I looked up and whispered, "Jet... please... kiss me."

He cradled my face with his rough-skinned hands, brushed his lips on mine, tugged at my lower lip, and then gazed into my eyes.

"I know how vulnerable you are right now," he said. "I don't wanna..."

I reached up, pulled his head down, opened his lips with my tongue and rocked my body against his. We stood kissing, glued together. My clit throbbed, my pussy grew warm and wet. I felt his dick growing harder with every second we explored each other's mouth. I dropped my hands around his ass and pulled him in, spreading my thighs around his muscular leg. My right hand came up on the front of his pants.

Abruptly, he pulled away, and drew the back of his hand across his face.

I gasped, rocked back on my heels, and stumbled. He caught me and drew me into his embrace.

"Not now," he said with incredible calm. "I want you healthy and whole, and then we can explore... who we could be together. You're sweet... so sweet."

"So are you," I panted and pushed him back so I could gaze into his eyes. "This is so foreign to me... every man I've known wanted sex first, before anything else."

"Let's be fishing buddies for now," Jet said.

"I can do that," I lied as the heat between my legs subsided.

"You can," he said. "Lillian knows what's she's doing, and when it gets tough and crazy, stick to it; don't give up. Dig in your heels and hold on to the dragon's tail."

He kissed my cheek and was gone.

# CHAPTER 25

AFTER JET LEFT I rolled up my pant legs and walked down to the creek. The air was warm and inviting; dappled sunlight shone through the trees. I put my right foot into the water and quickly withdrew it -- the water was ice cold. Stepping back, I dug my toes into the pebbles and stared at the smaller rocks barely covered by water. There were several dark grey stones with similar markings. I fished them out and held three in my hand. The sunlight revealed tiny flakes of silver over the surface of each stone and a layer of brighter rock formed a perfect circle on each flat surface.

"A circle in the stone," I said aloud. "The possibilities are endless." I carried them back to the porch and lined them up on the railing, wondering how they were formed.

It was time to call Lillian. Her answering machine picked up, so I left her a message along with my number. Tiredness overtook me; the early morning activities and my failed attempt at seducing Jet were taking their toll. I lay down on the couch, snuggled up with Sam and quickly fell asleep.

*Dad pulled into the driveway, opened the car door, and fell on his knees in a drunken stupor. Mom and I ran down the basement steps and out the cellar door; she locked the door behind us. "We can make it to Grandma's house before he sees us," she said. She held my hand and hurried us down the alley that led to my grandparents' home two blocks away. "Don't look back," she whispered. "Don't look back."*

I squeezed the stuffed animal against my face, and the sensation of its fur on my lips brought me out of the dream. I sat up, ran my fingers through my hair, and massaged my scalp. How many times, I wondered, did my mother and I run from the drunken fuck that was my father? It seems I'm still running.

I went out to the porch and re-examined the stones.

"Son-of-a-bitch!" I cried out in anger. I picked the first one up and threw it as far across the creek as I could manage. *Smack!* It hit a boulder and the sound was piercing. The second one hit another boulder and ricocheted back across the creek. "Screw this sentimental stone bullshit," I shouted and the last one slammed against the side of the mountain.

The telephone began to ring.

"Arrgghhh..." I screamed. "I... can't... talk... now!"

The phone went silent and I sat down on the porch floor and covered my face with my hands. So much anger welled up inside me. What if Dad had been sober? What if he had encouraged me to be strong and confident? Who could I have become? I got up from the porch, feeling weak and defeated. My patterns and pain ran deep.

Can Lillian help me?

The telephone began to ring again. I answered in a state of trepidation. "Hello?" It was more of a challenge than a greeting.

"Marianne... it's Lillian."

"Oh, Lillian." My voice was shaky.

"Are you okay?"

"Um... sure, thanks for calling."

"Robin and I had a great conversation this morning."

"Already?"

"She gave me the authorization to start working with you. Do you need more time to think about it?"

"No, no... the sooner the better."

"Do you like horses?"

"I do," I said, "although I haven't ridden since I was a kid."

"You free tomorrow?"

"What do you have in mind?" I asked.

"I'd like to take you for a ride in the morning, nothing wild, just a slow walk in the woods."

"Sounds delightful." My pitiful, sorry state began to dissipate. "What time?"

"Can you be here at nine?"

"Absolutely."

"See you in the morning."

—⚹—

As I drove to the top of Lillian's mountain, the sun's rays filtered through the trees, creating a mosaic of light on the gravel road ahead. I pulled into the parking lot and saw Lillian standing with a tall, slender boy wearing camouflage pants, a white t-shirt, and a cowboy hat. When I parked and got out of my car they came over to greet me. The boy's hatband was decorated with colorful beads, and a black and white feather was tucked into its side.

"Good morning!" Lillian said. "I love it when people respect their appointment time."

"My aunt Mary taught me that when you're on time, you're ten minutes late."

"Let's have a hug," Lillian said. We embraced, and she turned to the boy. "This is Tyler."

He took off his hat, placed it over his heart, and gave me a quick nod. "Ma'am."

"I'm so pleased to meet you," I said. He looked like an Adonis – six feet tall, curly blonde hair, muscular arms, and eyes that were a blend of blue and green with flecks of gold.

Lillian wore riding boots. I held out my hiking boots for inspection. "Will these work?"

"Yes. We're in for an easy ride."

Two foxhounds appeared at the top of the hill, and the larger, darker one began to bay. His nose reached for the sky, and with each soulful howl his front feet lifted off the ground.

"Those are my boys," Tyler said. "Dylan and Keats. My mom's an English teacher. She begged me not to call them Spot or Buster."

"Let's head up to the lodge," Lillian said.

The steps were railroad ties buried deep into the soil. A handrail made the steep climb somewhat easier.

"I had no idea we could go higher than your house," I said.

"The lodge, sweat lodge, barn and trails are all up here," Lillian replied, pointing.

When we reached the top, acres of flat land surrounded by trees spread out before us. We stood, not speaking, while I took in the view. The hounds circled us, stopped, and sniffed my feet and legs. Directly in front of us was a long, white building with five large windows along its side.

Lillian walked before us and gestured. "This is the main lodge."

We walked up to the lodge and found the double-door entrance unlocked. Once inside, I saw that the foyer opened into a large hall. A long table, like the one on Lillian's deck, sat in the middle, surrounded by twelve chairs. An office space, two restrooms and an open kitchen were on the left side. A couch, two stuffed chairs, and plants comprised the right. At the end of the open area was a hallway.

"Remarkable," I said.

"Lives have been changed here," Lillian almost whispered. "This mountain is sacred land. Let me show you the guest rooms."

Tyler stayed in the kitchen and rummaged through the refrigerator. Down the hall, several doors opened to reveal bedrooms, some with bunk-beds, and each one had its own bathroom. She opened the last door and showed me a large room with double beds. Black-and-white Ansel Adams prints hung on the walls, and the room smelled of lavender.

We headed to the kitchen.

"Tyler," Lillian said, "we're ready."

Outside the lodge we walked south past a dome about ten feet in diameter made of metal poles. It was not tall and I wondered what purpose it served. Just past the dome, a majestic totem pole rose twelve feet out of the ground. Three wooden heads were carved into the thick wood, each brightly painted. A yellow eagle, complete with wings at its side, was at the top. Next was a blue horse head, then a red fox, its head detailed in every way, down to its pointed nose.

"I've only seen these in history books," I said.

"Every animal has a powerful spirit," Lillian said, "and its own talents. Your power animal chooses you, not the other way around. Eagle came to me and filled me with the spirit of creation, and soon after that I built my lodge."

At the edge of the trees, standing in the shade, two quiet horses were tied to a hitching post. Nearby was a small, two-stall barn with a tack-room and wash rack attached to the outside of the building. It was surrounded by a split-rail fence and opened up to a field. We heard a noisy crash coming from the woods and the dogs took off down the trail in the direction of the sound, howling all the way.

The horses were fitted in large, comfortable-looking Western gear. One was a pristine white mare with a flowing mane and tail. She looked over at us and nickered.

"Hello, Paris," Tyler said. She nickered again and shook her head side-to-side then up and down. "That's her way of saying hello."

The other horse looked asleep, his eyes half-closed and one hind leg resting on the tip of its hoof.

"This is Bobby," Tyler said. "Don't let his look fool you; he can get spirited."

Bobby was a tall chestnut. Both hind legs had white socks, and a long white blaze covered most of his face. Tyler approached him first.

"Wake-up, Mr. Bobby, it's time to go to work." He moved to his neck, rubbed it briskly under his mane and massaged his ears. Bobby shook his head and let out a long sigh.

Lillian and I stood together and watched Tyler. He untied Paris and led her in a circle for a few minutes.

"I'll take Bobby out," Lillian said.

Tyler stopped Paris, rested one stirrup on the saddle horn and pulled the girth tighter. She took a few steps away protesting the increased pressure. "Now then," Tyler said in a gentle voice, "be still."

Lillian repeated the same routine with Bobby. Tyler walked Paris over to me and handed me her reins.

"Lillian will guide her behind Bobby on the trail," he said. "Just sit back and enjoy."

"How do you keep her so clean?" I asked.

"Baths and brushing," Tyler said.

"I'll be doing all the work after Tyler leaves for college," Lillian said.

"College?" I asked. "When do you start?"

"I'm taking some time off, working for Miss Lillian to earn extra money."

"Do you know what you want to study?"

"Forestry," he answered. "I want to manage forests."

"Sounds admirable," I said, "and fun."

"Yes, ma'am," he said. "I like being outside." He was so polite and poised, just adorable.

Tyler turned to Lillian. "Miss Lillian, is this a trust ride?"

"What do you mean?" I asked.

"This ride," Lillian said, "can teach you a very important lesson -- while blindfolded."

She must have seen the look of terror in my eyes, she said, "Remember, we don't see nature with our eyes; we see her with our hearts."

"I'll do it," I told Lillian, before I had any opportunity to change my mind.

"Tyler, the mask is in the tack room."

"I know right where it is," he replied.

Tyler disappeared, returned with a black mask, and came to stand at Paris's head.

"I'll take the reins," he said, "and give you a leg up." He offered his clasped hands for my foot and boosted me into the saddle.

Lillian mounted Bobby and stepped over to Paris. Tyler handed her the reins. "No peeking," he said, grinning, and handed me the mask.

Lillian pulled Paris up to the back of Bobby's rump.

"I'm not going to talk," she said. "Trust the horse's movement, hold on, and relax."

I slipped the mask over my eyes and adjusted it. It was a very uneasy feeling being six feet off the ground, blindfolded. May the force be with me, I thought.

Lillian clucked to Bobby and we jolted forward. I grabbed for the saddle horn with both hands, got into the tempo of a slow walk, and melted into the leather. You got it, girl, I encouraged myself. Soon I began to be aware of different aromas, and speculated as to whether I smelled wet leaves or decaying trees. The air was thick and rich, earthy, like mushrooms growing in moss next to a stream. Pretty cool, I thought.

We began a descent and I slid forward, leaning back in a panic. Paris let out a sigh and Bobby nickered in response. We leveled off and I heard the gentle bubbling of a brook. By the sound of the horses' hooves in the water, I judged it to be shallow. Paris stumbled slightly and I lunged to the right with her misstep. I regained my seat when her head rose up and we were back in rhythm. What am I doing here? I wondered. What could this possibly accomplish? I grew more uncomfortable as Lillian reined the horses to a stop in the middle of the stream. I resisted the temptation to throw off my mask.

Being blindfolded pushed my senses to a deeper level. I imagined tiny waterfalls because the sounds were softer than the water in front of my cabin. I heard gurgling, not the roar of deep water over boulders.

Lillian clucked again to the horses and we moved to the other side of the stream. I felt branches brush against my leg. I was tempted to slide the mask up over my eyes and catch a glimpse, but I knew Bobby's hind legs were only a few feet from Paris, and Lillian would catch me cheating. Okay, I trust Lillian, I thought, but why should I trust this horse? The feel of more branches against my ankle made me flinch, and I squeezed my legs into Paris's sides. To her it must have been a signal; she quickened her pace and bumped into Bobby.

"Whoa," Lillian said. She pulled the horses to a stop once again. "Relax, Marianne. Don't tense up; you're confusing her."

Sure, I thought, don't tense up? Yeah, right. You try the blindfold. My bodyweight shifted to the back of the slick saddle as Paris followed Bobby up an incline. I felt myself leaning forward, gripping the horn tighter and using the balls of my feet to resist. The trail evened out and then another incline took us to the right.

The sounds of baying hounds in the distance grew louder. I began to panic.

"Lillian? Lillian?"

"Stay calm. They're just passing through."

I felt my horse's head being pulled to the left and heard Bobby snort and paw his front hooves aggressively. Paris reared and leapt forward.

"Hold on!" Lillian screamed.

Both horses took off at a full run. There was no opportunity to remove the mask – I latched onto the saddle horn with a death grip leaning into the wind. I couldn't breathe; I was on a blind roller coaster ride to hell.

"Jesus, Lillian, help! Heeelp!" I screamed at the top of my lungs.

I felt myself about to fall as the horses snorted and raced up the hillside. Branches slapped my face and I ducked lower, my chin just above my hands. It wasn't low enough. Another branch hit me on the top of my head. Giving up the saddle horn in sheer panic, I grabbed the horse's mane, burying my face in her neck.

"Hang on!" Lillian's command was muffled by the roaring wind.

I couldn't speak. I couldn't hear. The horses' galloping labored, bringing us higher and higher up the mountain. I feared for my life.

Paris finally slowed to a stop, breathing and snorting heavily. She flung her head about as though she wanted me off.

"Marianne?" Lillian called out and roared with laughter.

I threw off the blindfold and exclaimed, "What's so funny? We almost died!"

Lillian couldn't quit laughing and finally it was contagious. All I could do was laugh along with her. Yes, I am still alive!

"Slow walk in the woods, you said," I sneered.

"Congratulations," she replied.

I squinted into the sunlight, heard the dogs approach, and saw Tyler running over to us. The horses were still agitated and frisked around each other. At least I could see this time.

"What the hell was that all about?" I asked.

"A trust ride is a trust ride," Lillian snickered. "I didn't quite plan it that way, but I think you graduated at the top of your class."

Tyler came over to Paris's head and gripped her bridle.

"I'm so sorry… I should've had those dogs under control," he said, wide-eyed.

"We all need to cool off," Lillian said, "humans and horses."

"Miss Marianne, you need help getting off?" Tyler asked.

"No." I lifted myself up in the stirrups, swung my right leg over the saddle, kicked my left foot out of the stirrup, and promptly fell on my ass.

They both laughed. Tyler came over and helped me up.

"I got it," I said. My arms and legs shook from all the effort of staying alive.

"Are you hurt?" Tyler asked.

"My ass is okay," I said, "but my pride..."

"You should be very proud," Lillian said, dismounting. "You didn't fall off."

"But I just fell down. So much for a trust ride," I laughed.

Tyler took Bobby's reins from her, gathered up Paris and walked toward the barn.

I was still quite wobbly.

"Tell me the truth," Lillian asked, putting her hand on my shoulder, "you hurting anywhere?"

"I'm not... but I was scared shitless."

"Maybe a cup of tea? Let's get back to the lodge and talk about what you want to accomplish. You're racing right along, literally. The next decision is how quickly to move you through the process."

Process? As we walked down the stairs I wondered: what does she have in mind, blind swordfighting? What Jet had implied, or hadn't implied, had had an air of secrecy. This therapy was way beyond sitting on Robin's couch and baring my soul. The only risk I faced there was running out of tears. Process?

When we got inside Lillian said, "Put the kettle on. I'm going to my office to get some paperwork and then we'll get started."

I found everything we needed. The kettle's whistle blew and I filled two mugs with tea bags, hot water and honey, bringing them both to the table. Lillian returned with a binder and several paperback books. She sat down next to me and gazed warmly into my eyes before she spoke.

"Feel better?"

"Beginning to."

"My ancestors lived in these mountains. I returned here to use the healing rituals of my tribe. I know you practice yoga, but are you in touch with your spirituality?"

"Um, not really, church was not big in my family. My dad was always too drunk to go."

"But surely you must..."

"After my parents died, I was raised by an aunt. She was a some-time Catholic." I laughed nervously.

"What's funny?" Lillian asked.

"I don't know, I'm uneasy talking about God-stuff. I use the term 'universe' a lot."

"Universe?"

"You know, like, the universe opened these doors for me."

"I have books for you, describing a sweat lodge ceremony and a vision quest. The sweat lodge is mandatory. As for the vision quest, it'll depend on how fast you want to get to the bottom of your stuff. Robin affirms that you have co-dependency issues. Also, childhood trauma."

"Yes."

"I'd like for you to stay here for the next seven days."

"What do I do next?" I asked.

"Pack a bag," Lillian said. "Bring your warmest clothes, any jack-ets, and food. The lodge is always open; choose a room and settle in. No more contact with my home. The work begins here. Start reading the workbook and do the written exercises."

"When do I start?"

"Anytime tomorrow," Lillian said. "Don't expect me. I'll join you at nine the following morning."

"Nine a.m. seems to be your favorite time of day."

"It is."

# CHAPTER 26

I PACKED FOR my stay at the lodge. I chose t-shirts, jeans, heavy socks, underwear and toiletries. I made a separate pile of sweatshirts, long-sleeved shirts and my woolen cap and decided I was ready for the elements. I locked up the cabin – to keep the bears out -- and set off to the Piggy Wiggly.

At the supermarket I bought microwavable meals, whole wheat bread, peanut butter, and fruit. How much can I eat in seven days? I asked myself. Quite a lot, I answered.

I returned to the cabin, unloaded the groceries, opened my last bottle of wine, and poured myself a glass of merlot. I thought about the liquor store, but something told me a case of wine would not be appropriate for the sweat lodge. *Rats!*

It was twilight and unseasonably warm. I sat on the porch and tried to wrap my head around all that had transpired in the last three weeks. Was Jet the "knight of wands" Sarah had foreseen in my Tarot reading? The devil – time to confront my personal demons -- and the tower destroyed had indicated a swift and dramatic change. I knew in my heart that Lillian was the empress, the healer. But then there was something else, something Sarah didn't want me to know.

God – or was it the universe -- created the world in seven days. Perhaps, with Lillian's guidance, I could create my new world in a week's time. I decided to head over to the lodge the next day in the early afternoon. That would give me time to review the workbooks she had given me to study.

An owl hooted from a nearby tree signaling the approach of nightfall. After one more glass of wine, I showered and went to bed.

———ᴍ———

In the morning I loaded my car and decided to call Ray. He might worry, I thought, if he calls and gets no answer. I dialed his number and, at the sound of the tone, began my message. "Ray, this is your cabin guest. I've met the most amazing woman and she invited me to stay at her lodge for a week. She does healing work. I'll be there until November first. I'll call when I get back to Betty's Creek. Oops! Are you in California?"

I called the Mountain Bar and Grill. I wanted to tell Beth I wouldn't be around and for her not to be concerned.

"Mountain Grill," a young man's voice said. "Is Beth available?"

"No, she'll be in at five."

"Can you give her a message?"

"Sure, let me grab a pen." After a short pause he said, "I'm back. What's the message?"

"This is Marianne. Tell her I'm off for a short adventure, and Jet can explain."

"Will do," he said. "Have fun on your adventure."

Finally, I unplugged all the electric appliances except the refrigerator and locked the door behind me.

I stood on the porch and spoke to the creek. "Thank you, my friend. Your music has restored my soul. See you in a week." My farewell was joyful and lighthearted. I was in a playful mood.

The October sky was a deep blue; long, feathery cirrus clouds floated in the high atmosphere. It was a perfect fall day, and my drive to Scaly Mountain flew by without anxiety. I parked at Lillian's, and then realized I'd be hiking up and down the steps several times, carrying all of my stuff.

"Shit, this is going to be work. Where's the valet?" There was no sign of Lillian, or anyone else. I got busy unloading and carrying all of my things to the top of the hill, and from that spot I made trips back and forth to the lodge.

There on the long table was a vase of wild flowers and a note that read, "Welcome! A surprise for you in the 'fridge." The words were circled with a heart.

I opened the 'fridge door and saw what looked like a shallow pie on the top shelf. I took it out, broke off a piece, and a medley of tastes exploded in my mouth.

"Yum... yummy." The filling was made of figs, crushed nuts, raisins and dried cranberries. I had never tasted anything like it before. Two small bites were completely satisfying.

I piled my journal, books, pens, and legal pads on the hall table, then carried my things into the lavender room. Within an hour I was settled in. I'm getting good, I thought, at making myself at home in other people's accommodations.

Finding tea bags and honey in the kitchen cupboards, the thought of a strong cup of tea was comforting. The first book I opened began with an explanation of the "sweat lodge ceremony." Each sweat had a specific purpose, seeking physical or emotional healing, a vision, or a chance to honor someone's death. Native American warriors would sweat in preparation for battle.

Reading the details made me anxious. I scanned a few dicey paragraphs, then decided to stay a virgin. Hadn't Lillian told me, *the devil's in the details?* Maybe if I went into the ceremony uninformed, I could take it in as I went along, without expectations.

I was getting hungry. I put down the book and made my way to the kitchen. While I fished out some of my food I found some carrots and decided to visit Paris and Bobby after dinner.

Even though the lodge was large enough to accommodate twelve people, I wasn't overwhelmed by its spaciousness. It felt like I was staying in an exotic home, filled with unlimited opportunities, surrounded by nature and protected by a totem pole.

Paris nickered as she saw me approach with the carrots. Bobby didn't even look up. I opened and closed the gate behind me and Paris moved in my direction.

"Hey, old girl." I vigorously rubbed her forehead. She tossed her head to remove my hand and stretched out for the carrot. "Oh my, aren't we aggressive." She chumped off the top and crunched loudly. Bobby lifted his head off the ground and walked over to us quickly, his tail swishing rapidly back and forth in anticipation. "So... you are hungry after all."

As I petted and fed the horses, the afternoon light faded and the field took on a dream-like quality that was bucolic, soothing, and restful. Seven days, I thought. Monday morning we go to work. All this new stuff did feel like work. What would Lillian have me do? What day would we sweat? I wondered too if Jet would be the "fire keeper" I had read about. My heart was torn between wanting him with me during the experience and keeping my distance until this week was over. Lillian would make the right decision about the fire keeper; it was not mine to make.

—ɯɯ—

I was brushing my teeth when I heard Lillian call out from the hallway.

"Good morning," she sang out. "Anybody home?"

I rinsed out my mouth and yelled back at her, "I'm here!"

The door was open. When I came out of the bathroom Lillian and I hugged like sisters.

"I slept *sooo well!*" I said dramatically. "Can I move in?"

"Maybe," Lillian said. "Have you had breakfast?"

"You'll be proud of me: an hour of yoga before breakfast, and a shower."

"I am. Let's get started."

We walked down the hallway together.

"I fed the horses carrots last night. I hope you don't mind."

"Mind? I'm thrilled," she said. "Tyler helps me out, but they really do need extra attention. I'm just too busy. So much for retirement."

We entered the main hall, where I saw that she had arranged an assortment of "tools" in front of the windows on the left side of the building. Two blankets lay on the floor at a ninety-degree angle. There were two drums in the middle of the area between the blankets, along with sage, candles, and matches.

"Are you up for more drumming... and a meditation?"

"Yes... I'm ready."

"Sit comfortably on whatever blanket you choose, and sit close to the center of the circle."

I sat cross-legged on the blanket closest to the window. Lillian sat down across from me.

"We'll be doing two separate meditations," she said. "One will help you find your spirit guide. The other is to identify your power animal."

"Help me understand what you just said. Power animal?"

"Your power animal is a land animal, air or water creature whose energy finds you and blends its power with yours."

"Oh...really?"

"You've seen mine on my totem pole -- eagle, horse, and fox."

"I love dogs," I said. "Could it be a deceased pet?"

"Anything is possible when you're drumming and meditating. When an animal appears to you, simply ask it if it's your power animal."

Sure, just ask it, I thought.

"We'll drum together. Stop whenever you feel led to. When we've both finished drumming, we'll lie back on our blankets. While you're in meditation, take your mind to a sacred place in nature with some form of water that you've experienced before. Follow it along its edge and travel down a corridor that has been carved out of stone. You'll go to an open area and wait for your animal or animals to appear. When you have closure and feel awake, sit up."

She lit the large stick of sage, waved the smoke from it around our bodies, and put it out in a metal ashtray on the floor. Then she picked up her drum. I picked up the other, smaller drum. Her beating was slow and measured; I chose to follow her lead. Lillian stood and danced around our circle; I was glued to my blanket and drum, following her rhythms. She slowed her movements, sat back down on her blanket, and lay down. I continued to drum for another minute, then I also reclined.

While meditating, I found that my sacred place was the river where I had caught my first trout. Standing in the tall grass, I walked over to the riverbed. There was a tall stone wall covered in thick moss. I held my palm against the side of it and walked down a steep, stone-covered path, at times almost losing my footing. Finally, the path leveled off and I walked into a large cave with a wide gentle stream running along its farthest wall.

On the right an entrance opened to another dark area. My power animal, I thought, a horse? Seconds later a large, black, shiny stallion with a small white star on its forehead ran from the darkness and slid to a stop on the shore of the river.

"Are you my power animal?" I asked as though the question was sane.

He shook his head side to side then stood perfectly still.

Maybe a crow? I remembered the crow which had left me a feather as a gift. Suddenly a crow flew out of the back of the cave and landed on the top of the horse's head.

"Crow, are you my power animal?"

Comically, both the horse and the crow shook their heads simultaneously in a negative response.

A loud roar sounded from the far chamber opening. I was suddenly terrified by the thundering growl. A large male lion with stout, muscular legs, a long tail curled in the air, and a brown-and-tan colored mane stalked out of the area, his eyes locked on me.

I froze. He walked slowly closer, baring dripping teeth. I wanted to run but I was too petrified to move. Right in front of me he dropped on the ground, turned onto his back, and rolled back and forth playfully, like a kitten searching for a sweet spot on the lawn.

He sat up, placed his arms and legs in front of him like a sphinx, and looked at me intently. "Lion, are you my power animal?" I asked. He yawned, placed his head on his paws, and closed his eyes. The desire to touch him was overwhelming. I reached slowly towards him -- he didn't move.

Next to his neck, I gently placed my hand inside his thick, fluffy mane. His head moved to respond to my touch. I rubbed his head more intently and ran my fingers through his tendrils. For several minutes I enjoyed bonding with my lion.

I stopped rubbing his neck and stepped away. He got up, walked to the back of the cave, and turned to face me. Was he smiling? Then he turned and disappeared. I walked back to the entrance of the cave. The horse and crow were gone, and I was ready to re-enter reality. As I made my way up the stone path and back to the meadow, my breathing became slower and deeper. I began to see the sunlight and my surroundings. I found Lillian sitting lotus-style across from me when I came out of my meditation.

Neither one of us spoke. I took in the hall. The colors were brighter; my sense of smell more acute, and Lillian was smiling at me from across the circle.

"How do you feel?" she asked.

"Is it... can I tell you... my power animal?"

"Only if you want to," she answered.

I told her about my journey and we both laughed about the horse and the crow.

"The animal chooses you," she said. "Lions symbolize the assertion of creativity, intuition, and imagination. Do you want to do another meditation to find your spirit guide?"

"My God," I said, "can we do them both so close together? I feel overwhelmed."

Lillian laughed. "This time is for you – you tell me when you're ready. There's always tonight or tomorrow. Take your time... you decide."

"Is it similar to the last one? That wasn't so bad."

"Yes," Lillian said. "We'll begin again at our special place, but we'll travel up instead of down. Spirit guides live in the ether."

"How far up?" I asked with trepidation. "I need some water... and air."

"Good idea," Lillian said.

We got up and walked out of the building into the bright sun. It was hot.

"Record highs for this time of year," Lillian said. "It's more like August these days. I like the heat and the sun."

"Just beautiful," I said and walked toward the metal dome. I looked back, but Lillian had gone inside the lodge. Her dome fit the description and dimensions of a sweat lodge I had read about. I was beginning to feel the excitement and anticipation of a sweat. After a few minutes Lillian came back and handed me a bottle of water.

"The water will help ground you," she said. "I'll leave you alone to enjoy the weather. Come back in when you're ready."

I stood taking in the sunshine and the view of the horses grazing. I spread out my arms and roared like a lion, "*Roooaarrr... Roooaarr!*" Magically a crow circled and cawed. I looked up and responded, "*Roooaarr!*" An inexplicable feeling of power surged through me.

When I re-entered the hall, Lillian was sitting on her blanket shaking a rattle made of two small turtle shells. I took my place on my blanket and listened to the quick succession of short, sharp sounds she produced.

She got up, danced around us, and then settled down on her blanket.

Oh no, I thought, here we go again. What if I don't have a spirit guide?

"During this meditation," she said, "you'll stand and look into the sky. At some point the clouds will open and a staircase will appear. It can be anything, a ladder, golden stairs, a wooden staircase, or a set of steps. You'll climb up and enter a space that's protected by a membrane. Gently push into it: it'll give way, and you'll enter a chamber. Be still and wait; your spirit guide will appear to you. This guide may or may not speak, but you will communicate."

We sat in silence. Then Lillian spoke. "Marianne, you and your guide and power animal will merge into one. Spirit will tell you when it is time to return. Then leave your guide, descend, and come back to consciousness."

We picked up our drums. I chose a slow light tapping, tom...tom... tom. Lillian's was faster but just as light. I didn't beat long; I wanted to go back to my meadow. I lay down on my back, got comfortable, and breathed in and out deeply.

By the end of the fourth breath I was back at the river's edge, looking up at the sky. An escalator appeared from thin air. I smiled and thought, this is going to be an easy transition. I stepped on and within seconds I was looking down at the meadow from a dizzying height.

The escalator stopped. I reached over my head into the cloud and touched a squishy surface like an inner-tube. I followed Lillian's advice and pushed into the soft layer above me. The membrane gave way, and my arm entered the space. I walked further up the escalator's steps, through the marshmallow surface, into a dimly lit chamber that held a lucid stillness. Experiencing a newfound peacefulness and strength, I felt invincible. I was a visitor in this place, a young knight searching for the Holy Grail.

A faint twinkling light appeared in a corner of the chamber. As it moved closer it became brighter, like a hand-held sparkler. When it was about six feet from me, the light became more of a solid illumination, and it grew into a large oval shape, the size of a full-length mirror.

"Welcome. I am Hiawassee, your spirit guide." The voice was soft and tender.

The misty figure of a beautiful young woman formed inside the light. She was dressed in a white beaded gown; long, thick braids of black hair hung on both sides of her chest to her waist. Her face was the most distinct portion of her image.

"Lion is my brother," she said. "We have chosen you; we offer you power and protection."

"Will you always be with me?" I hoped it was true.

She smiled. "We will protect you, no matter what you face."

"Face? What will I face?"

She looked at me with compassion. "There will be trials. You seek the truth. But with truth comes pain. You must face your past and conquer your fears. Listen to your shaman."

The oval shape dissipated into mist and disappeared. There was enough light for me to find the opening of the chamber. I got down on my knees, supported myself on the soft surface, and slid down to the steps of the escalator. It moved downward at a steady pace and returned to the river. As soon as I stepped off, the escalator vanished, and I opened my eyes. I was at Lillian's lodge, on my back, staring at the ceiling. I rubbed my face with my palms and sat up.

Lillian sat across from me and smiled.

"How long," I asked, "have I been gone?"

"Spirit doesn't own a clock," she said with a chuckle. "Let's get up and have some tea."

We remained silent until we were both seated on the couch with our mugs on the coffee table in front of us.

"Lillian, that was amazing. My spirit guide… her name is Hiawassee."

"Hiawassee, in Cherokee, means meadow," she said, sipping her tea.

"I started in a meadow. The meadow Jet took me to."

"Jet took you to that location; you felt the energy and purity of the water and the fields. Hiawassee's spirit was drawn to you. How do you feel now?"

I took a deep breath and let it out slowly. "I'm ready for… well, whatever."

Lillian put down her mug and moved closer to me on the couch. "Can we hold hands?"

"Of course," I said and extended my hands out to hers.

We held hands and she said, "Would you pray with me for guidance?"

"Yes." I wasn't sure what to expect.

We sat quietly for a moment. Then she began. "Great Father Spirit, Mother Earth, we come together this morning and give thanks for Marianne's visions. We are grateful for Lion and Hiawassee. Guide us in all future decisions concerning ceremony; guide us now and every day of our lives. And so it is… Hokh! Mitakuye o'yasin Hecetu welo!"

She squeezed my hands, signaling the end of her prayer.

We sat back on the couch and I reached out for my mug.

"What were those words you spoke at the end?"

"All my relations, it is indeed so."

"And so it is," I answered.

"It is indeed," she said.

"Yes, indeed… it is," I said. "Your turn."

She lightly slapped my upper thigh, then stood and said, "How about a sweat tomorrow?"

I was drinking my tea and almost choked. "So soon? I only just got here. Am I ready?"

"What advice did Hiawassee give you?"

"She said to listen to you."

"Smart spirit," she laughed. "You've committed to seven days under my guidance. A seven-day series of ceremonies is the fast track. But, we'll do this only if you are absolutely sure... or you could do my weekend workshop in December."

I felt a quick punch to the gut. December... the last day of my leave is November thirtieth, I thought. Why not get on the Autobahn of healing?

"I'm really feeling this work," I said. "I feel as if I'm watching a movie."

"It *is* a movie. And you are in it, not watching it. You have the starring role. Today your spirit guide and power animal found you. That is very important. Tomorrow we sweat. Then we have two days of rest and preparation followed by a vision quest that ends daybreak on Sunday morning."

"Daybreak... Sunday morning?"

"You can stop any ceremony at any time," Lillian said. "You'll fully understand what to expect on a vision quest. In fact, tomorrow if the sweat gets too hot, you can leave and listen to our words outside the lodge."

"I want to be a warrior princess," I said, "and live in the mountains."

"You are a warrior princess," Lillian said and we hugged.

She gave the most amazing hugs; they were robust and full of vitality.

"You've done enough work today. Have fun outside. It's another beautiful day. Our Grandfathers are protecting the mountain from rain. Tomorrow will be a good day to sweat; I'll arrive at eleven. There are two other women who are searching. One is Tyler's mother, Marie. Her own mother recently passed over."

"Oh, will Tyler be here?"

"Yes, he'll be our fire tender and gate keeper."

"And the other woman?"

"Her name is Zoe, she owns a bed-and-breakfast. You'll like her; she's a massage therapist, a Mayan record keeper, and a Reiki master. The lower level of her building is a small day spa complete with showers and body treatment rooms."

"A healing spa in the mountains," I sighed wistfully. "Sounds like a dream."

"It's called The Garden," Lillian said. "I go once a month for a facial and massage. She definitely has a healing touch."

"Your skin is absolutely radiant."

"I do declare," she said in a dramatic Southern accent. "I think I'm blushing."

We laughed and hugged again.

"It'll be important for you to eat lightly the rest of today and tomorrow morning," Lillian said. "The heat from the fire will purify more than your soul, it's cleansing for the body as well. After the sweat we'll have a potluck feast at the lodge. Think of something you can make and share."

"Will do," I said. "Can I ride Paris today?"

"Do you know how to saddle her?"

We walked to the entrance together. "Um, I'm not sure."

"Put in a bit?" Lillian asked.

It was difficult to envision the process, but a lot of teeth came to mind.

"I… I think I'll just go up and pet the horses," I said sheepishly.

"We can give you a few lessons in the coming weeks. You're here for a while, aren't you?"

"Yes."

"Then we'll have plenty of time."

The rest of the day floated by. I put Lillian's rattle, candles, sage and drums in her office, then walked out to the horses with some carrots. While standing next to Paris, I leaned my entire body against her side like a human blanket. She allowed me to stay on her without moving. I breathed in her wonderful horsey smells. She was like an enormous stuffed animal.

What a day, I thought. I wonder how many people find their power animal and spirit guide in the same day. I was both humbled and amazed. I couldn't even imagine what might come next, but for the first time in my life, I felt courage...not pretend bravado... real courage.

# CHAPTER 27

I DRANK GREEN tea for breakfast and plenty of water throughout the morning. After I baked frozen lasagna for our feast and stored it in the 'fridge, I waited for Lillian on the porch.

"Good morning, sunshine," she said.

"Morning."

"Isn't this the most beautiful day?" She was carrying soft canvas shoes and a white t-shirt that looked long enough to be a nightie.

"I'm a bit nervous about the sweat."

"Of course you are," Lillian said.

"The little I've read sounds more like roasting lobsters... and having visions."

"Do I look roasted?" She smiled. "I've done lots of them."

"Okay, but I'm still nervous."

"Let's sit for a while," she said, "and enjoy the fresh air. We have lots of time."

Lots of time, whew... my anxiety receded.

"Relax," she said.

I closed my eyes and whispered, "Thank you."

A strong wind rustled through the trees; a shower of leaves blew from their limbs, fell in a dance, and swirled around us.

"It's time," Lillian said.

"Already? But I thought you said..."

"Let our hearts be thankful for this time of preparation."

"Can I ask for another of your magnificent, life-affirming hugs?" I asked as we stood.

"You never have to ask," she said. "Just come and get one."

We hugged for a long moment. Then she backed away and looked me over.

"You'll need loose-fitting clothes before you go into the sweat lodge, preferably cotton. We'll stay in our jeans while doing prep work, change here, and walk back together. I'll say some prayers, smudge everyone, and then we'll go in."

"I'd like to go now," I said, "and pick out something to wear."

"One quick question," Lillian said. "Have any things in nature called to you recently... maybe a rock or a tree?"

"*Yes,*" I delivered the word enthusiastically. "Feathers. I've found *two* feathers. One was personally delivered to me by a crow while I was walking in the woods."

"What's the other one from?" she asked.

"A red hawk."

"Don't assume it's a red hawk just because it's red," she said. "It may be a turkey feather."

"I have them both here."

"I'm glad you listened to your intuition. There's an earthen altar at the base of the totem pole. You can place the feathers there."

Going through my clothes I decided on a white and pink flowered nightgown that went just past my knees. The flowers were tiny rose-buds connected by dark green stems. I set out a bath towel and my running shoes without socks.

As I made my way outside Lillian was already at the fence-line, petting the horses. Bobby was pushing Paris's head out of the way, so he could get some attention, too.

"He's such a brat," Lillian said as I approached.

"But he's so handsome," I said.

"Yes, he is. My big, handsome boy."

We walked together to the bare aluminum frame.

"How does this work?" It didn't look like much of a sweat lodge to me.

"First we decide where the opening will face," she said. "Then we cover the frame. Each direction has power. North is the grounding energy of the earth. I am leader of this sweat, so I'll sit there." She moved instinctively around the dome and stopped at the north curve.

"Have you decided where I will be?" I asked.

"South," she said without hesitation. "South will give you focus and concentration. Zoe sits east for the dawn and new beginnings. Marie will be west, to heal from her grief and loss."

We heard a "'yoohoo" yodeling from the top of the stairs. Two women and Tyler appeared.

"And now we are complete," Lillian said. She shouted back at them, "We'll meet you at the main lodge."

Lillian and I walked quickly down the path. Tyler met us on the porch.

"Ladies," he said and, with another profound obeisance, tipped his hat.

"Hello, my young man," Lillian said, and they hugged. "I'm so happy you're with us today."

"Helping with a sweat is cool," he said. "My buddies and I want to do one."

"And I'll be your gate keeper and fire tender," she said.

"That would be *great*," he said. "Thank you, Miss Lillian."

"You know the drill, Tyler," Lillian said. "Dig out the pits and we'll start gathering wood."

"Yes, ma'am." He was off to the barn.

Lillian took my arm and we walked together, joined at the elbow. My heart filled with pride as I walked close to her. She was so beautiful and brilliant, and she took an interest in me. Knowing this filled me with a deep sense of self-worth. I do matter, I thought, just on my own, not because of what I did or who I had in my life. I matter because I'm here with Lillian.

We parted and walked inside.

"Marie, Zoe," she announced, "this is Marianne."

They stood at the kitchen sink and turned to face us.

Zoe spoke first. "Are we not so blessed," she asked, "to spend this day together?" At five feet tall she was thin as a rail, a mere wisp of a woman, and half my size. She had a thick head of gray curls that fell to her shoulders, held back with an elastic headband. She wore an angelic smile.

"Hello," I said, extending my hand. "So good to meet you."

"You as well," Zoe said. Her handshake was firm and steady. I moved over to the next woman.

"I'm Marie," she said, "Tyler's mother." We shook hands. Her grip was soft; only our fingers touched. There was a sharp contrast between her greeting and Zoe's. Marie had reddish blonde hair cut in a short bob. Her eyes were deep brown like Lillian's and she smelled of rosewater.

"Have you both settled in?" Lillian asked.

"Yes," Zoe said. "We're sharing room number two. I *love* sleeping in the top bunk."

"I like the cavern feeling of the bottom bed," Marie said. "I feel more secure closer to the ground."

"I've sent Tyler to start on the fire pit, just outside the sweat lodge," Lillian said. "Marianne, while we are gathering wood and stones, we'll speak in low tones or not at all. It's important that we stay in our private thoughts, review in our minds what we want to accomplish today, and respect each other's desire for silence."

Accomplish? I thought.

"Has any wood been cut?" Marie asked.

"No," Lillian said. "We'll gather limbs that have fallen and are dried out. I'll pick small pieces for the bottom layer, and the three of you will choose limbs, maybe two to three feet long."

"Is there still a pile of stones?" Zoe asked.

"Mr. Turner delivered some granite last week. Each of us will select four small stones, nothing larger than a cantaloupe. Let the stones speak to you; you'll know which ones to choose."

Speaking stones? I remembered a Bible verse my mom used to say: *If they keep silent, even the stones will cry out.* I was never sure what it meant.

We followed Lillian out of the main lodge without speaking. The treetops swayed from lofty winds, and some clouds began to gather in the sky, but the temperature remained in the high sixties.

The four of us split up and went in different directions, and the space between us allowed me to feel a peaceful solitude to consider: *What do I want to accomplish?*

I wanted to solve the biggest puzzles in my life: why my father had been so cruel, and whether or not he caused the car crash that killed my mom. I needed an explanation. Robin had blamed it on PTSD, but that didn't help much. PTSD or not, how could he terrorize his own family? And why, why, why? I couldn't imagine being cruel to a child. Those questions haunted my soul. It hardly seemed possible that a cleansing sweat could decode my past.

I'll ask Hiawassee for help, I thought. Perhaps she can facilitate some way for me to see inside his head. But could I ever forgive him? No. As a result of my co-dependency I had chosen losers... so I could fix them... because I couldn't fix my fucked-up father. Robin had helped me see that, too. Focusing my attention on other people's problems was the way I ignored my own need for growth and maturity.

As I carried back my first load of wood, I saw Lillian and Tyler drape a black canvas tarp over the dome. Then they positioned two king-sized blankets over the tarp, allowing a flap cut-out of the canvas to open and drape back against the blankets.

Neither of them looked up from their task. I liked this veil of silence; it was as if we were communicating on another level, far from the exchange of words. I dropped my wood, headed back into the forest for another load, and passed Zoe on the trail. We smiled at each other. This must be how it is at a monastery, I thought, when monks pass each other, a simple reverent nod.

The limbs I picked up were light. My father once said aged wood made the hottest fires, because there's no sap to interfere with the burning. By the time I gathered the second armful and walked back to the fire pit, everyone was there.

"It's time to choose our stones," Lillian said. "As a tribute to Marianne's first sweat, we will allow her to go to the pile of Grandfather Stones before us and pick out the ones that call to her."

"Thank you," I said blushing. "I'm honored."

I walked slowly to the pile and knelt down in a gesture of respect. These stones, I thought, will turn red hot and, with water, create a purifying steam. "Cleanse my mind and my body," I whispered to the rocks. Unfortunately, they didn't answer back. Am I worthy? I scanned the pile with my hands and chose the first one. I picked it up and cradled it to my heart. "Hello, Grandfather," I said and placed it away from the others. It only took a minute to find the other three that begged, "Pick me, pick me, pick me." I'm talking to stones, I thought. I walked back to the pit and laid them down next to Tyler's shovel and pitchfork, hoping I was doing everything correctly.

Zoe went next, then Marie. Lillian stood with her arms stretched out to the sky, eyes closed. After a few minutes she opened her eyes and made her way to the pile. Quickly she chose her stones and rejoined us.

Tyler had changed into a white t-shirt and traded his hat for a bandanna tied on his head like a pirate's scarf. He placed the smaller kindling at the bottom of the fire pit, which was located near the dome, then stacked the limbs, creating a pyramid-type structure. Tucking the stones in amidst the wood, he struck a match and set the pile on fire, stepped back, crossed his arms against his chest, and smiled. He seemed very pleased with his success. The flames grew quickly and licked the larger limbs. Soon we had a roaring blaze.

Lillian called out, "Women of the earth, let us prepare to enter the womb of our Mother. Return to the main lodge and change into your dress."

The four of us made our way back to our rooms without speaking. I donned my nightie, draped the towel around my neck, slipped on my running shoes, and carried my feathers back to the main hall.

When we were all there, Lillian spoke. "We give thanks to the Great Spirit for this day and for our time together. If you have an offering for the altar, place it there before you come to the sweat lodge."

I ran the spines of my feathers between my fingers and felt joy in knowing that I would place my fetishes on the altar.

"Some time will pass before the stones are ready," Lillian said. "Continue to walk the land in silence, remember your intentions, and meditate."

Once outside we split up again. After an hour had passed, we instinctively joined each other at the sweat lodge. Tyler stoked the fire with a pitchfork and moved the stones around in the hot ashes. The stones glowed with a brilliant luminescence. I could feel their heat as we approached. I walked to the altar and placed the feathers on its surface.

"Help me get through this," I whispered.

I rejoined the circle and Lillian raised her arms and began to speak.

"Greetings and thanks to each other as people. To the earth, mother of all, greetings and thanks, to all the waters, waterfalls, rains, rivers, and oceans, to all the fish life, greetings and thanks. We give thanks to all animals for their teachings. We give thanks to the trees for shelter, shade, fruit and beauty, and to all birds large and small. We give thanks to the four winds for purifying the air we breathe and giving us strength.

We give thanks for all creation, for all the love around us. And for that which is forgotten, we remember and we end our words. Now our minds are one."

The only sound was Tyler raking the coals. Lillian lit a large stick of sage, approached each one of us, and waved smoke around our bodies. Then she took ashes from a small bowl and smudged them across our foreheads and down our cheeks. When she was finished she walked over to the sweat lodge entrance and said, "Great Spirit, watch over us and protect us as we enter the womb of Mother Earth."

Lillian entered first and moved in a clockwise direction. She sat near the entrance, next to a wooden bucket of water, a rattle, a talking stick, a pair of large deer antlers, and a ladle. As each one of us entered and searched for our positions we were told to say, "Mitakuye o'yasin."

It was dark and eerie inside. I was only able to see after my eyes adjusted to the dim light. Lillian gestured to each of us as we took our seats.

"Fire keeper, bring us our stones," Lillian called out.

Tyler moved quickly as he entered the sweat lodge with a glowing rock positioned on his pitchfork. Lillian used the antlers to guide the fork, and Tyler dropped the stone into the pit in the center. They repeated the process three more times and then Lillian called out to him, "Gate keeper, gate keeper, close the gate!"

Within seconds we were sealed inside total darkness except for the dim glow of superheated stones. I smelled aromas of sage, tobacco, and maybe cedar, I couldn't be sure. Lillian had placed the blend on the hot stones. The smell was exotic… other-worldly.

"Hoy! Grandfathers!" Lillian called out. "Welcome, Grandfathers."

She ladled water on the stones and an intense steam rose from the pit and smacked me in the face. I tried to turn away, but it was useless. The heat was overbearing. My instinct was to run. Sweat lodge? I was too hot to sweat. It was more like a pressure cooker. Can I take this? I asked myself. I had endured the pain of watching my mother's beatings, so yes, yes I can. I tried to relax.

"We are here together as sisters," Lillian said calmly, as if we were sitting on the porch drinking tea. "I hold the talking stick, so I will speak first. As you hold the stick and share, no one else speaks. We listen with our hearts, and without judgment. But this is not a place of oppression; we may laugh and sing together as Spirit moves us."

After a few moments of silence, Lillian spoke again. "I am Lillian Wilson, keeper of this mountain. I give thanks for my sisters. We share and heal together. Great Spirit, bless us."

She poured another ladle of water on the rocks, producing another blast of steam. It pierced my nostrils and I couldn't avoid coughing. There was a tiny breeze of air coming up through the bottom of the canvas. I felt the coolness on my ankles and moved my face downward, as close to the ground as I could. Finally, I could breathe.

Zoe took the talking stick. "I am Zoe Palermo. I search now for a new beginning. I ask the Great Spirit to bring me a business partner, one I can trust. I long to travel and visit the land of my ancestors. Great Spirit, clear my path, open doors, bring me peace."

She passed the stick to me and Lillian poured another ladle of water. The steam was oppressive; I choked and couldn't speak. My skin was on fire, but I was determined and struggled to utter a word.

"I'm… um… I am Marianne Sobieski." I gritted my teeth and swallowed to arrest my coughing. "I'm here to seek… answers… about my father's cruelty." It was all I could say. Miraculously, the air seemed to cool. A tiny twinkling light appeared in the left corner of the lodge.

"Do you all see that?" Lillian asked.

Marie spoke excitedly, "Yes, yes, I see it."

The ambiance of the sweat lodge suddenly shifted. Instead of feeling claustrophobic, the atmosphere expanded into an extreme spaciousness.

"It looks," Marie said, "as if the vault of heaven has opened."

I felt a presence. "Hiawassee," I said aloud. "Can you help me know my father?" I wanted desperately to hear an answer. No words came, only a flashback of a photo; it was my parents together, smiling, dressed in tailored suits, and standing in front of a 1952 Chevy.

I tightened my grip on the stick and raised my voice, "I ask my Spirit Guide, Hiawassee, into this lodge. Can you tell me... my father?"

Lillian poured another ladle of water onto the rocks. The steam enveloped us and for some odd reason the heat was gone. The tiny light that shone in the corner of the lodge distracted me, and, momentarily, I forgot the blast-furnace of steam. Was it her, Hiawassee?

I stared at the light trying to make out an image and handed the stick to Marie.

"I am Marie Rich. I seek a deep knowing that my mother's spirit has transcended... that she is basking in the glories of afterlife."

Lillian poured the water again, and again we were engulfed by a scorching cloud. I ignored the pain and focused on the light.

Marie held the stick a few minutes longer then passed it to Lillian.

"Gate keeper!" Lillian called out. "Open the gate... open the gate!" Suddenly the flap flew back and a burst of sunlight and cool air entered the lodge. I was blinded by the daylight, and heartbroken. Hiawassee was gone.

"Glory... glory halleluiah!" Marie sang out.

The three of them laughed, deep belly-shaking laughs, but I felt like I had been kicked in the gut. What happened? I wondered. I was so close.

"Oh, this air feels good," Zoe said.

"Is everyone okay?" Lillian asked. "If at any point you want to leave, do it quietly. There is no shame in leaving the sweat lodge. You can listen to the remainder of the ceremony outside. Honor your needs."

"I'm still in," Marie said.

Because she was a natural redhead, her skin glowed like a ripened tomato from the heat and steam. I felt my cheeks with my palms and realized that much of the heat from my skin had been reduced from the circulating air. My nightgown was soaked.

"You know me," Zoe said, "I like to sweat."

I nodded a "yes" and gave the thumbs up. It was all I could manage.

"Fire keeper!" Lillian called out. "Bring us more stones."

# CHAPTER 28

TYLER APPEARED AT the entrance of the sweat dome with a hot stone, and he and Lillian repeated the process. Four new hot stones were added to the pit.

"Gate keeper," Lillian cried out. "Close the gate, close the gate."

Tyler shut the flap, and once again we were immersed in darkness. Lillian poured on a ladle of water. The temperature skyrocketed.

Marie gasped and coughed. Some dim light from the glowing stones of the pit allowed us to see each other, but just barely.

Lillian picked up the rattle and began to chant; after a few rounds we joined her words. *"Hey! YoYo... Hey! YoYo."* She stopped the rattle and poured another ladle.

Marie began to cry. Lillian handed her the talking stick. "Mom," Marie said, sobbing, "do you know how much Tyler and I miss you?"

The flap began to shake. Marie closed her eyes and gripped the stick with both hands. She rocked ever so slightly back and forth with her head turned toward the ceiling.

"Mom, I pray from my heart that your spirit knows my deep love for you. Not the many times I told you here on earth, but now, with you on the other side, knowing the strength and energy of love's vibration."

A wave of coolness and subtle energy flowed around us. "Ahhh..." escaped from Zoe and me simultaneously in recognition of the perfect feeling of peace.

The four of us sat in silence. I remembered pristine sunsets, moonless nights looking up at the bright trail of the Milky Way, the sounds of ocean surf.

Marie stopped rocking, opened her eyes, and burst into laughter and tears. "Did you all feel that?" she asked excitedly. "My mom! She's here!"

"There is definitely an extra presence in this place," Lillian said. "One of the strongest heart vibrations I've ever felt."

I began to panic. My story was one of darkness and death. I sure as hell didn't want to bring my brute of a father here. I just wanted answers.

Lillian poured; steam rose up and scorched our faces and arms. I could feel every pore in my body, every hair on my head, even my teeth and gums were affected.

"We are grateful and aware of the strong love that surrounds us," Lillian said.

Marie let out a deep sigh, "I love you, Mom."

"Gate keeper," Lillian hollered, "open the gate."

The cold air surged in, and the stark contrast between sweltering heat and fall mountain air was shocking. Hot to cold. Cold to hot.

"Cold plunge," Zoe called out.

My heart began to race violently. Will it pop out of my chest? My body's sweat turned into a sheath of chill-bumps. I vigorously rubbed my arms, neck and shoulders with my hands, trying to thaw out my skin.

"My goodness," Marie said, "what lesson is there in this?"

"There is one here whose story is also of love," Lillian said. "But first there must be truth; cold brings clarity."

She can't mean me, I thought. Love?

Lillian called out, "Fire keeper, bring us more Grandfather Stones."

The process was repeated for the third time. "Gate keeper," Lillian repeated, "close the gate."

Instant darkness was followed by the sound of water spitting over hot stones. Even under the assault of the fiery steam Marie managed to hand me the stick. I could feel the wetness from her palms on its exterior. The baton of courage was over a foot long, and my fingers found the subtle curves in the wood.

"Speak your truth, Marianne," Lillian said. "We will not judge; there is only love and acceptance in this lodge today; draw from our strength."

Truth? Yes, I had come here to find the truth, but the prospect of an encounter with my father scared the shit out of me. What do I ask?

After a few moments I gathered my courage and gave myself over to Spirit. Deep breathing and concentrating on the pit's stones led me to the room where I first met Hiawassee. Lillian poured more water and I did not feel its effects; I was in another place.

"Welcome back," Hiawassee said to me. "Your father... he is here."

"Oh no," I cried, "I don't want to see..."

"You seek answers," Hiawassee said. "He wants to speak."

I swallowed hard. The room was cloudy like a dream – in my mind I pictured him standing in front of that old Chevrolet.

"Yes," I said, trembling.

A tall, handsome, dark-haired man appeared, clean-shaven, and dressed in the same suit he wore in the photo. His raincoat was draped over his arm. He wore a grey fedora pushed back from his forehead, and he was holding a lit cigarette.

"Hello, my girl," he said lovingly.

"But you're not..."

"This is who I was... before the war. The man you never knew."

His lips curved into a smile. It was a kind, humble expression, and his light brown eyes shone brightly. Could this be my father?

"I want you to know, it was my rage, it destroyed me. I couldn't control it."

"Dad," I said, "I miss the man who took me hunting and taught me to shoot a bow and arrow."

"Those are the moments I cherish," he said. "You were so much like me."

Tears streamed down my face. "Why, Daddy, why? You hated us! You beat us! I was just a helpless child!"

"The war. My friends, all blown apart, so much blood. I wanted to be numb and forget. I drank all I could... blacked out almost every night."

More flashbacks played in my head. I relived my father beating my mother in the living room and throwing us both out onto the porch, her face swollen and bloody from his fists.

"How could you beat my precious mother... hit her in the face... you were a monster!"

"I was lost." Tears streamed down his face and he sobbed. "I wanted you both to suffer... the way I suffered. I knew no boundaries."

"Daddy," I said pushing the tears from my eyes, "did you ever love us?"

"Yes. I loved you... and your mother, so very much. I love you, my girl, with all my heart. Can you remember... the good times? I tried so hard, but the demons won... and you lost."

I had to ask, "The car... did you cause the accident?"

I heard more steam come up. The cloud density increased, he started to disappear, and then, the scene unfolded like a motion picture.

My parents were in the front seat of the car, fighting, screaming at each other.

I couldn't hear their words. Dad leaned over and grabbed my mother's hair and began to beat her head into the dashboard. She flailed about and reached for the steering wheel. With purpose she pulled on it, and the car jerked off the road and over a high embankment. It sailed into the air.

I screamed in terror and the vision dissipated.

Lillian poured more water, and the intensified heat brought me back to the circle.

I continued to sob and Zoe began to sing *Amazing Grace*. Marie and Lillian joined her. They were angelic voices singing to heal my broken heart. I rocked back and forth, hugging myself, weeping. My crying quieted and I was able to join them as they repeated the first verse.

*... the sound that saved a wretch like me... I was lost... but now I'm found... was blind but now I see.*

I used the damp hem of my gown to dab my face.

"Open the gate, open the gate," Lillian called to Tyler.

The flap opened and the sunlight blinded me once again. My eyes were inflamed from the heat and from crying. The cold air jolted me back into reality. I felt dizzy.

I leaned back and turned my face to the ceiling of the lodge. "Oh, God, oh my God!"

"What's the matter?" Lillian asked.

My brain exploded in a collage of dark images. There was the Tarot card, the one Sarah had tried to hide from me. And then I saw it, it was my worst nightmare.

The sunlight didn't block my vision.

"You alright?" Marie asked.

"Mom, Dad!" I screamed. "I see them... the car is falling... exploding in flames! Oh no, get out! Get ooout! The flames... they're burning... screaming... hands waving in agony! The flesh, it's burning away from the bone. I can smell it. Oh my God, my God! Now... now they're still." I buried my face in my hands and bawled.

Zoe leaned over and rubbed my back. "You're here with us, Marianne, you're safe here. The burden, the weight will be lifted."

"We want to help you," Marie said.

"I need help," I whimpered. The tears finally stopped. I rubbed my eyes dry with my hands and sighed. "Whew... this is all so intense." I felt sick. I wanted to throw up. I handed the talking stick back to Lillian.

"Breathe, Marianne, breathe," Lillian said. "Are you able to stay for the final round?"

"No, I don't think... well, maybe, yes," I said as I exhaled. "Yes."

"Fire keeper, bring us our Grandfathers," Lillian called out.

Tyler brought in the final four stones and for the last time he shut the gate.

"Zoe, the stick is yours," Lillian said, and handed it to her.

Zoe cradled the stick next to her heart as she spoke. "The perfect person I seek is now ready to join my practice; our minds and hearts will be as one... I welcome this soul and pray The Garden continues to flourish. Great Mother Earth, hear my prayer and make it so."

Lillian poured water, and the heat and steam were unrelenting. I never thought I could get through all four rounds of the hellish vapor, but here we were together, each of us speaking from our core, remaining resolute, and receiving answers. I felt a sudden surge of momentum. In the darkness as I listened to Zoe's prayer I wondered, whom does she seek? If only it could be me. I hated the resort. I yearned for change and loved the mountains and the people. I thought of the old woman in the pick-up truck who stopped to check on my well-being, Jet, Beth, and now Lillian. But, no, she's seeking a business partner.

Zoe began to sing an old Crosby, Stills, and Nash song, *Teach Your Children Well*. We all knew the words and joined her at the second verse. Halfway through, we were swaying back and forth against each other's bodies, laughing and jazzing up the melody.

"All together, now," Zoe sang out and we started the song again from the beginning.

No Ordinary Fire

When we ended our song Lillian hollered out to Tyler, "Open the gate!"

The flap flew open and Tyler stood at the entrance, looking in. "Sounds good, ladies." He began to applaud.

We crawled out of the lodge charcoal-cooked to well done. My legs were weak from sitting so long. I stumbled and Tyler caught my arm. "Whoa, now, Miss Marianne. Coming out into this bright sunlight can be tricky."

"It's your first sweat," Marie said. "You'll get better with practice."

The four of us found our towels and shoes and dried off our heads and bodies.

"I think I lost five pounds," Zoe said.

"Let's head back to the main lodge," Lillian said, "shower, and put those five pounds back on. Tyler, please attend to the fires, the blankets, and the tarp. When everything is safe, come and join us."

Tyler smiled and went about his business. There was a quiet intensity and depth about this young man. His presence was commanding yet gentle; he was someone you could trust. I was happy to get to know his mother... and his grandmother?

The four of us walked back to the lodge and Lillian headed down the stairs to her house. We joked about our singing, the twinkling light, and Marie's passed mother paying us a visit. There was no mention of my scene of horror.

"Of course," Zoe said, "now we are cosmically joined at the hip."

"Hip? Just take some of my hips away," Marie said. "Marianne, you look like you could use a few pounds... how about some of mine?"

"Absolutely," I said. "But I get to choose where it goes."

"No problem," Marie laughed.

We split off to our separate rooms, showered, and changed clothes. While taking off my nightie I was surprised by my body odor. I smelled like a construction worker, or worse. The sweat had opened pores and lots of stuff had poured out: those nasty alcohol toxins. But

243

I was sure some of it was all the emotional poison I'd been carrying around for years. While I was in the shower I yelled out, imitating a Christian evangelist, "Get out, Demon! In the name of Jesus Christ, get out!" The vision of my parent's death was sickening for sure, but I had faced my demons and survived. Finally, I knew the truth.

I put on my most comfortable clothes, a soft cotton hooded sweatshirt, yoga pants, and heavy white socks. I looked in the mirror and my skin looked like a baby's butt, all shiny and new. I smiled at myself and felt joy, pure bliss.

In the kitchen I found Zoe and Marie putting out food on the main table.

"I hope you don't mind," Zoe said. "We found your lasagna and microwaved it back to life. This is going to be a perfect meal. I brought salad, Marie has a broccoli dish, and Lillian is bringing fresh fruit for dessert."

"I'm so happy to be here," I said. "It's all so overwhelming."

"Sweats with Lillian usually are," Marie said. "I'm happy Tyler is spending time with her. She's a good influence. He's grown spiritually."

"He's an awesome young man," I said. "And today, well... that kind of sealed the deal for me. Fantastic kid."

"Thank you," Marie said. "I am proud."

"You should be," Zoe said.

Lillian appeared with a giant bowl of fresh fruit cut up in bite-size pieces.

"Here we are, ladies."

We continued to arrange dishes and silverware and, as we gathered around the table, Tyler opened the front door.

"Am I too late?" he asked.

"No, honey," Marie said, "here's your seat." She patted the chair.

"Thanks, Mama," he said. "I'm starving."

"You should be," Lillian said. "Are we hungry? Let me say a blessing: Good food, good meat, good God let's eat."

I had to laugh. The conversation through dinner flowed seam-lessly. We shared stories and related to each other's experiences. That led us to yet another layer of appreciating of who we were.

After dessert I stood and announced, "Don't worry about the clean-up here, I'm on it."

"Oh, no," the chorus replied and we all turned into busy bees cleaning up the kitchen and dining room.

Finally we all sat together in the main lobby on the couches and recliners in front of a huge fireplace.

"Would you like another fire?" Tyler asked.

"You would do that?" I asked.

"Of course," he said.

"You're off the clock, Tyler," Lillian said. "But you can build a fire if you want."

"It's dropping to thirty-eight tonight," Tyler said.

"A fire would be lovely," Zoe said.

Tyler disappeared out the front door for kindling and wood.

"I have a treat for us," Marie said. "Could we have a champagne toast, Lillian?"

"I looove champagne," Lillian said.

"Wow," I said, "we *are* celebrating."

"Where are the glasses?" Marie asked.

We stood up together, moved into the kitchen, and had fun pop-ping the champagne.

"I propose a toast," Zoe said. "To Miss Lillian Wilson, our sha-man, our teacher, and our friend."

"To Miss Lillian," we said together and touched the rims of our glasses.

"I have an old toast my father used," Marie said and raised her glass in the air. "Here's to cheating, lying, stealing, and drinking. We cheat to cheat death, we lie to save our friends, we steal our lover's heart and drink to our friends' health."

"Hear, hear," Zoe said.

"I'd like to make a toast, too," I said, and everyone turned in anticipation. "I am grateful for the truth I have been shown, for both my parents, and for my new friends. Na Zdrowie! That's Polish for Cheers."

"Na Zdrowie!," we all said together and drank our glasses empty.

Tyler brought in wood, stacked twigs and small limbs into a bundle in the fireplace, and started the fire with newspaper and matches. I found a comfortable chair and settled in. It was unusual for me to be in a group without some kind of chatter going on, but we were comfortable enough in each other's presence. We did not feel the need to talk, especially after the sweat.

I stared into the fire, mesmerized.

Zoe moved over to my chair and sat on the ottoman. "Lillian tells me you're a massage therapist."

"I am... in Atlanta."

We chatted about my level of experience and she asked if I would be interested in a job at her spa.

"Are you kidding?"

"No, I truly need a partner I can trust."

I floated two feet off the floor. "I'll get you my resume," I said, trying to remain calm. I didn't want her to think I was flaky and neurotic. I also didn't want to take advantage of her.

"There in the sweat," Zoe whispered, "out of the steam, I saw a face."

"You did?" I was amazed. "But who..."

"It was a beautiful woman."

"Your Spirit guide?" I asked.

"No, as a matter of fact, it looked a lot like you."

# CHAPTER 29

I JERKED AWAKE and sat up in bed. The feelings of confusion always returned whenever I slept in a new place: Where am I? What time is it? *What day is it?* I looked around the room and gradually remembered everything: the sweat, my visions, a hot shower, and conversations at dinner. It was eleven o'clock in the morning. I had not slept this late since I was a waitress working weekends.

I crept into the main lobby, investigated the premises, and was relieved to find that everyone had left. I wanted to see Lillian sometime today, but not now. I needed her guidance as I processed the images of my father and the sickening details of the accident. Was I t real?

I made my usual strong pot of coffee and used extra sugar and cream in my cup. The sweetness was comforting and the caffeine turned my awareness up a notch. My gloominess turned into curiosity. Had I exorcised my father's demons? Had the ugly truth set me free? Could I trust what had been revealed? It all made sense, the beating in the car, my mother trying to defend herself, and the horrific crash. It had seemed so very real, but... how... how could I know for sure?

I took a second cup of coffee back to my room and found my copy of Rumi's work. He always seemed to have an answer when I most needed it.

## *Shadow and Light Source Both*

*How does a part of the world leave the world? How does the wetness leave the water? Don't try to put out a fire by throwing on more fire!*
*Don't wash a wound with blood.*
*No matter how fast you run, your shadow keeps up. Sometimes it's in front. Only full overhead sun diminishes your shadow. But that shadow has been serving you.*
*What hurts you, blesses you. Darkness is your candle.*
*You must have shadow and light source both.*

I put down the hardback and moved to lie on the floor with the intention of meditating, but I couldn't get comfortable. It was hard to quiet my thoughts, and my feet were cold. I had too much caffeine in my system. Giving in to all the distractions, I put on my jeans and a sweatshirt; I needed to get outside in the sunshine. I needed to see my shadow.

As I made my way up to the barn, a slight breeze chilled the air, but it felt good. I breathed deeply, stopped and looked up into a cloudless sky. Two large birds circled high above the fields. Buzzards? I wondered. Is something dead?

When I got to the barn, Lillian had Bobby in the cross-ties inside the wash rack. She was singing in a low voice. I didn't understand the words, but the melody sounded Native American with its long, drawn-out lyrical sounds. She smiled when she saw me and came over to give me a hug.

"I'm so happy to see you," I said.

"I wondered how you were doing," she responded, rubbing my upper arms, "but I didn't want to disturb you." She went back to brushing Bobby and I sat on a bale of straw, watching her.

"Disturb me? You could never..."

"How was your night?" she asked.

"I slept like the dead, woke up late, and now I've had too much coffee." I held out my hands; they were shaking.

"Would you like to talk?"

"Yes, I have questions, but not just yet. Could we meet later today? I do best when I'm... well, you know, in a room, sitting down. Some of my most insightful moments with Robin came when I was sitting across from her on her comfy sofa. Oh yeah, and while holding my stuffed animal."

"Stuffed animal?"

"His name is Sam."

"Of course. Sam," Lillian said. She unclipped Bobby and led him back to the field. When she returned, I stood up, shielded my eyes with my hand, and looked up in the sky.

"What kind of birds are they?"

"Those?" she asked, pointing. "That's Fred and Ethel. Eagles. This mountain has been their home for maybe three years. Eagles mate for life, you know."

"They're so majestic," I said.

We stopped looking at the birds and faced each other.

"If a lion is your power animal, you may feel drawn to have the eagle as part of your totem," Lillian said. "Eagles are messengers from heaven."

"Lion, Hiawassee, eagles," I said. My heart filled with optimism.

"You're flying into the sun," Lillian said, "seeking a higher path, one of purity." She reached her hand over to my face and brushed away random strands of hair from my cheek. "Once you start to live... for *you*, with integrity and balance, you'll be surprised how easy it can be."

"What time can we meet?" I asked.

"How about four o'clock," Lillian answered, "at the lodge."

"In time for tea," I said in my best imitation of an English accent. "Will there be scones?"

"Don't push your luck," Lillian laughed.

—ɯ—

I had just put the kettle on the stove when Lillian came into the lodge.

"It's starting to really chill down out there," she said, taking off her jacket. "Instead of scones I brought homemade peanut butter cookies."

"Much better," I said as I pulled some cups out of the cupboard. "You baked my favorite cookie. How did you know?"

"Ahhh," she said, "we shamans have our ways."

We fixed our tea and sat at the table eating cookies while I told her about Zoe's offer. Her eyes widened as she took in the details of our conversation.

"How does it feel to be asked to work in the mountains with someone of Zoe's caliber?" she asked.

"I don't know," I said. "This job could be the answer. I've dreamt of working in a place like hers for years, a true healing spa, not just an assembly line like the resort. I like Zoe. I guess it would be *perfect*."

"Not everything is perfect," Lillian warned. "We all have a shadow side; Zoe's no exception. She has an Italian heritage and a Sicilian temper. That's why she's looking for a business partner, maybe someone a bit more calm. She's planning to spend Christmas with her family in Italy, and then go back for the summer. I think she'd like to semi-retire. She loves her work, but she also loves the idea of living in a villa somewhere in Sicily."

"Yeah, who wouldn't?"

"Well, me for one. I guess this mountain is my Sicily."

"Before I came up to the barn," I said, "I was reading Rumi, his poem called *Shadow and Light Source Both*."

"Let your darkness be your light?" Lillian said.

"Darkness is your candle," I corrected her.

"Even after all these centuries he's still an inspiration to the light chasers. Now then, fetch Sam and I'll pull up a chair in front of the couch. Let's talk."

"He's there on the couch. He told me he didn't care much for tea but he might need a glass of wine later."

"We'll see about that," Lillian said.

I settled into the cushions of the sofa, relaxed, and anticipated our conversation with high hopes and an eager heart. Lillian sat down, leaned in and spread her hands.

"Well, how are you feeling... after the sweat?" she asked.

"Kinda like dropping a tab of acid," I said. "I'm wondering if the visions were hallucinations... or were they real? Frankly, I didn't think I'd make it, with all that steam, but with Marie and Zoe there, I decided I could.'"

"Did it feel competitive?"

"No," I said, "more like camaraderie."

"And what about the accident, and your father telling you how much he loved you?"

"How do you know... what he said... what I saw in my mind?"

"Well, I would claim shaman clairvoyance, but you were pretty verbal."

"Oh."

"The important thing is, do you believe?"

"On one level I'm suspicious of the whole thing. I mean... could this be what really happened to my parents, or did my subconscious create the story? I want to believe my father did love us."

"Victims of abuse will often doubt their recollections and think they've made it all up. It's a survival mechanism, but it halts the healing process. It's the fear of moving forward. Pain is all they've known, the only thing they can trust."

I sat holding Sam, not sure of what to say next. There was some comfort in the unknown. If there are no expectations, I thought, there can be no failures. I allowed myself to feel the soft cushions, my legs folded under me, and Sam's velvety fabric in my hands.

"But, is it true?" I asked.

"You know in your heart what is true."

"Okay, but what do I do with all of this, Lillian?"

"Do you understand the importance of what you've been shown?"

I closed my eyes and squeezed Sam against my chest. My heart ached but I knew I had been given a great gift. *The truth will set you free, the truth will set you free,* the mantra flashed over and over in my mind.

"I understand that my father didn't intentionally kill my mother, although the beating in the car was horrendous. I know now, too, that he didn't want to be the monster he had become. Yes, I even think he loved us once. He really was two men, one good and one evil."

I buried my face into Sam's fur, felt the tears welling up in my eyes, and started to cry. Neither one of us spoke for several minutes. Lillian got up and brought me a box of tissues. I reached over to the box and dried my eyes.

"On my thirteenth birthday he gave me a twelve-gauge shotgun, a Beretta, and he taught me to shoot skeet. I remember warm autumn afternoons going to the skeet range, riding in his truck back to the house listening to polka music on the radio, and talking about how bad the shooters were that day. Then... three months later I came home from school and the gun was gone. So was he. He'd pawned it off to buy booze."

"That must have been painful," Lillian said.

"I felt betrayed. It was at that moment I began to really really hate his guts. I decided to never go with him again. I would spit in his food any chance I got."

"How do you feel about him now?"

"I'm not sure. I realize that he was a victim too, the war and all. This does give me some relief from the pain. And now, I guess, I'm supposed to forgive him. Forgiveness is part of the deal, right?"

"Do you want to forgive him?" she asked.

"Can I forgive the bastard who sold my gun and love the man who taught me how to shoot?" We sat in silence for a few minutes. My tears started again. I sat Sam on the next cushion and reached over for another tissue.

"When we are born," Lillian said, "we are angels on this earth. Then life happens and we forget who we are."

"Newborns," I said with a half-smile. "They shine with joy and innocence."

"On a vision quest," she said, "when you are in the wilderness, you will have an opportunity to be reborn. You go there to conquer the evil that lives in you."

"Evil... lives in me?"

"Unfortunately, we inherit the sins of our fathers. Your father's rage is imprinted on your soul. That's why you choose men who abuse you. Did you start fights with Tom when he was sober -- just to fight?"

I thought for a moment. "Well, um... maybe. Yes."

"It's time to face your demons," Lillian said. "That's what the vision quest is all about."

"So, what are we talking... camping without food?"

"Something like that," she laughed.

"I did a three-day fast last year," I said. "My senses were heightened. Everything became more acute, my sense of smell and my vision."

Lillian stood and said, "Tomorrow we rest, and I'll give you the details. Then you can decide if you want to participate. It begins Friday morning and ends on Sunday."

"Alone in the mountains?" I said. "I don't know, it seems so extreme."

"Not any more extreme than your father beating you and your mother. You survived that."

A huge lump formed in my throat. I looked up at the ceiling and fought back tears.

"Am I ready, Lillian?"

"Now that you know the truth... you are ready."

# CHAPTER 30

I WOKE UP buried underneath the blankets, stretched my arms above me and bent my body first to the left, then slowly to the right. As I let out a long sigh, my stomach growled and my thoughts turned to pancakes, hot and soaked in maple syrup.

My talk with Lillian had had a powerful effect on me. All of the steps I'd taken so far seemed to be paying off. I felt sure I could do a vision quest. Lillian's words replayed in my head, *Plenty of men and women have done a vision quest on this mountain. You can sleep in the wilderness and not die.* The idea of sleeping out in the forest in the rain had a strange appeal. I liked to look up into the sky when it rained; so many people looked down, hiding under umbrellas. "We're going to get wet anyway," John Muir said, "so why not welcome the feel of rain on our skin? The only way to appreciate a storm is to get out in it."

The clock confirmed my suspicion that it was early in the morning... six-o-five to be exact. I got up quickly, well rested and hungry. Do I really want to do all the work to make pancakes? I decided to drive to the Scaly Mountain community. There was a diner on Route 106. After dressing, I brushed my hair and threaded my ponytail through the back of a Falcons football cap.

Three massive, four-wheel-drive pick-up trucks, and a gray sedan that looked as if it had survived a demolition derby were in the parking lot. The diner, about the size of a single-wide trailer, was a classic Ffties design with sleek rounded aluminum sides. I bought a newspaper out of a box at the front door and entered. The waitress smiled and waved her hand. Ahhh, I thought, there is nothing like the smell of breakfast.

"Anywhere you like," she said.

As I made my way down the narrow aisle, four men sitting in a row at the counter turned in unison and watched me. They all wore canvas Macon County Fire Department jackets and smiled on queue. The second one nodded. After I passed, one of them murmured a comment, and a low chuckle emerged from the foursome. Rather than harbor feelings of resentment, I decided these poor country boys just weren't used to seeing a real babe at seven o'clock in the morning. I could feel four pairs of eyes undressing my backside.

Choosing a corner booth against one of the windows, I saw the waitress approach, coffeepot in hand.

"Coffee?"

"Absolutely. And just so you know, I'm a heavy cream user. Please don't tell anyone."

"Don't worry. Your secret's safe with me." She turned my coffee cup right-side-up and poured.

I shrugged off my jacket and opened the paper to the crossword puzzle. The waitress made the round trip and put down a menu.

"By any chance," I asked, "do you have buckwheat pancakes?"

"We do." Her name tag said "Karen," and we shared a love for buckwheat cakes. "Would you like chopped pecans on top? It's real good... gives them character."

"Let's give it a try, and can I have a large glass of milk?"

"You bet, sweetie, I'll make sure it's extra cold."

I looked over at the men and noticed how handsome they were, those big, beefy boys from the fire department, especially the red-head sitting at the end.

I sipped my coffee, worked the puzzle, and from under the brim of my hat stole glances at Red. When my pancakes arrived, I cut one bite-sized piece at a time, soaked it in syrup, and savored each forkful. The cake and syrup dissolved into the very essence of comfort and sweetness. I closed my eyes and chewed slowly, taking in the added sensation of crunchy pecans. *Heaven!*

When the men got up to leave, Red moved across the diner and sat down in my booth. He was even better looking close up, with sparkling blue eyes and a mischievous smile.

"Great morning, isn't it?" he asked.

"It is." I put down my fork and reached for the coffee cup.

"Falcons fan?"

"I have to be. I'm from Atlanta."

"You here for the colors?"

"Colors?"

"You know," he said, "the leaves."

"A little more than that; I'm here to relax and meditate."

"Oh. So… you're a new-age chick."

I laughed. "And you're a redneck fireman?"

"I am," he chuckled.

We grinned at each other, big "you-are-so-cute" grins.

"Marianne Sobieski," I said, extending my hand over my plate.

"Scott Roberts." His hand was large and calloused, I assumed from the hard work of firefighting.

"There's a Halloween dance," he said, "Saturday night at the Clayton Civic Center."

"Sounds like fun," I lied. Yeah right, I thought, there is no way on God's green earth I'd go to another dance in Clayton. Besides, if all went well, I'd be on a mountain Saturday night with Hiawassee and Lion.

"It starts at eight," he said. "Come… I'll buy you a drink."

Let's see, I thought, he'd buy me a drink, we'd dance, drink some more, kiss passionately in front of people at the bar, and decide if we were into each other enough to have sex -- but where? Yeah, we'd go to my room at the lodge, because he already has a wife. He would ravish my body as if there was no tomorrow, and I would have multiple orgasms. Or, Lillian would find us and kick me out of the program. My past life flashed before me. I turned to look out the window and felt myself blush.

"Uh, hope I haven't offended you," he said. "I sat down here because you're so pretty, even with that ball cap on… and you're not wearing a wedding ring."

He's not a redneck, I thought. Rednecks don't talk this way. He's a gentleman.

"You're very observant," I said holding up my left hand. "And no, you haven't offended me. It's just…"

Scott stood up abruptly and said, "Nice to meet you, Marianne."

"You too. It's a small town," I added. "We may see each other again."

"I'd like that," he said and walked away.

My pancakes were still warm. I dug in and Karen stopped by with the coffeepot.

"Refill?"

"Please tell me," I asked, "who's the hunk?"

"That would be Scott. We were all watching him hit on you from the kitchen," she snickered. "The standing tease around here is, 'Help! Help! I'm on fire! Call Scott!'"

We laughed and shared a knowing smile. No matter how tempting Scott Roberts was, I had bigger fish to fry.

—◊◊◊—

When I returned to the lodge Lillian was in the main hall, arranging camping equipment on the floor.

"Hey, lady," I said as I came in and collapsed on the couch. "I just had the most amazing stack of pancakes."

"Carbo loading for the big race?"

"I got up at six," I said, "wide awake and ready to go."

"Have you made a decision about tomorrow?"

"Yeah, I woke up this morning and thought, How can I pass up something so exotic? Vision quests don't come along every day, you know."

She sat down on the floor across from me and said, "This is huge, Marianne. It can be life-changing."

"Sounds like fun," I said rolling my eyes.

"Well... you'll see."

"What am I in for?" I sat up. "Are there bears in these mountains?"

Lillian laughed. "Yes, my dear, there are bears. But don't worry, their eyesight is poor. If you encounter one, back up slowly, stand up tall, wave your hands, and roar at the top of your lungs. Use your lion roar. They're more afraid of you than you are of them."

"Yeah, yeah, I've heard that one before," I said with sarcasm. "And if one decides I look more like lamb chops?"

"No way," Lillian said. "Relax."

"Any other life-threatening creatures?"

"Oh," Lillian said, "maybe a few timber rattlers, ticks, a spider or two. No wild boars or cougars or anything like that. Humans are more dangerous. Here, I've got some things I want you to take a look at."

Yikes, I thought, I hate spiders. Snakes? Lyme disease? Oh well, it's probably safer than a Friday-night dance.

Giving Lillian a hand up, I walked with her over to the items arranged in front of the fireplace. There was a tightly rolled sleeping bag tied to the bottom of a metal-framed backpack, a coil of rope, a clasp knife, a box of matches in a plastic bag, two bandanas, two one-liter plastic bottles, a whistle, and a folded blue plastic tarp.

"These are your essentials. We can talk later about what else will go into your backpack."

"What's the whistle for?" I asked. "Will I be leading a parade?" I noticed one thing missing: food. I would breathe, drink water, experience nature and starve. Yep, sounds like fun.

"Do you know how to tie-off a tarp shelter," Lillian asked, "to protect you from rain?"

"I'm no city wimp. I've camped out with friends, but we had all the conveniences – you know, like food... and toilet paper. Where's the toilet paper?"

Lillian ignored my serious question.

"Lean-tos are easy," she said. "First, find two trees close together. You'll have this eight-by-ten tarp; the fabric is light but extra strong. High winds would eat up a flimsy tarp. Tie double knots to secure the corners to the trees; use limbs as anchors. Four feet high would be ideal. The tarp should slant down to the ground, and you'll secure it with rocks. You'll be safe from the elements. Use pine needles to make padding for your sleeping bag, and you'll sleep like a baby."

"What will I do for water?"

"There's a water station at the threshold."

"Threshold?" I asked.

"It's where you'll leave the compound and walk into the wilderness, just off the riding trail, about halfway down the mountain. We'll hike down there today so you can get a feel for the area. You can practice tying a tarp."

"Fabulous!" My confidence level rose.

"It may not even rain this weekend," Lillian said.

"Still, I'd like to learn."

"Good. I've got to run errands this morning, but I'll be back by noon. Let's meet at the stables at one. I'll bring day packs and a few water bottles. You'll be fasting for two days, so eat something light the rest of today and tomorrow. And take some time to meditate."

This vision quest business sounded pretty cool, but there was something about the tone in her voice that told me I should be a lot more worried. My thoughts raced to ask more questions, but nothing much came to mind.

"But what about… the spiders… rattlesnakes?" My voiced wavered.

"Not likely. Just stay alert and be careful."

"And what if I run into some mean looking hillbilly with a shot-gun and no teeth?"

"No, no. Your only enemy is inside your head."

"But…" I swallowed hard.

"Marianne, remember, thousands of people over the centuries have gone off alone to fast and pray, not just Jesus and Mohammad. Your time has come."

# CHAPTER 31

PARIS AND BOBBY were grazing in a section of the field far away from the barn. I sat on the top rail of the wooden fence, watched them, and chewed on a short piece of straw. As my saliva softened its outside I could taste the pithy material dissolve. I crunched it into tiny bits, and then spat them out.

A faint smell of smoke hung in the air, and that, along with decaying leaves and grasses, gave the atmosphere a subtle richness that only fall can produce.

As Lillian approached, I jumped off the fence and headed her way.

"Are you dressed in layers?" Lillian asked. "The high may hit sixty by three. If we're sweating, we'll need to adjust."

I had remembered the layering/hiking rule. "Good to go." I gave her a thumbs-up and took the light pack she handed me.

"We'll hike until sunset, then go to the lodge and get your backpack ready." She lifted the other pack over her shoulders and positioned it on her back.

I put on my knapsack. We remained quiet as we walked down the trail. As the decline became steeper, my boots dug into the soft ground covered in dried pine straw and withered leaves. I slipped and faltered but didn't fall.

"It gets a little dicey out here," she warned. "The ground cover can hide a hole, or rocks."

We walked farther down the trail, and off to the right I spotted several tall birch trees on both sides of another path's opening. They still had a few yellow leaves on their branches, and white and black trunks rose from the ground. Their limbs swayed from the high winds and bent inward to create a natural archway. The birch bark peeled into long horizontal strips that curled at the ends. We stopped, looked up at the trees, and listened to the sound of wind whistling through the branches.

"This is the threshold," Lillian said. "We're about to walk upon the hallowed land of the Great Mother."

She turned and faced me. "Have faith that you'll receive answers on this quest. You've decided to leave everyone behind and set yourself apart. Every action you take will have some kind of ceremonial importance."

I followed her through the trail's opening, then over to a pile of stones.

"This is how we'll communicate with each other," she said. "Sometime Friday afternoon you'll move a stone from the pile and place it at the trail's opening. I'll come by in the early evening to make sure you've moved a stone. Then I'll place another stone next to yours. You and I are linked by this quest."

"Lillian, you said I'd cast out my demons -- but how?"

She dropped her pack, knelt down, and opened a water bottle. I followed her lead, and we drank together.

"Rituals," she spoke slowly. "Trust the process. Passing through the threshold is like walking through an invisible door. Your transition begins here."

She drank until her bottle was empty, stood up, and repositioned her pack.

"Let me show you the water station and then we'll move to higher ground."

I followed her past the stone pile to a crude wooden platform about four feet high holding a bright orange construction-site water cooler.

"Here's your water source. It's safe and pure. Stay hydrated," she advised.

We continued to walk, this time side-by-side, until the pine trees got too thick, and then I followed behind her. Just below us, a narrow run- off ditch was blanketed with an array of light gray flowers resembling lace curtains. Their tiny flowers, freeze-dried by the frost, were still exquisitely delicate. We emerged into an opening surrounded by a mixture of pines, hardwoods, and underbrush. We walked across this stretch of land to the other side.

Lillian stopped and said, "Sshh, can you hear that?"

I closed my eyes and listened intently. It was running water, faint bubbling sounds. "A creek?"

"More than that," she said. "It's a waterfall."

We hiked down the hill and the landscape transformed into an enchanted area, the kind of place where pixies and water sprites lived. One side of the bank was steep and heavily forested. The creek was about five feet wide. Moss and ferns covered the earth, and shoots of smaller plants dotted the sloping hill.

An eight-foot-high wall of granite strata protruded at varying angles, causing the water to bounce off the rocks, producing spray and mist. I breathed-in the moist air. The cascading water created a deep pool, the water was clear, and I could see tiny minnows swimming in circles.

She took off her pack and pulled out a small blanket. She spread it out on the ground, sat down, and patted the empty space next to her.

"Let's take a breather and enjoy the water."

I slipped off my pack and sat down. Neither of us spoke; we listened to the light splashing of the falls and the water gurgling over the rocks.

"This is old news," I said reluctantly. "I'm still afraid of predators, and I won't have a gun."

"Embrace your fear and dance with it." She put her hand on my shoulder.

Lillian removed her hand and went inside her pack, extracted a Native American flute, and began to play tender, melodic sounds.

As she played, the forest was transformed into a cathedral; the light through the trees became something unfathomable, something holy. The music was a combination of long soulful notes and high staccato accents, and the effect was heavenly. I tucked my legs underneath me, closed my eyes, and began to breathe deeply, and my anxiety subsided. She continued to play for several more minutes.

Then, putting down her flute, she said, "It's normal to feel frightened."

I moved my legs and knelt at her side. "Am I going crazy?"

"Anyone going out on the mountain alone for two days and nights *is* a little crazy, don't you think?" She laughed. "Let's head up and look at more of the forest.

We packed up and hiked away from the waterfall. Its sounds diminished, the walk upward was invigorating, and I started to feel more optimistic. The hillside was a contrast of greens, grays, and browns, like a patchwork quilt sewn with random scraps of material. When we arrived at the top of the hill, we stopped at another small clearing. The sunshine filtered through the trees at varying angles, creating shadows at the forest's edge.

"There are three rituals that are very important to the quest," Lillian told me: "building a fire, receiving the gift of a name, and the cry for a vision. Sometime during the first night, build a fire. The key is to create a ring of stones large enough to enable you to move around your fire pit. Choose stones that speak to you, like the stones of the sweat."

I looked around and began to spot twigs and limbs that were old and dry. There were plenty to choose from.

"The fire will show you that your old life is being destroyed and that you can move forward to a new place, a new consciousness."

Farther into the woods, we took off our packs and Lillian extracted the tarp, a knife, and a roll of rope. We walked over to a symmetrical row of pines. She put down the items, then unfurled two ends of the tarp up into the air and let them glide to the ground.

"You'll tie one end of the tarp to an old limb about four feet high, adjust the length of the rope, and pull it taut. Thread the rope through the eyelets and secure it to the other tree, cut off the excess, and *voila!* The construction of your lean-to has begun. Find some rocks to hold down the bottom of the tarp. You may choose to create a wall by stacking branches. That way you'll be even more protected from the weather. I don't want us to build one today. I only wanted to give you the basics. Do you have any questions?"

"I don't think so. I'm feeling pretty good about this tarp business. I apologize for the constant melt-downs and whining."

"Whining is like being trapped in purgatory," Lillian said. "And frankly, it's just not attractive."

"All the more reason for me to stop. The flute music was amazing. Thank you."

We refolded the tarp.

"It's the Lakota song of courage. My shaman taught it to me."

When we returned to the clearing, Lillian spread out her blanket on the ground again. We sat together and watched the sunlight change into a rich, elevating glow.

"When we're born," Lillian said, "we're given a name. But now you will have the opportunity to choose one that will identify who you really are, your talents and your spirit."

"What's your name?" I asked.

"Angel Warrior. I see and feel myself as a spirit moving among those who are broken."

Who am I? I wondered. I love to run and to practice yoga. These two activities had kept me sane throughout the madness with Tom.

"How do I choose my name?" I asked.

"As soon as you cross the threshold become hyper-aware of your surroundings. Empty your mind and listen."

"When will I know my name?"

"It can come at any time. But when you receive it, you'll know without any doubt and your heart will sing."

"It's been a long time since I've felt that much joy."

"On your last night, build a fire and think of your circle as a womb. When the fire is burning its brightest, consider the death of Marianne, and surrender to the flames. You are to be reborn."

Reborn sounded okay, but I wasn't comfortable with the death part. I was too embarrassed to ask her to explain. Surrender to the flames? The whole thing was beginning to sound foolish, but I trusted Lillian and hoped I would find the courage to survive.

We sat together and watched the sun's rays bathe the western sky in random shades of red.

# CHAPTER 32

I SAT WAITING for Lillian on the middle step of the front porch with my backpack leaned against the rail. The first light of day prompted the birds to begin their morning songs, and I felt numb… so afraid of this final step. I heard Lillian singing before I could see her. It was a song in Lakota.

"Miye toka heya anpetu owakinyelo.

"Wanbli gleska wan heyaya u welo.

"Miye toka heya anpetu owakinyelo"

I walked out to meet her, we both stopped, and she continued to sing. She leaned on the long, brightly colored walking stick in her right hand.

"As the sun rises, I am first to fly.

"A spotted eagle is coming saying this,

"As the sun rises I am first to fly."

She held the staff out to me and said, "Here, a talisman from Jet."

"Jet?"

"He made it for you."

I walked closer to her, reached out and felt the weight of it in my hands. About two inches in diameter, it was a beautiful branch of white oak, long, slightly curved, but solid. I leaned against it.

"I could beat the shit out of someone with this," I said.

I held it like a baseball bat. Jet had woven leather strips around the top as a hand grip, and the stick itself was painted with yellow and white birds, green turtles, and a gray coyote.

Lillian and I walked together to the lodge.

"A magic wand of sorts," she said, her voice enthusiastic. "It will help guide your quest."

Her tone cheered me, and my mood lightened. When we got to the porch I handed the staff to Lillian, retrieved my backpack, and situated it on my shoulders. Then she handed me back the walking stick.

"It's tradition to hike to the threshold in silence," she said. "Hold your intentions for this quest in your mind and in your heart as we make our way down the mountain."

She moved in front of me, and I followed, our steps plodding along in unison. As we descended down the mountain path to the birch trees, guardians of the threshold, Jet's staff gave me more balance in the difficult spots. I liked the feel of the soft leather grip.

As we walked I silently composed a mantra. *I release any negative energy. I make healthy choices. I practice self-acceptance and total acceptance of others.* The words had a kind of rhythm, and repeating them over and over took my mind off the fact that in less than ten minutes I would be entirely on my own in the wilderness. The birch trees came into view and my stomach tightened. When we arrived, we faced each other and smiled the most galvanizing expression of unconditional love. Lillian took out a stem of sage and a lighter from her shirt pocket. She lit it, breathed it softly to life, and created a swirl of thick smoke.

"My sister," she said, walking around me, waving the sage around my body, "on this quest, work the rituals, ask your questions, seek the answers, and have faith."

She stopped in front of me, tapped out the sage under her boot, cast it aside, and rested her hands on both of my shoulders.

"Remember your guides and call on them; their strength will be your strength."

Tears filled my eyes. I blinked and they trickled down my cheeks. She lovingly brushed them away.

"Lillian," I struggled to speak and reached out for her. We held hands like a bride and her bridesmaid before a wedding, beaming at each other from some shared secret place. "There are no words to express my gratitude. I *want* to build a sacred fire and burn away my past."

"Good," she said.

We let go. She turned away and walked slowly up the path, not looking back.

I felt a stab of panic. I wanted to shout, "No, no… wait for me!" I stood still, barely breathing, and watched the last glimpse of her vanish.

Suddenly I was drowning in silence. I looked in every direction, wondering what secrets the forest held. Crossing through the birch trees, I slid my pack off, reached into the side pocket, pulled out my feathers, and stood trying to decide what to do next. The trees, I thought, my feathers will stay here with them. My clasp knife opened easily. I walked over to the first tree on the left and used the sharp blade to cut a small but deep groove into its smooth bark. I slid the hawk feather into it. At the farthest tree to the right I made another incision at eye level. I guided the crow's feather into the notch, closed the knife and placed it back into my hip pocket.

"There, that should do it. Rest well, my feathers, and hope for my return."

I stood between the trees, lifted my hands into the air, and called out to my guides in a strong and fervent voice, "Hiawassee, walk with me side-by-side. Noble Lion, protect me from harm." A soft echo gave my intonations a mystic ring.

I'm getting the hang of this, I thought. Satisfied that I had prayed well, I shouldered the backpack, got to the water station, and set it down again. This time I dug out the water bottles and filled them. The cooler's water tap was damp from the morning dew. Cold water flowed into the bottles and chilled them as I screwed the caps back on. Putting the heavy bottles at the bottom of the pack, one to the right, and the other on the left side, maintained a strong center of gravity. Now the pack seemed easier to carry. With it on my shoulders, I turned to the path ahead.

Somehow everything took on a deeper vibe; my senses heightened. Tree bark appeared a deeper brown, tree branches were illuminated in silver, and the North Carolina pines added a lush, opulent green. I felt more resilient and self-assured with each step. My pace quickened and after a short time I realized how far away from the threshold I had traveled. I stopped and turned, looking up to the eastern sky. My best guess was that it was ten o'clock in the morning. A soft pastel luminosity bathed the path ahead, and I continued on, this time more slowly. A large pine grove emerged to the left; it was twenty or thirty trees deep. I wanted to make it to the top of the bluff by noon, so I continued to follow the steep incline upward.

I repeated my mantra aloud, "I release any negative energy. I make healthy choices. I practice self-acceptance, and total acceptance of others." I wondered if the birds were listening.

One of the things I wanted to rid myself of was my knee-jerk reaction to everything. Up and down, up and down, it was exhausting. The past two months had been a rollercoaster ride. Half-way up the ascent my breathing became more labored. The backpack no longer felt light; it was time to take a breather. I looked back at the valley below; it was beautiful.

I set down my pack, got comfortable in the soft grass, and stretched out my legs. I noticed what appeared to be a moving twig, but there was no wind. What is this? At the edge of the path, close to where I sat, was a mix of tall weeds. I spotted more movement and stared in its direction. The dancing twig was no twig at all, it was a gray and brown, long-bodied insect, blending in with the rocks and soil.

On cue a grasshopper landed just inside the grass nearby. The twig turned and assessed its prey. I knew this bug; it was a big praying mantis, cannibalism at its finest. I watched with fascination.

Twig froze, motionless, its front legs folded together as if in prayer. Eerily moving its head back and forth, the mantis decided to strike. Faster than the blink of an eye, Twig lashed out. The spikes of its front legs pierced and pinned the grasshopper in its grasp. Twig held it with a deadly grip, pulled the grasshopper to its mouth, turned its body, and began to eat it like a cob of corn.

The grasshopper continued to struggle while it lived, fiercely kicking away. But after only a minute, it was still. The ruthlessness of the attack reminded me how violent nature can be. Twig continued to chew slowly, enjoying his meal. Is he sporting a smile? When he finished devouring the choice portions of his prey, he began to groom himself like a cat, one leg at a time, nibbling the spines. Finally, he resumed his fixed prayer stance, perfectly camouflaged.

I leaned my torso back away from Twig's exhibition and he turned to face me. His triangularly shaped head, bulging eyes, and long antennae looked like an alien. Comically, he straightened his six-inch long body and struck a Kung Fu fighting pose. His front legs whirled in circles, challenging me, and his head bobbed back and forth like a boxer in the ring.

"Are you serious? You're a bug!"

But he continued to hold his ground and test me. I entertained the idea of flicking him with my index finger; sending him through the air and into a thicket of weeds. But I wasn't a part of his world, and I had no right to interfere. Besides, I admired his hunting capabilities and sharp teeth. So I let him continue to show off, watched him for a few more minutes, stood, and grabbed my pack.

"Come on, girlfriend, let's get a move on. Jesus, now you're talking to bugs." I slid the straps over my shoulders and charged ahead.

The incline became steeper and I used my stick like a third leg, for stability. The ground vegetation changed. The frost had killed most of the weeds, but they were still beautiful. Dried, gray grasses and light russet colors surrounded the resilient emerald underbrush. The air was cool, and a breeze flowed down off the mountain. The gentle wind was energizing.

Soon the path disintegrated and I followed a faint trail lined on either side with granite and quartz rocks. One rock in particular caught my eye and I knew immediately it needed to be in my sacred circle.

Using my staff like an icepick at the rock's base, I dislodged it from the ground. It was about the size of a softball, and I cradled it in my hands, testing its weight and inspecting the raised areas of quartz. The rock was a microcosm of the granite mountain, and the exposed surface was varying shades of white crystals sparkling in the sunlight. I arranged the pack on the ground and placed the rock inside. The extra weight was a burden of joy.

The mountain continued to incline. I heard the waterfall and rejoiced.

"Hello, waterfall!" I shouted in its direction. "See you later."

When I arrived at the summit the sun was directly overhead and the wind rustled through bare branches, offering their welcome. The expanse was much larger than I remembered. Walking toward the edge of the pine trees I paced off the area's circumference and guessed it to be sixty feet wide. There were no signs of other fire pits or sacred circles. Vision questers had left no signs of their presence. "Leave the area pristine," Lillian had told me. "It's your duty not to scar the land."

I focused on the spot Lillian had proposed for my lean-to, felt assured in my camp-making skills, and chose an area three rows back into the woodlands at a slightly higher elevation than the entrance of the grove. If it rained I'd stay drier under thick pine branches on the raised surface.

"Let's rest here," I said. I put the pack down and knelt on the pine straw. Opening the front pocket of the pack and taking out the tarp and rope, a live wire of excitement sparked inside me. I thought about Dannie – the same kind of jolt. We'd get silly and embellish our intonations, and now it seemed fitting to do it again.

Oh my God, I thought, this is really happening.

# CHAPTER 33

I FUMBLED A bit but eventually tied the tarp securely to the trees, found heavy rocks nearby, and used them to fasten down the back end of my shelter. This time my tone was straight to the point, "Time to unpack.'

I untied the sleeping bag from the pack's framework, fluffed up the pine straw, and situated the bag on top of the pile. Climbing onto my new bed it sank down two inches and felt great.

"Good job, Marianne... but don't get cocky."

I brought in my pack, opened it, and began to set up housekeeping. My stomach made noises I hadn't heard in years. I felt some light, abdominal cramping. It wasn't painful, but the sensations reminded me that food was nowhere to be found. I needed a mushroom-Swiss-bacon double cheeseburger with extra mayo. Thoughts of Beth's Mountain Grill made my mouth water. I chugged the last of my water and promised myself I would have one soon.

I put both empty bottles into the day pack, gathered up my staff, and started my journey back to the threshold to move a rock -- my signal to Lillian that all was well.

The steep decline was an easy hike; I made it to the threshold in no time. On the trail in front of me I spotted a flurry of color in the air. As I got closer the flurry became a group of six light-brown moths. They flew in small circles, diving and soaring, playing a game of tag. I crept cautiously forward and they allowed me to get close enough to touch them. I held out my right arm at shoulder height.

Closing my eyes and breathing deeply, I wanted to experience the sensation of being as light as the wind, like a tiny moth, flying with friends in the afternoon sun.

I felt movement, opened my eyes, and turned my head ever so slowly to the right. Magically, two moths were perched on my thumb and index finger. Their forewings were the color of chocolate, but iridescent green-blue at the base, with a pattern of white spots in the shape of an "O" from the middle to the tips. They held their wings at rest against my fingers. It was a touch so light it could have been blades of grass; I could barely breathe.

Their antennae twitched forward and back, sensing the breeze, the heat from my hand, and their friends' movement nearby. I was awe-struck and mesmerized by my visitors. It was like swimming with dolphins, or falcon hunting. The intimate proximity to these delicate and fragile creatures was ethereal; certainly the fairies guided them to me.

Simultaneously they flew off my hand, rejoined the others, and continued their acrobatic dance. I moved my stick in front of me and rested both hands on it as they flew away.

"Hiawassee, thank you for this gift."

As I continued my walk, the rock pile came into view, and stones of various shapes and sizes beckoned to me. I was drawn to a large round granite rock, gray with white and silver speckles; it was about the size of a cantaloupe. My palms massaged its bumpy, smooth exterior. I walked it over to the other side of the threshold, found a spot with some remaining green grass, and placed it there.

"Lillian, I am happy, healthy, and hungry."

At the water station I decided that by drinking enough water, I could convince my stomach that food wasn't necessary. I filled the first bottle, leaned against the station platform, and took long gulps until more than half the bottle was gone. My stomach immediately rebelled; nausea overwhelmed me. I doubled over, grabbed my sides, and puked out the liquid as quickly as I had drunk it.

"Shit!" I exclaimed, wiping my chin with the back of my hand.

Just like the dancing moths, I thought, this is a reminder to slow down, trek through this quest carefully. I walked gingerly in a small circle until my stomach calmed down. I'd be sipping my water from now on.

Refilling both bottles, I picked up my stick, and headed back up the trail. When I returned to base camp the sun was at midpoint in the sky. It would set at six, followed by twilight and dusk. I'd have time to visit the waterfalls, but first I needed to create my circle.

I retrieved my foundation stone, the crystal quartz, from inside the backpack, headed out to the open area, and oriented myself east. Carrying it to its resting place was humbling. I stood and tried to decide how big the circle would be. Ten-by-ten, I thought. Perhaps Hiawassee is channeling important information to me.

"Ten-by-ten it is."

I began my search for stones to the south, away from my imaginary circle. About an hour later, I needed just one large rock, or several that were medium-sized, to complete the project. I walked down a hill to an area I hadn't hunted in and found a large black rock hiding under some leaves. I pushed it with my boot and it barely moved.

"Fuck, is this going to be worth the effort?"

I answered my own question. "Come on, lazy bitch, get going."

The walk up the incline was taxing; my legs burned and my whole body ached. Half way up the hill I stopped, leaned against a thick pine tree, and caught my breath. Back at the circle I dropped the stone with a thud, sat down, and admired my work. Hot and sweaty, I noticed blood on my forearm. The stone had gotten its revenge. I hoped it wasn't a bad omen. I wanted to make a trip to the waterfalls before dark.

At camp I filled my daypack with a bottle of water, my drum and beater wrapped in a hand towel, a washcloth, a change of underwear, socks, and a long-sleeved shirt. I wondered how cold the stream would be.

I walked slowly downward, spending extra time studying the trees. One large, smooth-barked tree stood on the right, resembling a curved female body with arms stretched upward, embracing the sky. Fallen branches littered the ground and my staff kept me safe as I maneuvered the landscape. The waterfall's lyrical sounds filled my ears and my pace quickened, driven by enthusiastic anticipation.

A small sandy beach was at the edge of the waterfall's pool. I knelt down and tested the water.

"Brrr... oh, shit. Freezing!"

I stripped down, carried the washcloth with me, and braved the pool up to my ankles. My feet went instantly numb, and my entire body puckered.

"Make it quick. Goddamn... make it quick."

The icy washcloth against my skin was like a shot of adrenaline.

"Whoa baby, this is cold! So cold!"

I rubbed my face briskly with the icy cloth, then my breasts, arms, and tummy. After another dunking I wrung out the cloth and cleaned my lower torso -- total time in the water, about thirty-five seconds. Once out of the pool I used the hand towel to dry off, redressed, and relished the sensation of clean, dry clothes. The fabric warmed my skin and my body stopped shaking.

Sitting down to put on warm dry socks, I laced up my boots and gathered up the sweaty clothes. I reached over for my drum and beater and began to drum. It was time to raise the spirits.

"Tom, tom, tom, tom...tom, tom, tom, tom" The beats were quick and sharp. Lillian's words blended with them, *"Work the rituals, work the rituals."*

I stood, repeated the words, and walked back and forth in front of the falls. Eventually I stopped and raised my arms to the heavens, holding on to my drum and beater.

*"Hello, Hiawassee,"* I sang. "I'm here!"

The only sound was the splashing water. No wind, no birds, no small animals scurrying in the underbrush. I felt contained in a dome or captured in a snow globe. My perception of time altered. Each moment seemed to spread across an entire lifetime.

The supporting wall of the falls and the surrounding topography exploded into detail and texture. Clumped mosses hugged the surrounding rocks, thick fuzzy vines snaked around tree trucks, and fluorescent green lichen covered dead branches on the ground.

The sun had moved closer to the horizon. Must be around four, I thought. I should have two or more hours of light. I chose to linger a little while longer. The sun's rays created long shadows across the pool. I knelt down at the edge and saw my reflection along with the trees above me in perfect clarity. Patches of sunlight shone through the water, revealing the creek's rocky bed.

Suddenly the amount of water flowing from the precipice exploded, the pool began to rise, and I sat back on my haunches, frozen with fright. A brilliant cloud appeared. It sparkled, pulsated, and emitted light beams.

"Hiwassee?" I gasped.

"Yes, daughter."

Amazed by her presence, I tried to gather myself. Eventually I was able to breathe and speak.

"Is this... a miracle?" I asked the luminescence.

"Put your hands in the water and keep your eyes on me."

After placing my hands in the stream, her image became more focused, and a cascade of stars traveled from her through the stream, surrounding my hands with a golden glow. I trembled, forcing myself to hold my hands submerged.

"Who am I?" I asked. "What is my name? Why am I here?"

"You are... Hands of Water. You are on this earth to heal others. Be at peace." Her voice was angelic, warm and affectionate.

My body tingled and my fear vanished. This celestial bridge formed between us transcended space and time.

"I am… Hands of Water?" I needed assurance.

"Hands of Water."

The stars eventually faded and the stream of light diminished. As my hands transitioned from water to air, the glow remained momentarily, dwindled, and then disappeared. I looked up and Hiawassee was gone. Sitting back, tucking my legs underneath me, I began to cry into wet hands.

"Thank you," I whispered.

I spent the next twenty minutes in meditation, holding the image of Hiawassee and my new name in awareness. My hands swayed in a starry sky, touching clouds and moonbeams. They caressed the planets, and I felt the solar winds pass through my fingers. Everything dissolved into a gilt liquidity. Slowly I returned to consciousness, felt my body, rubbed my hands together, and opened my eyes, dumbfounded by what had happened.

Disconnected from my surroundings, I splashed water on my face and promptly became more focused and centered. I used my hands to dry my face, cupped them, and took a long drink from the stream. There were three white pebbles that caught my eye. I reached in, picked them up, and carried them back with me. I put them inside my pack, loaded up and hiked back to the camp.

The gnawing hunger in my belly roared.

I focused on the forest and walked slowly, counted every sixth step and stopped, taking in every detail, listening to the wind in the trees and the birds tweeting as they sang to one another. Or, were they singing to me?

As the routine continued, there was movement in the leaves to my left about ten feet up the trail. Motionless, I fixated on the spot. There it was – a red fox looking back at me. She was the size of a small dog. We locked eyes and neither of us moved. Her body, tail, and the top of her head were a shade of reddish-orange, her underbelly white, and the tips of her ears and lower legs were black. Her tail was longer than half her body; it extended in rigorous attention. She bowed her head forward at a slight angle and lifted one paw. Her expression was one of shyness; her shining eyes begged to know: "Should I run?"

I stood completely still, not wanting to spook her. I'd never been this close to a wild predator. The hair on my neck stood on end as we continued to appraise each other.

A chipmunk ran across the woods and my fox was gone in a flash, hunting for dinner. I watched as she leapt away -- small, red, orange, black, white, soft and fluffy. So much magic in the forest today, I thought; what will be next?

# CHAPTER 34

CONTINUING UP THE hill, I saw that sunset was approaching, and I still needed to find wood and rocks for my fire pit. At camp, I unpacked the new stones and set them in the western sphere of my sacred circle. At the lean-to I shoved my pack against one of the trees and stood the staff next to it. Then I scoured the mountainside for more rocks. The pit would be relatively small, about thirty inches wide, so not many rocks were needed. But I wanted them to be beautiful, and stacked sufficiently high to safely contain hot ashes. I searched diligently and found the perfect candidates; they were granite and crystal, as shiny and colorful as the others already in the boundary.

Lillian had instructed me to kneel in front of my fire pit and make an affirmation while digging it out. I used one of the circle's smallest stones as a tool and burrowed into the ground.

"I am Hands of Water. I heal others." I loved the sound of it.

As I cleared the space of grass and leaves, memories of hunting with my father flooded my thoughts.

We hunted grouse and pheasant in the fields of western Pennsylvania with Springer spaniels, and I was never allowed to play with the dogs.

"They are hunters," my dad said, "not playmates."

One Saturday morning, we were up before dawn and I met Dad in the kitchen. He made coffee and appraised my sleepy state.

"You need to be extra alert this morning, because we're taking both dogs. You want to try a cup of my joe?"

I poured some coffee into a cup, added a tablespoon of sugar, and poured in enough milk to turn the mixture into a creamy brew. I sipped and grimaced at the bitter taste.

"More sugar?" he laughed, pushing the sugar bowl toward me. "You'll be wide awake in ten minutes."

Once outside, we loaded the guns and ammunition carefully into the space behind the truck's front seat.

"Let the dogs out."

I dashed down to their pens. Both dogs were eager, tails waging. I opened the gates and they sprinted up to the truck.

"Duke, Rex... sit," Dad commanded. They obeyed.

He dropped the truck's tailgate and opened the doors to their cages. "Come to me, boys." Both dogs jumped up, went into their cages, and lay down. Dad secured the latches, shut the tailgate, and we were off.

When we arrived at the mowed cornfield, the sun was beginning to shine across the landscape. I scrambled out of the truck, dropped the tailgate, and released the dogs. They busied themselves sniffing the ground around the truck.

Dad came out, whistled, and they bounded up to him. "Sit, lie down... good boys."

We slipped into our orange and tan vests, filled the pockets with shotgun shells, loaded the guns and put them on safety. As soon as the dogs saw the guns they jumped up and wiggled with excitement.

We walked out to the field with the dogs running ahead of us, noses to the ground. I glanced over at my handsome father. We were at first light, sharing a walk through the field, hunting birds. Nothing else mattered except this moment, and I wanted him to know how much I loved him.

He had taught me everything I knew about guns. Holding my shotgun made me feel powerful, as powerful as my dad, and I felt immense gratitude.

"Hunt 'em up, Duke, Rex. Hunt 'em up," Dad said.

They immediately got to work. The stubby corn stalks stood about a foot off the ground, high enough to conceal pheasants scurrying along the rows.

We walked side-by-side. Dad reached over and placed his hand on my shoulder.

"Listen carefully to every sound; keep your eyes on the dogs. Remember to watch them work, and when they start to circle, click off your safety. They'll bring the bird to you."

Our boots crunched into the frozen terrain. The air was crisp and clean. At this moment my father was my teacher, friend, and hero.

"Sweep to the right, Marianne. Follow Rex."

Rex began to circle an area ten feet in front of me. "Get a bird, Rex. Get a bird," I said.

I clicked off the safety and pointed the gun in front of me. Rex rushed in and a pheasant flew into the air. I moved my sights just ahead of the bird and squeezed the trigger.

*Crack!* The shot echoed and my body felt the kick of the shell's explosion. The dead bird sailed to the ground as both Rex and Duke sprang over the stubble to retrieve it.

Dad hollered out to me, "Good shot!"

I slid on the safety. Duke ran faster than Rex. He gingerly picked up the bird, ran to my father, and dropped it at his feet.

"Good boy, Duker," he said. "Good Duke."

Dad reached down and picked up the bird by its neck, shaking it aggressively, loose feathers spread on the ground. He turned to me.

"First shot of the day! Not bad, come and get your prize."

I jogged over to him with both dogs nipping at my heels. As Dad handed me the pheasant, Rex jumped up and tried to bite it. I held it high into the air and grinned at my father. I was triumphant, euphoric, and proud to be my father's daughter.

I choked with emotion as the memory faded. I placed the small digging stone back into the circle and started my search for wood. Twigs and small branches were easy to find. I piled the slender kindling in the center of the pit and decided to add medium and large branches once the fire got going.

As I scouted out downed branches, important people from my past presented themselves with each choice I made. A three-foot long branch was Mrs. Bosco, my first grade teacher. Her voice was always calm and comforting, and she made learning fun.

A thick, two-foot branch, four inches in diameter, carried the weight of Mrs. Edwards, my seventh grade English teacher. Her infectious smile and mnemonic devices for spelling and grammar remained in my thoughts. "Stationary with an 'a' is like static with an 'a'. Stationery with an 'e' is like paper with an 'e'. The principal is my pal."

A willowy, elegant branch from a downed oak tree was Aunt Mary. While holding the piece of oak I distinctly felt the presence of my mother and father. They were happy once; that was before Daddy went off to fight the Nazis.

I placed this offering of branches near the pit, made my way back to camp, and studied the open sides of my lean-to. There was plenty of brushwood; many of the branches still had leaves. I found branches that stacked easily and fit inside each other like pieces of a puzzle. Twenty minutes later my shelter had three sides. I crawled inside, knelt on the pine straw bed, and felt protected from the elements. Rummaging through my backpack, I extracted my sweatshirt, the small box of wooden matches, Lillian's flashlight, and my drum and beater.

On my way back to the circle I saw tall cumulus clouds forming in the sky, with flat, dark purple bottoms. The last rays of the sun lit up the billowing peaks, turning the tips an immaculate white. Twilight was near.

Inside the perimeter I slipped on my sweatshirt, sat down in front of the fire pit, placed the other items next to me, and looked up at the sky again. The air was lush; I smelled rain.

My day had been packed with a multitude of rich and resonant encounters: my stones, water from the mountain stream, and my new identity, a gift from Hiawassee. Touching the moths was a whisper from God sent on the wings of angels. The mantis represented the violent reality of nature. Each experience tied me to the elements of earth, water, and air.

And now I was about to introduce the fourth element of my quest: the lifeblood of ancient man – fire. Picking up the drum, I beat out a random rhythm, looked up at the sky, and watched the purple billows blend into a black line of ominous hell. Will it storm?

"*You have time for a fire,*" Hiawassee whispered.

I knelt down and struck a match under the dried leaves and kindling. The flames struggled; I panicked and threw four more matches into the mix. The kindling burst into a tiny sulfur explosion, I breathed gently into its center, and an infant flame was born.

Carefully, I balanced tiny twigs in a pyramid frame around the flames. They quickly caught fire, and a small area of the pit became an intensely red incandescence. I snapped a medium sized branch in half and placed it on either side of the small burning pile. The fire burst into a glorious blaze. Steady flames of orange and red grew inside the sacred fire, and as I added more branches, it soon became a beacon for me amid the approaching dark.

My intention for this ritual was to honor my past and revere the people who had nurtured my childhood. My favorite teachers had already tapped into my awareness; now I felt Mom, Dad, and Aunt Mary here with me as well. A sense of reassurance settled in around me. I no longer felt lost or afraid, but empowered by the growing bonfire.

# Erika Jantzen

Twilight descended into dusk, and I chose my next branch. Its bark was eroded and revealed the ashen wood inside. I looked up into the sky and watched inky clouds part to reveal a crescent moon well above the horizon. I turned my attention to the fire and relaxed, knowing that only thirty feet separated me from my lean-to and a comfortable bed. Once I'm inside my nest, who can hurt me?

Picking up the next branch to fuel the fire, I became more contemplative, praying that this fire would bless me with the clarity to know that my parents loved each other and me, despite all the struggles they faced when Dad returned from the war. He drank, they fought, but there were summer nights when we sat together on the back porch while Dad smoked cigarettes. Mom would slide her hand under his shirt and scratch his back.

Before I started the first grade, Mom and I walked hand-in-hand five days a week to attend the early morning Mass, sunshine, snow, or rain. In March the sun rose at about six-thirty and the early-morning daylight gently pushed through the trees and onto the houses and streets we passed.

"Mommy, look!" I said, pointing to a brilliant star sparkling in the eastern sky, with a crescent moon hanging slightly above it.

"That's Venus," she said. "It's a planet, but it's so far away, it looks like a star. The moon is keeping it company."

When I reached the age of twelve, Bishop Mahoney officiated at my Confirmation. Aunt Mary was my godmother and walked behind me to the altar. The thick smoke of incense filled the church, and light from the candles created a shimmering glow over the parents sitting in the pews. I knelt in front of the bishop, afraid to look at him directly. Instead I stared at the huge, jewel-encrusted cross hanging from his neck. He extended his hands over my head, prayed, and then anointed my forehead, making the sign of the cross with oil that smelled of frankincense.

"Be sealed with the gift of the Holy Spirit." He slapped me lightly on my left cheek, signaling that I would face pain and adversity as a Christian professing her faith to the world.

"I confirm you with the chrism of salvation, in the name of the Father, the Son, and the Holy Ghost."

Aunt Mary's hand lifted off my shoulder, and we walked together down the aisle. In the third pew my mother and father sat close together, beaming at us. I wondered why Mom was crying.

That night Dad gave me a gold chain and holy medal with the image of Saint Catherine, the patron saint of my Confirmation. I was now Marianne Catherine Sobieski. No one knew I had chosen the name of Catherine because I was in love with the history of Catherine the Great of Russia. The Catholic faith had plenty of secrets, and this was mine.

And now, I had a new name, Hands of Water.

I set one of the limbs across the fire pit; it warmed against the growing coals, intensified, and burst into flames. I threw on another branch and it immediately responded to the heat. Molten coals worked on its bark and it yielded to the high temperature, producing more light and more heat. I thought about Aunt Mary flipping pancakes, wearing a herringbone skirt, black turtleneck sweater, and pearl earrings and necklace, her cigarette burning in the ashtray on the counter.

"Mimi, I'll do that," I said. "Sit down and finish your smoke."

"Thanks, sweetheart."

She headed out to the sunroom to read the Sunday paper. When I went out to tell her breakfast was ready, she was asleep on the chaise lounge.

Now, sitting by the fire, tears dripped from my eyes and I hugged my knees to my chest. Aunt Mary would be so proud of me. The fire was beginning to die. The first part of my quest was complete.

Experiencing the serenity that accompanied my happy memories filled my heart with peace.

Darkness surrounded the circle, but the fire shed enough light for me to see the boundary rocks. Crystal quartz once again appeared, this time reflecting the fire's dying flames and red-hot ashes.

"Hello, my friends. Goodnight."

# CHAPTER 35

THE FLASHLIGHT CREATED a narrow tunnel of light guiding me through the brush, over the rise, and back to camp. Thirsty and exhausted, I crawled inside the lean-to. It felt cozy, like a bear's den.

Slowly drinking a quart of water, I did not want to repeat my earlier "too much, too soon" episode. I splashed a little water on my face, wiped away some of the soot with my hand, and dried it on my jeans. Unlacing my boots, I pulled them off with my socks and massaged my feet. Every subatomic particle of my body ached. I unzipped the sleeping bag, rolled inside the soft flannel cocoon, and instantly fell asleep.

Sometime during the night my snoring woke me up and I heard Hiawassee's whisper.

*"Put on your rain suit."*

Disoriented and confused I could only wonder why. A deafening clap of thunder answered my question, and a bolt of lightning turned darkness into day. Seconds later a sonic boom shook the earth. I almost jumped out of my skin.

I found the flashlight, pointed it at my backpack, and spotted the bulge of the rain suit in the outer pocket. The wind howled and my lean-to fluttered. The trees around me groaned against the fierce onslaught, and the tarp pulled against its moorings. Throwing back the upper portion of the sleeping bag, I reached down for the rain suit, and bolted outside. With shaking hands I pulled the pants over my bare feet and up to my waist. The heavens opened just as I slid the plastic hoodie over my head. Several bolts of lightning exploded, creating a strobe effect against the trees. Thunder followed with a high-pitched cracking, like cannons firing in the distance.

Once back inside I put on my socks and boots. My heart raced as I began to imagine the worst. The tarp would be ripped from the ropes; I would be exposed to the bone-chilling torrent and gale-force winds; and a final bolt of lightning would put me out of my misery. I was as helpless as a child.

"Mom! Dad! Help me!" I could barely hear my voice over the constant roar of wind and rain. "Lion, Lion where are you? Hiawassee?" I screamed at the top of my lungs. "Stop the rain, stop the rain!" So much for my romantic illusions of walking in the rain.

I moved the pack to the front of the lean-to, scooted the sleeping bag as far back as I could, and sat on top of it. The plastic suit kept me dry as the tarp's surface bounced off my head from the buckets of rain plummeting down from an angry sky.

"I don't want to die!" I buried my face in wet hands.

Tears of lamentation flowed down my cheeks like the rushing rain that formed a gully outside the lean-to. A sudden flash of lightning revealed every detail, like an X-ray of a broken bone. The temperature must have dropped ten degrees; my breath was visible with each exhale. I remembered this level of anxiety and fear from the times my father had threatened us with our lives.

"Hiawassee, please, stop the rain," I whispered.

The downpour began to let up. It transformed into a hard, steady rain with occasional lightning and thunder.

"Thank you."

I rubbed my hands together briskly, dried my face, and crawled forward, listening to thunder echoing in the distance. Then the rain stopped completely.

Once outside, I used the flashlight to inspect the tarp and my immediate surroundings. The knots had stayed true, and my wall of branches had stopped much of the water from penetrating the interior. The water that did enter had been absorbed by the pine straw. I shined the light on the trees and watched big drops falling from the high branches. They looked like gemstones floating to the ground. Shivering, I removed the rain suit, shook off the water from its exterior, and folded it in half. Everything will dry in the morning sun, I thought, if there is a sun.

I rearranged my sleeping space and propped the wet backpack between my bed and the entrance after I had taken out another pair of socks, my woolen cap, my jeans, and a second sweatshirt. My body began to warm after putting on extra clothes, and the inside of the sleeping bag was a dream come true – soft, warm, dry and welcoming. I snuggled down into the bag, covering my head with the top layer of the flannel insert. The second pair of jeans became a pillow, and I lay comfortably in the darkness, trying to determine what the storm had to teach me. Perhaps it was a baptism of sorts, I thought. With my new name, I have been immersed in holy water and purified.

My thoughts went black in a deep, deep sleep.

—⟋⟍—

At the first light of day, I awoke and heard the high notes of birds tweeting and thrilling in the pines that surrounded the camp.

My body was dehydrated from sweating. I slipped off my cap, stretched, and poked my head out of the sleeping bag. Then I lay still, ignoring my thirst, wanting only to listen. I heard a cacophony of scurrying and tried to guess which one of nature's creatures was making each noise.

How much noise do I make? I wondered, as I listened to my stomach growl. I recalled times when I had interrupted people and pushed for details, not valuing the integrity of their story, interjecting questions: Which hospital? Do you remember the surgeon's name? Any long term side effects? I had annoyed a lot of people with my noise. Perhaps I could cultivate the gift of genuinely listening to others.

Tonight I would build an enormous fire and burn away my childhood fears, pain, and uncertainty. I planned to be born again, this time by fire.

Once I was out of the shelter, the sweat on my skin evaporated and chill bumps rose on my arms. Abundant sunshine filtered through the trees, and I rejoiced, knowing that the camp would soon dry out. The chilly air was invigorating; everything was covered in tiny drops of water that glistened in the sun. I walked to the circle, crossed over the stones, and stared into the fire pit. A wet goo of gray ashes and water lay at its center.

I had no more water to drink, and it was time to move a rock.

Back at camp, I placed the pack in the sun, draped the rain suit and sweatshirts over branches, filled my day pack with the empty water bottles, found my stick, and started down to the threshold. The familiar ruts and stones on the path led me downward. As I walked a gust of wind kicked up. Clouds began to form in the sky, resembling large pieces of cotton. A faint cawing sounded in the distance.

I was at a place in the forest where tall trees stood on either side of the path, like skyscrapers lining a street. The cawing increased and I turned and looked up. Out of nowhere a huge flock of crows descended, blocking out most of the sunlight. They spiraled around me, gliding a few feet over my head, then rose upward and swooped back down again. I heard words in their calling, as if an ancient choir was chanting hymns in a hypnotic, Latin cadence.

*"Kill the beast. Kill the beast. Be strong... be strong."*

"What beast?" I shouted up at them. "What beast?"

"Caw... caaaw."

I wasn't afraid, but mystified by the immensity of the flock, and the varying pitches and quality of sounds. Their magic was like Creation calling to me.

*"Be strong, kill the beast."*

They were a sea of black in motion, waves of birds dancing in the air, delivering this message to me. What did it mean?

Within seconds the crows made an amazing exit. Flying one last circle above me, they formed a tight, straight line and soared into the heavens. When I shielded my eyes with my hand to watch the dark ribbon of feathers disappear, a roar sounded from deep inside the forest.

"The beast!" I gasped.

There was a more familiar roar. "Lion? Lion... my friend!"

He was there, in the edge of the trees.

A resounding roar gave me great comfort. My power animal, the one who had met me at my sacred place near the river, watched over me from the forest. I looked more closely and he disappeared.

I wanted to cry but I had no tears. I felt unsteady and lightheaded. My mouth was completely parched and my palms dry. I held onto my staff and tried to steady myself; it was imperative to get more water. Shuffling and in a daze, I made my way to the water station. The rock moving could wait, but I needed water now.

Kneeling down and sliding open the tap, I splashed water over my face. It was heaven. I closed it and rubbed my face with my hands and massaged my nose, eyelids, eyebrows, forehead, scalp, ears, and neck with the tips of my fingers.

I wasn't hungry, only thirsty. Hunger was a memory. I was experiencing a heightened state of awareness; my body felt light, not confined by the earth's gravity, and it had transcended the need for food. I half-filled one of the bottles and said a prayer, "Great Spirit, I am grateful for this journey."

I finished the bottle and then refilled them both. This would be enough for the rest of the day before I returned to check for Lillian's rock.

I stood and walked over to the rock pile. I used my stick to poke at them but none appealed to me. This stone had to be extra special; it represented the last rock I would choose on my quest. A sense of finality tugged at my soul.

A large stone caught my eye; it was covered in moss and partially buried in the ground. It looked heavy. I used my staff and scraped away some of the dirt from its foundation, then pushed under it. It didn't take much effort to shift it out of its resting place. Space on either side opened up and I was able to slide my hands underneath.

"Okay, big boy, let's go."

From a squat position I lifted with my legs, feeling the strain in my quads, lower back, and biceps. I took one baby step at a time to the threshold and dropped the hefty load. It made a loud thump when it landed. I made fists and lifted my hands over my head like a winning prizefighter.

"Lillian will marvel at my strength." I dropped my hands down to my waist. "Or she'll be amazed at this ridiculous waste of energy."

At the water station I rinsed off my hands, picked up a water bottle, faced the threshold, and made a toast.

"Here's to the sublime absurdity of moving a heavy rock when a little one would do. Saluda!"

After a long satisfying drink, I felt pride and wondered aloud, "Beast? Bring on the fucking beast."

# CHAPTER 36

AFTER ARRANGING MY gear I decided to visit the waterfalls before heading back to camp. The day was warming, and my body temperature had risen from the heavy lifting and now the brisk walk. Just as I heard the falls, a mockingbird flew overhead. Her long gray body was streamlined with white undersides, and there were flashy white patches under her wings. She followed me down the trail.

"Chrip, chrip... chrip, chrip, chrip." The song was enchanting and cheerful.

Close to the creek I heard rustling sounds in the trees. And then, about thirty feet away, I saw him, a shiny black bear on all fours. It wasn't the biggest bear in the world, but it was big enough. I wanted to run, but I tried to remember what Lillian had said. His coat shone like glossy black satin. Gray hairs surrounded his muzzle, and a patch of white marked his chest. He seemed so docile grubbing for acorns until he stood up and sniffed the air. He was bigger than I thought. The hair along his spine rose into a ridge, signaling alarm. His ears went back and he snorted in my direction.

"Jesus!" I stood immobilized, stricken by fear.

Suddenly, with no warning, he charged. Lillian's advice came to mind and I stood tall, raised my staff and roared at the top of my lungs. The bear swayed slightly and slid to a stop He raised up again, challenging my posture, so I roared again. To my amazement he went down to all fours and turned sideways, his body language saying, "Go away. You're too close."

"I am human," I said in a calming voice.

He held his ground and continued to watch me. I stepped back slowly, speaking in soothing tones. "Mr. Bear, I'm going home now. Enjoy you're breakfast… have an acorn for me. You're sooo gorgeous. I love you."

The bear's eyes blinked lazily and he slowly turned away. I watched him saunter back to the oak tree and continue to scrape the ground for nuts.

I kept walking backwards. When I felt safe I turned and ran through the tall grass, wanting to be invisible from any further threats. I sank to the ground and covered my face with shaking hands. My paralyzing fear melted into disbelief. A large lumbering black bear had charged and stood in front of me only fifteen feet away. And I was still alive.

Was this the beast? My gut said no. I had stumbled onto a black bear, eating acorns nothing more. One missed step and I would've died a violent death, a horrible ending, shredded by powerful teeth. I shivered at the thought and rubbed my arms, ironing out the goose bumps. This bear was not the beast.

—–∭–—

Returning to camp, I found that my plastic rain suit was dry, hot to the touch, and the backpack looked good as new. I put away the suit, rearranged my bed, and stowed the pack in the lean-to.

"Find the compass." Hiawassee's words gently entered my thoughts, like a whisper. I obeyed and searched inside the pack for Lillian's compass. It was in a three-inch aluminum oval case, with a lid that protected the face. I popped it open, turned it in my hand to point north, recapped it, and slid it into my back pocket.

I got comfortable on top of the sleeping bag, felt my body's weight press into the soft pine-needle bedding, and let out a heavy sigh. A noisy bird made a racket in a nearby tree and cried out a heckling call, as if to mock me. I was still shaking. The bear had scared the crap out of me, but he had provided no answers. What if no answers come, I thought, and I remain imprisoned by my own repetitive behavior?

I rubbed my eyes to stop the onslaught of tears, and then positioned my arms at my sides, palms up, eyes closed. The crows and the bear had consumed my morning and sapped my strength. A gentle wind rustled the tarp and produced calming sounds like ocean waves. My breathing deepened, my chest rose and fell with a steady rhythm, and I drifted off to sleep.

*I stood on the edge of a high mountain cliff and gazed at a village full of small cottages in the valley below. The streets were divided by some kind of green space filled with blossoming Bartlett pear trees. Their white petals drifted to the ground and lightly covered the grass like snow.*

*I floated down, a body without wings, and inspected the houses. Each one had a wide wooden door, window flower-boxes planted with cascading pink petunias, and red brick sidewalks. One cottage stood out. Yes, I thought, this one will do nicely. Finally, a place I can call my own, a calm environment, one without turmoil and strife... home.*

*I placed my hand on the shiny brass door knob; the metal was cool and the door opened effortlessly. Pristine hardwood floors, large sun-filled windows, and a bright yellow kitchen met me inside. I belong here in this unspoiled place, I thought, a new home for Hands of Water.*

The intense light of the afternoon sun shone through the lean-to's side branches, bounced off the tarp's silver lining, and prompted me to open my eyes. What a lovely dream. My supplication had been answered, and my heart was overflowing with peacefulness and equanimity.

I brushed small chocolate specks of dried leaves off my shirt and crawled out of the lean-to. Going to the threshold and rock-checking were late afternoon tasks. I had about four hours to search for tonight's firewood.

I wandered into the forest and within fifty feet of the camp discovered a mound of dry leaves and small pine branches perfect for kindling. Pulling my shirt outward from my belly, I used it as an apron to gather and transport the material. I made three trips, and then thoroughly swept the prickly needles off my clothes.

I examined the pit more closely, touched its gooey bottom and discovered that it was still damp. A new fire would take extra effort. A real platform was needed, a raised surface to protect the kindling from the damp ground. Last night's thunderstorm had soaked the downed branches lying in open areas. To find dry lumber, protected by the thick canopy, I would have to go deeper into the woods.

I made a mental note to head north. The path I chose was less cluttered with underbrush, and the grass was worn down. Probably a deer trail, I thought. Walking further and further into the woodland, I asked Hiawassee for help.

"Speak to me."

The high-pitched descending scream of a hawk echoed through the forest. I stopped and searched the trees, hoping for an appearance. About fifteen feet above me, I spotted his broad white chest and watched it puff up as he screeched again. The hawk spread his wings, shook them, and then settled back onto a slightly swaying branch. His belly and the feathers under his wings were white, speckled in black; his tail feathers were a cinnamon red. He was majestic.

He dove off the branch and flew away, skimming the treetops. I watched him land about fifty yards away. I made several twists and turns on the trail, trying to keep him in sight. Then just ahead and to the left, a massive decaying oak appeared. The ground around it was littered with lumber, and there were ten or twelve large limbs stretching toward the sky, branchless, misshapen, and ghostly white.

The body and limbs of the tree reminded me of Durga, the Hindu goddess of intelligence, wealth, and power. I knew her story from Mamata, an Indian friend. She was a devotee of Durga, drawn to the image of a young girl with ten arms who had the power to destroy or create the universe.

The branches beneath the huge dead tree were all bone dry, and a large piece of bark had fallen off the trunk and landed on the ground like a tray, a perfect platform. I studied the areas where giant limbs had broken off. One large circular scar was like a three dimensional star, complex with geometric details. Rumi said, "Scars are where the light comes in."

I stood in front of the tree and raised my arms. "Thank you, Mr. Hawk. Thank you, mighty oak. There is going be some kind of a fire tonight."

My elation was once again followed by panic. Where the hell am I? The return path was not clear. Everything in every direction looked the same, dark and foreboding. Hiwassee, I thought, the compass. Guessing that the distance back to the camp was about a quarter of a mile, I knew the direction -- due south. I pulled the compass out of my back pocket, and it gave me the answer. I turned around one-hundred-and-eighty degrees from north and proceeded. Looking for the broken underbrush I had created coming in made navigation easier. Getting lost in the woods was not an option.

Transporting the wood out of the forest was an arduous process. The smaller pieces were easy to handle; my shirt served as an apron once again. But while walking back I wondered if there might be a less time-consuming way to transport the larger pieces. A lot of firewood would fuel a hotter fire. This fire must burn insanely hot, I thought, hot enough to burn away my childhood.

Plowing through the brush on several return trips, I thought about the beast. The mantra, "Kill the beast, kill the beast," was frightening. It sounded like something from *The Lord of the Flies*. How can I kill anything? I am unarmed. And what will it look like? A pack of dogs? Another bear? Or maybe a slobbering dragon spitting fire and snarling teeth. I would visit the waterfall again before nightfall and ask Hiawassee for answers.

Within my purpose circle, I had accumulated an impressive wealth of burnable lumber. Tonight's fire will be visible in Atlanta, I beamed, like the aurora borealis in Alaska. I felt a little light-headed, and my mouth was dry. The angle of the light signaled that it was time to make a trip to the threshold. I gathered up my staff and day pack, added the empty water bottles, and headed out.

It was a relaxing hike down, no flocks of wild birds, bears, or lions, only me. The cool air made the walk downward a breeze, and as a cadence to my steps developed, the tension in my muscles released.

When I arrived at the rock pile it was clear that Lillian had trumped me. Four small round stones, about the size of golf balls, were lined up east to west on the surface of my oversized rock. How clever. It reminded me that small efforts can circumvent large obstacles.

After filling my bottles at the water station, I noticed two small finches twirling aggressively around each other. Are they playing or fighting? A pale green finch danced before me, spiraling from tree limb to tree limb, and his yellow-feathered friend followed him. Eventually, reality set in. The sun was setting and I needed to move on.

Hiking upward, I heard the waterfall before long. The familiar rhythmic patterns of descending water produced a smile, along with endorphins that slowed my heart rate and steadied my pace. I had never felt so alive and yet so peaceful.

The last time I'd tried to visit this place, a bear had interrupted my plans. Slowing to a crawl and listening intently for any sound that might indicate a predator, I warily pushed branches out of my way, not wanting to disturb surrounding limbs. I chose my steps cautiously, stalking the waterfall.

Making my way through two more thickets, I saw her – a beautiful white-tailed doe. Her ears twitched, she dropped her mouth to the edge of the stream, took a drink, and her head rose. Water dripped from both sides of her mouth. I remembered that Lillian once said, "A deer will open doors for you."

I could've stood there for hours taking in every detail of the doe's deep red coat and white-collared neck. Her legs were muscular, her body lean and powerful looking, and her nose ended in shiny black nostrils flaring at every sound. There was a loud rustling near the falls and she raised her head in that direction. Instantaneously, she was off, bounding across the stream and into the woods, her white tail swishing vigorously as she leapt over small bushes and out of sight.

The edge of the falls was even more beautiful than I'd remembered. I found a dry area of medium-sized river stones and sat down, wiggling my butt onto them. Each pebble was unique in smoothness and color. Dark rose, pink, and crystal clear quartz were in the majority, but there were darker brown stones as well.

I slipped off my pack and took out a water bottle. After taking a drink, I settled into a relaxed lotus pose, closed my eyes, and centered my breathing.

"I am Hands of Water. I am here with a humble heart to ask questions and call upon your spirit. Hiawassee?"

A long silence was followed by a single crow cawing twice in the distance. The flow of water slowly diminished to a trickle and Hiawassee's resplendent glow manifested itself in the cave.

"I feel your presence, daughter. Speak to me."

"The beast," I said, "I fear it. How will I survive?"

"Do not step out of the circle, no matter what happens."

Her light began to fade and I called out. "Wait, Hiawassee, I have more questions!"

The stream's current swelled as her voiced echoed, "Do not step out of the circle."

I jumped up. "No. Wait! The beast?"

Bursting into tears, I was filled with self-pity. I buried my head in my hands and mumbled, "Please come back, please." The mumbling turned to sobs, sobs to sniffling, and then I dried my eyes. A pang of anger shot through me.

"Don't step out of the circle? What a load of shit!"

An unexpected microburst blew down from the hill, causing a fierce onslaught of leaves to swirl around me.

"Do not mock me." Her voice floated in the air.

I felt embarrassed. But what was I to do?

I raised a fist and shouted to the sky, "Can't you see how much I need you?"

There was no response, and my fears were compounded. It was time to move on and embrace my journey. There was a beast out there somewhere, and I would have to face it. Tonight I had to push forward and pray for a vision of strength and resolve. There was no turning back.

# CHAPTER 37

WALKING BACK TO camp I recited my mantra, "I release any negative energy. I make healthy choices. I practice self-acceptance, and total acceptance of others." I took an oath to be more observant of other people's words and gestures, and not to fear holding someone's gaze while in a conversation, even if it meant I'd blush from the intimacy of sustained eye contact.

I reached the top of the mountain, walked past the ring of stones, and tossed my light pack inside the circle. I twirled the staff like a seasoned majorette making my way to the lean-to. I tossed it in the air, caught it, and laughed joyfully. A strong sense of self-confidence permeated my entire being. Smiling and feeling light as a feather, I gathered up all my belongings and carried them inside the circle.

Sitting on top of my bag, hugging my knees to my chest, I rested my head on top of them, studying the piles of wood and the fire pit. This is the last step of my quest, I thought. An entire spectrum of emotions churned inside of me: happiness, accomplishment, fear, uncertainty, anticipation, and sadness.

"When will you come, beast?"

On the downside of my emotional roller coaster, deep inside my bones, I felt the real possibility of death. I wanted someone to hold me, comfort me, and be here when I lit the fire. In the recent past, every time I found myself in trouble, there was some man to bail me out. Not now. Now it was only me. Whatever comes, I thought, I must persevere.

The cloudless sky was changing from sunset to twilight. Brilliant pink fingers of light spread across the horizon, and within a few minutes the colors changed to crimson and deep yellow. As the sun sank, the colors faded.

Kneeling at the edge of the pit, I heaped dry leaves and tiny branches on top of each other and arranged a wall of larger brushwood on either side of the kindling. Loading additional sticks perpendicularly and sprinkling in extra leaves, I added a third layer of branches and finished the pile.

I held the small box of wooden matches in my palms, brought them up to my lips and whispered into folded hands, "Please, let this fire start with one match."

Sliding open the box, I lit the match's blue sulfur head easily and set flame to the powdery leaves. A high-pitched crackle began, and a symphony of tiny explosions followed. Infant flames licked smaller twigs, turning them into branches of light. As the limbs continued to burn, the top layer fell inward, joined the burning heap, and established a strong foundation for my bonfire.

Handfuls of medium-sized branches thrown onto the blaze were quickly consumed. Bright daffodil-yellow flames swayed in the light wind, leaping higher with each addition of oxygen and fuel. I pitched several small limbs onto the stack; tiny orange sparks floated into the air and quickly vaporized in the darkness above. The sight was mesmerizing. By this image, I thought, the ancients found their power.

The wind delivered Hiawassee's words to me: "You are a child of mother earth... rest in her."

I spread out my arms and closed my eyes. "Stay with me, mother. Allow me to die gracefully."

"Do *not* leave the circle." The sound of her message was bleak.

I *was* going to die. There could be no other way. Lillian's prediction of me being reborn seemed like a dream... a fantasy. To be reborn, I thought, one must die. Still on my knees in front of the fire,

I wept in long, loud, mournful cries that reverberated from my belly and lungs.

"Hiawassee, Lion, stay with me!" I hugged both sides of my body tightly in fear of what was to come. "I don't wish to face this alone." My only defense was to build an inferno.

Three medium-sized limbs set across the growing embers in the shape of a pyramid quickly caught ablaze. The fire was now my source of warmth, light and protection. No beast would come near it.

I walked back to my sleeping bag and found the plastic bottle. My eyes felt scratchy from tears and smoke, so I spilled water into my hand, raised it to my right eye, and pressed my palm securely against it. The cool water seeped into my eye socket and brought immediate relief, and I repeated the process for my other eye. I sat down on the bag, picked up my staff and caressed it with both hands, slowly turning it over and over. Touching the irregular surface and the raised bumps of paint was like reading Braille. I thought of Jet. Oh God, if he were only here. I wondered if he knew my circumstances.

"Jet, what was your vision?" I whispered. "You survived. Will I?"

I heard a noise out in the brush and made for the circle. Back near the fire, I felt some measure of safety.

Stars, barely visible, began twinkling. I lay back, studied the sky, and held the wand between my breasts, my left hand over my heart. I listened to loud snapping and popping as the wood blazed in the pit. My racing mind calmed.

"Hello, my friends," I spoke to the stars. "Soon I'll be able to tell who you are. Vega, Hercules, and Orion? You're a sparkling mantle as I lie in the darkness."

Smoke began to travel along the ground in my direction. I rose, used the wand to steady myself, and walked to the wood pile. I stoked the burning heap with the staff, pieces of well-burnt wood fell together and formed a pile of glowing red coals. Flames engulfed another large log that I placed crosswise in the pit, and the fire's temperature increased, scorching the surrounding limbs. I kicked unburned ends of limbs into the center. The burst of heat slapped me in the face. I took off my cap and backed away.

A third of the wood was already spent, and a big blaze would need fuel to keep growing. I organized the limbs according to their size and threw in three more logs. On the far side of the pile, a stark contrast in air temperature between the fire and the tarp developed.

Newly added limbs ignited, and sparks flew thirty feet into the blackness. They descended as ashes and floated onto my sweatshirt. I brushed them off, added more wood, and walked from the brightly burning pit into the darkness.

There it was, Orion's Belt in the southeast sky.

"So there you are."

It was too early to see Sirius. She'd make her appearance in the eastern horizon just before dawn.

A pack of coyotes began an eerie howl. Their yelps sounded like young women who were being tortured -- high-pitched and terrifying. Overcome by fear, I returned to the fire's edge and held onto the staff with a sweaty grip. A noise here and a rustling there made me pivot back and forth. It was difficult to convince myself of Lillian's wisdom, "They are more afraid of you." I only hoped the fire would hold them at bay.

The coyotes' barking faded and my body relaxed. I knelt in front of the fire and situated the wand in front of me. Rough images seemed to dance before my hypnotic stare. Inside the embers two fiery balls materialized, one azure blue and the other faint amber. They rotated around each other like a moon captivated by its planet's gravity. A third crimson globe formed inside the rising smoke, expanded outside the pit and enveloped me.

My heart raced, and I wondered: Are these hallucinations from lack of food? The other two spheres infiltrated the cloud, and I melted into a serene state of consciousness. I lay on the ground, after a gentle push from an unseen hand, and gazed at the orbs moving in different directions, creating a strobe effect.

Inside the cloud, the entirety of my physical mass illuminated. The cloud elevated and I floated in space. The cloud's wall served as a movie screen and I watched flashbacks of my mother and father: Dad setting up my swing set, Mom kissing my cheek while tucking me in at night, Dad carrying me on his shoulders at the county fair while holding my mother's hand.

More scenes of them together came into view. Honeymooning at Niagara Falls, they smiled at each other seductively, two young lovers finally alone, about to consummate their marriage. Dad held me at the hospital soon after my birth and we recognized each other, two souls united to resolve our karma.

While drifting, the colors and light turned into darkness and the fire's sounds and smoke filled my senses. The cloud had transported me back to the fire and the wand was in front of me, just as I had left it.

The fire commanded my attention, and while I threw on extra logs, loud rustlings echoed from the forest underbrush. Picking up the staff and following the sound I was careful to stay within the circumference of the circle. Moving laterally, I stopped when it stopped. Whatever it was out there sounded as though it was right in front of me, stalking. *Crunch, crunch.* I could hear the footsteps.

A voice bellowed from the darkness, "Marianne!"

Jesus, I thought, who the...

"Marianne! You and your whore mother come out here now!"

My God... it was my father's voice.

"Did you hear me, you little bitch? Get out here now!"

Out of the darkness my father staggered toward the circle's edge. My pulse beat against my eardrums, *bump, bump, bump.* I opened my mouth but no words came.

"Get out here... you heard me!"

I raised the staff like a baseball bat, hyperventilated, and delivered my threat, "I'll kill you… if you come into this circle. You are not my father. You're the *bastard* that swallowed his soul."

He held out an open fifth and poured its contents into his mouth. The whisky spilled over his cheeks and he used his forearm to mop his face. After dropping the bottle, his blood-red eyes met mine and he fell backward, flat on his back with a thud.

The fire popped, sparked, and hot embers hissed. Fear pierced my heart. I studied the body. The air grew damp and heavy from smoke. I was breathing soot and dreading what was to come.

A loud whirling sound filled the night. At the spot my father had fallen, a creature ascended. A gigantic badger stood with a wide mouth that snarled, showing bright pink gums and razor-sharp teeth. It was huge. It paced back and forth, staring at me, its hideous sounds intensified. I watched as the whites of its eyes turned red. I backed up to make sure I was in the circle. Its lethal stare felt painful and piercing; its glare tore my heart in two. The eyes changed again, growing smaller until all I could see were tiny, glowing slits.

"No!" I shrieked. I trembled in fear.

The beast snarled, pounced towards me and snapped the air. It seemed to bounce off the edge of the ring as if there was an invisible shield. "Don't leave the ring," Hiwassee had said.

A fierce and powerful bellow sounded from the forest. Oh my God! I thought. What next?

Slowly Lion walked out of the woods, stopped, and roared again. He looked massive and invincible. The beast turned to face him. They traded vocal challenges and began to pace around each other. The beast rose up on its hind legs, boxed the air, and charged. They ran at each other and attacked violently, tearing away flesh. Droplets of blood peppered my face.

"Lion!" I shouted. "Save me!"

Somehow the beast got the advantage, jumped on Lion's back and grabbed him by the neck. There was a loud squeal and blood spurted from the wound. The beast turned to look at me as though he wanted to make sure I saw his power.

"Lion!" I screamed again. I was frozen in fear and cringed at Lion's heartbreaking howl.

The beast sank long fangs into his victim and clawed at his back.

I have to do something, I thought, but what? I flung a rock at the beast with no success. I flung another.

Lion cried out in agony. It was a sound from hell, the primordial sound of death.

"You fucking bastard!" I screamed. I ran out of the circle and held my staff high.

The beast looked at me as if he had already won. He left Lion, lowered his head and took a few steps in my direction

"I'm going to fucking kill you!" I screamed again.

He charged.

I sidestepped his advance but tripped and fell on my back. Shit, I thought, I'm dead. But, no! This is it. It is my time. I *will* fight to the death!

I rolled out of the dust and stood once again looking for the steely eyes of my enemy. The beast came at me again, and I swung the staff into him. I could hear breaking bones and he fell forward, one front leg bending off at an odd angle. It did not seem to stifle his resolve. He dipped his head, growled and turned my way.

The beast charged me again. I closed my eyes and swung the staff with all my strength. His other front leg shattered, and he piled into the dirt face first, wailing in pain. Without thought or hesitation, I attacked with full force. I straddled his back and pounded away at the head of the creature, like chopping wood. Over and over again

I drove the staff into him without mercy. Soon all I could see was a mess of hair, brains and blood, and, finally, the beast was still.

I stepped away and pivoted to look for Lion, fearing the worst. He simply got up and walked away toward the forest. He turned and gave me a knowing look and disappeared into the darkness. When I swiveled back to the beast, there was nothing but a spinning ball of light.

I fell to my knees and went face first into the dirt. Exhaustion overcame my elation. After catching my breath, I rolled over and looked into the heavens. A falling star blazed, more followed, and the ether began to light up as though a huge bolt of lightning flashed across the sky. Small, sparking lights saturated the atmosphere. Each ball of light carried with it an illuminated tail that stretched far beyond its core. There were hundreds of them, each one patterned after the other, and they fell silently to the earth. Searching the battlefield, I found was no sign of Lion or the beast. I was left alone with only the crackling of the fire.

"Lion," I called into the darkness, "are you safe?"

A guttural "Rooarrr!" gave me the answer.

Arms flaying, my body twirled in a rhythm, and my face pointed upwards. I was consumed by emotions. Finally, I managed to find the words.

"I won."

Dizzy with happiness and continuing to dance, I sang out the words of a John Milton poem, "Come, knit hands, and beat the ground, in a light fantastic round. Trip the light fantastic!" I shouted. "Trip the light fantastic!"

The falling stars were gone now. Still laughing, I dropped to the ground, rolled like a playful puppy, and eventually stopped and stared upward. Orion's brilliance was fading and its belt pointed to Sirius shining faintly in the east.

Oh my God, I thought, dawn has come, and I'm still alive. Continuing to revel in my well-earned independence, I sat up, positioned myself once again on my knees, and held my hands in prayer.

"Thank you," I whispered. "Thank you."

I stood and repeated the song Lillian sang while she walked me to the threshold.

"Miye toka heya anpetu owakinyelo."

Running and jumping over the stones with my arms spread like wings, I sang ecstatically, "As the sun rises, I am first to fly. *I am first to fly!*" My voice quivered with excitement. "*I am coming home!*"

Out of breath, I calmed down, held my palms against my heart, and remembered Lillian's directives. "At the end of your vision, remove the stones from your purpose circle, and scatter them."

With energy abounding, I pitched small stones like baseballs away from the circle. Each stone represented a particular memory of where I had discovered it, the walking trail, the waterfall, and the forest floor. I chucked the final stone into the tall grass and began my last chore before packing up camp.

At the fire pit dying embers glowed from a small concentration of red and black coals. I scooped up some of the dirt from one side of the fire's edge and heaped it onto the core. A thick haze of grey and purplish smoke filled the air, causing me to cough vigorously into the curve of my elbow and forearm. Using one of the remaining branches, I stirred the coals and covered them with more dirt. The smoke decreased significantly, and after several more scoops of soil, the fire was completely extinguished, except for a slight wisp of smoke escaping into the early morning air.

# CHAPTER 38

—— ⁓ ——

WHILE PACKING MY things, I felt as if I had just awakened on Christmas morning with every gift I had ever imagined waiting for me under the tree. My father, my loving father, was now indelibly printed into my being. The monster who had consumed his soul was dead, never to reappear. I had new eyes to see, a new confidence permeated my soul, and I held a burning rhythm in my heart to become the woman I was meant to be, whole and expectant of the very best life could offer.

The morning light intensified and my hike to the threshold was effortless. There in the distance I could see Lillian and Jet on the other side of the birch trees. Is that Bobby? Jet held him by a single lead, no saddle. The beautiful horse bobbed his head up and down as I approached. Bobby whinnied and my pace quickened.

Passing by the stone pile, I stopped at the birch trees. No one spoke. I removed the feathers from the bark and stuck them into my ponytail. I could have passed for a homeless person, smelly and dirty, with feathers in my hair. My welcoming party was only a short distance away. I froze. Lillian was the first to come forward.

She held out her arms and said, "As the sun rises, I am first to fly."

I slid off my pack and ran to her. I cried tears of joy, and we embraced. I took in every fiber of her essence. She smelled of sage; her hair was like silk; my arms around her strengthened me. I was back in the real world, I was home. She pushed back and looked into my eyes.

"You have completed your journey, and now... go live."

Jet and I looked at each other. It felt as if it was the first time I had ever seen him, a man whose heart was pure. He walked over to me with Bobby in tow.

"I'm so proud of you. Welcome home."

He held his arms open and I hugged him long and hard. Bobby pushed his head against my arm and I let go of Jet and laughed.

I rubbed Bobby's forehead and said, "Don't be jealous, my dear friend. There's so much love to go around... for everyone."

"Let me give you a hand," Jet said. "I'll give you a leg up."

Lillian nodded and picked up my pack. "I've got this," she said smiling.

Jet cupped his hands at Bobby's side and hoisted me up on his back. It was more than I could bear, so much love and affection. Jet led Bobby forward and Lillian followed.

Lillian began to sing.

"Miye toka heya anpetu owakinyelo. "Wanbli gleska wan heyaya u welo. "Miye toka heya anpetu owakinyelo."

The morning sun rose higher in the sky and we continued our journey to the lodge. My soul sang out to the heavens.

I was grateful... and I was free.

55568674R00194

Made in the USA
Charleston, SC
28 April 2016